T4-AQJ-012

## "You're not a spirit. You're a person."

"Of course." Elinor's gentle brow knit slightly.

"That first day I met you, remember? On the trail up the side of the bluff, that little clearing." Wade Travers paused and waited for Elinor's nod. "I scared you, and you dived over the side and vanished. No sound, no rustle, no movement, no monkeys or birds telling me where you were. It's possible to slip through the forest silently, I suppose. Indians can. But even they can't fool troupials and howler monkeys. How'd you do that, anyway?"

Elinor's fair ears turned pink; her pale cheeks flushed. This lovely lady was actually blushing. Her foggy blue eyes flicked up for the briefest moment and cast themselves earthward again.

"Well?"

"I didn't run away. I ducked aside and hid, less than two yards from you. I followed you to the top, watching you. I was right behind you. But I didn't have time to wait for you to come back out of Mr. Tweed's house. I had other errands."

"But I didn't see . . ." Wade scowled, confused. Surely if she had been that close, he would have detected her. "Why? Why did you follow me?"

"Because, even though you startled me, even though I was afraid to speak to you, you fascinated me." She paused. "And you still do."

FIRST BRETHREN CHURCH LIBRARY
Nappanee, Indiana

# Jungle Gold

## SANDY DENGLER

Serenade/SuperSaga
**BOOKS**
of the Zondervan Publishing House
Grand Rapids, Michigan

Other Books by Sandy Dengler:

*Summer Snow*
*Song of the Nereids*
*Winterspring*
*Opal Fire*
*This Rolling Land*

A Note from the Author:

*I love to hear from my readers! You may correspond with me by writing:*

Sandy Dengler
Author Relations
1415 Lake Drive, S.E.
Grand Rapids, MI 49506

JUNGLE GOLD
Copyright © 1987 by Sandy Dengler

Serenade/SuperSaga is an imprint of Zondervan Publishing House,
1415 Lake Drive, S.E., Grand Rapids, MI 49506.

ISBN 0-310-47781-6

Scripture quotations are taken from the King James Version of the Holy
Bible.

All rights reserved. No part of this publication may be reproduced, stored
in a retrieval system, or transmitted in any form or by any means—
electronic, mechanical, photocopy, recording, or any other—except for
brief quotations in printed reviews, without the prior permission of the
publisher.

*Edited by Sandra L. Vander Zicht and Anne Severance*
*Designed by Kim Koning*

*Printed in the United States of America*

87  88  89  90  91 / DP / 10  9  8  7  6  5  4  3  2  1

**FIRST BRETHREN CHURCH LIBRARY**
Nappanee, Indiana

*For our Lord
and for the people who serve him,
be it in cities or in jungles.*

# *Prologue*

HE STOOD ON THIS NAKED, JUTTING LITTLE LEDGE, suspended between two utterly alien worlds, and from it, he could gaze upon them both. Behind him, mountain peaks stabbed the clouds. Tonight, their icy flanks would send cold winds downslope past this ledge. But now, in mid-afternoon, a warm, muggy breeze moved upslope from the east.

Before him the mountains fell away so rapidly that even the nearest foothills huddled far beneath him. And the river—the river.

Upholstered in green velour, the flat and endless Amazon lowland filled his mind and eye. Raw moisture frosted the distance and blurred the horizon. Raw heat set it shimmering. Pure, wild, humid rain forest stretched away forever from the peaks behind him.

And this ledge hung between.

Wade Travers squatted on his heels a few minutes, partly to absorb the matchless view around him, mostly to explore his own thoughts. Why should this river have such an hypnotic effect on him? It wasn't really exotic, not anymore. He had traversed it several times from various directions. He knew it intimately as few men do, Indian or white. *Amazon* might mean "mystery" to most; to him it meant simply another opportunity to seek adventure and wealth.

He dug out his plug of smoking tobacco and absent-mindedly shaved some strands off it with his pocketknife. He rubbed the shreds with a thumb into the palm of his hand, breaking them up, loosening them. Methodically, he packed them into his pipe.

The Andes were behind him now: the past. The river basin, rich and vibrant, rippled and glowed before him. It extended beyond the horizon, beyond eyesight, beyond imagination: the future.

He struck a match and momentarily shifted all his attention to the task of getting his tobacco evenly lit. Beyond the horizon lay Manaos. Seventy years ago that bit of flat lush jungle produced most of the world's rubber. Then Britons and Dutchmen, who sought adventure in ways other than Wade's, started plantations of rubber trees in Southeast Asia. Now nearly all the world's rubber came from somewhere a globe away, and Manaos lay dying in the dank, tropical heat. And yet Wade Travers would find his fortune in Manaos. The rubber was past and Manaos's glory flown, but there was still gold.

To the north and east of Manaos, on a little tributary of the Rio Negro, rumors insisted there was gold. Gold so abundant that the rivulets in the sandhills glowed shining yellow. Gold so pure you could gather a pocketful without picking up a pebble of dross.

Of course, for centuries Indians on two continents had held out to white men the promise of distant gold, like a carrot in front of a goat. But Wade should trust this rumor. He had spent nearly a year with Indians of that area. In their own language (salted liberally with Portuguese) they had described the unique low ridges of the region so vividly that Wade was certain they were talking about quartz outcrops. You might pan a little gold from a sandy streambed, but the source—the mother lode—would occur in quartz seams. Unschooled Indians wouldn't know to describe a quartz reef if it weren't really there.

This intelligence about gold, volunteered by Indians, he had kept to himself for three years. Now it was time to seek, to find, and then to get the blazes out of the jungle and settle down. He was not a young man anymore. Sooner or later his senses would dim and his reaction time lengthen. He wouldn't survive long in this business of adventuring once age slowed him.

He stood up and stretched. Why was it so hard to tear his gaze away from the endless green splendor dissolving itself in the mists? He ran his fingers through his dark hair and squeezed his eyes shut a few times, waiting for the magic to fade. The mist sent hints and warnings up to him on the muggy breeze. *Beware, Wade Travers. You'll change. If you come here, you'll die. You think this land is yours, to walk where you will. It's not!*

What nonsense! He turned his back on that verdant vastness and clambered up the rocks into the close, embracing woodlands.

## chapter
## 1

WADE REMEMBERED HEARING SOMEWHERE that the first scheduled steamship line had begun operations on the Amazon almost seventy years ago, in 1853. And in all that time not a thing had changed. The same crotchety old boats plied the same muddy, changeless river. This mailboat from Iquitos to the border was an insult to the eye, the nose, and the ear.

Probably at one time she had been a pretty little thing, all sparkling white in the tropical sun. Now she offended the eye, for not an inch of her sixty-five-foot length had escaped the rust and grime. The white had yellowed and grayed. And the smells. It wasn't just the ballooning black smoke that poured from the single stack. One also noticed the unwashed passengers milling on deck and smelled whatever it was that had died in the hold.

The noise, though, annoyed him most. The vessel itself constantly orchestrated a discordant cacophony of creaks and moans. The boiler pipes clanged. The smokestack roared. A troop of howler monkeys announced the boat's arrival a hundred yards before it reached the dock, and a colony of large wading birds took flight, screaming.

A half-breed boy, butternut-colored, squeezed beside Wade at the rail, glanced up at him self-consciously, and looked off toward the shore. An Indian woman crowded him from the other side, and someone who desperately needed a bath was shoved up against his back.

Wade picked up his swag, roughly one-third of his worldly possessions, and waited. Two hundred yards ahead, the docking crew yelled things in foreign languages as they watched the mail boat approach shore. At the bow, a black-skinned fellow gathered the mooring hawser in giant hands. The boat shuddered as it reversed itself with a wild swirl of frothy tan water. Wagging drunkenly, the old clunker nudged into the dock timbers.

Then the noise really started. The iron hull lolled, swishing, as it clanged against the dock. The hawser lines thunked. A score of voices chattered in Portuguese, Spanish, Italian, and at least one Indian dialect Wade had never heard. As the deckhand opened up the railing, it grated with a sound that could destroy teeth. With pained moans the gangplank stabbed thin air and fell, *pung,* against the dock. Wade braced himself against the rail and waited until everyone else had scurried off.

Well, almost everyone. The butternut-colored half-breed boy hung back, so Wade shouldered his swag and walked from swaying deck to solid land. Riverboats were fairly stable, but he preferred terra firm—the firmer, the better.

"Way-ed Chrah-ffers?" He was a customs officer of some sort. Wade recognized the uniform, in this case about the same color as the boat. "Your pahssport, pliss?"

"Right here. Somewhere." Wade lowered his swag to the dock and fished through pockets. It seemed the smaller the customs station, the more passport-minded the officers became. He handed his battered black booklet to the gentleman.

The man opened it, studied it, nodded gravely, smiled a bit. "Yes. Mr. Chrah-ffers." He turned on his heel and marched off toward the little customs shed.

Resigned, Wade hefted his swag and followed. He was on the Colombian side of the river where, by international agreement, a small corridor of Colombian territory extended south, squeezed between the twin bulks of Peru and Brazil to give Colombia access to the Amazon system. This was a diplomatic error on the part of Brazil, as far as Wade was concerned. He was constantly battling Colombian customs. By comparison, the customs officers of Peru and Brazil were absolutely magnanimous.

As Wade approached the shed, a minor officer jogged toward the dusty road leading up the river bluff. Here, as in most of the Amazon Valley, the human habitations were all crowded together "upstairs" so to speak, along the lip of the bluff a few feet above the river. The lowland was left for the river to flood annually. Only the Indians played it smart by building their wooden huts on floating platforms.

The customs officer perched himself on a tall stool and reached brusquely for a log book of some sort. He leafed from page to page, running his finger down the lines, until Wade was ready to explode with dazzling obscenities.

Minutes passed. Finally Wade could contain himself no longer. "Is there some sort of problem? I've been through several times. Maybe I can help."

"Problem? No, señor. No problem."

"Then may I have my passport back, please?"

"No, señor."

"Then there's a problem."

"No, señor."

Wade counted to ten mentally as he thought. "Okay. You don't have a problem. But I do. Where's my passport?"

"His Excellency Tweed has it, señor."

"Who's he?" Wade suddenly remembered the lesser official who had gone jogging off toward the bluff.

"His Excellency governs this district. He requested to see your pahssport." The fellow flashed a smile full of teeth.

"Why *my* passport?"

"His Excellency do not say."

"Bet his Excellency dropped some kind of hint. *Why?*" Wade put a sharp edge on the "why."

The toothy smile disappeared. "Your services are famous. He is in need of services, perhaps."

"You're sure he wants Wade Travers? I have nothing for him."

"Talk to him, señor. He has your pahssport. He shall clear all."

"Top of the hill, right?"

"Top of the hill, to right. Right."

"Mind this," Wade snapped, and stuffed his swag in a corner of the customs shed before the fellow could object. Wade stomped off toward the bluff, so boiling mad he nearly ran over the butternut-colored kid.

The beaten path tunneled through a lush green tangle of trees, ferns, and glossy-leaved bushes. The vegetation reached out to brush his arms on both sides. The heavy canopy of trees overhead blocked off most of the daylight. A flock of noisy, agile little toucans scolded him from somewhere above, but the idyllic scene was wasted on him.

Every step he took along the trail ignited another little fire of anger in his mind. Famous services, huh? If the local bigshot needed services, let him hire someone at a fair price instead of trying to coerce Wade Travers into working for cheap, or perhaps even for free. He was an American citizen with a valid passport, and these officers had no right and no authority to pull a stunt like this.

It wouldn't matter quite so much if he weren't three months late on the trail already. Because of lousy connections and unseasonal storms and a host of nickel-and-dime delays, it would be another month before he would get to where he wanted to be at the beginning of the dry season. This minor bureaucrat couldn't have picked a worse time to cause trouble.

He stopped. All those little anger-fires had united into a considerable blaze, and a hot head would get him nowhere. He'd better slow down and cool off.

He continued for another hundred feet up the path. He was nearly halfway to the top of the bluff. A hole pierced the forest's denseness, an opening where the ferns and low brush had been beaten back, although the canopy high overhead still hid the sky. It had been a clearing once, but the jungle was reclaiming it plant by plant, leaf by leaf.

Nearby, well off the trail on the uphill side of the clearing, a kapok tree thrust out an inviting "knee." Wade sat down on the buttress and forced himself to relax. He was so angry he almost fumbled his tobacco plug.

A troupial perched across the clearing scolded him for pausing. The noisy bird reminded him of the bossy Baltimore orioles back in New York state. Home. A long time ago. At his feet little black ants skittered. Ants. Always ants. The Amazon belonged to the crocs in the river and to the ants ashore. Possibly even the river belonged to the ants. They were everywhere. Soft, brown butterflies flitted here and there.

He packed his pipe as he watched the aimless insects. Interesting. He could not recall seeing these particular brown ones anywhere except in man-made clearings. He almost fumbled his matches, too, but he was calming down a little.

He struck a match.

The troupial must have forgotten Wade. It sounded a sharp chirp to warn of an intruder and flashed, all golden, across the clearing to settle in the branches above Wade's head. It realized its error almost instantly and disappeared into the green.

Someone was indeed approaching. Wade's match stopped a foot short of his pipe bowl as he stared, dumbfounded.

She came down the trail toward him, floating, for the crowded little bushes in the clearing hid her legs and feet. All he saw was a slender and graceful young woman in some sort of very plain, modest white dress. Hair so blond it was nearly white. Skin so pale it was nearly as white. Eyes the soft milky blue of the sky on a hazy summer day. He had never seen anything like her. Her hair, cut very short around her ears, lifted and fell lightly in the vagrant breeze, almost a radiance. The vision of her burned itself into his mind so fiercely it quenched the puny little fires of his former anger.

The burning match reached his fingers. He yelped and dropped it.

Those opalescent eyes flew open, dinner-plate wide. Like a startled brocket deer she froze, terrified in mid-stride. Then she wheeled away from him and in two long strides melted silently into the green gloom.

He bolted to his feet. "Wait!" He repeated it in his next-best language, Portuguese, *"Espére!"* as he ran across the clearing. She was gone. Not so much as a moving leaf betrayed her passage down the steep and tangled hillside.

*You fool! You supreme donkey! You scare the wits out of that poor young woman and then you double her terror by running after her!* He jammed the cold pipe into his shirt pocket. The anger that had

15

flared against Tweed, whoever he was, was nothing compared with the rage he felt towards himself.

The vision of her emerging into the clearing—

Who was she? Surely any local would know. She was unique. Was she married? He saw no ring on her finger, in fact no jewelry of any kind. But then, that didn't mean much. All he remembered clearly was her face, so pale against the dark of the forest. She had a childlike aura to her, the kind of delicate pallor you might expect to see on the face of a street urchin in London, or on a shy little girl peeking around her mother's skirts. She looked so fragile. Vulnerable. And yet, she had just disappeared as quickly and perfectly as a jungle-born Indian. Or a ghost.

She haunted his memory, all right. A wood wraith. Fox-fire.

He returned to the trail and strolled on up the hill. What if she didn't exist at all? It almost seemed he had imagined it. After all, he'd never seen a woman quite like her before, and he'd seen a lot of women. She was so silent. Except for that troupial, who was upset anyway, she hadn't raised any noise from the birds or monkeys— those sentinels who are always so quick to announce who's in the neighborhood—and exactly where. Why, right now, a troop of howler monkeys were notifying the residents of the area that Wade Travers was passing along the path below.

He remembered the spooky feeling on that ledge as he was looking down on this rain forest. *What's going on here?* he thought. *This is the sort of stuff you read about in those pulp mystery magazines. Pure malarkey!*

Defiantly he pulled his pipe back out of his pocket, but his fingers shook a little as he struck another match.

She was probably a daughter of one of the many Dutch or Germans living here, he assured himself. Or some Scandinavian.

Wade lifted his head, absently putting out the match. Actually there weren't that many Germans here. In Manaos, yes, and in Belem. Not in Iquitos. Certainly not on the border. And there were no Scandinavians at all. *Who was she?*

Suddenly he found himself standing on top of the bluff. He could not remember walking all the way up. Now that's dangerous! In this country one dare not switch his senses off for a second, and he must have gone a quarter mile with his brain adrift. Thinking about what? Her. That apparition. That fox-fire.

He didn't bother to ask directions to Tweed's place. The fanciest estates would hang off the rim of the bluff, overlooking the river. He angled right and followed the edge of the mesa.

Here it was—the only wrought iron gate with a uniformed guard and no brass nameplate. He scowled at the guard, and the guard scowled back. He spoke his name. Expressionless, the watchman ambled to a little sentry house and tugged sharply at a frazzled rope hanging from its ceiling.

A flock of red-faced green parrots came jabbering through the trees, in one end of Wade's consciousness and out the other.

Eventually, from far beyond the gate, a ridiculous-looking fellow came walking up the unpaved path. Dressed in Indian attire, he wouldn't have looked the least bit silly, for his features were the classic chiseled profile of the mountain Indian. Were he dressed in formal wear with an ambassadorial ribbon down the front, he'd look perfectly dignified. Were he stark naked, he'd have looked magnificent, for underneath the clothes he was powerfully built. It was the dainty knee breeches and coat of eighteenth-century livery that made him appear foolish.

If he were self-conscious in that absurd red-brocaded garb, he showed no sign. Morosely, he approached the gate and nodded. The sentry opened it enough to let Wade slip through.

Wade followed the Indian down the winding path among manicured strawberry guava bushes and marveled at how some people out here in the middle of nowhere, once they get a little money, imagine themselves to be lords and kings. Livery attire on an Indian servant indeed!

Wade had to admit the mansion itself looked pretty impressive. Whitewashed, with a red-tiled roof, it sprawled out a mile wide. He was abandoned on a sun porch with wicker furniture. His escort disappeared elsewhere. Wade picked out what looked to be the most comfortable chair, a well-cushioned piece with a broad fan back, and settled in. He would relax and pack his pipe and wait. These people with pretensions might be bored stiff and playing solitaire when you arrive, but rest assured they'd make you wait a while.

Fifteen minutes later, the uniformed Indian ushered Wade into an airy, expansive office. The imported furniture, ornate Victorian with thick plush upholstery, surrounded a desk big enough to play soccer on. Huge windows—banks and banks of tiny panes—looked out across the Amazon, the jungle, and most of the rest of South America.

Wade could have described Tweed just by seeing his servant in the brocade livery. Overweight and paunchy, his Excellency did his best to imitate Frank Buck with his jodhpurs, high lace boots, and a riding crop (not a horse in the whole Colombia corridor, just a riding crop). From a nearby hatrack hung one of those pith helmets Teddy Roosevelt had popularized twenty years ago.

Tweed rose from behind his acre of desk. "Mr. Travers. Be seated."

Wade sat down without saying thanks for the privilege. The fires of anger were rekindling, and he could not keep them banked. Wade had dined with men of power, true heads of state. Who did this bush mogul think he was? "So what is it you want?"

"Two things, actually. Small things." Tweed settled his oversized body into his oversized chair, sat back with his elbows planted on its arms, and laced his fingers together. "I understand you have an excellent record for rescuing important people from the clutches of scoundrels."

"You mean getting that old rubber baron away from the *Cangaceiros* over in northeast Brazil?"

"A feat of courage and great cleverness, I'm told."

"My record for rescues is one for one, and it's going to stay that way. I paddled a dugout eighteen miles with a broken leg and spent seven weeks in the hospital in traction because of that one. My leg still aches in the rainy season. From now on, rubber barons are all strictly on their own."

"Ah, but this is not a rubber baron, as you call them. The prime minister's legate to certain Indians has encountered problems with natives of a bordering district in Brazil. We need someone fluent in Portuguese, Spanish, and our local Indian dialects—someone who knows enough of the terrain and local custom to extricate him and bring him safely back here."

18

Wade shook his head. "This is the deepest I've ever penetrated the Colombia corridor. I don't know the terrain or the language or the Indians. As for—"

"No matter. I have maps. And you've been other places; the Indians are all alike. The job shouldn't take you more than three or four weeks at most. They're not that far north of here. And the second little thing is even easier. I need a good man who knows aviation to choose the location for an airstrip here and supervise its construction."

"What makes you think I know beans about flying?"

"You recovered a lost bi-plane less than two years ago."

"Right. But the plane wasn't airborne. It had crashed somewhere within a fifteen-hundred-square-mile chunk of rain forest, and I was hired to find it. You don't have to know diddly about aviation to find a pile of junk in a tree."

"No matter. You have enough general expertise to handle the task. My staff here does not. You'll have to take the jobs one at a time, commencing with the legate. That one cannot wait, and the airstrip will require your constant supervision."

Wade pulled in a deep breath and let it out slowly, buying some time to think. "Pay?"

"Negotiable."

"That business in Brazil netted me eight thousand cruzeiros plus a hefty bonus. The bonus was gobbled up by the hospital bill incidentally. Two thousand plus expenses to find the plane. Five hundred fifty a month plus expenses to blaze a trace northeast from Manaos capable of taking heavy trucks in the dry season, which is close as I've ever come to building an airstrip."

His Excellency spread a crocodile smile across his face. "Mr. Travers, you must master this nasty little habit of expecting to be overpaid. The rate of pay will depend upon the condition of the legate upon his arrival here. He must be alive and in speaking condition. One hundred pesos for the airstrip, regardless of the length of time involved. Total expenses including labor and materials not to exceed one thousand. My staff assures me the task can be completed for eight hundred."

"You just said your staff can't do it, so how would they know?

You're expecting me to spend the whole dry season here doing your odd jobs for a couple centavos."

"As good here as anywhere. I happen to know you are without employment at the moment."

Wade was too hopping mad to think, so he silently counted to a thousand to make it appear he was thinking. "Five hundred in advance against expenses. And I need my passport for this. I'll be moving back and forth across the border."

"Two hundred should comfortably cover expenses. The passport stays in my hands until you've completed the work. I'll provide letters of passage enabling you to move within the area we discussed." Tweed shifted his weight; his burdened chair creaked. "I see you are, to use my father's phrase, a man of a wandering foot. I would regret hearing you had gone wandering before my little chores were completed. I have no idea what vague and distant voices call you onward, but I am certain they are many. I need a device to still those voices temporarily."

"Not much I can do about it then, is there?"

"Not unpleasant tasks, either of them. They are work you do well, work from which you must derive great personal pride. I am simply giving you the opportunity to tuck more feathers in your cap, as the English say."

"My cap doesn't need feathers. My pocket needs money."

"The legate is a charming man. When you meet him, you will be glad it was you sent to his aid. He will thank you warmly."

Wade stood up, suddenly weary. "You said maps."

Tweed stood also. "In my office. Tell them I sent you."

Wade took two steps toward the door and stopped. "The name of a local girl? Slim, about five-five, very pale blond, age . . . age . . ." He tried to pick a number. He could not. "Between fifteen and fifty. Ageless."

"I wouldn't know." The cold, flinty edge to Tweed's voice told Wade he certainly did know.

"Just wondered. Reminds me of a girl I knew in Rochester." Wade nodded toward the pith helmet, approximately, and walked out the door. The Indian saw him to the veranda and stood watching as he walked up the lane to the gate. Nobody trusted nobody.

He paused outside the gate. Ten feet away stood the butternut-colored kid. "You, boy." Wade addressed him in Spanish since he'd come from Peru. "You got on the boat at Iquitos. You stood around beside me at the dock, and you obviously followed me here. What do you want?"

The boy's eyes widened but he held his ground. "I am to say . . ." His tongue stumbled in broken Spanish. "Mama say . . ." He took a deep breath, gathering his courage from the four winds where it had flown. "I am to tell you that I am your son."

*chapter*
# 2

LIFE DID NOT OFTEN LOSE its happy smile toward Wade Travers; but today, life was sneering. With his passport in Tweed's hands, Wade could count on at least six months' servitude to the fat blob.

Of course, Wade could write a letter to his embassy, but embassies are known for their tortoise-like lack of speed. They would cajole Tweed with a few polite letters, and, by the time they started making serious noises, the rains would be here, and Tweed wouldn't need Wade any more. A whole year would be wasted, essentially a year without pay.

He could file for a new passport, but that would take months also, and heaven knows how much red tape. That wasn't worth even thinking about.

And the girl. That girl. Tweed knew who she was, so at least she was not a figment of his imagination.

And to top it all off, here stood a butternut-colored snippet who wanted to call him "Papa."

Wade snarled more at Life than at the boy. "I don't need this. I don't need any of this." He stuffed both hands in his pockets and shuffled off along the dusty, palm-lined road.

The boy fell in beside him with a little double-step and spoke in Spanish. "You have no questions to ask me?"

"Not at the moment, kid."

The lad was as full of brass as a munitions factory, but he wasn't all that rotten—at least, he didn't seem so. Wade wasn't angry at the boy; he was angry at Life in general and Tweed in particular. Why take it out on a kid?

"Keed! Tha'ss English! I spick English alzo."

Wade glanced at him anew. "Do you! Where'd you learn it?"

"Meeshin. Eh-school at meeshin I go. Tree years. Learn reet, write."

"Reet. You mean *read*."

"*Si*. Goot eh-school, learn lots to reet."

"Mmm. Take a piece of advice from a man who grew up in New York state speaking real English, kid. Stick to Spanish."

The boy ignored the advice. "Not so bad. You get stuck with lots worse keed mebbe, eh?"

Laughter exploded out of Wade, and laughter had been the farthest thing from his mind. "Maybe."

They were somewhere in the midst of the settlement, such as it was. Probably no more than two dozen border police were stationed here, counting the Colombian and Brazilian contingents together. That the village existed at all was simply happenstance: the Colombia corridor met the river here and not elsewhere. Iquitos to the west, where the Maranon might now be called the Amazon, was a major city. So was Manaos to the east, where the Rio Negro joined the river. Neither metropolis needed this border settlement. Wade certainly didn't.

He stopped to look around. A few crude huts blended into the forest here and there. Two military compounds had been cleared and fenced off. Their buildings were covered with the corrugated metal roofs that were getting so popular. A few women vendors sat under low trees, their wares spread around them on blankets.

"Ever been here before, boy?"

The boy frowned and hesitated. Perhaps he was concocting an answer that would fit with the rest of his story. He shook his head. "Iquitos. Meeshin. My veelage. No here. No so down rio."

"You mean never this far downriver before."

"*Si*." The boy smiled brightly. His were the loveliest teeth, smooth and white and even.

"Got any money?"

"No money. All money go boat Iquitos here. Pay boat come."

23

"How'd you expect to get along with no money?"

"Steal." He said it with the same nonchalance he would have used were he planning to dig ditches or tap rubber. Wade knew instantly that the boy was already well committed to what would be his lifetime occupation—avoidance of authorities.

"Not while you're with me, you don't." Wade wandered over to the nearest vendor offering food and dropped down on his heels to look from bowl to bowl. Grinning, the Indian woman swept her hand across the vessels. A black cloud of flies lifted so that he could get a better look at the contents.

He combined Spanish with a pointing finger. "Two of those, a couple big scoops of that, and four eggs. Hard-boiled?"

*"Huevos duros, sí."* She wrapped the lunches separately in two sheets of newspaper.

Wade didn't ask now much. He dropped a couple centavos Colombian into her hand and watched her eyes. She didn't seem displeased, so he thanked her before she could start dickering and handed the boy his lunch. Together they wandered over to a shady tree in what would be a plaza, if this settlement had a plaza. It seemed that so far all the building funds had gone into Tweed's residence.

Wade started with his big scoop of "that," hoping it was rice. It was. "What's your name?"

"Pato."

"That's all? Duck?"

The boy giggled. "Meeshin teacher, he called me Pato all time. Say I walk wiggle."

"Waddle like a duck. And what's my name?"

"Wehd Trahfferss." The boy paused. "Mama tell me."

"H'm. You also happened to be within earshot when the boat steward at Iquitos pronounced it and when I was talking to the customs officer here."

"So I know iss you, eh?"

Wade twisted around to stare at him. In this half-grown little runt lurked the mind of a Machiavelli. "How old are you?"

"Old? *Viejo?* Very, I hope."

"No. How many years do you have now?"

"Oh. This my twelve dry season."

"Twelve. *Doce*."

"*Doce, sí*."

"And your mother's an Indian."

The boy nodded violently.

Wade finished his rice and started on the "those." It was probably a monkey arm. "And she says you're Wade Travers's son."

"*Sí*." His mouth was full.

Wade polished off the drumstick and wiped his mouth on his arm. He cracked the first of his two eggs. "Y'know, Pato, I've had a lot of close scrapes, but none of them was ever caused by carelessness. Know what I mean?"

"No."

"Sometimes I have to take chances, but they're always calculated chances. I try never to do anything that's going to get me into trouble I can't handle. Like mess around with Indian women, for instance. Best way in the world to get a poison dart in your back. So I've never touched 'em. I have a solid reputation among the Indians for leaving their women alone."

He could feel the nerves tensing in the bundle of energy beside him.

"Also," Wade added, "I came down from the states in 1910 and made my first trek up the river here in 1911. That was, let's see, eleven years ago." He twisted around to look Pato right in the eye. "So now what—*son*?"

Those dark, dark eyes climbed the hill to meet Wade's and quickly slid down again to study the grass. "One of us don' count numbers too good mebbe, eh?"

"Maybe." The luncheon partners fell silent. Wade leaned back against the tree trunk and closed his eyes. "Why me, Pato?"

"Meeshin preech God, no more reet, put me work fields. No Mama gone." The boy's voice was soft—frightened but not cowed. "I need goot man, strong father. Strong eyes you have." The voice hesitated again. "You my father."

Great eyes. Peachy. He heard the newspaper crumple. The boy had finished lunch. "You're awful small for twelve. Sick much when you were little?"

"Seek? *Sí*. Worms meeshin says. And malaria. You get malaria ever?"

"Quinine's my middle name." Wade pocketed his second egg for later and fumbled for his plug and pipe.

The soft voice hardened a bit with hope. "Leedle keed no use. No goot. Beeg keed I help you many things. Not so bad. Help you lots."

"What's a runt like you gonna do for me?"

Pato flipped around and up onto his knees to face Wade. "Ask me!" He grinned brightly. "Ask me. I do."

Wade studied him a moment. "Okay, hotshot. Coming up the hill here I saw a girl—just a glimpse. She's about this much taller than you, very fair skin—"

"Wha'ss fair?"

"Light. Creamy. Not dark. Very blond hair—*muy rubia* —and cut real short. Floats like a halo all around her face. Gorgeous eyes—huge, a soft smoky blue. Find out for me who she is and where she lives."

"Gotchit!" Pato bolted to his feet and with a cheery wave trotted away toward the path down the bluff.

Wade packed his pipe, torched it, and leaned back to sift options. Nasty in a way, sending the boy off to seek a will-o'-the-wisp, but what harm was there? It would keep him busy and out from underfoot. If it kept him busy enough, Wade might never see his "son" again, and Pato could latch onto some other luckless fellow.

And what if by some wild chance the boy did learn about her? Wade had no intention of following up on the information. He was curious, that was all. She was a ray of light in a very gloomy jungle, and he wondered how she happened to end up illuminating this particular dark hole. He thought about the way she moved, so soft and yet so arrow straight.

His pipe went out. Scowling, he drew a few extra times. He even had a match struck before he realized there was no tobacco left. He had been sitting here all wrapped up in pipedreams for . . . for how long? Long enough to smoke a pipeful without realizing it. She was bewitching him.

Nonsense!

He wasn't going to seek her out, but what *was* he going to do? He was certain what he would not do—rescue legates or scratch out airstrips. He told Tweed he needed maps. This afternoon he would devote to poring over his Excellency's maps. Studying decent maps was never a waste of time. He would line up a canoe, too, with a couple paddlers.

Tweed would be pleased that Wade was getting to work promptly. The fat fool wouldn't catch on until too late that Wade, plus canoe, had bolted for Brazil before the dawn's early light. Wade was pretty certain Tweed's sphere of influence would not extend beyond the Colombia corridor. Once in Brazil, Wade could move freely again, for his Portuguese was better than his Spanish and he felt pretty much at home there. In Manaos he could get the passport situation straightened out quickly.

Wade lurched to his feet and ambled off toward the downhill path. Things were still bleak, but not quite as bleak as before. He'd certainly faced far tougher problems—problems carrying the threat of death, not just inconvenience. He had even talked himself into a fairly good mood by the time he reached that vaulted little clearing where he had first seen the girl.

*The* girl.

It was stupid to think Pato might succeed in finding out about her, but somehow Wade wished he would.

He would at least like to learn her name.

# chapter
# 3

IT WAS AN ORDINARY TREE—as ordinary as trees in this jungle ever were—reaching only into the middle layers of the forest's understory. Still, it was home to a weirdly fascinating gaggle of creatures. Some of them—the dayfolk and the nightfolk—lived yards apart yet never in their lives saw each other.

Wade leaned his back against this ordinary tree and listened a few moments as day turned raucously into night. The toucans, howler monkeys, and varied parrot types were shutting up—finally. Now the night crew was coming on, and they were, if anything, noisier.

From the river shore a hundred yards away, a crocodile bellowed, booming as if it were calling from inside a tobacco barrel. A night bird shrieked in the branches overhead; Wade had never really familiarized himself with birds he could not see. The Indians knew them all, of course.

A faint rustle stirred the air high above him. It might be a *douroucouli* —an owl monkey—a gentle, wide-eyed little softy. They almost never made noise. Then again it might be a night hunter, one of the cats. They almost never made noise either. Maybe Wade was unwise to stand here any longer.

A bat flibbered by, inches from his nose, as a couple ants burned fire-dots on his left shin. He brushed so frantically at his leg that he barely heard the whisper of someone approaching. He wheeled.

She stood six feet away, illuminated by the small flame of a single match, and read in painful singsong from a notebook: "Dispense uh may, seen yore. Yo key air o hab lar cone oon hom bray say ah mah Twee dough." She was a white woman, but the yellow matchlight made her tanned skin look warm, like toast. Huge, dark, liquid eyes caught the tiny points of light.

Wade grinned. "Downstate New York, probably the City."

She gazed at him dumbstruck, her eyes widening still more.

He stepped forward and extended his hand. "Wade Travers, Rochester."

The burning match reached her fingers. Wade might have expected a demure yelp and perhaps an "Ouch!" What he got was an expletive he hadn't heard since he mustered out of the army.

She popped the finger into her mouth, then reversed it, and pointed it at him. "New York! I don't believe it! *New York?!*" She glanced at his extended hand, dropped her notebook, and grasped his hand in both of hers, as a monkey might lock onto a tasty guava.

She bracketed her "Am I glad to meet you!" with expletives. Without the matchlight Wade could barely see her, but it seemed she had dark hair done in those short little finger waves so popular these days.

"So what brings you to the middle of nowhere looking for . . . who? . . . Tweedo? Or is it Tweed you want?"

"Tweed? Is there really a Tweed, like Boss Tweed?"

"Bigger than life and twice as ugly."

"I'm supposed to see him about some kind of regional visa, a permit to go up into the corridor further and maybe cross into Brazil. Know anything about that?"

"I know there isn't any such thing, which means Tweed will sell you one for however much cash you have."

"Oh. It's like that, huh?" She unleashed another expletive. "Name's Marcia Lewis. You said Travers, right? You seem at home here. Is there anyplace to buy a drink?"

"Not recommended. In the local pub you'd be the only white woman in a vast herd of lonesome border guards feeling sorry for themselves. Well, almost the only one." And he couldn't possibly imagine *her* in a pub.

"I can take care of myself."

"Don't doubt it. But I have a standing policy to avoid trouble when I can, and I'd be with you." He picked up her notebook and started walking, very casually. He was suddenly quite curious to get this blaspheming beauty under better light, and the settlement's only streetlamp stood down by the dock.

"We're headed for the shorefront, right? I just came from there. Nobody ever heard of this Tweed. I already asked." She fell in beside him. "You live here?"

"Not if I can help it. How did you get here? You weren't on the mail boat from Iquitos."

"Private launch. Leased it in Santarem. The local steamboat line was too slow and didn't stop where I wanted to. Come on now. Quit avoiding my questions. What's an apple knocker doing in this Godforsaken neck of the woods?" She snorted.

He paused a moment, listening, as a soft rustle tickled the leaves ten feet to their right. Whatever it was shrank back into the blackness. He decided it probably wasn't human and walked on.

"I'm a businessman. My business would be called adventuring by some, I suppose, but it's a business all the same. Doing jobs no one else can do—at least, as well."

"Soldier of fortune."

"In a sense. Your stereotype soldier of fortune, though, has a reputation for recklessness. I don't."

"Yeah. I hear you won't even take a woman to the village pub for fear the locals will riot when they see her."

"Avoiding recklessness has made me what I am today."

"Which is . . . ?"

"Still alive." He listened again and changed his mind about that vague noise among the leaves. Someone *was* following them. "You spent most or all of your life in one of the world's great cities. So what brought you to the Amazon, which is as far removed from a city as you can get?"

"I'm a reporter. *New York Sun Telegram*. On assignment."

"And the *Sun* picks up the tab for launches and such?"

"I'm on an account, yeah."

"Ever think of learning a foreign language?"

"You understood what I was saying."

"Sure, because I'm from New York, too. Anyone from a Spanish-speaking country, though, might have a little trouble." Here was that solitary streetlight. Wade parked beneath it.

He was right about her wavy black hair. It shone. And there wasn't a thing wrong with the face or figure, either. She wore a dark dress shaped more or less like a potato sack. The women of Lima wore them, too, so it must be the fashion. Her black handbag was bulky, but not abnormally so.

He turned slightly and held her notebook up to the light so that he was facing the spot where he had last heard their follower. He leafed casually from page to page, reading at random and keeping an eye out for movement in the brush.

"Listen, Travers. That's none of your business." She grabbed at the notebook, but he held on. She gave up almost right away, so it must not hold anything sensitive or secret.

He handed it back to her. "Never saw Spanish spelled out in phonetic English like that before. Key air o. *Quiero. I want.* You ever decide to give up reporting, you can make a fortune teaching languages. Got a press card?"

"Sure." She cocked her head and studied him a moment. Then she dug into that big purse, fished out a wallet, and pulled a card. *Sun Telegram,* all right. The huge dark eyes flooded all over him. "Now that you've checked me out, how about going to work for me? Interpreter, local contact, agent, navigator; the clown who pilots this launch doesn't know down from up. I pay well."

"Tempting, but I'm otherwise engaged. That your launch there?" He waved toward a smoky gray hull lurking in the dimness beyond the lamplight. He didn't have to see her nod. The dingy boat was the only likely candidate on the dock. "As you said, I'm pretty much at home here. So take my advice, and go back to your launch for the night. Tomorrow morning climb the hill and turn right. Tweed's place is at the end of the path with the palm trees. Iron gate, sentry box. And don't let him sell you any bridges named Brooklyn."

She giggled with that delightful little lilt women manage to insert into their laugh. "Thanks. I will." Marcia Lewis extended her hand, and Wade accepted it. Her grip was as strong as any man's. She walked off, her hair and dress melting into the night.

Wade listened a long time. He heard the noises to be expected from the launch as Marcia boarded and closed herself in. On the periphery of his mind his ears took in all the normal sounds the night creatures make. And he listened for their follower. Nothing.

He slung his hammock out behind the customs shed—as good a place as any to settle in for the night. He wondered ever so briefly where Pato was staying, and then he slept.

Most of the next day Wade spent getting frustrated. Yesterday he had learned that Tweed's maps were next to useless. Now he learned that no one had any better ones. No problem for him; he didn't need a map to get to Manaos. But Tweed might expect him to become familiar with the country to the northwest, and surely Tweed was smart enough to know those maps wouldn't serve.

He had a terrible time finding a serviceable dugout and even worse luck finding a warm body willing to paddle it. What was the matter with Indians these days? Didn't they know the value of the peso? Tweed gave him a couple of absolutely worthless letters of introduction. Wade saw nothing of either Pato or that foxfire.

By mid-afternoon he smelled a rat. Besides Tweed's clear lack of cooperation, the lesser minions were eyeing Wade suspiciously. They seemed to be watching the launch, too. Something definitely was amiss; the day was coiled tight like an over-wound spring. Between the din of dawn and the noise of sunset, the jungle hangs relatively quiet on the senses. It seemed particularly silent today, and that didn't help the tension a bit.

The day exploded as Wade, still seeking dependable paddlers, was crossing the dirt path toward a jumbled cluster of huts. Gunshots over by the dock set off every bird and monkey in the jungle. A soprano voice cried out; men's voices shouted. Something the size of a truck came crashing through the undergrowth toward Wade.

Pato popped out of the ferns not a rod away. The boy slammed against a tree trunk and clung to it gasping. He was naked except for a dirty loincloth, and injured somehow; blood flowed from a gash just above his right knee. The "truck" noise dissected itself into the thrashing of two or three men unaccustomed to moving through dense growth.

Wild-eyed as a trapped animal, Pato spotted Wade. "Papa!"

32

Wade bolted to the boy and scooped him up as his pursuers, three of Tweed's border guards, came floundering out onto the path. Wade glanced over his shoulder. Hang if one of the guards wasn't raising a pistol! It was no warning shot, either; the man disappeared in a black cloud as a chunk of bark flew off a tree by Wade's cheek. The gunshot upset all the jungle loudmouths anew and did nothing good for Wade's nerves, either. He wheeled and ran.

Pato might be a half-grown runt, but he weighed a ton. Wade really must be getting old. Ten years ago he could have outrun those three while carrying twice the weight. Not now.

Another gun roared behind him.

He could take refuge in the undergrowth or among these huts. In the jungle, birds and monkeys would betray his position. His best bet was to get some buildings between himself and them, and then take to the bush. When it was clear, maybe he could sneak up the hill and get Tweed to call off his goons.

His lungs burned. They couldn't suck in the dank air fast enough. He'd better pace himself or he'd collapse short of safety. But he dare not slow up—those clowns were too close behind.

He raced around the nearest hut, plunged past another. He dove between two hovels and jumped a brush fence into a pig sty. A huge, cantankerous-looking sow lurched to her feet as piglets scattered in all directions. He hopped the far fence before she could reach him, knowing that an enraged sow could tear him apart.

He was spent. He had no more to give. Nor could he dump Pato in some safe corner until he could draw the guards off. The kid was latched on like a tick in a dog's ear.

She splashed across his vision like sudden light at the end of a tunnel. The wood wraith. Fox-fire. He came around a corner, and there she stood at the door of a modest little hut, watching him with those huge pale eyes.

He forgot Spanish. He forgot Portuguese. He forgot politeness. His tortured lungs barely let him squeak out "Help us."

How stupid! This child-woman knew no English. Yet he could not find the scrap of energy needed to say it right.

She hestitated only the slightest moment. Her pale arm whipped out and grabbed his. She dragged him through the door and into the middle of the single room. Her bare foot kicked aside a woven mat. With unexpected strength she yanked open a small trap door and literally stuffed the two of them down into some sort of tiny fruit storage cellar, barely a hole in the ground.

The trap door slammed shut; the mat whispered across it. Wade tried to gulp in the stale air without making noise. Pato stirred and seemed to know by instinct to keep silence. Wade groped around for his handkerchief. He'd better do something for that leg before the kid lost too much more blood.

Overhead, the woman was speaking in smooth, fluid Spanish. Her charming voice lilted soft and melodious. Men's voices responded, not the least bit charming. Wade couldn't make out the words. Hard-heeled shoes clacked across the floor, over the trap door. The whole floor must be elevated for the footfalls sounded no more hollow on the trap door than on the floorboards. Huts rarely had floors at all. Why should this one be so elaborate?

Silence above. Wade waited for days. Weeks. Longer. What was keeping her? But then, she knew what was going on up there. He didn't. He'd just have to trust her. He hated having to trust someone else, especially with his life.

Kinked grotesquely, Wade's legs started to cramp up. Pato's amazing weight half crushed him, pinned him to the musty dirt. The air grew thicker and heavier; it was putting him to sleep.

Dawn broke so instantly that the sudden brightness forced Wade's eyes shut a moment. The trap door yawned wide. Sunlight spilled into the cramped little fruit cellar. Fresh air brushed across his cheek like a draught of cool water.

Framed in brightness, her face peered down at him. She smiled as if he were a guest standing in her parlor. That sweetly musical voice spoke softly in unaccented English. "Good evening, Mr. Travers."

# chapter
# 4

"ELINOR. THASS HER NAME. Never I seen hair that much silky white. Not old woman white. Rubia white." Pato ripped a chunk of bread in half. "Local *bruja*—you know whass a bruja, eh . . . ?"

"Yeah. Magic woman. Lady witch doctor."

"*Sí*.Local bruja name Locha—Losha?—something like dat; she much eh-scared of Elinor. Real eh-scared. Say Elinor big magic, eh? Others, they say Elinor no a bruja. So who's right, eh?" Pato shrugged.

"Why're they scared?"

" 'Cause never *she* be scared. Either loco or big magic, see?"

Wade leaned back against a wall post and dug out his pipe. As he shaved the tail end of his next-to-last tobacco plug, he watched Pato. The boy was still stuffing his mouth, fifteen minutes after Wade had finished eating. Wade felt mildly embarrassed that the kid was putting away so much of this Elinor woman's food. Pato must not have eaten since yesterday when Wade bought him lunch.

"What else did you learn?"

"No much. Nobody don' know nuthin 'bout her. She come, go, help out here, there. Like a ghost, some say. *Una fantasma*."

Will o' the wisp. Fox-fire.

Wade lit his pipe with difficulty; his tobacco was damp.

Pato licked his fingers. "Hear dis by feeserman, he sell fresh feesh near custom shed: Tweed don' like her none."

"Tweed causing her trouble? Pestering her?"

"Pestering?" Pato frowned at what must be a new word in his tortured lexicon. "Trouble, *sí*. Like mans make now then. She, uh, she stay away. Don' get near Tweed."

"She here before he came?"

"Think so, *sí*. Tweed no here long, come border guards and stuff. Most pipples here first, 'fore Tweed. Nice veellage. Feesh, hunt, trade, don' need Tweed."

"Who does?" Strange. Maybe it was because Wade was just plain tired, but Elinor's little hut here made him feel so comfortable. At ease. Even the hardwood wall post felt good to lean against. Strange? No. Silly. Stupid. Why couldn't he even think straight when she was occupying any corner of his mind?

The charm of this tiny hovel certainly didn't lie in its furniture— there wasn't any. Elinor's bed was a hammock slung across a corner, same as everyone else's. She owned no table or chairs. The stove was a firepit, the pantry a curtained crate in one corner.

Pato sat on the floor with his plate before him. His injured leg stretched out at an odd angle. It didn't seem to be bothering him yet; perhaps he would escape serious infection.

The girl-woman herself entered, framed momentarily in the sunset-orange light of the doorway, her bare feet silent on this unusual wooden floor. She was carrying Wade's swag. Now how did this young lady manage to come by that?

Wade remembered his manners just in time and swung to his feet. "It'll be dark soon. We'll leave then."

"To where?" she asked pleasantly.

Wade sat down again and resumed holding up the wall post. "Sneak up the hill and find out what Tweed must be thinking of. Find out why his turkeys were shooting at Pato here."

"He stole a wallet of money from one of the guards. I learned that at the customs shed. Also, your bundle was rolled up behind the shed, so I brought it. I thought you'd want it."

"Yes'm, I do. Thank you." Wade glared at Pato. "A minute ago I felt sorry some guard's bullet ripped your leg. Not any more. I told you no stealing when you were with me, didn't I?"

Pato's huge cow eyes dropped. "*Sí*, Papa." The eyes drifted back to meet Wade's. "But was so eesee. There it sticks from his pocket, eh? Say, 'Lemme come with you, Pato.'"

"I'll return it to Tweed and see if I can get you off the hook. Where is it?"

"Don' know." The eyes slipped downward again. "Loss it somewhere. Don' know where. Dropped I run, eh?"

Wade closed his eyes. A bit of charity is nice, but this kid was fast outgrowing Wade's charitable intentions. He'd better dump the little troublemaker right now, before things got worse.

Elinor settled onto the floor mat near Wade's feet. "I'm not certain it would be wise for you to approach Señor Tweed. He seems to feel you are betraying him in some way—or about to.. At least, that's what Señor Tweed's cook thinks. Perhaps I should go to him in your behalf."

"No!" It burst out of Wade much more forcefully than he intended. He adjusted his voice downward a couple notches. "No, I don't want you to do that. He had me lined up to, ah, work on a few projects for him. Suddenly his whole attitude changes. Just a misunderstanding. We'll get it worked out."

She cocked her head. "Oh? Projects? What projects?"

Pato blurted some sort of abortive warning. The hut turned dark as a man in the doorway blocked the waning light of evening. A uniformed guard appeared, then another. The guards carried their usual sidearms, and one of them quite carelessly waved a 16-gauge.

With Elinor they babbled some sort of local Spanish that was all clouded up with stray Indian words and garbled syllables and key sounds left out altogether. Wade could pick up only snatches, and he was pretty good with Spanish. From gestures and tones of voice, he discerned one important tidbit of information: for concealing Wade and Pato, and perhaps for other reasons as well, this Elinor was in trouble just as deep as he was. Maybe deeper.

The shotgun waved in Wade's general direction. *"Tu tambien."*

"Me, too, huh?" Wade lurched to his feet and stretched mightily. He helped Pato stand up. These faceless army types were herding Elinor toward the door.

Outside, the cacophony of nightfall was beginning. Darkness comes rapidly, especially in the jungle, which is gloomy in the best of light. That would work to Wade's advantage; so would the fact that these neophyte border guards seemed like city slickers unaccustomed to operating in a rain forest. No competent woodswalker would crash through the underbrush, as those two had this afternoon.

Wade shoved Pato roughly toward the door. Elinor was just stepping outside. Two of the three guards were outside now. That shotgun, on one of its aimless circuits, was swinging toward Wade again. Elinor stopped and turned to protest something.

Now!

Wade lunged forward. He grabbed the barrel of the shotgun, wrenched it upward, rammed it back. The gun butt knocked the wind out of its wielder. One down.

The shotgun blast sent the treetops into bedlam as dayfolk and nightfolk together screeched and howled.

Pato turned into a frenetic windmill of arms and legs. His shrieks added to the mindless uproar. Already his flailing had given one would-be captor a bloody nose.

"To the river!" Wade yelled in English, and Pato was gone that quick, swallowed up in the forest.

Elinor was just standing there, frozen in place. Didn't she have any instinct at all for survival? Wade took a fast swing at the fellow coming at him and connected, but not well. He grabbed Elinor's slim arm and yanked. A pistol boomed behind him but the shot went wild. He dived for the bushes, dragging the woman with him.

She was objecting, struggling, resisting as he hauled her through the dense growth. Light and reason disappeared, and they were plowing through solid, leafy darkness, disconnected from reality. The din above and behind them quieted by degrees.

He needed his second breath. He flattened out against the trunk of a kapok tree, pulled Elinor tight against him, and spent a few welcome minutes simply sucking in air.

She started to speak, but he clamped his hand over her lips. He listened. The treetop loudmouths were calming down. He could hear no trucks, no elephants, and he was sure those border guards couldn't move silently through the night jungle. They would no doubt patrol the river shore, but they weren't following at the moment.

He glanced down at Elinor and felt instantly ashamed. She

couldn't move; she probably couldn't even breathe. He let her go and mumbled an unintelligible but heartfelt "Sorry."

She kept her voice low, midnight soft. "I will not be made a fugitive. I must go back, and you should, too. We can help the boy somehow."

"I'm on my way to Brazil," he whispered, "and if I can connect up with Pato, so is he." And then Wade found himself saying, "I want you to come with us. I've met a thousand Tweeds. They're all alike, and I know he's too much trouble for you to handle. Maybe you think that because you've done okay so far, things'll stay that way. They won't. You can't win. Please come."

She shook her head. "Everything I have is here—"

"Which ain't much. I've seen what you have."

"I don't mean possessions. Not things. People. People who need me; people I need, too. The cook up at Tweed's house has just committed her life to Jesus. I can't leave now; she needs nurturing. And the woman who lives on the dugout down beyond the customs shed—if I don't bring her bread and fresh fruit, who will? These and many other things I must do. No. I'm sorry."

Wade opened his mouth to argue and closed it again. Why was he arguing, for Pete's sake? He didn't want the responsibility of still another warm body—another fugitive, as she so aptly put it. Already he was stuck with Pato. Here was an adult capable of making her own way. What was it to him if she chose to stay? Her choice. She knew what she was doing.

He nodded. "Any back trails down to that little cove west of the shed? I stashed a dugout there earlier today. Couldn't find any competent paddlers, but I did turn up a canoe that doesn't leak—much."

"There is, but if you take it, you'll miss Pato. If he ran directly for the river, I think I know where he'll be. I'll help you find him." She turned and moved off through the thickness.

Wade could barely discern the diffuse lightness of her white cotton dress, hazy gray amid black. She slipped quietly through the tangle, but not silently. He remembered his first sight of her yesterday when she disappeared so perfectly and completely that not even the birds and monkeys took notice. Darkness, of course, made quite a difference. Still . . . how had she done that?

By the time Wade and Elinor reached the river, Tweed's minions had a boat out on the water. They were rowing here and there along the shore, trying ineffectively to beat back the darkness with a couple smoky torches.

Wade spotted a momentary flash of red just off shore—reflected light from a pair of eyes at water level. "You know," he mused, "I think I'd like this river better if it had a few less alligators in it."

"I've heard that about piranhas, too, and snakes and crocodiles and candiru. But not butterflies." She commenced walking, moving along the shore with the river to their right, floating effortlessly through the tangled night. "Yet God in his wisdom made them, you know—butterflies and crocodiles alike."

"He made Tweed, too, but that doesn't mean I have to like the bum." Here was the little cove where he had beached his new dugout. He groped a bit in the bushes, but he hated doing that— too many things with fangs waited in bushes. "It's not here!"

"They're coming this way," she whispered.

"It's not here anywhere!" Wade stood at the water's edge and scanned the sullen, slurping darkness. Now and then a ripple caught the tired light of the approaching torches. If his canoe were still here, he could surely see it.

She tugged at his sleeve. "Let's check downstream a bit, in case it drifted loose."

"I know how to beach a boat, lady." Wade instantly regretted saying that, but he didn't apologize. Instead, he followed her quietly, grumpily. Why couldn't local Indians show a little more respect for private property? They seemed to figure that anything they saw and needed was available for the borrowing, anytime of the day or—

"Papa!"

From somewhere out on the water, Wade's son of two days, the inveterate thief, came paddling toward shore, materializing out of nothingness. Wade heard him; Elinor heard him; the boatmen upstream heard him. They shouted and waved their torches.

Pato nudged the canoe's prow against the mud at Wade's feet; the kid was very good with a canoe, but then all the locals were.

With wild splashing, the boatload of pursuers headed this way.

They fired guns, but it was bluff—they could surely see nothing to aim at. That boat, though, had at least four paddlers, and Wade had only two—himself and a stripling. Here was a race he could not win. But he would not lose for lack of trying. He clambered in over the roughhewn bow. Pato curled into a knot as Wade crawled over him.

But when Wade grabbed the second paddle, swung around, and settled in the stern, it wasn't Pato seated in the bow. Elinor was there, and already she had usurped Pato's paddle to shove off from the bank. Wade dipped his blade deep and pulled the back end around as she stroked, driving the canoe forward. They were off on a fearsome and frenzied retreat.

"That way!" she whispered hoarsely, and a pale arm waved toward the left. Wade veered the canoe to port. The darkness was so thick now he could see nothing at all of land or water. The shoreline was obvious, though, marked by the random flashes of a million fireflies.

They cruised in close to the warm, dank trees. Softly the canoe nudged sawgrass; Elinor parted it, pushed it down with her blade. And now they stopped dead in the water in a thickly matted marsh, wrapped in perfect blackness.

Wade twisted around to watch and listen. Bits and pieces of red-orange torchlight flickered beyond the vegetation. With quiet sighs the sawgrass arched itself erect again. Tree frogs resumed their chirping. Out beyond the riverbank men shouted and waved their puny torches and brandished their guns. Here, within reach of shore, peace reigned.

They were safe.

Wade straightened front again and sagged against rough wood. He rubbed his sweaty face and whispered, "Thanks for the help. But it looks like you're with us after all."

"I suppose so. Your swag is still in my house."

"Nothing in it worth going back for." Wade grinned and pulled out his pipe. "Got all I need." The heady cheer of escaping Tweed's greedy claws faded; just barely, in the swimming blackness, he could see her wan face. The sadness showed even in the depth of night.

"Hey, look," he pressed, "you can do better anywhere else, believe me. You're not leaving behind that much."

She smiled wanly. "You're right, I'm sure. Still . . ." She sat back with a heavy sigh. Her fragile voice floated whisper soft. "Much too often I ask my Lord to lead me and then struggle against him when he tries. I must learn not to fight so when he sends me forth. It's difficult. Life was rich there."

Rich? A half empty hut, bare feet, plain dress? What could she possibly have that made her ache so with the leaving of it?

Wade groped and fumbled for his tobacco, his mind on this strange fair girl.

Reality dawned on him slowly, painfully: his only remaining tobacco plug was in his swag.

# chapter
# 5

NIGHT HAZE OBSCURED ALL BUT THE BOLDEST STARS and darkened what was usually a silver sky. The last-quarter moon was too old and feeble to soften this darkness much. The unbounded river picked up the sky color and spread it around them forever in all directions. They floated in endless gray-black.

This time of year the river current flowed at the speed of a strolling man. Without a lot of effort, Wade could do five miles an hour paddling alone. Six hours so far; thirty miles—and he had another four or five hours left of the night. By daybreak he could be fifty or sixty miles from Tweed. That thought felt so good it almost canceled the weariness.

Pato, curled up asleep amidship, was tossing a lot. No doubt infection was starting to catch up to him. He'd be restless and feverish for a couple days yet. Crazy kid. Wade watched him a few minutes, then looked past him to Elinor.

She ought to be asleep, too; she had worked as hard as he. She had reversed herself in the bow and now she rested, draped casually across the ragged wood. And she was looking at him, those great, glorious eyes wide open. Were it anyone else, Wade would accuse them of staring. Somehow, though she watched him steadily, she was not staring.

He picked up his pace; no use lollygagging. "I know nothing about you, and you seem to know everything about me. You even called me by name when you invited us to leave your root cellar."

"The soldiers supplied your name. Later, when I was talking to the woman who cooks for Tweed, I learned he is angry with you for some reason."

She shifted, stretched her back, and settled in again. "I learned also, from Manuel Perreira, the fisherman, that your son was asking everyone questions about me. Why am I an object of your son's curiosity?"

Well now. Should Wade tell the naked truth—that it was his curiosity being served and not Pato's? Or should he take refuge in a lie? And if so, which lie? For simplicity he chose the lie he had given Tweed. "You remind me of a girl I knew in Rochester so I set Pato to asking around. Thought it'd keep him out of trouble. Just goes to show how much I know about boys."

"And what did he learn?"

"Not a thing."

Nor did she seem inclined to volunteer anything. She melted deeper into the crease of the bow. She slept awhile; and yet, even when her eyes drifted to half mast and eventually closed, Wade could not shake the feeling she was watching him.

Does the rising sun arouse the howler monkeys, or do the monkeys wake up the sun? Wade had heard that conundrum bandied about quite seriously by Jivaro Indian philosophers, but the question was academic; the sun and the noise rose as one, even though the dugout was still a good quarter mile offshore.

Pato rolled over onto his back and stared up at the crystal sky. "*Cotomonos*," he muttered. Howler monkeys.

"*Sí, cotomonos*," Wade agreed. "*Amanecer*." Dawn.

"*Tengo hambre. Y sed.*" Pato's speech was thick and slow; he wasn't even attempting his fractured English. Yesterday he had been so proud of it he had used nothing else.

"Yeah, I bet you're hungry and thirsty. We're headed for shore now. We'll dig you up some breakfast somewhere."

"'*Stamos en Brasil todavia*?'"

"Yep." Wade was guessing, but surely they had to be well into Brazil by now. With only a few brief rests (why, oh why, had he left that other tobacco plug in his swag?) Wade had kept them moving. And after a few hours' sleep Elinor had taken up a paddle again. They had made good time. Very good time.

The sun broke loose of the horizon as they nosed in against the bank. They dragged the dugout into the undergrowth and out of sight. Breakfast hung from the trees, free for the taking, and Wade discovered Elinor was a better climber than he.

He slept over half the day.

It was no cartographer's oversight that the village of Bacalhau did not appear on any map, including Tweed's. The governor of Amazonas himself decreed the village out of existence; its reputation for villainy and corruption made it *urbs non gratis* in emergent Brazil, with her new and heady pride of nationality. This did not in the least, of course, prevent the village from existing.

Bacalhau was one of Wade's favorite places in the world. Especially now. Here no one would ask about his passport. Here he could buy a good dinner for a small price. Beds came with or without other people in them—your choice.

The dugout bumped against Bacalhau's lone dock very nearly at sundown. This first day's travel had taken longer than Wade had expected. On the bright side, they were now deep into Brazil. Tweed's arm surely did not reach this far.

He lifted Pato bodily onto the dock and gave Elinor a hand she didn't really need. He swung the dugout around to the muddy red shore and beached it high. He rubbed his hands together in anticipation. "Dinnertime."

Elinor took Pato in her arms like a mother would and pressed her palm against his head. "We can find Pato a comfortable accommodation here, I hope. He's not well."

"Yeah. Not far from here. This way."

She had not asked about a comfortable place for herself, he mused. So far she seemed totally indifferent to her own circumstances. He had trained himself, because of his peculiar line of work, to put aside discomfort. But Elinor didn't just put it aside; she didn't seem to notice it existed.

Wade herded his crew up the dusty little street to a place he knew, one of the less unsavory hostelries. The main floor of the establishment consisted of a barroom and a dining room. The kitchen was actually more of a pantry, for the cook did all her dirty work out back in rain, sun, and dark of night, on a stove made from an oil drum.

Wade could do without the surly types that tended to hang around the bar. As clienteles in Bacalhau went, this place catered to the top of the line. Still, you're talking about a shifting assortment of folk: smugglers, disenchanted fortune seekers, crippled old *seringueiros*, outcasts and half-wits.

The adjacent dining room consisted of four tables, a mongrel mix of chairs and benches, and three kerosene lamps. The only dining patrons were just leaving, headed for the bar. Wade picked a table in the corner with his back to the wall. Without trying, he could see everything in this room and half of what went on at the bar.

"*Ola*, Wade!" From the barroom came Rosy, a yard wide and a meter tall. Her acres of cotton skirts swayed like a ponderous bell. Before Wade could warn her not to, she smacked a gooey kiss on his cheek.

His ears burned hot, and that was not at all like him; he was hardly ever embarrassed by anything life dished out. "*Ola, Rosa. Jantar, faz favor.*" He squelched any trace of warmth in his voice.

"*Sim. Temos frango e iscas.*"

Wade turned to Elinor. "The choice is chicken or liver."

She smiled at Rosa. "*Arroz e legumes, por favor.*" There was nothing wrong with her polite Portuguese.

Wade ordered chicken for Pato and himself and settled back to figure out why this whole scene seemed like something those new modern artists would splash onto canvas. He was a frequent patron here, anytime he was in the area. They knew him and he knew them—and yet the place felt out of joint somehow. Maybe after he had eaten . . .

Pato definitely was sick. His appetite had dwindled to that of a couple healthy men. Elinor picked delicately at her rice and vegetables. Wade fought his chicken, an old bird tough enough to go fifteen rounds with the champ, to a hostile standstill. Rosy came and went, now grinning at Wade, now scowling at Elinor. At least she didn't make any more amorous advances.

Coffee came, that densely rich bitter-black coffee that is Brazil's just claim to fame. Wade cadged a wad of tobacco from Rosy and, for the first time since leaving Colombia, could bury his head in a thick, creamy cloud of aromatic smoke.

46

Elinor took a sip of her hot coffee and immediately laced it with another big dollop of sugar. "You mentioned yesterday about some projects of some sort for Tweed. What was so laborious that you would work this hard to avoid it?"

"It's the principle of the thing. He didn't want to pay what I'm worth. Besides, I have other plans for the dry season." Wade glanced at Pato, nodding off over his goat's milk. They must leave soon and tuck Pato into bed.

The soft eyes were watching him. He had not yet answered her question, and her eyes reminded him of that.

He continued without really meaning to. "One little chore was to build an airstrip on that ridge behind the settlement. The other was to rescue some legate. Neither job appealed to m—"

"Legate!" The huge eyes opened wider. "Morris Hurley?"

"Yeah. That's the name Tweed's lieutenant mentioned. You know him?"

She sat up straight. "We must go back! If I'd known you were the one chosen to help Dr. Hurley, I would have . . . I mean I would not have . . . Quickly, Mr. Travers! It's extremely important that Dr. Hurley be freed immediately. I don't quite understand why you were the one chosen, but I accept it. We can make it back in two days, even paddling upcurrent."

"Now just hold on!" Wade felt his insides tighten up like a watch spring. "Tweed's a pain in the pinstripe, and I owe him nothing. And neither do you. I told you, I'm not getting involved in that little project, and I mean it. No."

"Yes, you are." She said it so quietly, so matter-of-factly, so nonbelligerently, that he found himself speechless. How could this wisp, this frail and gentle woman, wear the mantle of impertinence so gracefully?

A burly chorus of appreciation rumbled in from the bar, nearly drowning out normal speech clear back in the dining room. Moments later Rosy came stomping in to gather up the dishes. She was mumbling something about too skinny. All the girls these days were too skinny. For good measure, she scowled one more time at Elinor.

"*Quem?*" Wade asked.

Rosy made an attempt at wrinkling her nose but all she did was rearrange her pudgy cheeks a little. "Mahshah, uh, Loosh."

"Marcia Lewis?!"

"*Si*. Mahshah Loosh."

Wade tossed some coins on the table without counting too carefully and stood up. "If she's with Tweed's people, we're in big trouble. There's a back way out. Let's take it."

In the barroom a female voice yelped, a shocked, surprise sort of sound.

Elinor's eyes widened. "I believe she needs help. You must go help her!"

"She can take care of herself. She told me so."

"You help me good fine," Pato offered.

"Yeah, and look where it got me."

There was that yelp again, more strident this time.

Much against his better judgment, Wade trotted over to the doorway. Rosy pushed past him out into the barroom with her load of dishes. She swooshed off into the kitchen.

Seven or eight scummy types stood crowded into a tight knot against the bar. Wade could just barely discern a dark wavy head among them. She didn't seem to be in any immediate peril. Wade would have turned and made a quiet exit through the kitchen, but Pato was blocking his way. The boy craned his neck, watching eagerly, and some of the old vivacity had returned to his eyes.

Wade could hear Marcia's voice now, and she sounded frightened. When a streetwise woman with a mouth like a longshoreman feels threatened, she's probably in trouble. With grim foreboding, Wade headed for the bar.

He forced some boisterous good cheer into his voice. "Hey, Marcia! Is that you?" He shouldered past an old seringueiro with a scarred face. "By cracky, it *is* you!"

"Travers!" A smile like sunrise broke across her face. She pushed past an unwashed fellow of uncertain ancestry and wrapped around Wade as a drowning person seizes a life buoy. For the second time in an hour he got a sloppy kiss on the cheek.

Wade attached a grin to the outside of his mouth; it was either that or let the worry show. "Out the back door." In Portuguese he babbled something about not buying her dinner until she had inspected the kitchen; this way, please.

A beached whale—tiny black eyes sunk into a blubbery face—blocked his way. The fellow was tall as well as bulky. He must weigh three hundred.

Wade stared straight into those cetacean eyes. *"O que aconteceu?"*

*"A tua mulher?"*

*"A minha amiga."*

"What's he saying? What are you saying?" Marcia gripped his arm so tightly his fingertips tingled.

"Later. Stay behind me. And let go of my good arm!"

She didn't unlatch fast enough. The blubbery chap commented briefly on the implications of the legal principle ofttimes referred to in lay terms as "finders keepers" and punctuated his discourse with a healthy swing.

Wade couldn't duck fast enough, let alone free his arm in time to return the favor. The fellow caught him in the middle and lifted him bodily onto the bar. The guy's second swing would have dumped him on top of the bartender except that Wade managed to knock the blob back a step with a lucky kick.

A shotgun blast out of heaven froze the world in place. Rosy the barmaid stood in the kitchen door and expressed herself in terms that would have brought a blush to Marcia, had Marcia been conversant in Portuguese.

Rosy marched across the room scattering patrons, grabbed the front of Wade's shirt, and yanked him off the bar. She jerked a thumb toward the back door as she turned her attentions to the whale. By sheer force of personality she was driving the lout relentlessly toward the front door.

Wade knew an exit when he saw one. It's not too dignified to walk around folded up like a carpenter's rule, much less to sneak out the back, but dignity take the hindmost. With Marcia still clinging to him, he pushed past the tin pots and plucked chickens hanging from the rafters and staggered out into muggy night air.

He about-faced and espaliered himself against the nice solid back wall. He couldn't straighten up. He couldn't breathe. With some difficulty he talked himself out of throwing up.

Marcia tugged at his arm. "I don't think we should hang around here. Come on; let's get out of here."

"Gotta go back inside. Elinor and Pato are still there."

"You can't be serious! Those drunks will tear you to pieces. Nobody's worth going back there."

"And you're not worth this, far as I'm concerned, so don't go telling me what's worth what, you hear?" He wanted to draw a deep breath; he wanted to stand up straight; neither was happening. Even feverish, Pato was quick and clever. Wade wasn't worried about Pato. But Elinor . . . and that besotted mob . . .

"Don't you get sharp with me. We'll go find a local constable and let him handle it. Let him retrieve your Elinor and whoever. I mean, whomever."

Wade lurched erect, more or less, but it wasn't Marcia who helped him stand steady. A stronger hand than Marcia's held his elbow.

Elinor smiled up at him. "I sent Pato ahead to the dock to tell the skipper of Miss Lewis's launch to make ready. I assumed she'll not want to stay here in town, in light of the general mood, so to speak."

And the three of them were on their way down the dusty road toward the river—sandwich style, Wade thought ruefully—two slim slices of bread flanking a hunk of Travers's baloney. There had been a day when Wade would have killed for the pleasure of walking with a gorgeous lady on each arm. This day, he'd be satisfied simply to escape mauling by a whale.

Marcia was yammering nervously. "When Harry sent me down here—Harry Landis, my editor—when Harry sent me down here I didn't have the slightest inkling how different this was going to be. I mean, I grew up on the streets, right? I know my way around. But these guys." She called up another expletive.

He could breathe again, finally, and walk upright like a proper, civilized man. But he didn't feel like wasting his precious breath on "I told you so."

The launch loomed in the darkness at the far end of the rotting dock. Almost there. Almost safe.

"So why *did* you come down here? You didn't say."

"Chasing a story. Why else?"

"I mean here in Bacalhau. You were headed up into the corridor."

"Some little fisherman told me I could find competent guides here. Sure didn't see any there. He told me a lot of people here are looking for a temporary job."

"A lot of people here are out of work, but most of them are that way on purpose."

"Speaking of which: you ready to reconsider working for me? I'm going to need help with the language. Tonight, for instance, a lot was going on, and I couldn't make sense out of any of it. And I'm having no luck at all finding some key contacts that I need."

"Such as . . . ?"

"I didn't get this from Tweed. Didn't get anything useful from Tweed at all, come to think of it. Anyway, the most important man I gotta find is a professor. A Dr. Morris Hurley." Her crackling black eyes looked up at him like a puppy begging for a treat. "You'll help me find him, wontcha?"

# chapter
# 6

"HOW'S HE DOING?"

Wade watched Elinor come flowing up from belowdecks. He tried to stretch his legs out, but the cabin on this little launch was pretty tight and crampy.

"Fine. Asleep already. Thank you, Miss Lewis, for the use of that bunk. Pato needs the rest and comfort."

"Happy to. The navigator can sleep on deck. I'm paying enough for this tub. Travers, how about it?" She poured herself another glass of wine. Either she was going to go dipsy-do in the next two minutes, or she could drink any sailor under the table.

Wade looked not at Marcia but at Elinor. "Who's Hurley?"

But it was Marcia who answered. "You know about that Putumayo business a couple years ago. Some businessmen, so to speak—rubber barons—were using Indians as slave labor and systematically killing them off. Or letting them die. Atrocities."

"Yeah, I know. Wiped out most of the Indians in the Putumayo area. Huitotos, Boras. The Ocainas are about gone. Dirty business, and the culprits got off. Politics at its ugliest."

"Newspapers uncovered the scandal and pressed for justice; you know that, too."

"Reporter named Roger Casement. I met him. British papers mostly. But that was six years ago. Why now? Why you?"

Marcia leaned forward. "Harry was assistant editor then, didn't have much punch. Now that he's chief—the big desk—he wants to get on top of this again."

"The Putumayo thing is over with."

"Harry's sure there's more. Not just the Putumayo district, but other places. Other tribes. Same dirty work. So he sent me down here to dig." She poked at the tabletop with her finger for emphasis. "Travers, I come back with the juice on this one, I got it made. Write my own ticket."

Wade turned again to Elinor. "Where does Hurley come in?"

She had a gift for draping herself fetchingly anywhere. She looked good in the bow of a dugout and just as good here on a little settee in a stuffy, smelly boat cabin. "An American church and its—" She groped for the word, the serene brow momentarily puckered. "—its affiliated school heard of trials among certain Amazon tribes, problems caused by white settlers and even by certain local churches. They sent a legation down to see if they could help."

"And this Dr. Hurley is part of it."

"He is in charge. Or was."

"And I can't find anyone who admits ever hearing of him." Marcia pointed at Elinor. "You know where he is, don't you?"

"No. I wish I did."

Her voice was so sad, Wade had to fight back a sudden urge to pat Elinor on the head, hug her close, and purr, "There there. Uncle Wade will fix everything."

"He was abducted, apparently for ransom, but that's not certain." Wade watched Marcia's face for any sign that it might not be new to her.

She flopped back in her chair and said a few of her favorite words. "I need that guy. Doesn't anyone at all know where he is?"

"Tweed does, approximately." Wade yearned for a draw on his pipe. He'd find some tobacco around here somewhere. "He thought I was the perfect man to bring 'em back alive. One of his lieutenants filled me in with everything they know, which is zip. Inadequate maps, inaccurate information, hearsay."

"In other words, you know everything Tweed knows." Marcia's eyes were bright, alert, like a hound on the fox's scent.

"Everything Tweed told his subordinates. They wanted me to go searching; I doubt they'd hold anything back."

"How close can you get to Hurley, do you think?"

"However far from Manaos he happens to be. I have no intention of chasing all over the bush looking for that guy." Wade glanced at Elinor.

The pale, lucid face was reposed, pleasant, and its eyes reiterated, *Yes, you are*. Her smugness—or was it confidence?—infuriated him.

"Money won't buy you. So what will?"

"Tonight? A plug of tobacco. Tomorrow, nothing. Forget it."

Marcia pawed rapidly through her voluminous purse. From its dark recesses she hauled a bundle and tossed it on his lap. "My boodle. And if the story's worth it, there's more where that came from. Where is this Hurley? I smell a big story here. A scoop. An exclusive. And I want it. I want to be there when he's found, and I want to bring him out myself. I'm hungry, Travers. You told me you specialize in jobs no one else can do as well. This is one of them. Name your price."

Wade thumbed through the bundle without untying the string around it. Colombian pesos, Brazilian *cruzeiros*, Yankee twenty-dollar bills. He paused to rub them between his fingers a moment. Nothing—no other money in the world—feels quite like U.S. greenbacks.

"It will do you no good to fight it." Elinor's voice crooned soft and gentle. "You've been chosen. I'll help as best I can. And Miss Lewis can provide resources we cannot."

"Chosen. Second time you've said that. Chosen by whom?"

"Why, by God, of course."

"Of course. And I bet it's because he admires great eyes, right?" Wade sighed and thumbed again through the bundle. He pulled half the Brazilian currency and tossed the rest of the wad back to Marcia. Wearily, he swung to his feet. "Be back in a couple hours."

She didn't question him. She knew she owned him. The "I won, ha, ha" look on her face said as much. He shoved the hatch back and stomped up the companionway, out onto the silent deck.

A pushy, overbearing reporter and a religious fanatic, not to mention a butternut-colored conniver with an infected leg. Why, for crying out loud? *Why me?*

On the other hand, this Lewis woman had enough money to buy

Bacalhau, if not Manaos. If she enjoyed that kind of clout—at least, if her paper did—she could grease some skids and get his passport back. Maybe she could do him some other favors. He had influential friends and acquaintances, sure; but none nearby when he needed them.

And Elinor. He walked up the street, among the scruffy houses. Elinor must have a personal interest in this Hurley fellow. Her tone of voice betrayed her feelings every time she mentioned him. Wade really wanted to help her. It wasn't just that she had sheltered Pato and him when they needed her, putting her own safety on the line. Even if she had never lifted a finger, he would want to help her, now that he knew her. His debt of gratitude merely reinforced it.

Okay. So he'd take a couple weeks and work on this Hurley thing, rake in some money from Marcia, and still have time to earn his retirement fortune. It was the airstrip that would have taken all season anyway. He was glad Elinor evidenced no interest in airstrips. The woman could bewitch him into just about anything.

The doorway of the Snake House stood ever open because there was no door on it. No matter. The Snake House never closed; it merely shifted emphases. At this time of night the bar and gambling tables formed the center of interest. Daytime patrons would incline themselves more towards meals and the exchange of various forms of illicit merchandise.

"Eh, Wehd!" The bartender, a jovial old man, both fat and black, addressed Wade in Portuguese. "Good to see you. How has fortune treated you?"

"Fortune is fickle, Manolo, but then I bet you already know that. Is Brelho the Rodent still around?" Wade was a bit surprised that his own Portuguese was somewhat halting. He must have talked English with the women too much—hard to shift gears.

"Not for a year. Nor has his boat been seen. We surmise he made some sort of misstep."

"*Cangaceiros or policial?*"

"Does it matter?"

"Not to me. Probably not to Brelho, either. How about Chao?"

Manolo shook his head sadly.

"Got any tobacco?"

"Straight or coca leaves?"

"Straight. Plug if you have it. Keeps better."

As Manolo dipped under the counter, Wade sensed a massive presence at his right side. The smell was familiar, too. It took all of three seconds to determine a course of action and only a fraction of a second to take it. He swung toward the presence and caught the whale in the nose with one fist; he planted the other in the fellow's belly hard enough to send him into a table five feet behind him.

He pointed a finger at the beached whale. "Finders keepers, huh? You don't have Rosy the bouncer to help you out this time, chum. Want to dance?"

Blank as a fish face, the fellow stared for a good half minute. He chuckled. He laughed. He squirmed among the table's wreckage a moment and hoisted to sitting. He let Wade give him a hand to his feet. Good. He showed absolutely no sign of recognizing Wade's toughness for what it actually was—sheer bravado unadorned by any hope of winning a fair fight with him.

Wade laid some coins on the bar and nodded toward the brute. He must be a regular customer; Manolo served him without further instruction.

"No Brelho, no Chao. How about Andre?" The bartender shook his head. "No? Humph." Wade turned to study the unkempt, swarthy man at his side. He wasn't fat. All that poundage looked to be muscle. Except for a white scar the length of his left cheek and the bloody nose so recently obtained, he seemed to have pretty much escaped the slings and arrows of life. "Want a job?"

'Doing what?"

"Helping rescue a kidnapped legate."

"A what?"

"Some ambassadorial type, I guess."

"From who?"

"Don't know."

"Where?"

"Don't know."

"How much?"

"Depends." Wade handed a bill to Manolo. "For the tobacco."

He laid another in front of his newfound chum. "An advance if you want the job."

"Colombia? Don't wanna go to Colombia."

"Neither do I. Don't think so. Think it's Brazil." Wade scooped four plugs of tobacco off the bar and, with a warm sense of relief, jammed them in his pockets.

The fellow enclosed the bill in a massive hand and stuffed it in his shirt. "Nothing else to do. Why not?"

"Sun-up. The motor launch out at the end of the dock."

The guy nodded. "What's your name?"

"Wade. Yours?"

"Tiny."

"Figures."

# chapter
# 7

SHE WAS SCREAMING EXPLETIVES above the rumble of the launch's engine, yelling loud enough to be heard in Panama. "What could you be thinking of? To hire that . . . that . . . He was the worst of the lot in that miserable bar! And here you pay him money to come aboard and leer at me!" She pounded her fist on the brass railing.

Wade leaned against the rail. "He was kinda drunk then. Be a little bit forgiving, huh? He's okay now."

"Okay!" She peppered the breeze with more of her basic vocabulary. Did she even see the beauty and serenity of the river in the morning, the cloud of wood storks flying out across the clear sky, the drifting sparkles where water turns the sun back? Probably not.

Reason wasn't likely to mollify this virago, but he ought to try. She was his boss at the moment. He moved a step closer. "Now stop and think. What do we have here? One man, a couple women, and a kid prone to getting in trouble. We're gonna need some heavy muscle somewhere down the line, and Tiny was the biggest thing in town. Besides, he's free at the moment."

"You mean out of jail."

"Unemployed. And unattached. You know what I mean. No responsibilities. I talked to him when he came aboard this morning. He's not going to explain Newton's laws of physics to you, but he understands surviving, and he takes orders okay."

"And what are we going to do when he starts pestering me?"

"He won't."

"Hah! What's to stop him?"

"He thinks I'll kill him if he tries anything."

She expressed herself with a real beauty of a word. "He outweighs you by a hundred and fifty pounds—and you have him cowed? He could flatten you just by sitting on you."

"Yeah, but he doesn't realize that. Told you he doesn't know diddly about physics."

She stared at him the longest time with eyes like liquid coal. She burst into laughter as loud as her former ranting. The laughter dissipated. She sagged against the rail. "So where's our mountain of muscle now?"

"Sleeping off his hangover." Wade leaned both elbows on the rail to watch the emerald wall slipping past them a hundred yards to port. Only moving branches and occasional flashes of color betrayed the abundance of birds and animals within. "Nothing else going on, least 'til we get to Minho."

"Wherever."

"If you thought Bacalhau was small, wait'll you see Minho. A church and a plantation up behind the village. The plantation population is bigger than the village's."

"Another little nick in the jungle."

Wade nodded. "The village is on the edge of a swamp in the dry season and under thirty feet of water during flood. The plantation takes up some high ground a little less'n a mile away—low clay hills. Long hot walk."

"I can hardly wait."

He raised a hand. "Word of warning. The man we're going to try to see doesn't talk much. You might even think he isn't listening. Don't let it fool you. You'll be talking to one of the smartest men in the world and absolutely the craftiest. Give him the least opportunity, and you'll be lining his pockets. Even so, he's got a—"

"Another crook. Isn't there anything but Tweeds on this insect-riddled continent?"

"You didn't let me finish. Not a crook or shyster. He's also got a crystal-clear reputation for integrity. He gathers in bucks no one knows exists because he sees the money hiding in the bushes where no one else does. He sees everything."

"He should bootleg in New York. There's the bucks."

"I said integrity, remember? He remembers everything, too. Every person, every word. Speaking of words, you'll be wise to tone down your language. He's an influential friend to have if you want to find your Dr. Hurley, and he likes the language clean, especially when a lady's using it."

"You make him sound like a— Look at that!" She gestured frantically as a flock of red and blue macaws burst out of the wall, a spray of brilliance across the solid green. Maybe she noticed more than he gave her credit for.

In the two years since Wade last came here, Minho hadn't changed a minute. The waterlogged little village still clung to the edge of its dank and stolid swamp. Beyond the villagers' front doors stretched miles of glades, floating meadows of grass, and water hyacinths so rank they could support the weight of a man or a hog. The forest nudged constantly at Minho from behind as if trying to shove the rickety little huts into the muck.

What Minho lacked in size and sophistication it more than made up for in docks. The village boasted not one but four, including a broad pontoon pier nearly two hundred feet long, capable of serving ocean freighters. Some seasons Wade had seen all four docks busy, as boats loaded the produce of Bernardo Martin Cruz's private empire.

He docked the launch at the dilapidated jetty nearest the plantation road. Why walk farther than you have to? Like a mother hen with chicks, he herded his companions up the wide, dirt way.

Within a quarter mile Marcia was stumbling a little. Her shoes were more sensible than some he'd seen in cities, but they certainly weren't bush boots. She poked his arm. "Why are we bringing *everybody*? This Cruz fellow surely can't be interested in Pato or Tiny. Or my launch owner, for Pete's sake."

"Yeah, he is. He makes it a point to meet every single person who comes anywhere near. Ten years from now, when Tiny's lost a hundred pounds and Pato's all grown up, he'll still know 'em. And he'll remember how they might be useful to him."

Wade glanced behind. The launch owner slogged step on step, obviously out of his element. Tiny waddled. Elinor floated gracefully, lightly, with the limping Pato close by her elbow. She was showing him some bushes along the roadside. And then she was pointing to a butterfly as Pato nodded vigorously. Despite the nature lessons, they kept up comfortably.

In the vast front yard of Cruz's hacienda, thick patches of leafy green welcomed the visitors. Beans, manioc, corn, potatoes, peanuts, and what-have-you lined the wide road on both sides. Wade didn't mind the jungle; but he relished these infrequent breaks in the constant canopy, where unfiltered sunlight could pour over him. Only on the river itself could you see this much sky all at once.

With a wave he summoned a small naked girl hoeing sweet potatoes. Shyly she mumbled answers to his questions in a stilted Portuguese only barely removed from a pidgin Indian dialect.

"She says Señor Cruz is out on a hunt. Been gone two days. Doesn't know when they'll get back. Since we're here, we might as well hang around a while."

"This place is too much like medieval England. The master of the estate goes hunting with his hounds while the serfs do all the work. What's that smell?" Marcia headed for the shade of a *palo de sangre* tree near the house.

"Dead fish. Notice how lush all those garden plots are? You're looking at the best vegetables in the Amazon Basin. The dirt along the river here is just about sterile, so Señor Cruz taught his people to bury fish with the seed. Fertilizer." Wade flopped down and settled his back against the tree trunk.

"Indians were doing that in Massachusetts before the white men showed up."

"Yeah, but the Indians around here weren't."

As Elinor fluttered to rest in the shade beside Wade, Marcia flipped a notebook open. "What's a local word for *serf? Peon?*"

"*Caboclo.*" Wade began the leisurely process of digging out his pipe and a tobacco plug.

With shrieks to summon the dead, half a dozen goose-sized birds exploded out of the thickets beyond the yard.

Marcia jumped so wildly she broke her pencil point. "What the h—, uh, blazes, is that?"

"Nice recovery." Wade pocketed his pipe. "Screamers. Common around here. They love marshland. I think our host is coming."

Horsemen came clattering out of the forest to the north, but Wade couldn't count them, so thick was the cloud of red dust they kicked up. As he stepped out into the late-afternoon sun, they pulled to a churning halt by the front door.

Wade walked over to a nervous little pack mule. Draped across its back was one of the biggest jaguars he had ever seen. He twisted its great, heavy head around to pull its lips back. Both upper canines were broken off, one of them at gum level.

He heard steps behind him and turned around to extend his hand. "Cattle killer?"

"Child killer. Welcome, Mr. Travers." Bernardo Martin Cruz, half an inch shorter than Wade, still seemed to tower over him. Wade had once guessed the man's age as somewhere on the sunset side of forty, but there was yet no hint of gray in the thick black hair, no sparseness to the dense black moustache. The slim body still moved with the disciplined power of spring steel.

Wade waved toward the others. "Señor Cruz, may I present my current employer, Miss Marcia Lewis, from New York."

She was gawking at the cat. "That thing eats children?"

"Not any more. Your servant, Miss Lewis." He nodded to Wade. "My house is yours. Come in. Refresh yourselves. Join me in an hour for dinner."

Wade muttered, "Thank you," but the man was already striding into the house.

Marcia stepped in close to him, her eye still on the cat. "I wasn't expecting English. Took me by surprise."

"Three years at Princeton."

The man leading the mule would have turned his horse to leave, but Pato was standing in front of it.

"Please, sir?" Pato stared at the cat. "How beeg the child? How size?"

Wade translated both question and answer. "About your age."

The hostler twisted his horse's head aside, and the jaguar was carried off in the dust cloud.

"God bless you, Señor Cruz," Pato murmured.

An hour later Wade leaned against the tiled fireplace in the parlor and mentally compared this place with the garish opulence of Tweed's new digs. Bernardo Cruz could buy anything in South America, Tweed included, and his home spread out as large as any presidential palace. Yet there was restraint here, almost an Oriental simplicity. Every detail, from the potrait of a woman on the far wall to the woven Jivaro mat above the fireplace, bespoke a quiet elegance. Wade felt very comfortable.

Marcia wandered over to study the portrait. "His wife?"

"Deceased. Three sons, all away at school. Forget where."

"Spain, Salamanca." Señor Cruz stood in the far doorway. Crisp tropical whites had replaced the sweat-stained riding clothes. "My cook tells me dinner is served."

The dining room was as Wade remembered it. He paused a moment to admire again the ornately carved mahogany chairs. The Indian servants wore clean, plain cotton instead of brocade livery. Score a couple more points for Cruz.

The *patrão* personally seated Elinor at his right, leaving Wade to hold his boss's chair for her. As he introduced everyone all around, Wade marveled privately at his motley crew. The launch owner looked nervous. Tiny, in his filthy shirt, looked dreadfully out of place. Pato looked plain scared. Wade reminded himself that the boy had just emerged from a Peruvian mission village where "sophistication" meant chasing the pigs out of the house before sitting down to eat. Marcia with her big-city polish fit right in. Interestingly, so did Elinor.

They were halfway through dessert when the patrão asked the question Wade had been waiting for. "What brings you to Minho?"

"To seek your advice, possibly your help. These ladies have succeeded where a local bureaucrat failed. A Colombian bigshot named Tweed tried to coerce me into looking for a kidnapped American named Hurley. A Dr. Morris Hurley."

"Doctor. *Politico?*"

"I don't think so." Wade looked at Elinor.

She shook her head. "His is a doctorate in theology, not medicine, and he had no political leaning."

"What is this Tweed's interest in him?"

Wade shrugged. "Might be getting pressure from overhead to find the man. Avoid the international embarrassment of losing a foreign emissary to ransom-hungry thugs. I don't know."

"A doctor of theology. Why the Amazon?"

"To investigate the plight of certain forest tribes and try to help them. He is sponsored by a church and church-supported school." Elinor sat back with a look of despair on her face Wade had never seen before.

Cruz settled deeper in his chair, his elbows on its arms, and laced his long, slim fingers together. *If he weren't a guitar player, he ought to be,* thought Wade.

Marcia opened her mouth, and Wade jabbed her. She closed it again. Three servants cleared dishes in the silence as two others poured cups of the patrão's legendary coffee all around.

"A man of God." The eyes that miss nothing turned to Elinor. "Your reputation has preceded you, in a sense, though you're more a rumor than a legend among local Indians. A woman who knows no fear because of the power of her God. A woman of God."

"I love Jesus and walk with him."

"You are conversant with God."

"Yes."

The dark eyes snapped to Marcia. "And you, Miss Lewis?"

She shrugged. "God minds his business, and I mind mine—if there *is* a God."

Wade tried to read something—anything—in that dark face. He could see no hint of what the man might be thinking.

Cruz stared at his neglected coffee. The fingers paused. "I often wonder of late how much my heart weighs."

Marcia shot a confused glance at Wade, as if he knew.

Elinor tilted her head in the charming way that was hers alone. "You mean on the scales of ancient Egypt?"

He looked at her and almost smiled. "You know the story."

"I don't remember the names. The Egyptian god of justice . . ."

"Maat."

"Maat. When you die, Maat places your heart on one pan of a balance, and a feather on the other. Your heart balances against the feather only if you have led a correct life. If it doesn't, you don't go to heaven—that is, the Egyptian equivalent. I don't remember what happens if you fail the test—if your heart is too heavy."

"You are devoured by the chaos monster, in the shape of a crocodile. The second death. Caimans. Crocodiles. The Amazon contains far more of such than Egypt ever did."

"But God never weighs the soul like that. It's not a matter of good outweighing bad. It's a matter of purity, and you're pure only when you're safe under Jesus."

"Perhaps. But the figure is vivid. Easily seen, clearly understood. The Egyptians had a gift for that."

Apparently Marcia could contain herself no longer. "What the— what the blazes . . . does that have to do with anything?"

"I have for many years been attending my own business and attending it well. I believe it's time I attended some of God's, lest selfishness weigh my heart down."

Wade at last saw where he was going. "Like coming to the aid of one of God's men."

"When I'm uncertain or ignorant in an area of expertise, Mr. Travers, I seek the advice of an expert. Many call themselves men of God, but few are. This woman who walks with God feels that your Dr. Hurley is genuine. I accept her opinion."

"This means you'll help us out, right?" Marcia grinned.

"Helping you out suggests working under your auspices, for your sake. No. I will help Dr. Hurley out, for his sake. But the end is the same. Yes, Miss Lewis. Together we'll rescue that man of God, Dr. Morris Hurley."

## *chapter*
# 8

FOR TWO WEEKS IT HAD LAIN HERE nearly motionless, its eight-foot length arranged in casual coils. The dry season, though, is lean season. Few creatures passed this way. Until the rivers overflowed again and covered their vast forested flood plains, animals had too much space to roam in. But they would be back, when the floods drove them higher into these hills. And it would be waiting for them then as now, with cold, infinite patience.

Earless and deaf, it heard no soft rustling in the ferns downhill. It felt the footsteps, though; minuscule vibrations in the forest duff spoke to it more clearly than did any sound to ears. Its tail tip flicked. Its tongue tasted the air. At last, for the first time in weeks, its heat-sensing pits picked up the presence of warm-blooded prey and unerringly homed in.

Its head lunged forward, more a reflex than a considered action. Three feet from its coils, the fangs struck home, sank deep, squirted enough venom to kill a horse.

It didn't hear the scream or shouts. It didn't hear the gun blast that ripped its head off. For hours longer the cool brown velvet body would cling to life, twitching and squirming. But the patience, the waiting was done.

Wade's hands trembled. He snapped the cylinder open, shook out the two spent casings and popped fresh shells in the chamber. Only when his pistol was ready to go again did he step forward for a closer look at the snake.

Marcia paused by his elbow, stared briefly at the writhing creature and jerked away. She got two yards back down the trail before she lost her stomach.

Cruz holstered his own pistol. "It get a strike?"

Wade tilted his head toward the shaken Indian standing a few feet away. "Tried for Tingido but hit his pouch instead. Must've sensed the warmth of that woolly monkey Tingido killed and stuffed in his bag a couple minutes ago." He poked the severed head with a stick to confirm identification. "Fer-de-lance. Didn't know they lived in this area."

"Pockets of them along the bluffs here."

Tiny made his own identification from five feet away. "*Jararaca*."

"Yep."

"*Pior 'un piranha*," he muttered.

"Lots of things worse'n piranhas, my friend," Wade said in English. Tiny grunted. He must have caught the gist of it.

Cruz and Tingido exchanged a few terse words Wade didn't recognize. Tingido nodded, hefting his blowgun. And now they were on their way again, winding through the dense, dark thickness, with the wily forest Indian in the lead.

Tingido was a good four inches shorter than Wade and a whole lot more deadly. His Dutch-boy bangs dropped down on a face plucked clean of hair. The only skin on his body not showing was that thin line of hide directly under the string wrapped around his waist. And yet he was not naked, for he wore the sole essential attire of his culture—the carefully painted marks on his face and arms. In them he stood adequately garbed before the world.

Quietly Elinor fell in beside Tingido. She laid a gentle hand on his shoulder for a moment. They muttered, heads together, and Wade was struck by the sharp contrast of dark Indian with pale Anglo, of nakedness with modest cotton shift, of the solid, competent hunter and the ethereal will-o'-the-wisp. And yet they were so alike—both barefoot, both silent and sure of movement, both totally, comfortably at home in this dank and dreary closeness.

Marcia crowded in beside him. "Nice shooting."

"Hardly. Missed with the first shot completely."

"Pshaw. You're just not used to Cruz's gun there, that's all." With the whole north side of the Amazon basin to walk in she was crushed hard against his arm. "We've been hoofing it through these weeds for three days now. So how come you haven't made a pass at me yet?"

"Another rule of life. Never fool around with the boss."

"Stupidest rule I ever heard. How about after all this is over? Or won't you reconsider your rules of life before then?"

"Let's see how it goes." Wade debated with himself a few moments and decided this was not the time to tell her he was about ready to chuck that nonsensical notion, which was not truly a rule at all. Nor was it the time to tell her how tempting she was, how close he had already come to suggesting something more than just a business relationship. He might possess a firm reputation for leaving Indian women alone, but independent and willing white women were quite another matter altogether.

She watched his face a moment and switched subjects. "Tell me, when you and Tiny first tangled, I asked what you two were saying, and you said, 'Later.' It's later."

"He asked if you were my wife, and I told him you were my girlfriend."

"Why'd you do that? If you'd said wife, he probably wouldn't have taken a swing at you."

"He might have decided to court a widow, too. I didn't know. Didn't know him, either. Girlfriend is less permanent."

"Is everything you do and say always that calculated?"

"I try."

Tingido up ahead stopped abruptly. He jutted his chin, pointing to the left off the trail. From the bamboo-like *caña brava* case at his waist, he pulled a dart. Silently he loaded his blowgun.

The hair on the back of Wade's neck prickled. He popped the safety strap on his holster and moved in beside Cruz. "*Quem?*"

Cruz shook his head. "Don't know. Definitely Indians." He wiggled a finger at the back end of the parade. "Pato? *Ven aqui momentito.*"

Wide-eyed, Pato slipped past Tiny, Marcia, and Tingido's two nephews. He pressed close to Wade. "*Sí, patron?*"

"*Hablas Tenumas?*"

"No, patron."

Cruz glanced at Wade. "You?"

"None of the Tenumas dialects. With a lot of hand-waving I can get by with Ocainas and Andokes, and I can talk to anyone south of the Uaupes with my hands tied."

Tingido's two nephews, a few years older than Pato, slipped in beside their uncle. Marcia pasted herself so tightly against Wade's arm, he could feel the motion of her breathing.

"This is creepy," she murmured. "There's nothing out there."

Tingido's chin jutted again, toward the faceless forest to the south of the trail.

The patrão nodded, his dark eyes watching everywhere. With a few brief words of instruction to Tingido and Tiny, he gave Pato a little push forward. Wade fell in behind them. At a casual walk they left the trail, shoving aside the bordering fronds and bushes. The forest opened up a bit, expanding visibility to perhaps a hundred feet.

Why was Cruz putting a stripling child in jeopardy by making him lead? But then, everyone here was in jeopardy—on the trail and off. And Pato was certainly a lot less threatening-looking than Tiny or some Indian with a blowgun.

Wade realized too late that Elinor walked beside him. He grabbed her arms and turned her around. "Go back."

"No." The mild face gazed at him fearlessly, pleasantly. Didn't she realize what they might be walking into? Her safety loomed in his mind much more importantly than he would have guessed— more even than his employer's.

Wade glanced behind them. Already the understory had blotted out the rest of the party. These four stood alone in an endless wilderness. A sudden nagging fear grabbed his stomach. He wanted to be somewhere else, anywhere else, even matching wits with Tweed. Why had he ever agreed to this insanity, anyway? This was running counter to his every survival instinct.

"Over there." Elinor pointed off toward nowhere. "Come, Pato." She took the boy's hand and walked off so firmly he fell in beside her, no questions asked. Above them, a troop of monkeys screamed the news of this foreign invasion.

"She's nuts," Wade muttered.

"No." An admiration, a wistfulness, colored Cruz's voice. The voice firmed up. "I see them. Light your pipe, eh?"

Ever so casually Wade dug out his pipe and tobacco in an effort to appear peaceful and nonthreatening. It's hard to shave a plug while trying to keep one's hands from shaking. He leaned against a rough gray tree trunk as he broke up the tobacco and stuffed it in the bowl.

He saw them now, shadow forms among the trees, and a most untropical chill ran down his back. They were forest Indians with face paint he had never seen before—wild Indians untouched by the axioms of civilization, axioms such as "Live, and let live."

With elaborate calm he struck a match and pursued the gentle art of lighting a pipe evenly. Sham. All sham. The tobacco was too loose to burn right. He glanced at Cruz.

The patrão leaned against a tree, too. He was quietly folding a slip of notebook paper into a small hard wad. He popped open his pocket knife and began whittling at the lump.

Elinor, in some mysterious way, had made contact. She stood fifty feet away with her back to them, both hands extended, as Pato cringed behind her. One Indian, then another, stepped within view. Suddenly a fellow in an erect red feather headdress dropped to his knees and bowed forward, his forehead on the mossy forest floor.

Wade gaped. "They're treating her like royalty!"

"Or deity."

Elinor sat down, dragging Pato beside her. From the vigorous way she was gesturing, Wade suspected she couldn't speak whatever dialect was involved here. She seemed to be getting something across, though, and receiving information back.

A sick feeling, a terror, kept gnawing on him from the inside out. At one time danger had excited him, gotten the old juices flowing. No juices flowed now. He was drained dry, from his mouth to his soul. Why did he still covet life so desperately when he relished it so little?

Painstakingly, Cruz unfolded his bit of notebook paper. A snowflake. Wade hadn't seen a paper snowflake in . . . in how long?

Pato glanced nervously back at them.

Cruz lurched upright. "The boy has a good nose for trouble, doesn't he?"

"Nose? The whole boy!"

"Flanking action. Move in a little closer?"

Wade nodded and pocketed his pipe. It was practically cold anyway. He started walking, swinging out in a wide semicircle toward Elinor's left, trying to see everywhere at once. The futility of his effort multiplied the terror inside him. He, Elinor, Cruz, the rest of the party somewhere behind them—all were within easy blowgun range of any hidden enemy unimpressed by the sanctity of human life. One didn't have to see the danger for it to exist.

Barely within view, Cruz wove among the trees in a broad swath to their right. The Indians were there, near Elinor. And then they were not anywhere at all. Wade ever marveled at the gift of forest Indians for blending instantly and invisibly into the dense growth.

Elinor climbed to her feet; Pato hopped to his. Eagerly Pato led the way as they started back toward the trail. Wade, trying to walk in one direction and keep watch in 359 others, tripped over a vine and very nearly got hung up in a strangler fig.

When he reached the trail, Elinor was already kneeling in the dirt, smoothing out a slate to write on as the whole gang watched over her shoulder.

"If this is the Putumayo and this the Japurá, Dr. Hurley and two of his group are being held along a large river about here." Elinor drew a scribble of lines in the dust.

"Oh, come on! There isn't any major stream there. They lied to you." That crushing sense of danger multiplied itself in Wade's breast. He was no longer interested in Elinor's Dr. Hurley, and he had never cared about the weight of his heart. He wanted only to escape this nightmare. And he could see no way out.

"I don't think so." Elinor stood up. "These people fear the Indians who abducted the doctor. They say they're renegades without regard for the gods. I think. I'm not sure. We had some trouble communicating exactly."

"You sure did. An imaginary river." Wade snorted.

"Not imaginary." Cruz stared at the ground. "The swamp at Minho isn't a swamp. It's a drowned river mouth."

"I thought it was just a *furo*—a flood channel."

Cruz shook his head. "Not navigable very far, though. The fall line is a few miles beyond the hacienda. Then it levels for perhaps a hundred miles before the next fall line. If her information here is good, they're beyond that second fall line."

Wade calculated crow-flight distances mentally. "That puts them in the Colombia corridor."

"Or close to it."

Tiny's pudgy face tightened. "Colombia?" In Portuguese he expressed himself extensively regarding the inadvisability of traveling that particular piece of geography. No one listened.

Wade's eyes scanned the sea of green around them and above them, and suddenly he hated it. Its dark closeness choked him. "How safe are we from your informants out there, Elinor?"

"Safe enough, I believe. They fear Dr. Hurley's abductors very much, and we can get rid of them. I trust that will buy us safe passage through their territory, all the way to that river."

"More slogging through this snake factory, right?" Marcia sighed. Much of the starch and vinegar were gone. She seemed less irritating. "I don't understand. Those savages could have wiped us out before we knew they were around. They could wipe out those whoever-they-are holding Hurley. They can blot out anyone they take a notion to. So why are they afraid?"

"Spiritual reasons, Miss Lewis. The abductors seem to be defying the gods with impunity. These Indians aren't afraid of the men themselves, but of their magic." Cruz looked at Wade as if for confirmation. "We should eat lunch here, then head in a general southwesterly direction?"

Wade nodded. He sat down against a *cedro* trunk, suddenly weary, and closed his burning eyes.

A warm body bumped his legs. Marcia settled into the moss beside him. "You look worried."

"It takes years to win the trust of these remote forest tribes. You don't just walk up to them and start talking."

"*She* did."

"Right. And you had it pegged. Why didn't they wipe us out before we ever saw them?"

"I assume the answer isn't 'charity.'"

"Safe assumption. But what is it?" Why couldn't he articulate this foreboding, this strange fear? He remembered that feeling on the ledge, months ago.

*"Beware, Wade Travers. You'll die."*

Nonsense?

# *chapter*
# 9

"IF I EVER BUY a green dress again, I hope lightning strikes me." Marcia batted absently at a passing leaf. "I detest green. Every shade of green known to man."

Wade corrected her. "Except for that found on United States currency."

"I'll write checks. Pink and blue checks. Maybe yellow."

He could see her point. They had been struggling through virgin forest for nearly two weeks. She had not yet developed the skill of seeing with her ears as well as her eyes, and her eyes saw only green. Wade's ears told him more than his eyes could, for they were unrestricted by the leafy closeness. He "saw" monkeys and coatis, an ocelot spiraling down some distant tree, a hundred vivid birds she didn't dream existed.

What did Marcia call that kind of skirt she was wearing? Coolocks? Culottes. Divided in the middle. She could ride a horse astride in that thing, were there a horse anywhere near. That and her baggy shirt were hardly what you'd call provocative attire. But there wasn't a thing wrong with the slim, supple body inside. He really should quit putting such a hard, sharp line between business and pleasure, between surviving in this primal wasteland and enjoying life. Surely there was room for both.

Strange. He didn't feel that same temptation when he looked at Elinor, and yet she was every bit as attractive as this caustic reporter. And, in many ways, he liked Elinor much better. He liked to listen to her smoothly cultured voice ripple in any of her three languages. He liked the way her soft hair lifted out when she turned her head. He liked simply watching her move and float. In fact, he liked stealing glances at her when he could.

Up at the front of the parade Cruz tilted his head skyward. "Sloth for dinner?"

"Do you know what those buggers taste like?"

"Only meat we've seen so far today."

"Yeah. Wonder why."

"Pato?" Cruz pointed straight up. "Think you can reach it?"

The boy pushed in against the patrão craning, squinting. "Oh. Dere tis. *Sí*, patron, I climb it up."

Cruz bobbed his head, apparently satisfied, and pulled his pistol. He aimed carefully, two-handed.

Wade got a sudden thought and laid a hand on Cruz's shoulder. "Let's let Tingido get this one. Quieter."

Cruz looked at Wade, studied distance a moment, and nodded. "No monkeys." He beckoned Tingido and stepped aside.

"No nothing. Barren."

Marcia pushed in close to Wade's elbow. "What are you two talking about, anyway? What do you mean 'barren'?"

"No birds or animals—except old slow-britches there. Something's wrong. They've vacated this area for some reason."

"And why does Pato have to climb up? Won't it drop if you shoot it?"

"No. Kill a hanging sloth, and it just keeps hanging there, even after the flesh rots. He's the ultimate anti-gravity device. Hangs upside down in the trees eating, sleeping, everything. Comes to the ground once a week or so for outhouse purposes."

Tingido had taken his time dipping a dart in the little gourd of poison at his waist. He arranged a bit of kapok fluff around it, casually slipped it into his blowgun, just as casually swung the long thin pole upward. The cheeks bulged, the air whispered. That was all.

"Wait a couple minutes, Pato. See if we get lucky and it falls." Wade watched with the others as the distant coarse-haired creature hung there.

Elinor's radiant head hovered by his shoulder. "There's evil near." She looked up at him, and her eyes were wary, not fearful.

Still, he couldn't resist wrapping a protective arm around her. "What? You feel something?"

"Not feel. Know."

"That's nonsense!" Marcia almost added one of her words but caught herself in the first syllable.

"I used to think so, too." Wade glanced at Cruz's face.

Clearly this man of power, who had tamed the most mysterious of earth's unknown reaches, believed Elinor absolutely. "Can you identify it?"

She shook her head.

Pato was still concentrating on the sloth. "No lucky, eh, Papa? Up?"

"Sure." Wade gave Pato an arm's-length boost up the trunk. Grunting and clawing, the boy shinned up the rough bark.

Somewhat enviously Tiny commented at length in Portuguese on the lad's speed and maneuverability. Wade saw fit to remind him that he weighed about three hundred pounds more than the nimble child. Tingido giggled.

Forty feet off the ground Pato reached the first limbs and paused to catch his breath. He scurried up to the second tier and paused again. He twisted and turned, looking in all directions. Wade could hear him sniffing. He began to climb again, faster now, for the branches were close enough to use as holds.

Marcia started to call to him that he had just passed the sloth's branch, but Cruz clapped his hand over her mouth. She frowned, puzzled, at Wade. Wade put a finger to his lips.

Pato disappeared completely into the green ceiling. Minutes passed. Then he came, scurrying with the agility of a spider monkey from branch to branch downward. The crazy kid might miss a step, but Wade dared not yell at him to slow down.

Tiny was waiting at the base of the tree, arms extended. Fifteen feet off the deck Pato jumped into those huge, waiting flippers. White scratches and oozy red marks covered his tummy, arms, and legs. His agility had cost a price in skin.

"Stop. Smell smoke. Up more. Still smoke. Climb top see . . . see . . . *sin arboles* . . ."

FIRST BRETHREN CHURCH LIBRARY
Nappanee, Indiana

"Clearing."

"*Sí*, clearing. Is them." He waved a puny hand off toward the southeast. "Them!" He slipped into the language he knew best. "*Conozco que 'stan los ladrones! Lo conozco!*"

"*Paz!*" Wade pulled him in and hugged him close. "Catch your breath. It's all right. You did well. Very well."

"*Verdad, hijo. Muy bien.*" Cruz rubbed the boy's hair affectionately and called Tingido over. They muttered head to head.

"*Tengo miedo,*" Pato murmured into Wade's shirt.

"I'm scared, too, but it's okay." Maybe Spanish would salve the boy's jangled nerves. Wade repeated it. "*Y yo tambien, pero 'sta bien.*"

Marcia's wide eyes glistened. "I think I'm in over my head. Maybe we ought to reconsider the whole business."

"Little late, isn't it?" Wade watched Cruz. He noticed Tiny was watching Cruz, too. Did Tiny know what was going on? He understood neither English nor Spanish.

Tingido and his two nephews turned away. Their brown bodies melted into the green wall instantly and completely. Amazing. Constantly amazing. Cruz and Tiny conferred briefly. Tiny nodded. He pushed past Wade and disappeared into the jungle. For as big as he was, the whale could move quickly and silently through heavy growth. Wade felt a momentary tug of pride in having chosen this ponderous mercenary, albeit at random.

Marcia looked from face to face. "So?"

"We wait." Cruz watched the green wall grimly.

Pato gestured toward the sloth.

Wade shook his head. "We want you down here with us, sport."

Somewhere up in the leafy rafters a bellbird began its measured, monotonous, repetitious call, bong after bong after bong after bong. Wade's nerves didn't need that. A ticking clock would be nice now, something less irritating than a bellbird with which to count the slogging steps of time.

Tiny surfaced. He wiped his sweaty brow and reported in Portuguese. "Ocainas, mostly half-breeds. Not wild, either—white-man Indians. Women, kids. Five houses. No sign of prisoners."

Cruz nodded. "Guns?"

"Saw none. No blowguns, either."

Wade stepped in closer to Cruz. "Walk right in?"

The patrão looked thoughtful. "You say you can greet them?"

"Yeah."

Cruz turned to Marcia. "Miss Lewis, this group may not know the whereabouts of your doctor. But, if they do, you will surely have to pay for the information."

"That's all right with me."

Wade tapped Pato's ear. "Changed my mind. Can you go shake that sloth loose for us? Little hostess gift to take along."

"*Sí.*" Pato hesitated frowning. "Dat means we don' eat still a while yet, huh?"

Wade grinned. "Napoleon claimed his army traveled on its stomach. You'd fit right in. Hop to. We'll eat soon."

It was Tiny who boosted Pato up the tree trunk this time. Tingido and his kin returned as Pato was climbing back down, and they were on the road again—were there a road to be on.

Settlements in forest clearings bear a likeness to each other. All share the same bare orangish dirt, pounded to soft powder; thatched roofs perched on poles, pretending to be whole houses; net hammocks slung from here to there; and, scattered all about, the bits of handiwork that prove the scope of human creativity: delicately carved little stools, children's toys, wooden bowls, mesh tote sacks, ornately woven pouches, presses of bundled sticks to squeeze the bitter water from manioc pulp, all fashioned from the forest primeval.

This particular settlement was typical in every way but one. It stood abandoned. Fires smoldered in carelessly dug firepits. A few cotton shirts hung from a cord under one of the roofs. A row of rusty tin cans under another held herbs and treasures.

As Wade stepped onto beaten earth, only a half dozen dogs greeted him, yapping at his knees. But then he didn't really expect to meet the inhabitants right off. Even so-called tame Indians— pure- or part-blooded Indians who have rubbed elbows so much with Europeans that they have lost their wild instincts—don't trust strangers. And strangers didn't come any stranger than this crew of which Wade was part.

Wade looked all around for weapons. He saw none, not even a blow-gun or fishing line.

As he hung the gutted sloth near the middle of the compound, Wade thought he heard a voice in the forest. A muffled baby's cry? No. It was a woman's voice.

"Travers?" Cruz stood staring at the ground on the far side of the clearing. Wade wandered over, keeping his movements slow and casual.

He dropped down to a squatting position and poked a finger through the little pile of metal bits. "Grenade pins?" He picked one up, turned it over in his hand. "What in blazes would these people be doing with a pile of hand grenade pins?"

"Not what you'd call the weapon of choice for hunting in dense forest. You can't throw a grenade very far without trees and branches deflecting it."

"No worse than blowgun darts or bullets."

"They won't come bouncing back off a tree trunk at you."

"True." Wade stood erect. Using exaggerated gestures, he held the pin at arm's length and with a solid, metallic clink dropped it back on the pile. Whoever watched from behind the green wall must know he wasn't stealing anything. "That'd explain why the forest is barren around here. Except for the sloth."

Cruz nodded. "The noise from a few grenades would clear just about everything out. Another advantage of blowguns."

He and Cruz saw her at the same time. A girl with a baby stood at the edge where bush met clearing. She watched the men as a mouse watches a cat, poised to bolt. She wore a dusty blouse in a faded floral print instead of the usual sleeveless, sack-shaped black dress most "civilized" Indian women preferred. Her eyebrows were fashionably plucked, but she wore no marks, no paint.

Her scrawny baby hung slack in her arms. It drew up its legs, fussed a bit, and went limp again.

Like iron to a magnet, Elinor was there. She purred, she smiled, she lifted the naked baby gently from the girl's arms.

"Marcia! Stay back," Wade warned.

Too late. For a fraction of a second the girl watched Marcia moving toward her, then snatched her baby, and disappeared beyond the brushy forest edge.

Marcia stood with a frustrated scowl in the middle of the clearing. "What'd *I* do?" she whined to no one in particular.

Tiny crossed to one of the fires and stirred a bubbling pot of something, lest it stick. *How incongruous,* Wade thought, *the massive whale demonstrating domesticity!* He picked up a woven fan and gave the fire a bit of encouragement. Pato sat down very close beside the pot to gaze longingly at someone else's lunch.

Wade took a deep breath. Another. He walked over to the nearest house pole and gripped it with both hands just to feel something solid. This whole scene was a splash of surrealism—a thing painted by one of those Dada artists who could see no sense to life. Nothing was real; everything was out of whack and that frightened him. He'd never felt this way before. *Do you experience such weird forebodings just before you die?*

He glanced around self-consciously.

Cruz was staring at him. "You all right?"

Wade lied. "Yeah." With some reluctance he unmoored from his solid anchorpost and crossed the compound to the one stable ray of light in this gloom. Elinor.

She turned and smiled at him, and the world aligned itself aright again. "She'll be back, I'm sure. They'll all come out before too long, I expect. And I believe I know what's wrong with her baby. Too much fresh fruit. Diarrhea. I've seen it so often." Those wistful eyes flicked off toward the dark trees. "I do hope she comes back soon, though."

"Often? Are you a nurse? You realize I don't know a solitary thing about you."

"What's to know about me? I went through two years of nurses' training during the war. Then the war was over, and they didn't need so many of us. So I'm not a nurse. Not exactly. I *have* learned quite a few Indian cures for various things, though. Surprisingly effective, jungle medicine. And I know most of the common ailments in this part of the world. Infant diarrhea is one of the commonest. So sad, too. Many babies die when their deaths could be prevented."

He leaned against a housepost. "Is that what you left behind in Colombia? Nursing duties?"

"Partly. Opportunities, if you will." She studied the ground a moment and then skewered his eyes with her own. "I don't expect you to understand this fully. You have no . . . how shall I say it? . . . spiritual insight, as such. But I'll try to explain it in simple terms. Jesus always was and always is and always will be—all at the same time." She watched Wade's face carefully. Was she expecting some encouragement from him, or evidence of boredom, or what?

"Keep going."

She nodded. "For a certain length of time, however, Jesus took on manhood so that he was just as much a man as any other man. During that time he was, uh . . . his own presence. He was Jesus; I don't know how to explain it. He healed with his own hands, he taught with his own lips, he cried his own tears.

"But, after his death and resurrection and ascension, that part—the part of being man—ended. There was no more need for it, you see."

Wade didn't see exactly, but he nodded anyway.

Encouraged sufficiently, she continued. There was a lively lilt to her voice. Obviously she was talking about what she loved best. "Now we who love him are his presence here on earth. His humanity. When he heals he often uses our hands to do it, and to teach he uses our lips. And, when he cries, it must be with our tears."

"You were his presence in the Colombia corridor."

"Yes! That's it exactly. The villagers there had accepted me, and believe me, it took a while. I could walk freely. They trusted me. Oh, the local brujas didn't trust me, of course, because they belong to Satan. But the others—the people Jesus loves—I could do so much for them there."

"But you're not a spirit. You're a person. Human."

"Of course." The gentle brow knit slightly.

"That first day I met you, remember? On the trail up the side of the bluff, that little clearing. I scared you, and you dived over the side and vanished. No sound, no rustle, no movement, no monkeys or birds telling me where you were. It's possible to slip through the forest silently, I suppose. Indians can. But even they can't fool troupials and howler monkeys. How'd you do that, anyway?"

The fair ears turned pink; the pale cheeks flushed. This lovely lady was actually blushing. Her foggy blue eyes flicked up for the briefest moment and cast themselves earthward again.

"Well?"

"I didn't run away. I ducked aside and hid, less than two yards from you. I followed you to the top, watching you. I was right behind your Pato. But I didn't have time to wait for you to come back out of Mr. Tweed's house; I had other errands."

"But I didn't see . . ." Wade scowled, confused. Surely if she had been that close, he would have detected her. "Why? Why did you follow me?"

"Because, even though you startled me, even though I was afraid to speak to you, you fascinated me." She paused. "And you still do."

# *chapter*
# 10

FIRST YOU FIND a cassava bush, see? With a plain old stick, dig to China, and you can eventually rip out its yard-long roots. After you wash the roots off, you chop them up and pound them. Pound 'em 'til you're purple. Then you rinse lots of water through them to flush out all the acid, because they're not edible. You squeeze as much of the rinse water out as you can, dry what's left, and then pound a whole lot more to turn the tough gray mash into tough gray flour. If you dry it, forming farina, it will last forever.

This manioc flour can be mixed with different things to make into porridge or cakes or whatever. And after all that, you can watch a half-sized butternut-colored boy eat a good two pounds of your hard work. And Tiny was nearly as bad—a bottomless pit.

Wade sat cross-legged, his elbows on his knees, and packed his pipe as he watched the end of dinner and the diners. This meal was as far removed from that elegant repast in Cruz's half-acre dining room as is the south pole from the north. The contrast lay not just in tiled floor versus raw dirt, rambling home versus thatched roof, ornate furniture versus no furniture at all, or European tableware versus rough wooden bowls. The most profound of contrasts existed among the diners themselves. Pato was his old comfortable self, unfettered by the strictures of civilization. Tiny slurped, and no one noticed. Marcia looked absolutely lost. Only Cruz and Elinor retained their elegance, for elegance reigned innate in both of them. What a glowing, gorgeous lady, Elinor.

The sun had dropped instantly out of ken, as the sun does in these tropics, leaving behind dank darkness. The moths and mosquitoes, nightbirds and bats were taking over. Probably about half the total population of this settlement had returned from hiding in the woods. By dawn tomorrow the others would be back, casually pretending they had never left.

The woman and her baby were here again, along with seven other women. They gravitated to Elinor and seemed totally indifferent to Marcia. Wade heard murmurs more than once of "*Mujer de luz.*"

Woman of light.

Woman of light who found some sort of fascination in Wade Travers? Oh, come now! Still, it tickled him, for she was nothing short of fascinating herself. He struck a match.

Cruz came wandering over. He hunkered down beside Wade and waited silently until a solid curl of smoke drifted up from the pipe bowl. "Learn anything?"

Wade shook his head and the match both. "Something's up, though. These people don't have Hurley. I doubt they know where he is. But there's a link somehow. They're part of the same web."

"How so?"

"I can't explain it. A funny feeling about the place. I've been in a hundred little forest settlements like this. They all felt . . . well . . . relaxed. Easy-going. Nothing so important today that it can't wait 'til tomorrow. Except dances and observances, of course. But these people? They're strung tight, like guitar strings."

"They admit any worries to you?"

"No."

"Me either. In fact, a number of things they refuse to talk about at all."

Wade nodded. "Like who they know among white men, where they get their shirts and tin cans, who they trade with."

"You mention grenades specifically?"

"Not yet."

"Nor I." Cruz pondered for a while the patterns of wavering firelight on the beaten earth. "I don't believe they are the evil Elinor mentioned."

"You think there's someone else nearby."

"Has to be. The only blowgun in camp is Tingido's. There aren't even any fishing spears. These people are totally dependent on someone, probably someone Peruvian or Colombian—Spanish speaking. No one here seems to understand Portuguese."

Wade sighed. "When I told Marcia and Elinor I'd help them dig this Hurley out of the bushes, I figured at most it'd take a couple weeks of derring-do. Finish the job quick, and get on with my own business. But it seems everytime we take another step closer to the good doctor, he moves farther away. The problem just keeps getting more and more complex."

"Business of your own?"

The question was so casual, so innocuous-sounding, that Wade almost answered it without thinking, almost mentioned his plans for a golden retirement. Fortunately, he caught himself in time. "Maybe I'll explain later, if I need your help. Might, too, if the rainy season comes on us before this is done."

"Then we'd best hurry. You haven't much time left." The playful, slightly sarcastic edge to Cruz's voice told Wade the wily Spaniard was doing now what he did best—sniffing out money. Wade had better not mention future plans again.

Notebook in hand, Marcia was headed this way. She sat down so close to Wade their knees touched. She flipped back a page or two. "How's this? *Key air oh en cone chrar ah el doke tor* Morris Hurley. *Poo aid ee oo sted eye you dahr may?*"

"Spoken like a native. You been asking around like that?"

"Yeah. Nothing. Native what?"

"Long Islander."

"Thought so. Don't these men talk to women, or am I asking the wrong question?" She looked past Wade to Cruz. "You understood what I said, didn't you?"

"Clearly." Cruz paused for the briefest moment. "Of course, I lived for three years in New Jersey."

She glared at Wade as she snapped her notebook shut. "*You* talk to them, huh? That's one of the things I'm paying you for—translator, spokesman. Find out if they know where he is, and if they don't, let's get moving."

"You're in a hurry, Miss Lewis?"

"Yeah, I am. You bet I am." Her voice softened. "I'm afraid we're going to work like slaves and break our necks in this wretched wilderness and then find out he's already been rescued. I want to be the one who brings him out. I want his story. Front page and exclusive. And I'm scared someone else is gonna beat me to him. Get there before we do while we wallow in filth and snakes and alligators. I'm scared this will all be for nothing."

"I see." Cruz studied her with dark, unblinking eyes. Wade didn't doubt for a minute that Cruz did indeed see, for Bernardo Martin Cruz saw everything. "And you received no response to your questions."

"Most of them just ignored me or turned away. A couple of 'em even walked off into the woods. Rude, if you ask me!"

Walked off into the forest? Wade looked at Cruz. They both nodded in unspoken agreement.

Cruz climbed to his feet. "I'll talk to Tiny."

"Elinor can handle a watch safely, too," Wade suggested. "She doesn't seem to need much sleep."

"Watch? As in 'stay awake and watch'?" Marcia eyed Cruz's departing back. Her voice dropped a notch. "You know, Travers, I'm not so sure I trust your buddy there. He's creepy. You ever notice? He doesn't really say anything. Like just now."

"He says enough." Wade's pipe went out.

"What's he talking to Tiny about? What are you two talking about? You're as bad as he is. I'm paying for this safari. I want to know what's going on."

"Your rude Indians who disappeared into the woods—we think they might be running off to tattle on us." Wade turned his pipe over and rapped it on his boot heel.

"Tattle to whom?"

"Elinor's evil ones."

"You know, you're as creepy as he is."

"So we're setting up a double watch tonight, just in case."

"Just in case what?"

"Just in case someone pulls the pin on a hand grenade."

She gawked at him. The stare hardened into an angry glare. She blurted one of her very favorite words, but Wade didn't blame her too much. Hand grenades were news to her.

No doubt one of the reasons Cruz could build a mighty empire out of a soggy, unexplored flood plain was his gift for organizing any enterprise anytime, using anyone available. With only the limited resources of this motley crew, he set up a system of two-hour double watches that was both effective in its form and beautiful in its simplicity—assuming that Marcia didn't fall asleep simultaneously with Tingido in that heavy-eyed hour just before dawn.

Marcia and Tingido, though, never took over their predawn watch because about two A.M., when Orion's fierce dogs are snapping at Columba, the dove, among the stars overhead, the world exploded.

The first pistol shot brought Wade bolt upright in his hammock, and the second sent him over the side. He flattened out on his belly in the dirt and groped for his sidearm, trying to shake off sleep and figure out what was happening. The vacant hammock swung back and forth above his head.

Fire and thunder burst across the compound. Where was Elinor? He couldn't remember where Elinor had been sleeping. A woman shrieked, but it wasn't she. Who was supposed to be on watch now? Cruz and Tiny—that was it.

Two of the thatched roofs across the way smoldered thick green smoke for a moment, then flared out in open flame. Dogs and Indians raced back and forth across the compound, silhouetted in the ruddy glow. A second grenade took half the thatch off the roof catty-cornered from here. Like spent fireworks, a thousand burning wisps and fronds came floating down.

Guns in the forest—at least three of them—were arguing loudly and heatedly. Wade lurched to his feet and started running forward, out into the compound, though he didn't have the slightest idea where he was going, nor who was friend nor where was foe. He could hear Pato wail above the howl of the fire, above the babbling screams of terrified Indians.

Marcia came racing out into the open. She stopped, turning this way and that. Wade saw a shadow figure on the far edge of the forest, thought he saw a figure raise a rifle. He dived forward, grabbed the slim little body, and kept going. She oofed as he landed on top of her. By the time his arm was free, the shadow had wheeled back into the blackness. Wade got a shot off, but he had no idea at what.

No more gunshots. Without them, the human voices keening, the fires crackling, the dogs barking and howling, all seemed more like silence. The warm and vibrant body beneath him struggled, and he rolled aside to let her breathe.

She gasped and coughed. Dirt, sweat, and tears masked the perfection of her tanned skin. She was sobbing almost too hard to speak. "Tiny's down. Cruz is down. I can't find Elinor, and Pato can't even hear me he's so hysterical. I don't know . . . don't know who . . . or where . . ." She choked, swallowed, and appealed to God, and this time, somehow, it wasn't just an expletive.

"Cruz is down! Where?"

"Over . . . over . . ." Her fragile arm waved aimlessly.

"Take me. Come on." He dragged her to her feet and gave her a shove in the general direction she had come from. She stumbled, clinging to his arm. Then some of the old starch returned. She stiffened up and started running.

The muggy blackness of a million trees and bushes gulped them up, shielded them from the raging hell out in the compound. Wade felt vulnerable here, subject to attack from myriad dark and unknown enemies, even though his head knew that, in the forest, he was actually far safer.

She stopped, jogged a few steps farther, stopped again. She looked out at the compound, then on the ground. "I . . . He was right . . . I thought . . . Somewhere around here—"

Pato's voice cut through the darkness beyond.

"This way." Wade gripped her arm firmly and led her off, beating a path through denseness, wondering what creatures with fangs or plant with poison spines was waiting for him.

In the gloom of broken, shifting firelight knelt the beached whale, sitting on his heels and grunting. Pato tugged ineffectually at one arm, and Cruz was trying to get any kind of grip on him at all.

Wade dropped to one knee in front of him. "*Onde?*"

"*Cos . . . cost . . .*" Tiny coughed blood. He didn't have to finish the word. His ribs.

He gave the whale a little shake and asked in Portuguese, "The river. Can you get down to the river?"

Tiny bobbed his head.

"Where's Elinor?" Wade looked from Pato to Cruz.

"*No sabemos.*" Pato looked absolutely stricken. Wade was almost afraid the boy would go into total hysterics, and they'd have two impossible situations to deal with.

Why wasn't Cruz coming up with the perfect brilliant solution? Why were they all looking at Wade? He was too muddled to think; he'd just have to let his instincts take over.

Wade stood up and tried to see something—anything—in this tangled forest. "Let's go throw him in a boat. Then I'll come back for Elinor, see what happened to Tingido and the others. Cruz, can you clear the decks for us?"

"My gun's empty."

"Here." Wade handed him his own and hooked his arms under Tiny's vast armpits. The blood-soaked giant swayed to his feet. "Marcia, help me!"

"Wait!" Instead of helping, she was standing here arguing! "Let me hold the gun, and Cruz can do it. He's stronger than I."

"Cruz can spot danger quicker. Now grab on here. Give him something to lean on. Pato, stay near Cruz. You'll be in charge of the dugout when we reach the river."

One thing about blood—it spreads. By the time they had skirted the compound and covered the hundred feet to the river shore, Wade's whole right side was sticky. Marcia was covered with blood, too. Even Cruz, just ahead, was well besmeared.

Pato darted past Cruz to the riverbank. He ran twenty yards upstream and came running back. "*Aqui, patron! Esta!*" He laid hands on one particular dugout among many. With the skill born into all river people, he gave the thousand-pound dugout a shake and a heavy shove. It slid down the mud into sullen dark waters.

Tiny sloshed three steps into the water and tipped gracelessly into the boat. It wagged, slopping, but Pato didn't let it swamp. Wade snatched Marcia up and unceremoniously dumped her in the bow as Pato leaped aboard and grabbed a paddle.

"Wait for us downstream, sport!" Wade pushed them clear of the grasping mud. They disappeared almost instantly into the blackness.

Cruz was already headed back toward the orange glow.

Wade ran to catch up. "Where were they sleeping?"

"Elinor in the house with the tin cans, Tingido and his nephews in the one with the yellow dog." Cruz tripped over a vine or something that threw him to his knees. He hesitated the slightest moment and scrambled back up.

"Tingido may be gone; his hut got hit first. Who'd you see?"

"Five, at least. Two whites with rifles and three Indians. I put down one of the whites, and I think . . . stop. Catch our breath." Cruz slammed against a tree trunk and just leaned there a moment dragging in air. "I think Tiny took out one other. Three left.

Wade welcomed the pause. Leaping from a sound sleep to a dead run hadn't done his lungs a bit of good, nor had hauling that whale half way across the state of Amazonas. "I may have hit a rifleman zeroing in on Marcia. He was wearing white man clothes."

"Two, then. Somewhere."

"Yeah. Somewhere."

Two of the three fires had about burned out. The third still roared. A fourth roof was smoldering, ready to burst into flame, no doubt ignited by the flying, drifting firebrands. The dogs barked yet, but the human sounds had changed. They were moans and mournful wails now, and the lusty crying of terrified children.

Children.

"If she's up and moving, she'll be there." Wade pointed.

"Yes, of course! The children."

And she was. The blond head bobbed among many dark ones, a churning confusion of mothers and children huddled under one of the few undamaged roofs.

Wade pushed through the sweaty, bleeding, sobbing human wreckage and pulled Elinor to her feet by one arm. "Come on! We have to get out."

She yanked free. "No! There's too much to do here. Look at them! You go on. I'll catch up. They need—"

He cut her off. "What they don't need is another attack, and those people are still out there. The quicker we leave, the safer these folks will be."

"No. I'm not—"

"Elinor, the best thing you can possibly do for these women is to get as far away from them as possible. The grenades and the guns are meant for us, not them."

For the longest time those brimming, bottomless eyes locked onto his. She shuddered, swallowed, and began working her way step by step, out from among the frightened sufferers.

He pulled her clear and, half dragging her along, started for the river. "Cruz is looking for Tingido and his nephews. Have you seen them?"

"No. Or the others, either. Where's Pato?"

"Safe. We—" A bush rattled twenty feet to his left. He swung around and jerked Elinor behind him. How would he defend her with no weapon? Who was there? He saw no one.

Cruz.

The patrão must have snagged on another vine. He fell to his knees, but this time he didn't scramble up again. Elinor reached him before Wade did. He stood up slowly, wagging his head. "They aren't there, but no bodies, either. They may have escaped. I didn't look everywhere, though." His face was sweaty, tight.

Tiny down. Cruz down. Marcia had been right, and Wade hadn't even seen it until now. How could he have been so stupid? When was the last time he saw Cruz pause to catch his breath, let alone trip over anything?

"This tears it. Tingido's on his own. So's Hurley. We're getting you out of here, all the way out. Climb on that river and ride it clear home."

"We won't leave without Tingido." But the ring of authority was gone from Cruz's stricken voice. He offered no resistance as Wade propped him up and started him toward the water.

"Patrão!" Silent as a moonbeam, Tingido materialized at Wade's elbow. Had he been an enemy, he could have dispatched Wade in any of a dozen ways, and Wade would never have known what happened. One of the nephews, even less visible from the darkness of smoke and blood, appeared.

Tingido took Cruz's other side and in mournful tones related some sort of news.

Cruz cleared his throat. His voice wavered. "He says he can't find one of his nephews. He'll come with us."

"Want me to help him?" Sheer bravado. Wade dreaded the idea. He probably couldn't make himself do it.

"No."

Relief, of a sort. But it lasted only a fleeting moment.

If Tingido could slip up on him undetected, so could any of these other Indians, or the Indians Cruz had seen attacking, or . . . That bulging lump of fear welled up in Wade's chest again. The fear itself frightened him, for he knew that if his mind and reflexes were crippled, he was doubly vulnerable—from the dangers he could not detect and from those he would have seen were he his old self.

So he fought fear fiercely—as Tingido helped him bring Cruz to the water's edge and as they pushed out onto the river, not in a well-chosen dugout but in the first one they happened to find.

Fear. There was a day, and not long ago, when he had been immortal. Death, even ennui, was for others. Never for him. Stay alert, follow precautions, take no unnecessary chances, and you'll live forever! Adventure tasted sweet then, and victory gave hot, rich zest to life. Tonight the acrid smell of smoke and death stole the sweetness, quenched the gusto.

Fear. Not long ago the intensity of this night would have piqued his enthusiasm and set his blood racing hot. There was a day not long ago, too, when he would have relished the likes of Marcia Lewis. Even that had lost its savor. What was happening to him?

What had all this accomplished? Nothing. What had it cost? Pain and suffering and quite probably lives, before all was done.

And so he fought fear valiantly as the hideous orange glow fell farther and farther behind. From the far and dusty echoes of his memory he tried to call forth the old times that had stirred him so. He tried to relive the glories, to rekindle the flame.

No use. The fear remained, weighing him down. Some time or other, when he wasn't noticing, the last embers of elán had flickered and died. The fire was gone.

Only fear and futility remained.

Life had gone cold.

# chapter

# 11

FLAT BLACK WATER lay without a single ripple for a hundred feet from shore to shore. The endless green wall rose straight up from each bank and hung out over the water a little here and there. The larger trees arched up and in to nearly close out the sky overhead. Nearly, but not quite. Wade could still see some early morning blue.

Sometime within the last year, a jungle giant had fallen. The tree lay half in the glassy water and half out. It didn't know yet that it was dead; although most of its branches were bare, a couple still bravely sprouted leaves. Wade walked out a few yards along the broad, inviting trunk over the water and settled down cross-legged to watch the jewel-bespangled neighborhood go about its business.

He knew who was strolling this way even before she had come around the bend. Only Marcia, city-bred Marcia, would crash through the woods like that. He followed with his ears; no need to twist around. She paused when she spotted him and tried extra hard to be silent as she approached.

He waited until she reached the fallen tree before he spoke. "Morning, Boss. Watch your step coming out here. The bark is starting to slough off by that dark green bush there."

"How'd you know it was me?" she snorted. "I told you, you were creepy." She scuffed and shuffled and yipped once or twice. He watched her reflection in the silky water as, like a circus star, she tightroped the six feet out to him, her arms stretched wide. She sat down on the rough bark and dangled her legs over the side. Her clothes were pasted tight against her skin, soaking wet.

93

He twisted around to look at her directly. "Fall in?"

"Laundry time. No soap or shampoo, but at least I rinsed everything." She salted her "Was I ever filthy!" with a few choice expletives. Wade agreed with Cruz's dislike of foul language, particularly in a woman. In a way, it tarnished the image. The image was a pleasure to behold, too—firm, youthful, and very obvious to the eye under that semitransparent laundry.

He forced himself to turn around straight again. "Remind me to get you some soap."

"Where?"

"Roots of one of the plants around here. Scaly bush about this tall." He held out a hand. "I used some last night to wash my stuff out."

"Yeah. I noticed you weren't blood-caked. What a mess that was. Even puddled on the floor of the canoe. You read about gun battles and stuff in those western novels, but they don't mention all the blood. I mean, so *much* blood. They don't tell you how everything gets all . . . Let's talk about something else."

"Learned a lot since you came down here, I see."

She chuckled bitterly. "Bet I don't know it all yet, either. I thought when I first hired you that most of you was idle boasting— that stuff about doing certain jobs better'n anyone else can do them? But it wasn't bragging. You're as good as you think you are. Better, even. And you know everything about the jungle. Everything."

"No. I know a little bit. Elinor knows everything."

"That woman irritates the h— . . . bothers me a lot, but I gotta admit she knows her stuff. Weird leaves, branches, bark, roots. Pounds together these stomach-turners, and her potions actually work. At least, her patients don't show much sign of infection yet. Seen Tingido this morning?"

"He'll be gone for a few days. Wanted to sneak back up to that settlement and find out about his nephew. If he's dead, whether they handled the body properly."

" 'Handled' . . . you mean, disposed of the body."

Wade nodded. "Burned it with proper reverence and dispersed the ashes. They wouldn't save his ashes in the tribal pot, since he wasn't a clan member."

She hunched her shoulders and shivered, and it probably wasn't because of her soppy clothes. She studied her reflection for a few silent minutes. Wade watched one of the local jewels, a sapphire dragonfly, as it cruised along a yard off the deck, close enough to catch small insects near the water and high enough to avoid the jaws of leaping fish.

She broke the silence. "You know, I'm really impressed with the sense of loyalty in this outfit. Pato wouldn't leave Tiny. You and Cruz sent us off and went back for Tingido. Tingido wouldn't leave his—how do you call it?—*patrown*? He could have run all the way home if he wanted to. And he doesn't have any stake in this game. 'Specially not one worth dying for. You and Cruz both treat him like . . . well, like a real person."

Wade twisted around to stare at her.

She met his eye squarely. "I admit it. I'm guilty. The way I grew up, you don't treat Negroes and Indians like white people. They're . . . something different. But not here. Not with you two." Her eyes fell away, and she resumed her study of the reflections.

The dragonfly had zig-zagged up the river, but a far larger jewel, a turquoise motmot, left its perch and darted out over the water. With a swoop it snatched a fly out of the clear air and flew back to its tree. Wade heard a little muddy-brown antbird rattle and scratch in the loose bark near the base of the fallen tree, but he didn't twist around to look.

Good thing, too. She shrieked as she jumped and latched onto him so hard she very nearly dragged them both off their tree and into the river. Had he been off balance . . .

She pointed wildly. "A crocodile! Look at that!" She addressed the creature in terms to curl your teeth.

Its dark scaly back broke the surface, making the morning's first ripples. Silently, serenely, it cruised under their log, then sank from sight in the black water. Wade guessed its length at around eight feet.

Her grip wasn't loosening a bit.

"It's called an arapaima. It's a fish. Lives in the shallow backwaters mostly. Skims along the surface every now and then 'cause it actually breathes air. Has one big lung. That fish's about full size, but I've seem them longer."

"Who does it eat?"

"I don't know. Not a hunter, though—too sluggish." He thought of asking her to turn him loose, now that the so-called danger had disappeared into the dark depths, but he didn't mind the warm body pasted against him. Not a bit.

She shuddered for the second time that morning. "This was a mistake, I can tell. The whole trip's a mistake. Blood by the bucketful. Wild Indians. Eating off dirt floors. Snakes long enough to reach a second-story window. Fish the size of a touring car. No indoor plumbing since we left Minho. I'm just not up to coping with this . . . this . . ." She clamped her lips together. Her head sagged against him.

She was going to pull him off this log yet if he wasn't careful. He swung his legs around and hung them over the side beside hers, for better balance. Still clinging to him, she sighed mightily and stared off at nothing.

He wrapped an arm around her shoulder and noticed in passing that the employer-employee relationship was flying right out the window. "No Spanish or Portuguese. No preparation, it looks like. City-born. Why'd you come here, really? I mean, why you?"

"Because Harry can't stand me. He said so. Said I irritate the h— . . . that I irritate everybody I meet, and a reporter can't be that way, not and get any good stuff. I'm expendable. He said that, too. If I dig up something down here, the paper comes out ahead. If I get eaten by cannibals, the paper still wins, especially if it's a slow news day. That's exactly how he phrased it."

"You're safe. No cannibals here." He paused a moment. "Headhunters. No cannibals."

A blue word slipped out as she loosened up enough to draw her head back and look at him. "You're sure a bloody barrel of good cheer. So headhunters aren't just myths, huh?"

"Myths? No. Jivaros, mostly. Couple other tribes."

"Ever see one? A head, I mean."

"Almost ended up being one."

The dark liquid eyes grew wide. They sparkled as she grinned and plopped against his chest again. "And the closest I ever came to danger was playing stickball in a busy street. I mean, 'til now, at least."

"Wanna go back?"

"Yeah. I'm not afraid of busy streets." The voice softened almost to a husky whisper. "Here I'm scared. I'm so scared."

He kept the hug in place and rubbed the side of her head with his free hand, ran his fingers up into the short wavy hair behind her ear. Soft, incredibly soft, and nearly dry by now. Her long lashes just barely tickled his palm as she blinked.

She tilted her face up, or was it he who tipped her face up to his? Her cheek was as soft as her hair, her lips even softer. The harsh, caustic reporter had evaporated. He drew her tighter, or was she pressing tighter, for her frightened clinging had become an eager embrace, a very, very gentle distinction, nearly missed.

A subtle sound along the shore alerted his ear, ripped a part of his attention away from the situation at hand. Another sound, identifiable . . .

He sighed and lifted away without loosening the embrace. "Later, Pato."

His boss stiffened instantly. The moment fled.

Pato stood by the trunk, grinning like a cat festooned in canary feathers. "Papa. The lady say tell me you tell Tingido come and his blowgun. You get some feesh maybe."

"Can't you go fishing?"

"Jus' a leedle keed, no goot feeshin', eh?"

Wade was sorely tempted to borrow some of Marcia's words. He rolled to his feet, his whole day suddenly in tatters, and it was still only morning. "Go find a couple sticks for fish spears."

"T'ree sticks? You, me, her?"

"Why not? Miss Lewis says she probably doesn't know it all yet. Let's teach her to fish."

"I can hardly wait." Her voice rang hard and bitter; the old caustic Marcia was back. She rose cautiously to her feet, uncertain. He gave her a supporting hand back to shore, but she balanced with her free arm.

By the time Pato returned with the sticks, Wade had found a branching hardwood bush and from its forks had whittled three barbed hooks. They could go through all the hassle of fashioning some cordage from lianas, or he could rip the hem edge off his handkerchief. His hankie lost. He didn't feel like doing a lick more work than necessary.

Pato borrowed Wade's knife long enough to expertly cut just the right notch in his stick to fit the hook flush. "*Little kid no good fishing*" in a pig's eye.

Pato studied the results. "Beeg hook. Arapaima?"

"Saw one a while ago. Good backwater for arawanas, too. I've seen half a dozen turtles along here, mostly on the other side. See what you can scare up over in those shallows."

Pato splashed into the quiet river with all the enthusiasm of tender youth. He paused, knee deep, and studied the dark water. "Candiru?"

"Could be, so don't take the chance. Stay up. Last thing we need is that."

Marcia eyed Wade suspiciously. "Last thing we need is *what?*"

"Candiru's a skinny fish about this long—couple inches at most. Real thin. Its scales are spiny, and the spines point backwards. Once it hooks a victim, it's there to stay 'til you cut it out."

She glared at him. "And you expect me to wade in that?"

Keep on the alert, and you'll be fine." He turned his back on her quickly, because if she saw his grin she'd *really* be fried, and for some reason he didn't want the final shreds of her tenderness—the last vestige of that moment—to be destroyed.

Wade sloshed slowly along the edge, trying to see down into those niches and half-hidden galleries formed where land and tree roots meet the water. He scared up another turtle, but it wasn't big enough to keep.

"*Mir'!*" Pato slashed at the surface with his spear.

A dark form in the dark water sliced toward Wade. He thrust out without thinking, calculated without dwelling upon it how the water makes a fish look like it's here when it's actually there. He pinned its tail to the bottom. It flopped powerfully. He dare not raise his spear lest he lose it.

"Pato! Nail it!"

Eagerly the boy came stomping and splashing. He thrust his spear blindly into the cloud of muddy water. "Gotchit!"

As one they swung their spears up, tossing the arawana out onto the bank. Together they sloshed to the safety of shore.

"Tiny eating yet?"

"*Sí*. Start so again, beeg eat."

"Then just one won't be enough."

Pato nodded and charged off upstream, fighting the shoreline tangle.

Marcia stared at the ugly two-footer. "Tell you what. You do the fishing. I'll carry the catch. Why are we going somewhere else? Scared away all the fish here?"

Wade popped his knife open and slit the belly. "Not scared away, *attracted*.Blood in the water might draw piranhas. They're almost never a problem unless there's blood in the water. It's safer upstream."

"Which Pato obviously knew without being told."

"He's a good kid. Smart, wise to the river. Good mix of brains and caution."

"Isn't it just a wee bit egotistical to boast like that about your own son?"

Wade smiled. "Guess so." He left the head on so that Marcia would have the gills to carry it with. The entrails he tossed out into the stream. Almost instantly the still surface erupted, boiling, churning with flapping little silver bodies. Then it quieted.

She stared as the concentric rings drifted wider and wider. "I want to go home."

"What! And miss all the fun?" He slogged off through the growth and listened to her fall in behind him stumbling.

Beyond the next bend Pato had already speared a pacu. His bright eyes twinkled; the grin spread as wide as Kansas when Wade praised the fish's size. Wade once fed on praise that way. No more. He envied Pato.

Among all the beauties that got away, they managed to land two more. Wade called time. They worked their way back to camp.

Elinor lit up like Christmas when she saw the fish. Maybe Wade wasn't quite as immune to praise as he thought. Tiny slept, and Tingido's nephew still looked pretty weak, so Wade crossed on over to the far side of the glade to say hello to Cruz. He settled cross-legged in the moss near Cruz's feet and dug out his pipe and a plug.

The patrão hoisted himself to a half-sitting position and propped his shoulders against a tree. "Pacu. You provide the best."

"My son's contribution. My boss tells me I shouldn't boast about my son. Egotistical, she says."

"Well, it's true." Here came Marcia. Uninvited, she plopped down near Wade. "Like father, like son. I couldn't see a thing, and there they are, spearing fish like crazy."

Cruz gave Wade a bemused, knowing look. He knew how long Wade had been in the Amazon, and he knew how old the boy was.

She wrinkled her nose as a whiff of pipe smoke drifted by, but it didn't slow her monologue. "I didn't realize at the time how truthfully I was speaking, of course, because I thought then that Travers was mostly hot air. But when I told Tweed I'd hired Wade Travers to take me backcountry, I sort of laid it on thick how good he was as a jungle guide, and Tweed didn't—" She frowned at Wade. "'What's the matter? Quit staring!"

"You said *what*?!"

"I said you were a crackerjack jungle guide. And you are."

Wade pointed an accusatory finger. "When you talked to Tweed, I'd just turned you down! You lied to him!"

"Not permanently. You're working for me now, aren't you? And what's so bad about lying to that rascal? You know what he wanted to charge me for a nonexistent permit? Then he starts making noises about a reporter's license, for—" She caught herself in time and glanced guiltily at Cruz.

Wade slammed a fist into his knee because it's ungentlemanly to clout a woman. "No wonder he thought I was double-crossing him! One of his not-too-slick spies watches us talking that night by the docks, and the next morning you tell him you've hired me. If Elinor hadn't yanked us out from under his boys' noses, we'd be cooling our heels in his municipal hoosegow. Or worse. Thanks a bunch, Petunia."

"Don't blame me. I didn't know—"

"Tweed comes across as a fool, but don't count him short. He's deadly. All those bush moguls out in the weeds and far from the head office are like that. They have just enough power to do what they want and not enough brains to be noble. He wouldn't mind a bit if people he doesn't like disappeared."

"Tweed have any hooks into you?" Cruz was probably enjoying the little employer-employee spat.

"Took my passport."

"I'll radio Manaos when we get back. Ramão Basteiros owes me a favor."

"Radio? Wireless? You have wireless?"

"Telegraph isn't dependable enough, especially at flood. We have an airplane now, too, with an airstrip on that high ground out behind the cattle barns. Usable year round. Minho has leaped into the twentieth century since last you worked for me."

"Look, Travers, it's unfortunate if I accidentally caused you some inconvenience with Tweed there, but I'm not apologizing to you or anyone else. It's the way it goes sometimes." She stood up. As she walked away, she brushed herself off.

He watched the way she moved as his memory lingered on the softness. It was gone now, the softness.

Gone. Along with so much else.

# chapter
# 12

He yawned. He stretched. He rubbed his face with both hands. He took a couple deep breaths. He scratched. He opened his eyes. He had just run out of things to do. Might as well get up.

He sat up and arched his back. Elinor had kept watch during the first half of last night, and here she was, already up and at it. Didn't that lady ever sleep? Apparently Pato had been fed. Over in one corner of the compound, he was fluffing up his bed of fronds and rushes, preparing to sleep until noon. Wade was proud of how the stripling accepted the adult responsibility of sharing watches through the nights.

Wade stood up, stretched one more time for good measure, and wandered over to the breakfast bowl by way of Pato's pallet. He gave the loose matting a kick. "G'night, sport."

Pato grinned. "G'night, Papa." And he turned his back on the world.

Elinor smiled, a sunbeam on what was essentially a cloudy morning. "You slept well?"

"For the first time since we holed up here. What's on the list for today?"

"Tiny had trouble getting to sleep, so he worked on hammocks some more. He has the long cord measured and tied for four, and last night wove some short cord into one."

"So one's nearly done."

She nodded and flipped his breakfast—fried plantains—on her

ironwood grill. "But he's nearly out of cord, both weights. Perhaps that might be the first order of business today. Bring in more *cañamo* and such."

Wade nodded. "Be glad when we can get Cruz up off the ground, and Pato. Too many creeping things out at night." He watched Elinor work, almost effortlessly cooking, with no utensils at all. He recalled a magazine article he had read in the hospital in Recife while his leg was knitting. It listed the essentials of the modern kitchen, those tools no cook can do without. Sure.

She tipped his plantains onto a fresh leaf, gave him his breakfast, and scurried off on some unknown errand. He settled down with his back against a pole and stretched his legs out. This wasn't what you'd call elegant dining, but it surely was comfortable. In fact, this whole compound was getting comfortable. In a scant two days they had cleared an ample area of trees and underbrush. Of course, there weren't any large trees, which made the achievement a bit less grand, if you look at it that way. Apparently this spot had been an Indian settlement in the not-too-distant past. The Indians did that—cleared a spot, lived in the area until game and wretched soil gave out, then moved on.

Here were rain shelters built in a single afternoon, not unlike the open unwalled roofs in that ill-starred settlement they had fled. The beds weren't snake-proof like hammocks, but at least they were half a foot off the ground. Tiny, using only his knife, had hacked out two wooden bowls for Elinor and now had started on the hammocks. The whale with the busted ribs was almost chipper now that his lung had quit bleeding.

The only thing this camp needed was a sign saying MINHO MEMORIAL HOSPITAL, and Wade was half tempted to make one.

He finished the last of his breakfast and crumpled up the leaf. He licked his fingers on the way down to the river. The second time he lost his swag—about seven years ago—he had vowed to carry a straight razor in his pocket and never ever put his pipe in the swag. Not once had he regretted that vow.

Especially now. He answered nature's call, washed, stropped the razor with his belt, and shaved, all without benefit of swag or indoor plumbing. The self-sufficiency provided him a certain smug satisfaction. Good. He needed all the satisfaction he could lay hands on now, for precious few were the things that gave him any satisfaction at all any more.

For a moment he studied his reflection in the flat and sullen water. He saw the same Wade Travers as always. Average in most ways. Half the men in the world called him "Shorty," and the other half looked up to him. Most women called him good-looking, and a few who knew him well called him things that are best left unsaid. The outside, the external, was intact. What had happened?

He stood up and tilted his head skyward. Was his weather sense on the fritz, or would the flood season come early this year? Up until now the patterns of sun and sudden storm had cycled upon themselves normally. Just what he needed—to get bogged down in this futile project while the floods washed away all his well-laid plans. He wiped his razor on his shirt tail, folded it down into its handle, and headed back toward camp.

Cruz needed him now, though. The one man in the whole world whom Wade respected totally, without reservation, depended on him. Elinor could live off the land, but she didn't know the area. And woman of light or not, she was vulnerable to attack by the marauders she so tersely heralded with her "Evil is near."

Heaven knows, Marcia depended on him! Marcia couldn't get a quarter mile on her own, nor find a bite to eat. Tiny was doing better, but Wade had gotten him into this, and Wade was bound by honor if not law to help him out of it. And Pato—a game kid and able, but not ready yet to face life alone. Injured companions, women, and kids. It seems the only thing left that didn't depend on Wade Travers was a pet dog.

Marcia was sitting on her pallet looking like she'd just tasted a rotten pickle. She scratched those soft curls and scowled at him. "Bring me that comb thing over there that Elinor made."

"Sure." He obediently fetched the makeshift hairbrush.

Here was another problem. Marcia. What should he do, if anything, about what they had started yesterday? Keep the relationship strictly business until this mess was over, or reap pleasure while he may? The pleasure advantage was obvious, but what would it do to the fragile web of relationships within this whole crew, for it wasn't just a matter of two people minding their own business. Any change in the relationship between him and Marcia would alter everything, and not in ways that Wade could predict. He'd seen it happen before. How much, if at all, would a little extracurricular fun affect their chances of surviving this predicament?

All he had wanted to do was go prospecting up that backwater behind Manaos. Now look how complex life had suddenly become. A pox on Tweed and his little projects.

"You said something about getting me some soap."

"Want it now?"

"Yes, I want it now."

"Coming up. Don't hold your breath, though. I gotta go dig." He picked up the stout stick he'd found yesterday. As he headed out into the forest, she flopped noisily and disgustedly back on her pallet.

The muggy air was getting thicker, heavier. It would rain today, and before it was supposed to. When life dealt low blows, they came one right after the other.

It took him twenty minutes to find what he was looking for and another ten to dig enough roots to suds up both the lady and her hair. He took them down to the river to trim and wash them. They weren't exactly the perfumed bar one could buy at the druggist's, but the less they looked like dirty old tree roots, the better the city girl would receive them.

The thinnest of them he wrapped around the others to form a neat bundle, easy to carry. He turned toward the camp and froze. On the faint path right in front of him stood a dog. He recognized it, too—the yellow cur from the Ocaina hut that had burned first during the attack.

The Ocainas had traced the party here, to this hiding place! And if they were here, the evil owners of hand grenades were surely here as well. He dropped the soaproot and yanked his pistol. Perhaps the Ocainas had not yet reached the camp. Perhaps they were still tracking, still searching the way. They were too civilized, too tainted by white men, to have retained the sharp sense of smell with which some forest Indians can track men. They might even have lost some of their forest savvy. Perhaps.

No such luck. Wade knew better than to trust fairy tales. These Indians had found them out. His only hope was to stop them before they found the camp. He was surely too late already.

He whispered to the dog, "*Eh, perro. Trae tu señor. Ve!*"

The dog seemed disinclined to fetch its master, and Wade didn't know enough Ocaina to do much more than ask how the hunting was to the north, or how its day was going. The mutt lost interest in Wade and began exploring the various bushes along the path.

Now what? He dare not return to camp. If they had spotted him by now, he'd lead them straight in. He backed up motionless against a tree, and let his eyes and ears tell him what to do next.

"Amigo." A hoarse whisper floated out of the denseness—from where? Somewhere. "*Eu sou Tingido.*"

Wade swung around pistol first toward . . . toward where?

The voice asked in fractured Portuguese about a name Wade thought sounded like Tingido's nephew's.

"*Onde esta?*" Neither eyes nor ears were telling Wade anything. Zillions of leaves and trunks and branches, and not a living thing within miles, it appeared. Then Tingido deliberately moved, and there he stood, fifteen feet away, his hand raised in the universal gesture of friendship. Wade's eyes and ears had betrayed him.

His senses were fallible; still, he had nothing better to fall back on. He continued watching and listening, wondering who and how many had returned with Tingido.

Tingido used the nephew's name again and said something about fear. Then he turned away and strode off right toward the camp. The dog bounded ahead of him and dropped to a trot, its nose to the ground.

Wade waited, watching, listening. Nothing. Eventually he sought out the bundle of soaproot and followed Tingido. If Tingido was not alone, his companions were too slick to be spotted.

When he reached the compound, Marcia was sitting on her pallet crumpling up a leaf and licking her fingers. Wade dropped the soaproot on the mat beside her.

She stared at it blankly. "That's it?"

"Pure castile. Here's how to get suds out of it." Wade explained, demonstrating, but his mind was on Tingido.

On the far side of the compound, the wily Indian sat in earnest and animated conversation with Cruz. Cruz caught Wade's eye.

Wade gave Marcia a pat on the shoulder. "Enjoy the bubbles, boss." He hopped up and crossed to Cruz, ignoring the protests behind him. As he hunkered down by Cruz's shoulder, he got his first good look at Tingido. The man's face was tight and drawn, very grim. Very sad.

"Tingido says you gave him quite a start down by the river. He was afraid you were going to shoot him. He thanks you that you didn't shoot first and check identity afterward."

"I gave *him* a start, huh?" Wade smiled.

"Tingido, as you know, developed a close acquaintanceship with the family who owned the yellow dog. Three of the family members died in the attack."

"And his other nephew?"

"Injured severely. Ran and hid in the forest, where he died the next day, alone, before anyone found him."

The tribes south of the Uaupes used traditional gestures and a little dance to express sympathy or grief. Wade had no idea, though, what custom Tingido might observe, so he simply laid a hand on the man's shoulder and used good old Portuguese.

Marcia came storming up behind him, interrupting. "You work for me, Travers, remember? I said I need you. I'll be hanged if I'm going to pound roots. That's what I hired you for. Now quit chewing the fat with your buddies and come along."

Wade nodded tersely toward Cruz. "'Scuse me a minute." He was tempted to comment in Portuguese on the amused twinkle in Cruz's eye and voted against it.

He hopped to his feet and engaged Marcia nose to nose. "What you hired me for, *Miss* Lewis, was as a crackerjack jungle guide to find your Dr. Hurley and keep you alive in the process. And that's exactly what I'm doing right now, the matter of survival being first on the agenda. If you want maid service, put an ad in the paper."

The eyes of liquid coal widened and crackled. "Don't you ever speak to me like that again, you g—"

He clamped his hand down so hard on her mouth it forced her back a step. "And don't you ever use your favorite names on me again, you hear?" He softened his voice a couple notches. "You're such a beautiful woman. Don't let your tongue spoil your beauty."

She sputtered, she fumed, and her ears and cheeks turned vermilion. She opened her mouth to speak, but he raised a warning finger in front of it. Angry beyond words—well, beyond decent words—she wheeled and blazed off across the yard.

Wade took a few deep breaths and rubbed the back of his neck, bringing his own fire under control. With a sigh he hunkered down again, back to the business at hand.

Cruz wasn't looking bemused now. "Yours is a gift I have long admired and never possessed—the ability to manage intractable women."

"Don't I wish. So we inherited the dog from that family?"

"In a sense. They feel responsible in part for the death of Tingido's nephew. And because both Tingido and the boy liked the dog, the surviving family member gave it to him."

Had he been musing that the only responsibility he lacked was a pet dog? Apparently there was a God up there with a very wry sense of humor. "They feel responsible? How?"

"For not warning us. More than just failing to warn us, they refused to mention the grenade-throwers even when we asked about them, however indirectly."

"Then it wasn't just a language problem."

"No."

"The grenade-throwers. Renegade Ocainas?"

"Tenumas." Cruz turned his attention back to Tingido, using a stuttering, halting mix of Portuguese and whatever Tingido spoke. They did a lot of talking for the amount of information conveyed, it seemed. Wade could make no sense of it. Whatever bits of Portuguese he picked out meant nothing without the alien words between.

Eventually Cruz closed his eyes and rearranged his battered body. Wade would be glad when they could get the man slung comfortably in a hammock again. The dark eyes opened. "As Tingido understands it, the Ocaina clan is enslaved, in a way. The Tenumas hold them in a grip of fear."

"I can see why."

"Yes. Not just the superior weaponry—the utter disregard for their lives if they step out of line. The Tenumas use them as intermediaries between themselves and the outside world, because the Tenumas are being hunted. Outlaws. They're slavers, supplying Indian forced labor for rubber-tapping, lumbering."

"Do they have Hurley?"

Cruz started in again with Tingido. Wade sensed someone nearby and almost expected another attack by the boss, but it was Elinor. She stood silently on the periphery, listening, as she stripped *cañamo*. He felt a twinge of guilt. He went soaproot digging, and she had to go find her own *cañamo*.

Cruz nodded to Tingido. "Apparently not. Might Dr. Hurley be considered a warrior saint by low-contact Indians?"

"A university professor? Warrior?" Wade shook his head.

But Elinor said, "Yes." She stepped in and dropped down beside Wade. "There are many kinds of warriors."

"Oh." Cruz nodded toward the *cañamo*. "Tingido brought down a dugout with two swags and some hammocks—the ones not destroyed by fire. Also Miss Lewis's notebook. The Ocainas prefer not to have any of our possessions or totems around."

"Understandable. I'll help him unload then. What about a warrior?"

"The Ocaina clan has heard rumors of a warrior saint protected by a ring of his people, his believers. The Tenumas want to reach him to kill him but cannot. And Tingido thinks the white men behind the Tenumas—the men who buy the slaves and supply the explosives—want the warrior saint as well."

"Tweed said Hurley was a ministry legate to certain Indians. By which I assume he meant a certain tribe. Said Hurley was kidnapped, being held hostage. How does that add in?"

"For ransom? Did Tweed mention ultimata? Terms for release?"

"No." Wade leaned both elbows on his knees and pondered the point a bit. This part, at least, was falling into place. "Tweed said he wanted me because I rescued an old rubber baron last year. That was strictly a sneak-in-and-grab-the-guy situation. No negotiating, no trading. The way Tweed talked, I'd say this is the same kind of situation."

"And the situation, as you call it, is getting more critical." Elinor's cloudy blue eyes looked anxious, almost frightened. "We must reach him soon."

"Why?"

"I'm not sure. But I'm certain we must."

Wade twisted around to look squarely at her and felt an unexpected twinge akin to jealousy. "Who is he to you, anyway? How do you know him?"

"We share the same Lord and Master, Jesus. We're fellow servants, if you will."

"Yeah, I know all that. I don't mean that. I mean, where did you meet him? And when? How close is he to you? You talk about him like he's a relative of some kind, or a good friend. A real good friend. He means a lot to you."

"Of course he does. Spiritually, we're brother and sister, sharing the same Father. But know him? Not personally. I've never met him."

"But then why are you so sure . . . ?" Wade dropped it. It seemed to be just one more mysterious addendum to that weird feeling he experienced on the ledge. Spiritual mumbo-jumbo, whispered voices in undiscovered corners of his mind.

He sensed a real and practical spiritual bond between Elinor and the unknown Hurley (did Hurley know how lucky he was?). And if she felt this bond with a man she never met, how much tighter must such a bond be with a known friend who shared her spirituality? Wade had never guessed until this moment that this sort of bond could exist.

Maybe this was all beyond him and always would be. He wished he could escape the tangle these puzzlements made of his thinking and just go down to the river, an obedient employee, to help Marcia soap up.

But Elinor, like a light in the forest, would not go away. She lingered powerfully on his thoughts. No futility in her life. Purpose. And she was not alone. Never. How he yearned for a bond—for anything—that would give him that assurance.

# *chapter*
# 13

THERE HAD TO BE A THOUSAND kinds of bats and birds and dragonflies and spiders and unknown night stalkers who specialized in eating mosquitoes. A thousand kinds wasn't nearly enough. And why did mosquitoes persist in preying on Wade in the rain? Didn't they know that if some stray raindrop blipped them, they'd be knocked right out of the air? Or would they? Wade probably wasn't that lucky.

He squashed his latest assailant as it was poking a proboscis into his arm and stood up to stretch. All comfortably slung in his own hammock again, Cruz napped nearby. And beyond the protection of the roof, hard mid-afternoon rain pelted down. It drummed against the moldering thatch. It pounded the lax dirt of the open compound. It had long since quenched the fire out in the open pit.

Flood season must be here, all right. Wade's left leg ached, and it did that only in extra-damp weather.

Pato and Tiny, Tingido and his nephew all dozed under the shelter next door. An afternoon rainstorm can put you to sleep quicker'n a politician's speech. And under the shelter across the way sat the two women with their heads together, black and blond, doing something or other to the hem of Marcia's culotte.

That's what Wade could do—bug the women awhile. Between his chores and hers, he had seen Elinor for only a few minutes today. On the other hand, he didn't particularly went to go running out through the rain. He'd be soaked before he got six feet.

"Travers?"

He turned around and smiled at Cruz.

"Time for a war council."

"You think you're ready to travel?"

Cruz nodded. "While you were fishing this morning, I walked out as far as that shale ridge. No problems. So long as I pace myself and take it a little easy, we should be able to move normally."

"Now?" Wade checked himself. Why not now? "I'll bring the others." He dashed next door to Tingido's shelter and played town crier, awakening and notifying. Then in a brilliant stroke of the sort of genius that reveals true leadership, he sent Pato across the compound in the drenching downpour to call in the ladies.

They gathered by Cruz's hammock. Wade picked the nearest housepost, sat down, and settled back against it. Considering the haste with which he and Elinor had set these posts, they were quite sturdy. Pato settled cross-legged close beside him. Had the boy grown this last week? Not in size, but he seemed older. The yellow dog waddled over—he appeared to detest hard rain as much as Wade did—shook all over everybody, and splacked down at Tingido's feet.

Marcia sat down close to Wade's other leg. Her rain-soaked shirt clung provocatively.

Cruz scooted back in his hammock, closer to sitting. "We are ready to move. The question is—which direction."

Marcia scowled. "What do you mean, which direction? When we came here and built this camp in the middle of nowhere, you said it was because you and Tiny couldn't travel any farther until you mended some. You even apologized. I thought you people knew where we are. Now you don't know which way to go?" She waved a hand. "Tingido left us and found us again. Surely he's not lost."

Wade clarified. "Back to Minho, or try again for Hurley."

"Then there isn't any question. We're going back. To Minho and straight on to civilization. And the sooner the better."

"No." Elinor's voice had its usual velvety sound. "I can't turn back. I'm sorry. But I understand that the rest of you should. Dr. Hurley isn't your responsibility. Isn't your problem. Except . . ." She looked right at Wade with those smoky blue eyes. "Except that you've been chosen. Called."

112

Marcia tightened. Her voice rose. "Travers works for *me*, not you, and don't you forget it. He goes where *I* say."

Cruz looked at Tingido.

The Indian said something unintelligible, but Wade heard Hurley's name. The nephew nodded and dipped his head toward his uncle.

"Thank you. Tiny?" Cruz spoke in Portuguese.

The whale studied Wade as he spoke. "I work for him and the lady. What they say."

"Yeah, but we hired you to help find Hurley. So if you want to go with Elinor, you're still on the payroll." Wade was glad he was using Portuguese. If Marcia had understood that, she would have kicked him.

Tiny shrugged. "One job's good as any other. Find Hurley."

Wade heaved a private sigh of relief. The whale, for all his inability to articulate, was a splendid woodswalker. He would serve Elinor well. At least now she wasn't alone in her quest. But now, suddenly, when escape from this exercise in futility loomed near, Wade wanted to be with Elinor. He wanted to go with her, to help her, to share her crazy obsession. He didn't want to go to Minho; he didn't even want to go to Manaos any more.

"What's happening, in English, huh?" Marcia looked from face to face.

"What about you?" Wade nodded to Cruz and popped his pocketknife open.

Cruz addressed no one in particular, but he stared right at Marcia. "It is no longer a matter of the weight of one's heart. I didn't achieve what I've achieved, or built what I've built, by turning back. I have never at any time abandoned a project once undertaken, although on occasion I'll alter a project to make it profitable. I will find and free our Dr. Hurley."

Elinor closed her eyes, and her face absolutely glowed with happiness. Wade couldn't believe she had never met the man she was so deeply concerned about.

"You'll do it without me then. I'm on my way to New York, getting out of this putrid swamp. And you're taking me." She stared Wade straight in the eye. "All the way."

Cruz shifted in his hammock. "There is still one member of the party not heard from. Pato?"

Pato looked at his Papa, at Tiny, and mumbled, "I don' know."

Subtly, barely perceptibly, Cruz's demeanor changed. Wade saw it only because he had seen it before. Cruz had found another well of money from which to draw a profit. The crafty Spaniard folded his hands across his belt buckle and locked onto Marcia with eyes of steel. "Miss Lewis, it is time to deal."

"Deal? You and I?" She shook her head. "I don't intend to hang around your farm long enough to owe you anything."

"Deal. Nothing to do with Minho, which is at your disposal. There is no price tag on hospitality, or it would cease being hospitality. Concerning Dr. Hurley. You want the exclusive, the story. I will deliver your Dr. Hurley to you for a flat fee of three thousand dollars American, plus expenses."

She gaped. She nearly choked. "You can't be serious! I'm not about to fork out so much to . . . to . . ."

"Of course not. Your newspaper will. Plus expenses."

She smiled suddenly. "You're trying to get me to pay for something you're bound and determined to do anyway. I didn't miss the intent of your little speech about building what you built. No. You're going to bring him out whether I deal or not."

"Yes. But you'll never see him. Others will buy his story."

Those lips, so soft once upon a time, tightened to a hard thin line. The anthracite eyes crackled. For the longest time she tried to stare him down, to melt him with her anger. "Deal. Wait! Exactly what expenses?"

"I'll keep an accurate reckoning."

"I'm sure you will." She looked at Wade. "You said he knows where to find—" She caught herself. "I remember what you said about him, and I believe it. How long will it take?"

"Don't know. There's not a soul here wants to drag it out a minute longer'n we have to." Wade packed his pipe, but he didn't light it. He was down to the bottom half of his last plug. The more he could stretch things out . . .

She sighed grimly. "Deal. But only if I have veto power over the expenses."

Cruz casually dipped his head. "Agreed. By that I assume you're going with us."

"Do I have a choice?"

"Not if you want to achieve fame for yourself and your newspaper."

"Fame. Yeah." She relaxed, loosened, almost as if resigned. "When do we leave?"

"We have about three hours of daylight left. Let's pack up, garner extra supplies, and be ready to leave by first light."

In ones and twos the conferees wandered off. By the time the rain ended, Wade and Cruz sat alone.

Maybe he'd light this pipeful, after all. He struck a match against the post. "Three thousand."

"Frequently, if you make a thing appear valuable it becomes desirable. I doubt she would have acquiesced for a lesser sum. And she certainly would not have remained with us had I offered to pay her to come. I don't much care whether she accompanies us or not. It was you I was actually bargaining for. We need you."

"And you said you didn't have a gift for handling intractable women."

Silence. Cruz lay back with his eyes closed, but he wasn't sleeping; his breathing was too firm and frequent. Wade applied himself to the problem of where to go in pursuit of the hidden Dr. Hurley, but his mind kept drifting to Elinor, to her gentle determination, her strong sense of purpose. He realized what he was doing and forced his thoughts back to the problem at hand. Almost immediately they jumped the track, returning to Elinor.

Bewitched! Bewitching.

The dark eyes blinked open. "Tweed identified the general area where Hurley is being held."

"North of the border compound near the Brazilian line."

"Which agrees with our other intelligence. So we know approximately where to look. Who has him?"

"Not Ocainas. Not Tenumas. Not the grenade suppliers, whoever they are." Wade's pipe finally caught well.

"It would profit us to know who they are. We don't dare ask the wrong people for help. We must know whom to avoid."

"You think it's official? Colombian or Brazilian police? Maybe Peruvian."

"Some sort of authority with access to war surplus ordnance. Government officials or rubber growers."

"Rubber growers don't have much power any more."

Cruz nodded and studied the soggy underside of the thatch roof. "Did you know Peru is ceding the Putumayo-Loreto district to Colombia?"

"Then Peru probably wouldn't be in it." Wade shook his head. "I don't think it's official. The Colombian government isn't in the rubber business or slavery either, for that matter. Why should they supply Tenumas with grenades and otherwise risk being associated with dirty business? Nothing in it for them—nothing worth a big black spot on their international reputation."

Instantly the sharp eyes were on him. "That affair on the Putumayo. Thousands of Indians suffered and died to line the pockets of exploiters. Whole tribes decimated. Hideous atrocities. How did Peru and Colombia react when the story came out?"

Wade shrugged. "Lot of hand-wringing and official 'Oh dear me! How terrible,' but they didn't actually do anything about it. I'm sure you know that the Arana chief, Normand, Homero, Rodriguez—every one of them got off scot-free. Or escaped custody. In fact, probably with official help."

"Intense international embarrassment."

"Yeah."

"Now here we have an international situation. Dr. Hurley is an American, quite possibly a potentially embarrassing problem, much like the Putumayo affair."

The light dawned. Wade punctuated with his pipe. "Hurley stumbled onto something, and the government's trying to cover up. Which means Tweed wants Hurley not to rescue him, but to silence him. The government put it on Tweed's back."

"Let's go two steps further. Since Tweed is a minion of Colombia, we're talking about the Colombian government rather than Brazil. Also, since Tweed went to some trouble to obtain your services, and you are a civilian—"

"Not even a citizen of the country hiring me—"

116

"Exactly. The government itself is trying to stay as far away from the situation as possible. They'll use a foreign mercenary, and keep the official presence in the background."

Wade sagged back against the post. "If we're right, know what would have happened if I'd gone along with Tweed?"

"You and Hurley would have both died under mysterious circumstances as soon as you brought him out."

"I wouldn't have realized that Tweed was the real danger until too late." The fires of anger against Tweed, long banked, were warming up again. "Okay, so we know who to avoid. Now. Who has Hurley?"

"A circle of believers, according to Tingido's Ocaina friends, protecting him from his enemies but surrounded by the enemy. Unable to get him to safety outside their circle."

"If it's a small tribe, they might not know much about the world outside their territory."

"We do. If we can reach him, we can bring him out."

Wade wagged his head. "Slim chance of making it both in and out. Slim chance of even making contact with Hurley's circle of protectors, whoever they are. They'll wipe us out before we can tell them we're friends." Wade's pipe was going out too soon.

"A problem to be answered once we reach them."

"You're so optimistic." Wade started to climb to his feet.

"No." The *patrão*'s voice was so heavy, so sad, Wade sat down again to hear more.

Cruz stared at unseen sky far beyond any soggy thatch. "Do you read Scripture? The Bible?"

"Snatches, in the past. Never the whole thing."

"The book of Ecclesiastes. The Philosopher, or Teacher. Life is futile. Whether you be good or evil, the rain falls on you all the same. You eat, drink, make merry, try to be wise, then die just as dead as any simple fool—as any animal in your stable. You amass a fortune and leave it behind for someone who doesn't deserve it, who never worked for it. Futility."

"Elinor reads the same Book. I don't think that's what she found."

The dark eyes drifted down to meet Wade's. "I am a desperate man. You didn't know that, when you brought me Elinor, you gave me one final straw to grasp. One last chance to find any meaning at all in life. Life is hollow for me. But not for her."

Wade felt himself staring and couldn't find the presence of mind to quit. *Life is hollow for me*. That was it exactly. Hollow. Void. "You have everything."

"Which all becomes, once you have it, nothing. I was hoping, desperately hoping, that coming to Elinor's aid in this matter would somehow open a door, though what door I can't imagine. Provide some sort of meaning. I don't even know what I'm seeking, let alone how to find it. I know only that I'm lost without it."

"So you're not just hot on Egyptian religion and afraid of crocodiles."

"Which religion is the right religion? Is any? And how do you tell? Does anyone know? Anyone at all?" Cruz sighed to the depths of hell itself. The emptiness in his voice wrenched at Wade's heart. Cruz's nothingness was his own; Cruz, being more intellectual than he, simply articulated it a little differently. That was all.

It was high time to switch topics. Long past time. "We have to get around the Tenumas somehow, or through them, preferably without having to deal with more hand grenades. Any suggestions?"

"We have, in poker parlance, a hole card. Tingido and his nephew. They consented to remain with me if I chose to seek out Hurley. Both are forest Indians with very little white contact other than with Minho. And there I have used them for their jungle skills. I deliberately avoided softening them—civilizing them, so to speak."

"I see. You're saying the Tenumas are no match for Tingido."

"All his faculties are intact. Theirs are not, not any longer. We can use him to scout ahead and pinpoint enemy camps and operations. He can move through Tenuma territory without being detected. We cannot. He is the key."

"Marcia's gonna be thrilled to hear that."

Marcia. Intractable Marcia. Wade thought about the promises she made, about reaching civilization, about a lot of things. In essence, he had just turned them down. He could have talked her out of going on this wild goose chase as soon as he had seen where Cruz was headed. He did not.

And now he was off on a distasteful adventure neither he nor Marcia wanted. And yet he did want it. Elinor. But he didn't.

Hollow. Cruz was right. Life was hollow. Futile. But even Cruz had failed to mention that besides being futile and fearful, life is also confusing.

# *chapter*
# 14

COMPLETE DARKNESS. Utter blackness. Absolute nothing. Wade stood with one hand on a tree trunk, because he had learned years ago that you can lose your orientation, even your balance, in total darkness. Touching something solid prevented that.

Marcia was touching something solid, too. Him. She pressed closer. "How long yet?" she whispered.

"Probably fifteen, twenty more minutes. Patience."

"That long?" A warm hand touched his shoulder, his neck, the side of his head and drew him down into a kiss. He didn't fight it.

She lifted away. "Your heart's definitely not in this. I'm beginning to doubt your manhood."

"Well, don't. I have trouble paying attention when I'm surrounded by people with hand grenades who don't like me."

She sagged against him, and her hardness softened. "Why did I let myself get talked into this? It took me two days to realize what Cruz had done to me." She added a few words of reflection on the patrão's ancestry.

Cruz and Tiny were making their run about now. If all went well, silence should prevail. Wade kept his senses tuned, not so much toward the river, but toward the forest ahead.

The blackness was so thick that surely sound could never penetrate it. Perhaps the silence was—

The silence, the hope-inspiring silence, shattered. Up ahead men shouted in the forest. A gun went off. More shouting.

120

"They didn't slip through." Wade stood erect. "That's us."

"You said twenty minutes."

"I said 'probably.'" He felt around until he had her wrist firmly in his left hand and his pistol in his right. They must hurry now.

Another gunshot told him where the river lay. He turned his left side to the river and started forward in what can only be called rapid groping. The menace—the endless, mindless menace of a rain forest—clung close around his ears. Injury and death came so easily, so quickly. The forest didn't care a whit whom or what it destroyed. Somehow a danger that could pick and choose its victims seemed infinitely less dangerous than this random one.

The Tenumas could pick and choose, and they chose just about everybody, even their luckless thralls—the Ocaina clan. Wade paused suddenly. Marcia's free hand grabbed his arm and throttled it. The faint scritching he heard came from overhead. Somewhere up in the understory a cat or coati prowled across loose bark. He hastened on.

Dogs began to bark up ahead. Almost there. He fired his pistol skyward. He saw an orange glow beyond the trees. Bingo! He saw movement. He fired again and let loose a war whoop he had learned as boy in a Rochester scout troop.

Half a dozen Tenumas, some in face paint, were snatching up rifles and leaving the ring of orange light. Wade swung wide around the camp through the black woods, dragging his reluctant boss. He fired again. A shadow near the ring of firelight fell.

Keep moving. Stay back from the glow. Better to die by the bite of a bushmaster than by the hand of these savages.

Under a little frond shelter at this end, a man crouched beside a wooden crate, watching wild-eyed all around, a rifle at ready. Might this be the arsenal? Wade moved in twenty feet closer and stopped. He laid a hand on Marcia's shoulder—the stay-put signal—and started forward.

Cruz had been right about their hole card. Wade could never have approached Tingido the way he slipped up behind this man. He would never have gotten within striking distance. Any compunction he may have had about knifing a man from behind was blotted away by the thought of Tingido's nephew dying alone in the forest.

121

And yet, even as he held his breath and moved in behind the fellow, he couldn't go through with it. Killing was part of the rules of the forest, a necessary rule, for the first rule of all was survival. Wade had been both killer and intended victim more than once. But now for the first time ever, he had cold feet.

Tingido's nephew—mutilated, dying—flashed through his mind. No. An eye for an eye wasn't good enough anymore. He shifted the knife to his left hand and put all his muscle into a hard chop with his right. The fellow dropped instantly as if pole-axed.

Wade blasted two more pistol shots off towards the faceless trees beyond the clearing. He got a few wild shots back at him, but he was back in the darkness and safety, with both the rifle and the crate, before any of the unseen enemy could draw a good bead. These Tenumas were probably hot shots with grenades, but they couldn't hit barns with rifle fire. Crashing through the underbrush like an elephant, Marcia joined him. He passed her the rifle and emptied the crate into his pockets and his shirt. Disappointment: the box held only seven grenades.

Marcia led, struggling against the lianas and buttresses and tree roots. The forest wrapped them in velvet blackness. Wade fired again, wildly, for he saw nothing.

"Stop," Wade whispered. "Listen."

She even held her breath.

He could pick out by the sounds of battle about where the river lay. He handed two grenades to Marcia, and heard the whisper of fabric as she jammed them in her pockets. "River's that way. Here we go!"

This whole diversionary tactic was for no other reason than to divide the Tenumas' attention. *How well did it work?* Wade wondered. *Had Cruz and Tiny made it through?* He'd soon know.

A hint of gray light promised the river ahead. The forest opened a bit to a patch of moonless gray sky. The riverbank gaped suddenly, unexpectedly, at his feet. Almost home.

Now he must reproduce the baritone barking, grunting call of caiman, those alligators which at times form a reptilian carpet along river shores. His first attempt was all right, if you didn't listen too closely. Emboldened, he upped the volume and called again. A sleepy heron protested from twenty feet away.

Barely detectable, a canoe prow slipped in close in front of him, the blackness so intense he couldn't see Pato in the stern. He grabbed a gunwale, gripped the rough-hewn wood as Marcia climbed in, and hopped in himself. He was kneeling on the paddle, had some trouble pulling it free. And now they were off, silent in the silence, dark in the darkness, a part of the river and the night.

They paddled nearly half a mile before Wade whispered "Tiny and Cruz come through?"

"*Sí!* It works goot."

Silence. Darkness. The dim gray of moonless sky.

"*Mas allá de los arboles; el segundo.*" Pato's whisper was stretched thin and tight. The poor kid was scared spitless.

"Wa'd he say?" So was Marcia.

"The second bunch Tingido told us about are beyond the trees there. See the faint glow?" Wade was scared, too. Plenty scared. With the thrill of adventure absent, the terror had plenty of room to grow.

With those grenades in his pockets, Wade couldn't flex his legs to kneel properly in the canoe. He popped them out with difficulty, and let them roll around on the floor right in front of his knees.

They sliced on through black nothingness, keeping close to shore. The land's edge curved and snaked to their right, nearly undetectable but for the fireflies that flickered around the shoreline shrubbery, but for gently sloshing water now and then.

The sign was so subtle Wade nearly missed it—a patch of shoreline with no fireflies for a hundred feet. He pried out with the paddle, made one hard lunging stroke, and rapped twice on the gunwale as he folded forward. The faint rustle behind him told him that Marcia and Pato had both remembered the prearranged signal to duck.

Wade raised up high enough to stroke again. He very nearly didn't make it back down in time. A rifle flashed and boomed from shore. One slug struck the dugout. It wagged drunkenly. Much as he hated to, he rose up far enough to give the boat another push.

The canoe glided forward. Instantly it slammed to a stop as tree leaves whooshed. A leafy branch smacked Wade across the top of his head. Had they rammed the shore, or had a tree fallen out across the water? Either way they were in big trouble. The Tenuma scouting party on the bank knew exactly where they were.

Wade popped up, grabbed a handful of leaves, and stuck them in his mouth, tasting. He spit them out, satisfied that the dugout had not touched shore. This was not a shoreline shrub. It was one of the several kinds of capirono trees. That meant the tree was maybe a hundred feet wide. If the tree fell from close to shore, it could be blocking the whole river.

The angle of branching told him the tree had fallen from the south bank, from the left. If they could get around it at all, they must swing to the right—in close to that shore party. In total darkness.

Cruz and Tiny were right behind in the second dugout. How could he warn them in time? Futility and responsibility—they weighed him down so heavily, he was surprised the canoe stayed afloat.

The dugout lurched backwards, slipping clear of branches. Pato had thrown safety to the wind. He was up and paddling.

"We have to swing around it on the right, sport."

"But them . . ."

"I know."

A flash and roar marked the position of a rifle. Before Wade could pull his pistol, a rifle answered right behind him. Marcia was up, too. He had forgotten about handing her the sentry's gun. The canoe wagged wildly from the recoil. Her shoulder would be stiff tomorrow. If there were a tomorrow.

The canoe nosed into firm branches, backed off again. The faint crackle along the shore told Wade about where the Tenumas were. The river exploded hard by his right ear and sprayed in a geyser, straight up.

He thought he saw a shadow form and fired a shot at it. A rifle shot came back at him and struck the dugout. The prow pushed into leaves again. The branches yielded. Wade reached far ahead and grabbed leaves. He tugged mightily. The canoe jerked forward. Marcia's rifle blammed, and the canoe jerked sideways. He pulled, and they lurched forward again. Wade hand-over-handed through the thick treetop, driving the prow along, fearing all the while that somehow he would get the leverage wrong and dump them all in the drink.

The dugout wallowed apart from Wade's pulling. The whole shore exploded; men screamed. Marcia had tossed out one of her grenades.

Now the prow met no resistance. He grabbed his paddle and stroked. The canoe brushed limbs, waddled a bit, and slipped free.

In English he whispered to the blackness behind him, "Keep moving, Pato. We'll meet where we arranged. I'm going back to help Cruz through the tree."

"No! Wait!" Marcia hissed, but he was already over the side. Dank water drenched through to his skin instantly, armpit deep. He kept his pistol high and dry as he struggled back to the branches, trying to maintain silence. Involuntarily came all the memories he ever had of slinky, deadly, silent saimans slipping into the dank water with dinner on their pea-sized minds.

Moans and voices marked Tenumas along the shore. But which were down and which still dangerous? The truly perilous enemy was that without sound or voice.

The tree rattled ahead and to his right. Cruz and Tiny had arrived.

Wade yelled, "Down, quick!" as gunfire flamed from the shore. Was his warning in time? "Over here! You can get through here!" At least one of the gunmen ashore was firing at him. Slugs ripped leaves nearby.

Handy thing, English. He could speak freely in the presence of these Tenumas with scant chance of being understood. But Tiny wasn't going to get any quick messages either. Wade started working his way through the tangle of branches.

Somebody from mid-river blasted away toward shore. Months later, it seemed, the canoe nudged in close by. It backed off, rustled again still closer.

Wade groped forward and grabbed rough wood. In Portuguese he whispered, "I got ya. Stay down."

A humble human tugboat in a backwater of one of the world's great waterways, he yanked and dragged at the canoe prow. It came scraping and wallowing. Then it was free. He gave them a push upstream.

They were safe.

No, they weren't.

"Reinforcements!" Cruz barked. He cut loose with his pistol.

Wade heard them crashing through the forest. There must be a dozen out there, all fresh recruits for this unholy war. Tingido on his spy mission had said nothing about extra Tenuma troops.

Guns were going off like the Battle of Gettysburg. Unseen people in blackness blasted away at unseen people in blackness. A grenade exploded in the water near Wade, and the underwater concussion slapped his breath away. If they hit much closer, the shock alone would do him in.

The shore blew up, bright and loud. Marcia and Pato must still be somewhere close, and she was back to tossing grenades. The flash of light gave Wade a few chance targets—better to shoot at than general darkness. A few small bushes caught fire and flickered briefly before putting themselves out.

His gun clicked. Empty. He started swimming upstream. If he could reach Cruz's dugout . . . No, Cruz would be ahead somewhere if he were smart. The shore burst aflame again; Marcia had found the grenades he had left in the bottom of the dugout. Get her going and she was a one-woman army!

"Papa!" Pato wasn't but a couple yards away. Wade renewed his swimming efforts. Ashore, another grenade blew. Marcia's rifle blammed and blammed and clicked. Wade touched wood, lunged forward another stroke, and grabbed the gunwale.

"It's me!" he whispered hoarsely, just in time—in feeble half light from the shore, he saw Marcia hold her rifle high like a club, ready to repel boarders. She put it down instantly and grabbed handfuls of his shirt. She was stronger than she looked.

Pato counterbalanced as Wade hauled himself into the dugout and clambered forward. The kid was great! They followed the dim, gray-lit ribbon of open sky that marked the river. Then the night haze melted enough that a few bright stars burned through, all haloed.

"Papa! Bee-hine us!"

"I hear 'em. Faster!"

The Tenuma reinforcements had taken to the water, and they weren't far behind.

"Gimme your gun! Quick!" Marcia begged.

"Empty."

She loosed some solider-like, very unladylike words.

Cruz and Tiny should be a quarter mile ahead by now, for they were stronger paddlers than Pato. Instead, they were right here off Wade's bow. Now they were broadside, and now they had dropped back, just off Pato's stern quarter.

Tiny grumbled something about watching where you shoot, and Cruz murmured some platitude or other. He was reversed in the bow of their dugout, his pistol and right hand steadied by his left.

Wade was out of wind and sweaty enough to start the flood season without the Amazon's help. He must work harder, paddle faster, and yet he was paddling slower. He had nothing more to give, and they were losing ground to their pursuers. He heard Pato behind him, gulping air frantically.

Wade had always admired Cruz's iron nerves. He did so now. How tempting it must be for Cruz to just cut loose and fire into the darkness, hoping to hit something strategic. How tempting, in fact, to keep paddling, pretending he might win this deadly race. Not Cruz. While Wade and Pato tried their hardest to put some space between the enemy and their unarmed canoe, Cruz let Tiny work, and waited, his gun poised, aiming two-handed.

He opened fire, and the sudden noise shattered the air, the water, the jungle around. Monkeys set up a violent protest in the trees somewhere near. That disturbed Wade more than the gunfire—if the monkeys were screeching, dawn couldn't be too far away. They still needed the protection of darkness.

Monkeys? Perhaps they were crossing the frontier of the Tenumas' barren territory.

Cruz's pistol clicked empty. Instantly, he rotated and snatched up a paddle. Their canoe forged ahead, lunged abreast Wade's. He glanced back. Cruz had done damage, but not enough damage. In the gray mist of predawn came three canoes. No, four.

Futility.

A Tenuma warrior, amidships in the second canoe back, stood up, the better to get a good shot with his rifle. He raised the gun, aimed—there was nothing Wade could do about it.

Wade watched as the man stood transfixed, something of a surprised look on his face. He pitched forward, dropped across the gunwale, tipped the canoe gently and surely, and dumped his four companions in the river. The capsized boat hung upside down, then began casually to drift backwards, downstream.

Another rifleman took aim from a seated position. His gun blasted; Wade's canoe jerked as chips and splinters flew from the stern end. Pato yelped.

Two of the Tenumas had slumped over. And now another one. They yelled to each other, and as one, the three remaining dugouts swapped ends and headed downstream in full retreat, paddling as rapidly as they had come.

Tiny brought his boat in, thump, against Wade's. Pato reached out and grabbed their gunwale.

"Marcia. Latch on." Wade shipped his paddle and sat there, exhausted, drawing in a lot less air than his tortured lungs craved. He'd let Tiny keep them moving a while.

Marcia held onto Cruz's boat with one hand and wrenched herself around to look behind. "What made them drop over like that?"

"Blowguns." Cruz popped his cylinder open and glanced at Wade. "Any shells?"

Wade shook his head.

"Blowg— . . . but who? Oh! Tingido?"

"Them." Cruz nodded forward.

At first you saw only a dugout ahead, with three or four forest Indians in dress paint. But if you looked carefully, you could see the blowgun shooters ashore, nearly hidden by the growth. A couple more there, and still more over there. Both sides of the river, in the bushes, on the water, before, behind, everywhere.

Marcia's black eyes rolled wide. "They're not like anyone I've ever seen. The paint, I mean. Or . . . they're naked and . . ."

Cruz laid his empty gun on the bottom of the dugout. "I believe we have just made contact with Dr. Hurley's inner circle of believers."

# chapter
# 15

THE DEADLIEST CREATURE on earth is not a rogue elephant or fer-de-lance or piranha or crocodile. The deadliest creature of all is a forest Indian unsullied by white civilization who doesn't think you should be in his territory. They stood all round about Wade now—forest Indians without any garments, weapons, or adornments of exotic manufacture.

Why didn't he care more? Why didn't it concern him that he could die in the next few seconds, perhaps without ever knowing how his death came? He felt all washed away inside, yet not clean.

His breathing was finally catching up to the demand of his lungs. He leaned over the side, scooped up a big handful of water, slopped it all over his face and neck, then did it again. He picked up his paddle and helped Pato swing the dugout toward the south shore.

Tiny and Cruz beached their boat on a muddy little bank.

Cruz climbed out like an eighty-year-old pensioner and wiped his face. "I suggest using no Spanish. Spanish is one of the languages of the enemy. Hear, Pato?"

Pato hesitated the slightest moment. "Yes, *pat-* . . ." He looked at Wade.

"Sir."

"Yes, sir."

Pato planted the nose of their dugout in the mud next to Tiny's. Wade hopped out and steadied it between his knees, but it wallowed anyway as Marcia struggled forward and out. Like a lumberjack, Pato flowed out over the gunwale and helped Wade draw the dugout higher.

Cruz sat down heavily on the moss beyond the mud. He folded his arms across his knees and laid his head on them. The man had obviously overextended himself, and Wade could do nothing for him. He felt useless.

Futility.

One thing Indians absolutely lack is any sense of urgency. These men stood around carelessly, casually, pretending they were not even looking at the newcomers as they drank in every detail. Wade stood around, too, just as slack. Tiny sat down and leaned back against a tree, totally wrung out. Pato was comfortable with the Indian way. He settled down close to Tiny, prepared to wait. Only Marcia, city-bred Marcia, anxiously paced, awaiting action.

"Pato, you were a man this morning. We couldn't have gotten this far without you. I'm proud of you."

"T'anks, Papa." He looked almost embarrassed with his sheepish grin. He traced in the dirt with his big toe.

"Remember when we first met that morning, I said something like 'What's a little kid gonna do for me'?"

"Now you know, eh?"

"Now I know you aren't a little kid."

Two Indians had their heads together muttering. Good or bad? The stoic faces offered no hint.

Wade stuffed his hands in his pockets. With his fingertips he measured the length of his plug. He crossed over to Cruz, dropped down beside him, and laid a hand on his neck. No fever. Just weariness. He sat down and began the nerve-soothing ritual of shaving a pipeful.

Marcia paused in her pacing. "We waiting for something in particular?"

"For these folks to make the next move. Stick poison darts in us, offer us breakfast, whatever."

"How can you be so casual about all this?"

"Wish I knew."

Futility.

The sun had risen far enough now to call it "day." Wade was

outrageously hungry. He could just imagine Pato's starvation meter going off the scale. And poor old Tiny was probably ready to eat the dugout.

Marcia plopped down beside him. "Isn't it weird? These men are all standing around stark naked, and, uh . . . how do I say this? It doesn't matter somehow. Clothes, no clothes. You don't even notice."

"Going naked here means going without the proper paint. Nobody here is naked. You never go out into the forest naked. Just isn't done."

She giggled. "Not in New York, either. You never go out on the street without make-up."

"So much for cultural differences. What am I missing back home, anyway?"

"The prohibitionists pushed through no-booze laws. No beer, wine, hard stuff—nothing. You can't buy booze any more."

"I'll bet."

"Legitimately, I mean. The hard drinkers like Harry Landis haven't slowed down any. It's wild. And getting wilder. Harding's president."

"Yeah, I heard that."

"Music. Some real good music coming outta downtown. I love to go down, to some of those clubs. But you don't hafta go somewhere anymore, to listen to music. Everybody—just everybody—has a phonograph now. You know, a Gramophone. You get yourself a couple records, crank up the machine, and listen any old time you want. Everybody's getting a telephone, too. When I was a kid, they were curiosities. Now they're everywhere. Everyone's got an auto. Streets full of cars. Lot's changed in the last couple years."

"Sounds so."

*When I was a kid,* she had said. Was she that much younger than he? He'd been in South America now for more than a decade. Come to think about it, that *was* a long time. He subtracted ten years from her age and saw a little kid in grammar school—and he, even then, a man in his prime. The heaviness of encroaching age pressed on him anew. He thought of his plan to seek gold south of the Uaupes. Maybe next year. When he'd be a full year older. How did these things happen? And why him? Cruz asked unanswerable questions about religious philosophy. Wade's philosophical questions touched closer home.

An older man paused beside Wade. His paint marks were different, and the marks on his chest—paint and scars both—were unique. This must be a state occasion, for he had put on his macaw-feather headdress and a necklace of seeds, shells, and stuffed hummingbirds and barbets. The headdress plus his long, shaggy bangs half hid the crackling black eyes.

He squatted down in front of them. Cruz raised his head and straightened somewhat, though his arms still draped across his knees. Marcia tightened. Maybe she didn't care how they dressed, but they made her nervous.

Wade glanced beyond Cruz to Pato. Good old Pato didn't seem the least bothered, and why not? By blood, if not by totem, these were his people—half, at least. The boy watched with curiosity unabashed, totally unafraid.

"We hear you speak," said the old man in careful, measured English. "Now we know your speech. Your tongue. Now we ask. Why do Tenumas chase you? Why do they try kill you? Why do you try kill them? Why are you enemy?" And he settled in to listen.

Wade gave Cruz a do-you-want-to-take-this-or-shall-I? glance.

Cruz dipped his head toward Marcia and spoke just as slowly and distinctly. "Our friend, Miss Lewis, must find Dr. Morris Hurley. Dr. Hurley is known to her. Same tribe. American. Dr. Hurley is enemy to those Tenumas. So we are enemy to them, also. They do not want us to see Dr. Hurley. They do not want us to live. We try to kill them to escape from them. Get away from them alive. We do not hate them. They are not enemy to us."

Wade kept his face loose and even nodded as he marveled at how Cruz could say that. Cruz and Tiny ripped by bullets, Tingido's one nephew killed by a grenade and the other injured, and Cruz says that? Never mind how. *Why* would he?

"You are same tribe."

"No. I am Brazil tribe. Friend to Miss Lewis. For three floods, I lived with her tribe. Among Americans."

The half-hidden eyes flicked to Wade.

"I am same tribe. American."

The old man stared approximately at Wade's breastbone as he digested all this. Suddenly those eyes snapped back to Cruz. "Who is Jesus Christ?"

Wade caught himself gaping. It was absolutely the last question in the world he would expect of a forest savage.

Cruz never broke stride. "Jesus Christ is Lord of heaven and earth. Chief of sky and forest. He is Spirit."

No doubt Marcia, because she didn't know Indians, thought all those men standing around were simply looking off into space, their thoughts elsewhere. She probably did not detect that they were watching the newcomers most carefully. Nor would her untrained eye notice now that their attention had shifted from the outlanders to the old man. They were waiting for some sort of verdict, ready to follow his lead for the next move.

The brilliant red and blue headdress tipped toward Marcia. "Welcome. Come into us."

Wade caught Cruz's eye. "Now?"

Cruz held up his hand and counted off fingers. "You see five of us. But we are eight. Two men friends of me, friends of Miss Lewis. One woman, a sister of Dr. Hurley, a sister in Jesus. She is a woman of God. Some call her woman of light. Those three wait near the line, across the river there." He waved his arm toward the water. "They ask you: 'We come into you also'?"

The old man thought a few minutes, then nodded. "They come. I will do it."

"Thank you."

The old man stood up in one fluid motion. Age hadn't diminished his faculties the least bit, nor did he appear the sort who would want to build a retirement fund. He didn't seem bothered by futility, either, or any such nonsense.

Wade gave Marcia a hand to her feet as the old man turned away.

"Into us?" she murmured.

"Try 'among us.' No big difference. Invitation to stay alive a while longer." There was no walking two abreast through this tangle. Wade unlocked Marcia's grip and took her by the hand. He maneuvered her around behind him, but he didn't let go. Holding an attractive woman's hand was definitely a pleasant way to walk. He'd known that since grammar school. He heard Cruz and Tiny following.

Pato slipped in close. "Think we eat quick mebbe?"

"Maybe."

Such was not to be. With polite greetings the old man turned them over to the care of other Indians. After an hour of walking faint game trails, they were transferred to the aegis of still others. Cruz began to fade despite frequent rest stops, and Tiny was looking pallid. Indians came and went. When the old man said "into us," he wasn't kidding. They were into the thick of it and still walking.

Marcia was beginning to fade, too. The journey was taking its toll. "When that person said he'd do it, did he mean invite Tingido and Elinor?"

"Think so. You never really know. These folks tend to treat other people's languages pretty casually. With their own, though, they can get as nitpicky as a philosopher."

"How's he gonna find them? Where are they, anyway?"

He will. Forest Indians find forest Indians when no one else knows there's anyone there."

"Elinor isn't an Indian. On second thought, guess she might as well be."

The ferns rustled to the right, and Wade grabbed for his gun, his reflexes never thinking it was empty. With deep squawks a flock of hunchbacked gray birds burst out and away and scattered among the green leaves, some flying, most running rapidly on chicken legs.

"They look sorta like guinea hens at the Central Park Zoo."

"Yeah, they do. Trumpeters, they're called. Fairly common."

"Do you know every bird in the woods?"

"It's a crackerjack guide's job to know all the animals. No, I don't. That tell you anything?"

"Yes, and I don't believe a word of it."

The sun was nearly overhead somewhere beyond the dense green canopy when their latest guide brought them into still another settlement and called a welcome halt. Women and children, at least a dozen of each, eyed the strangers curiously. They seemed especially intrigued by Marcia's soft wavy hair.

At last these hosts put into motion the ritual steps of hospitality. Wade talked Marcia through the confusing parts. "That's called chiche. Don't ask what it is. Just drink it. And don't wrinkle your nose like that. It's quite an honor for a woman to be allowed to have some." "Your other hand. That's it." "First, you say thank you. Watch how Pato does it." But his mind was on other things.

This settlement was different somehow, but it was not a threatening or unpleasant difference. Indian villages in the basin looked alike. The same shelters and thatch, meager furnishings and utensils, storage baskets and dried herbs—all resembled such things Wade had seen in a hundred other places. What rang false? What changed the atmosphere here?

Finally they ate, and the meal was the same as that served everywhere else—manioc, monkey meat, fish, vegetables. It surely wasn't the food that differed.

Cruz was picking at his food half-heartedly, struggling to keep enough starch in his spine to sit erect.

Wade offered him a sweet plantain. "You feeling all right?"

"Yes. Tired is all. Thank you." He abandoned the catfish he was working on and sampled the fruit.

"How'd you know what to answer that fellow who asked about Christ?"

"Logic. Dr. Hurley is associated with not one but two religious institutions, a church and a university. Tingido's sources claimed he was protected by a circle of believers. Not just friends. Believers. It followed naturally to quote a basic tenet of the Christian faith."

"Logic." Wade finished off a chunk of fish and licked his fingers. "See? That's why you're the master of an empire the size of Texas, and I'm having trouble scraping together a little nest egg to retire on."

"I had wondered what that business of your own was that you had mentioned."

Wade recalled dimly the time he first explained to Marcia on the deck of her launch about Bernardo Martin Cruz—a man who saw everything and forgot nothing. Wade knew the man, had known him for years, knew his prodigious memory. Why did these little confirmations of Cruz's mental prowess always surprise Wade so when they popped up? How could so sharp a thinker taste futility so keenly? Did futility perhaps come in part from thinking too much?

At his elbow Marcia gasped and tightened up like a watch spring before bolting to her feet. Wade climbed to his and gave Cruz a steadying hand up.

For out of the green wall had just stepped one of God's ambassadors to earth. You wouldn't know it by looking at his slight build, his balding head, his pale skin, his uncertain and halting gait. You might not notice the genuine deference, even awe, in which his Indian companions held him. Because of their own stoicism, it was not obvious.

No, the glow came from elsewhere. The man's face radiated serenity and peace, just like Elinor's. He showed absolutely no trace of smug superiority or even leadership, although he was the only clothed person in the territory, except for the outlanders. Elinor called herself Jesus Christ's presence in the Colombia corridor. Here was Jesus Christ's presence in the depths of the forest beyond the Minho River.

Here was Dr. Morris Hurley.

# chapter
# 16

STICK A UNIVERSITY PROFESSOR out in a rain forest with no university for two thousand miles, and what would you expect? Books, of course—lots of books—all somewhat mildewed and insect-riddled. The Amazon is very hard on books. Personal papers in disheveled stacks. A brown-stained coffee cup. Reading glasses. A big padded armchair to cradle and swallow the lucky scholar curling up with a good book.

They were all here, even the chair. It was built of tapir hide, stretched tautly over a hardwood frame lashed together without benefit of metal screws or nails. The hair had been worn off in the areas of hard use, the seat curved and molded. Wade didn't try out the chair, but it was tempting. It looked not only comfortable, but civilized, a drop of the familiar in an ocean of exotica.

He stuffed his hands in his pockets and wandered around Dr. Hurley's study, an open rain shelter, as this afternoon's thunderstorm pounded on the thatch. He craned his neck sideways to read the spines of the three or four dozen books on these makeshift shelves. *Young's Analytical Concordance*. *Dispensational Truth*, by Clarence Larkin. *Foxe's Book of Martyrs*. Dr. Hurley must have liked Larkin. Here was another slim volume by the same author—*Book of Revelation*. The rain was letting up.

Cruz came jogging in, only slightly soggy from crossing twenty feet of open compound in the downpour.

Wade turned away from the books. Books had never genuinely interested him. "You look much better."

"I feel much better."

"Tiny still napping?"

"They all are, including our host. I'm surprised you're up."

"So'm I. Last night was rough."

It was clear that books intrigued Cruz. Instantly he homed in on the bookshelf, running his fingers along spines, pulling this volume or that for a closer look. Seeking. That was it. He was seeking, the way a busy coati forages on the forest floor.

Wade gave the armchair a fond and final glance—Cruz would surely want it if he found anything worth perusing—and settled into his next-favorite position: on the ground with his knees cocked and his back firmly planted against a house post. He had packed his pipe at dawn. Now was as good a time as any to torch it off. The drumming rain slowed to a casual whisper.

"Wha'd you find?"

Cruz shook his head and carried a book over to the chair. Cruz and the chair belonged together. He looked more scholarly nestled in there than Wade could ever hope to. "Dr. Hurley has the same quality Elinor has. Elán. And purpose. I was hoping it might be found here in his library."

"Lotta books to wade through there. Exactly how desperate are you?"

"Enough." Cruz folded his opened book on his lap and stared at infinity in the dirt near Wade's feet. "I searched for a year at the university in Salamanca and found nothing. I decided that schools in Spain have certain unintentional strictures to religious thought because Spain is basically a nation of only one religion. To find what I was seeking I needed complete freedom of thought. America and freedom of religion are synonymous."

"So you tried Princeton, in the land of the free."

"Yes. Excellent teachers and brilliant theorists at Princeton, but no answers. Perhaps what I was seeking came not from study, but from achievement. I married, built Minho, sired sons. By the strength of my own hand and mind, I achieved great things. As you so aptly put it, I have everything—except answers."

"Does it bother you that a mere slip of a girl half your age seems to have found the answers you've been searching for your whole life? Or do you suppose Elinor simply never asked the questions?"

Cruz mulled the matter a few moments. "We'll never know. Eighteen years of marriage taught me that women and men don't think in the same ways. Her questions quite probably aren't mine. But it appears the answers are the same."

"As are Hurley's."

Cruz's eyes for the first time met Wade's. "Yes. Precisely. So long as Elinor was the only one who seemed to have the answers, I couldn't be sure it wasn't something only a woman can accept. Answers only a woman, with her special way of seeing the world, can understand and live with. But, if Hurley has it, it's not beyond me. He found it. Therefore, so can I."

"Maybe."

Cruz's voice softened. "In some ways, my friend, you're more despairing even than I."

*Isn't that the truth.* "Lemme know what you find." His pipe was dying. He stared into the bowl a moment at the fluff of gray ash, then tried to draw a few more puffs of life from it. Why does tobacco burn so much faster when your supply is way down?

Wade lurched to his feet. Suddenly he felt this itch to move around, a restlessness. He left Cruz to his foraging and wandered out across the slurpy open yard. He missed Elinor. That realization struck like lightning, stopped him dead in his tracks. He yearned to see her near, to feel her presence even when they were a compound apart doing separate tasks. He was bewitched, all right, by that woman of light who shone like sunshine on the darkest of hours.

Was she safe? Cruz had given Tingido orders to guard her with his life. Confident in Tingido's loyalty, Wade was certain he would. But sometimes in the jungle, capable as Tingido was, that might not be enough. Would she come soon? Depended on how soon Tingido and Hurley's protectors made contact.

Wade was glad she hadn't run the gauntlet along with the two dugouts. They came much too close to losing that race. She was safer from the Tenumas by staying on land, by working her way through enemy territory. If anyone could slip through, Tingido and she could.

Still, he was worried. And he had never worried about anyone else before in his whole life.

Marcia leaned against a housepost across the way and beckoned him with a flick of the head. He took his time ambling over.

"Nice nap, boss?"

"Lonesome nap." She dropped her voice. "Don't you ever think about me? I mean . . . you know what I mean."

"Sure I think about you."

"Then why are you scared to get close to me? I can't believe you're so old-fashioned that you'd back off from a girl just 'cause she won't play hard to get. You think I'm predatory? Trying to trap some poor unlucky slob into marriage? What? "

He turned his dead pipe over and rapped it against the housepost right beside her ear. "Then there's some question about my manhood, too, as I recall."

"I admit my timing was a little off that night. I didn't realize we were so close to those whoever-they-are. The enemy. But we don't have any murderers breathing down our neck now."

"So it's about time I proved my manhood's above question. Like maybe we take a walk in the woods or something."

"Now you've got the idea."

"More ideas than you could guess." He blew into his pipe bowl—all clear—stuffed the cold pipe into his shirt pocket and buttoned down the flap. "Item one. I don't feel any pressing need to prove my manhood to you or anyone else, and it's none of your business anyway.

"Item two. That marriage trap hooey isn't a consideration because no woman alive is going to sucker me into something like that if I don't want it. I like to think I'm a little smarter'n that."

"Yeah, well, some men—"

"Item three. You keep forgetting the first thing you ever learned about me. I don't take any unnecessary chances, remember? I'll be the last man in Amazonas to turn down a little harmless fun now and then. The key word's *harmless*. Out here in the weeds, you let your guard down, quit paying attention for a minute, and the rain forest is waiting to nail you. It's dangerous to mix pleasure with business. Right now it's strictly business.

"Item four related to item three. Soon's you start monkeying around with personal relationships, you change the whole fabric of the group. Your survival and mine don't depend on just me. We depend on the group—Tiny, Pato, Cruz, the others, if they get here. So far the group's doing just fine the way it is, and I'm not about to risk my survival by accidentally upsetting something.

"Sure, I think about you. You're a pleasure to behold, cute as a kitten, and you let me know plainly enough how you feel. You also hired me to do a job, part of which involves keeping us both alive. So, until we're out of the woods, I'm not going to risk your pretty little neck—or my neck either—for the sake of momentary pleasure." He took a breath. "How'm I doing so far, boss?"

"Well, uh . . ." She shrugged helplessly. "I suppose . . . at least it's not some fuzzy moral scruple Little Goody Two-Shoes talked you into."

Wade felt his neck heat up. "Her name is Elinor. And, if I didn't have a couple stray moral scruples of my own—like a moral responsibility towards an irritating reporter with a head problem who's five thousand miles from where she oughta be—you would've been left to fend for yourself long ago already."

"Irritating, huh. You and Harry. You think I'm irritating."

"Yeah. Try bossy, selfish, and demanding while you're at it."

"The Red Queen maybe, in *Through the Looking-Glass*. Or is it the white one? 'Off with her head'?"

"Papa!" Pato stood by the corner housepost of the next-door rain shelter. "That Dr. Hurley thinks, he sess . . . uh . . . talk mebbe you want, eh?"

"Sure. Go tell Cruz."

With the exuberance of youth, Pato ran splacking out across the muddy yard. Wade locked eyes with his employer. He decided not to make some snide comment and walked away, her shrill and angry expletives yapping at the heels of his awareness.

Dr. Hurley sat beneath the rain shelter that was apparently his home, as opposed to the library, or office, Cruz and Wade had explored. He looked no better after his nap than he had before. His pallid skin seemed almost translucent, like the little tetra fish that lived among the reeds on the river shore. He moved with difficulty—cautious, deliberate. He settled into a chair similar to the one in his library and smiled pleasantly as Wade approached.

141

"Mr. Travers, your son is a delight. We've been talking a little. He's polite, and wise beyond his years. Twelve, he says?"

"Twelve. Yeah, I'm proud of him."

"He tells me your party has come to rescue me."

Wade heard Marcia come slopping in behind him. Pato bounded in from the yard.

Cruz entered soon after. He paused at the edge of the roof, glanced at a carved wooden stool, and looked at Dr. Hurley.

The doctor nodded. "There are no shaman stools here. Sit wherever you wish. You, too, Miss . . . Miss Lewis?"

"Thank you." She jabbed Wade and muttered, "Translate."

Wade held a stool for her. "Remember I said never sit down in a house unless you know it's all right? Some clans have stools for exlusive use of priests and high officials. Almost always they're carved with water animals—a turtle or something. And may lightning strike any woman or nonclansman who sits on one."

Wade pressed the legs of his stool into the dirt by a housepost so he could lean. "We're assuming you want to be rescued."

"I do, and I don't. I want my papers rescued. But I'm not so certain I would be worth the bother any more."

"Why not?" Wade settled in. Paddling all night last night was starting to catch up with him.

Tiny came waddling in to complete the group. He sat on the dirt next to Cruz and Pato. Just as well—few are the stools made sturdy enough to support a whale.

"I am close to death. Having no medical background, I can't say for certain what illness this is—consumption, I suspect, or what they've started calling tuberculosis recently. I can feel myself declining daily. I haven't long."

Wade stared at Cruz. "Elinor's sense of urgency!"

Cruz nodded. "Conversant with God."

"Elinor is the woman coming by another route?"

Wade dropped forward and parked his elbows on his knees, the better to keep from getting drowsy. "We made an attempt to reach you about a month ago and were repulsed. By common consent . . ." He looked right at Marcia. ". . . we agreed to try again. Elinor has been anxious to reach you since the beginning."

Cruz picked up the story. "We broke up into three small parties, two by land and one by the river, for a small party would have the best chance of penetrating Tenuma territory successfully. We hoped at least one would reach you. When Elinor and Tingido and his nephew make it, we will all have succeeded."

"I'm impressed—and very touched—by your perseverance. But I rather thought official channels would deal with the Tenumas and negotiate my safe conduct. American embassy, perhaps."

Wade smiled. "Private enterprise is the American way."

Dr. Hurley laughed, and it was the relaxed chuckle of a happy man, not a dying consumptive. Like Elinor, he didn't seem to be afraid of anything, nor did he seem to notice discomfort.

Cruz was muttering rapid-fire to Tiny, translating. Tiny nodded, then his face went blank. He didn't get it.

The doctor grew serious. "Have lives been lost on my behalf?"

Why lie? "One. A boy four years older than Pato."

"Children. You send children out on such a mission!"

"They might be considered children in the States, maybe. Not here in the forest. Pato pulls his full weight. So do Tingido's nephews. Tingido considers it training for future battles."

Marcia cut in. "You said you wanted your papers rescued. Memoirs?"

"Some. Studies also. And a partial manuscript on sensible methods for converting the Indians."

"This whole tribe is Christian, is it not?" Cruz sat forward on his elbows, too, his slim fingers lacing in and out.

The lithe Indian nearest Hurley's right shoulder smiled. "We call ourselves by Christ. We are Christians. We don't use the old name for our people any more."

"His people. Our people. What's left of us. These are a remnant who escaped enslavement by the Tenumas. Pahoa here told me about your arrival on the river. You're alive now only because they're Christians. They are, with some justification, quite xenophobic."

Marcia shook her head. "I don't understand."

"Faith in our Lord Jesus is strong, but so is the survival instinct. They've seen too many kith and kin die by the hand of strangers.

143

They're suspicious of Tenumas in particular and every one else in general. They tend to quietly remove trespassers, much as I plead against murder. Fortunately, you answered the questions rightly."

"What questions?"

"Who Jesus Christ is. And when they asked if you made enemies, you gave essentially a pacifist answer. There are very few of us pacifists in this region. It made you one of us."

Wade gaped at Cruz. The *patrão* ought to be looking downright smug. He didn't. He explained more to Wade than to Hurley, "Elinor is strongly pacifist and strongly empathetic with you, Dr. Hurley. A pacifist response seemed in order."

"These memoirs," Marcia pressed, "deal with the slavery? With involvement of white rubber barons and such?"

"Mostly. The tragic tale of the Putumayo atrocities a few years ago is being repeated."

"More than you realize." Wade leaned back; his spine was getting stiff. "The Ocainas lost eighty percent of their tribe then, and the Tenumas have part of what's left under their thumb now, using them as a connection with the outside world."

Dr. Hurley wagged his head. "I feel overwhelmed so often. So much injustice and here I sit, next to helpless to do anything."

"You *can* do something!" Marcia sat forward, perched eagerly on the edge of her stool. "You didn't ask my trade when we met this afternoon. I'm a reporter. *New York Sun Telegram*. I want to publish your story. An exclusive. Tell the world!"

"Ah, I see." Dr. Hurley melted back in his chair. Did Wade detect a twinkle in his eye? "Underlying my rescue, a profit motive."

Cruz nodded solemnly. "As we said. 'The American way.'"

# chapter
# 17

THERE'S NO WAY to be uncomfortable in a jungle hammock. It gently cradles every square inch of your anatomy. It gives under bulges and angles, supports everything equally.

Wade was uncomfortable.

He flopped one leg over the side and gave himself a push. He swayed back and forth. He laced his fingers behind his head. With a skill born from years of falling out of hammocks, he turned onto his side without dumping. Nothing worked. In desperation he got up and padded in stocking feet out into the open yard.

The fire had melted to a few coals swimming in a dull red glow. A full moon coasted high above the little hole this clearing punched up through the trees, overwhelming the puny red light with bright silver. Why wasn't she back? What had gone wrong?

He walked over to the edge between silver and black and let his ears tell him what was happening in the night world beyond. The bats were hard at work, here in the compound and high in the canopy. He couldn't hear the treetop bats, but he could see them when they crossed the little patch of open light above. A sudden startled scream in the understory told him an ocelot had caught a sleeping monkey. He heard rustling up high, then the unmistakable claw-on-bark sounds as the ocelot came spiraling down a tree trunk head first.

Where could she be?

Tiny started snoring. Wade looked that way, straining his eyes to see the hammocks in the darkness of the rain shelter. From Pato's hammock beside Tiny's waved a palm frond. *Fwack.* The snoring ceased.

He walked a few yards into the blackness and backed up against a tree. A mosquito found him. Silently he wiped the beastie out. His eyes began to feel tight, as one's eyes do when they struggle for a while to see something in total blackness. That creepy feeling—*Beware, Wade Travers, you'll die*—was coming back. Now, though, he was frightened not for himself but for Elinor. He tried to recall each little detail of her and was shocked to discover his memories blurred.

He smelled human sweat. It wasn't his own. Without thinking, he grabbed for his pistol. A warm damp hand out of nowhere gripped his wrist, held his gun hand tightly. He hauled back with his free fist and froze. The face he was about to punch was Tingido's.

The Indian grinned like Puck.

Wade sagged back against the trunk. "That's the second time you pulled that on me, you . . ." He was so happy he felt weak-kneed. Wait! "Elinor . . . ?"

"Here." She materialized by degrees as she came floating through the growth. The yellow dog trotted out into the compound to reacquaint itself with civilization, no doubt to seek treats and handouts. Tingido's nephew and two others followed Tingido into the settlement. Elinor paused before Wade.

He really and truly intended only to greet her in a prim and proper manner befitting her dignity. He laid his hands on her arms. Then his hands quit taking instructions. On their own they wrapped around her, drew her against him, pressed her so close she probably couldn't breathe, tried to fuse her to himself to make up for all the worry and the waiting. He mashed his cheek against the halo of moonlit hair. And for minutes, he could not let her go.

Belatedly, it occurred to him that the hug was not one-sided. She was wrapped around him just as earnestly, her head pressed hard against his shoulder. He kissed her forehead. Her face tipped up to his and caught the filtered moonlight just so.

And, when he kissed her lips, he learned something he should

146

have guessed months ago when first he ever saw her on that trail up the bluff: he was in love.

Hers was not the teasing, taunting kiss with which Marcia and others such made sensual promises. Her lips promised far deeper things, warm and caring things, the things that mark the difference between an eternal relationship and a shallow, passing fancy. It surprised Wade very much that he could discern the difference.

When eventually he lifted away, her cheeks were wet. His eyes felt hot, too, come to think of it. He kissed each of her dewy eyelids, and with one hand snuggled her head against him. Felt good. So good.

"I was worried."

She sniffed. "*You* were worried. All I could think about was one of those grenades blowing up too close to you. My head knew perfectly well that since you were chosen, you would survive and reach Dr. Hurley just fine. But my heart was so frightened for you."

"Any trouble getting through?"

"Not much. A few tense moments. I'm not nearly as good at moving about undetected as Tingido and his nephew are. But Tingido was very understanding and protective. How about the others? Did you have to take to the water?"

"Yeah. The Tenumas spotted the dugouts at that first major camp, so Marcia and I divided their attention. It worked. Then Pato picked us up. Actually, we didn't have any problems to speak of. Cruz got a little tired, is all. Pato acquitted himself well. Good kid. Sharp kid. Stronger'n he looks, too. I think he enjoys the adventure of it."

"Surely you do, too."

"Used to."

The radiant head pulled back to look him in the eye. She tilted it in that charming, inquiring way of hers. "I hear much more than that in the tone of your voice."

He pushed her head back against him. He liked it better when the glowing eyes were looking elsewhere. "Don't read too much into my voice. It's tired. Been a hard couple days."

"It's not your voice that's tired. It's your soul."

"You think so." Wade was starting to feel nervous. "Let's change the subject, huh?"

147

"I've been watching you—you and Señor Cruz both. Am I right that you've been plagued by strange thoughts? That things seem just a bit out of kilter?"

He pushed her away far enough to look into her eyes. "Now, why do you say that?"

"Ah. I *am* right. That's wonderful." And her eyes shone.

"Wonderful, huh? You should live with it a while."

"Don't you see? No, of course you don't. You don't have spiritual sight yet. The Holy Spirit is working on you. He's starting to move powerfully in your life. It is as it should be!"

"If you say so."

"Oh, I do! For reasons . . . perhaps someday I'll tell you. I don't dare tell you now." Suddenly she took his head in both her warm, dry hands. She drew it down to her lips and kissed him roundly, enthusiastically. She shoved away from him and darted off into the settlement with the agility of a spider monkey, left him standing there, trying to figure out what had just happened.

He never did sort out all the pieces.


Wade slept late next morning—something he never did—and no one woke him for anything, not even for breakfast. By lunchtime it was raining so hard you'd think God was trying to quench hell.

They ate lunch together, the rescuers and the rescuee. Dr. Hurley monopolized the conversation, and rightly so, telling what he had learned regarding the Tenuma mess. Eager beaver Marcia practically jumped up and down for joy. The bigger the holocaust, the better the story. Reporters!

Elinor sat near tears the whole time. Wade admired her sensitivity. When he tried to drum up a little admirable sensitivity of his own, though, he went dry. Nothing. There was a day, and not long ago, when his heart if not his eyes wept for the Ocainas and the dastardly hand fate had dealt them. He no longer cared enough to matter. What had happened?

After lunch Cruz called another of his war councils, gathered as before under a sopping thatched roof with rain pelting down. Dr. Hurley was in on this one, of course, since he was the reason for it all. His coughing spells persisted, seemed even worse today.

148

Marcia's body arrived, but her mind was elsewhere. Absently she rubbed her sore shoulder as she curled up in a corner of the rain shelter, part of the group and yet absent, poring over sheets and sheets of the doctor's notes. She seemed little more interested than the yellow dog curled up at Tingido's feet. No real matter. Everyone knew what she wanted—to get out as quickly as possible.

Cruz looked from face to face. "Suggestions? Comments?"

Dr. Hurley coughed. "My friends here could probably get me out, but neither they nor I would know what to do next. We wouldn't know where to go once we left familiar territory. We wouldn't know what officials, if any, to trust. In fact, since I can't tell Spanish from Portuguese, I wouldn't know which officials were which." He smiled sheepishly.

Cruz almost smiled. Almost. "We know where to go, and if fortune be with us, we have identified the foe, both in the forest and in the bureaucracy. But we'll not ask your friends here to bring you out. We must leave; therefore, we are at risk in any case. There's no point in placing your friends in peril as well. We'll bring you out with us."

"I don't see how. It looks hopeless." Dr. Hurley fell prey to another coughing fit.

Cruz looked from face to face. "Tingido, his nephew, and Elinor had difficulty coming through Tenuma territory. They're the most highly skilled of any of us, but they were only three. Miss Lewis and Travers had to take to the water almost immediately. I see no hope that our whole party could reach safety over land. The group is too large to move silently."

"By water, then. Anybody besides me notice the river's starting to rise?" Wade groped for the last of his plug. When this was gone, it was all gone.

Cruz nodded. "The *varzea* can work much to our advantage."

"The what?" Marcia looked up.

"The inundated forest during flood season," Wade explained. "More places to hide, more water surface, less chance we'll hit a problem like we did coming in, such as that tree."

Cruz looked at Hurley. "Is there a way of controlling your coughing spells, at least temporarily?"

"No. My friends tried several times to get me past the Tenumas. That was the constant problem."

"Dr. Hurley . . ." Marcia sat up straight, still staring at his papers. "This quote about Renaldo Morales. Can you substantiate it?"

"The Indian who provided it is dead now. But there are others on the west side who no doubt know about him."

"And the accusations regarding the prefect in Chehuapes. And this how do you pronounce it? *C-r-e-l* . . ."

"Crellado. Unsubstantiated. The Indians who know about it firsthand live about thirty miles from here, up a little side stream."

"How can we get up there? I have to talk to them."

"We're going the other way." Wade tried to put a note of finality in his voice.

"No, we're not! This is dynamite stuff. I'll be d—" She looked up with a guilty glance at Cruz. "I'll be dipped if I'm gonna walk away from a piece this size." She waved a handful of notes toward Wade. "Do you realize what this is? An investigative piece that will end up in every journalism textbook in the western world! It's a ton of pure gold. Ten tons. But I have to substantiate it—all of it—if it's going to have any teeth."

"Miss Lewis," Cruz reminded her wearily, "the doctor's condition is deteriorating. We must go now. And besides, you're the one who wanted to accomplish this project with all haste—to return to civilization as quickly as possible."

"Yeah. Yeah, I know." Marcia looked at Wade and her black eyes sparkled bright. "When we were paddling up that river just before dawn, and they were throwing hand grenades and I was throwing hand grenades and they were shooting and I was shooting back . . . remember that?"

"How could I forget?"

"That was . . . I never . . . It was wild! The most exciting thing I've ever done. You know why? For the first time in my life, I had just as much power as anyone else. They wanted to bomb me? Well, I could bomb 'em right back. All the rotten deals people ever handed me my whole life, and I could never pay back . . . Here were these people shooting at me and I could send the bullets right back to 'em with their own gun yet! It's . . ."

"An eye for an eye."

"Yeah! Something I could never do before. I can't explain, but it changed me. I feel changed. Now I want to go for all of it. Hurley's statements and charges and the proofs to back 'em up. I want it all! And I'm gonna get it."

Wade sighed. "That explains it."

"What?"

"When Dr. Hurley walked out to meet us, you stood up. Dumb me, I thought it was out of respect. Cruz and I stand up, right? Respect. Then you start jumping up and down yelling, 'We did it! We did it! We found him' and clapping your hands. So much for respect. Part of the change?"

She didn't look a bit embarrassed; she just scowled at him angrily, one of her commonest expressions. "Just remember who you're working for when it comes time to vote, Travers." She flexed her shoulder and went back to studying the papers.

Tiny, in his slovenly Portuguese, talked to Cruz a couple minutes. Wade translated for Dr. Hurley's sake. "Tiny wants to get back to territory that's undisputedly Brazilian. He's apparently in trouble with Colombian officials and doesn't want to be in or near that country. Uh . . . something about a jailbreak."

Cruz was looking at Wade. "How do we get the doctor with his coughing spasms past the enemy?"

Wade began shaving his plug. His brain worked better when his hands were busy. "You told me you have an airplane. I'll build us an airstrip here while Tingido gets you out. You fly in, and we waft him away on the wings of eagles." Wade didn't realize until after he'd spoken just what he'd said. Once upon a time he had bucked the prospect of building Tweed an airstrip. And now . . . fortune surely is fickle, as he had said in Bacalau.

"No." Dr. Hurley wagged his head. "An airstrip is too dangerous for these people. So many officials and developers have airplanes now. It would make this remote area too accessible, and remoteness is all that saves my friends."

"It is, however, a viable last resort." Cruz nodded slowly.

"*Jacaré* and crocodile is loud," Pato suggested. "Catch us a *jacaré*—easier to catch, not croc. Ever time the doctor makes noise we twist 'is tail, eh? *Jacaré* makes more noise than doctor mebbe."

"Bingo!" Wade jabbed his pipe stem toward Pato. "Perfect, sport! That solves that little matter. All's left is planning the best way to run the gauntlet down the river."

Cruz was staring at him. It gave Wade a silly, heady flush of pleasure. This was the first time Wade had ever gotten ahead of the *patrão*. The very first time.

Pato brightened like daybreak. "Like you call us in, come get you on the river!" He cackled delightedly.

Marcia came up for air, the usual frown on her pretty face. "What's a hacker-ay?"

"Alligator. Caiman. They make that baritone boom you hear along the river."

Cruz bobbed his head and looked at Elinor. "The Tenumas know you three joined us."

"Yes. We evaded them, but they were aware of us. They know, if they exchange information at all, that we are eight."

"They saw you? They know your coloring?"

"Yes."

"Dr. Hurley." Cruz started to twist around to look at the man beside him and stopped instantly. The wet weather must be working on his half-healed wound even more than it was affecting Wade's leg. "I was too precipitous in turning down your offer of help from your friends. Has their faith in Christ abrogated their traditional beliefs to the extent that they would consent to go out naked?"

Dr. Hurley finished a coughing fit and looked to Pahoa. "He wants to know with his long words if you would go out without paint."

"For you only. But for no other reason."

"Decoys?" With a twinge of regret Wade stuffed his pipe with the last of his tobacco.

Cruz nodded. "Indians painted with the markings of Tingido, a small man in whitewash to approximate Elinor in the darkness, others disguised as the rest of us—"

"There's no duplicating Tiny."

"Padding?"

"I doubt there's enough kapok in all of Brazil, but we could try." Wade translated for Tiny's benefit. The whale chuckled.

How sharp was Pahoa's sense of humor? Worth exploring. "About dugouts." Wade stared at Marcia. "Trade for some?"

Hurley started to speak, and Pahoa silenced him.

Pahoa nodded sagely. "Any manioc? A couple tapirs, perhaps? Bullets and guns?" He paused. "Women?"

"Just one. Hey, Marcia, stand up a minute."

"What?" She looked up. And to Wade's delight she stood up.

Pahoa walked over to her, walked all around her measuring by eye, poked her arm with a finger. "Strong?"

"Strong enough."

"Whaddaya mean, 'strong enough'? I can paddle my end of a canoe. What is this, anyway? I wasn't listening."

"One dugout maybe. Three-man."

"Extra paddles?"

"No paddles. Just canoe."

"I dunno. Cruz?"

Cruz studied Marcia gravely for a long moment and shook his head. "Not without the paddles."

Wade sat back. "No deal, Pahoa. You can sit down, boss."

Her face made Mount Vesuvius look like a smoky candle. "I don't believe this! I can't . . . It's a trick, right? A dirty rotten joke! You can't be . . . I'll show you whether your warped gags work. I refuse to get mad. So there!" She sat down with a plop. "And you." She jabbed a finger at Wade. "You're taking me up the river."

"I'll trade you for a dugout first." Wade pocketed his pipe unlit. "You can't find fame and fortune—in fact, you can't fight back on equal terms, if that's your fancy—when you're dead. And this whole trip's for nothing if we don't get the good doctor to medical help and give him at least a fighting chance."

For nothing.

Futile.

Wade didn't need another single lick of futility at the moment.

"Settled." Cruz commenced the lengthy preparations for lifting his wracked body from a sitting to a standing position. "Doctor, I suggest bundling the papers you want to take in oilskin and sealing them with tapir tallow, as waterproofing. All the books?"

"None of the books. They can be replaced. I've taught some of the adult men to read, and they're teaching others."

"Good." Cruz wrenched himself erect. "And now, if you have a few hours, I would like to discuss some of the things I found in your library."

Elinor looked at Wade. *Why don't you go, too?* her eyes asked.

But he didn't feel like discussing religion. He was more interested in getting through this ordeal—preferably alive. He might help waterproof bundles of papers. He might take a nap. He might even practice some *jacaré* calls.

# chapter
# 18

FROM A PICTURE RUN in the *Capper's Weekly*, Wade remembered Teddy Roosevelt leaning forward in the saddle as his horse lunged, muscles bulging, up a steep incline. Roughriding Teddy brandished his saber high, shouted, exhorted . . . Flags waved in the distance, the breeze just right to keep them streaming out. It was all so exciting, so thrilling. It was the kind of picture that sends a burly farm boy straight down to the army recruiter to sign up.

*Would that war were actually that glamorous,* he mused.

No waving flags, no sabers, no plunging horses, or encouraging exhortations, not even a hill to charge—Wade could use a little something to get his sluggish blood coursing, to build some enthusiasm for this harebrained attempt. He was always sharper when he was hot, and he wasn't hot now.

That warning voice kept nagging at him. Elinor attributed it to God's Holy Spirit working on him. Much as he would like to take her word for something like that, he couldn't believe it. He couldn't buy the idea that God was warning him he'd die. God was supposed to comfort you. Fat comfort that would be.

He handed his shirt to Pahoa and picked up the last of the waterproof bundles to be stowed in Dr. Hurley's dugout.

Pahoa wasn't used to buttons. It took him a while, but he eventually looked like a credible Wade Travers—at least he would at night. The really ludicrous decoy was an Indian named Moamo, the tallest of the clan, with fronds, horsetails, kapok, and a couple frayed old hammocks stuffed into Tiny's acres of shirt.

Pahoa's eyes were a little misty.

"Dr. Hurley's pretty much become one of you." Wade's statement acknowledged that he had noticed. "Thanks for letting us have him back."

Pahoa smiled, not altogether sincerely. "He belongs among his own. We cannot cure him. Perhaps his own medicine people can help." The voice dropped a notch. "He gave us great much—heaven beyond the sky and Jesus. His books in his language also take us far to new . . . new . . . not edges . . ."

"Horizons? The edges of the forest and the world?"

Pahoa nodded with a dip of the head very much like Cruz's. "When he goes home. When he goes to Jesus, I ask much to you. Can his ashes come to us? We put in our clan's jar."

"I'll try. They might come at you from the sky in Cruz's airplane. We'll see what we can do. But he's not dead yet. If we can get him out and get his story spread around, he might be able to stop the slave trade. Make you a little safer."

"His heart is very big." Pahoa studied the ground a few moments. "What is aah-puhlane."

"Hmm. Let's see. It's a mosquito as big as a rain shelter, and men can fly by riding on it."

"Then I just squashed a couple airplanes." Marcia tapped Wade's arm. "Come 'ere a minute."

Wade put down the waterproof package and followed her over to the trees. "Watcha need?"

"You're so sticky about what I hired you for and what I didn't. How about renegotiating the contract—not that there ever was a contract?"

"I don't think so."

"Salary or piecework. I don't care. These people will make it out all right; they don't need us. And I have Hurley's agreement right here."

"Agreement?"

"Exclusive rights to his story, written by me for the *Sun*. No one else is gonna scoop me on this, so now I have time to gather up enough corroborating evidence to convict all of South America. The people behind the slave trade, the people who let the Tenumas do whatever they da— . . . whatever they please and who sell 'em the arms. All backing up Hurley's original story."

"I doubt that we'd—"

She moved in closer. "That's not all. Loving's part of the contract. Whatever you want, whenever you want it." She brushed against him, blatantly sensual.

He hesitated and hoped she didn't notice the hesitation. "Too dangerous."

"Not with you. You know what you're doing and how to get along. With just the two of us, we can move fast, get what I need, get out. And then, Manaos, wherever—take a little holiday, you know?"

"If I get killed, you'd be a dead woman. You can't fend for yourself in the forest, don't know the languages, nothing."

"I'll take my chances. You might even find I'm getting better than you think out here." She brushed against him again, deliberately, with a softness that contrasted like night and day with her hard voice. He recalled the softness.

"I'll think about it."

"You do that." And now her voice was soft, too.

He watched her walk off, watched the way her body moved, the exciting way her hips failed to follow any straight lines at all, either in form or in motion. Why hadn't she come into his life ten years ago, when he would have leaped at the chance to grab her offer? Because she was still a school girl then, remember?

Pato was young; his cup of elán runneth over. Elinor was young. Elinor. She had no doubts at all about life. Cruz was old—well, older—and Wade was fast getting there. They were the desperate ones.

Could it be that what Wade needed most was a fountain of youth to restore, not the physical body, but the mental one? She didn't know it, of course, but Marcia was offering him far more than a job or an adventure or even a little indulgent fun. Perhaps, with her, he could regain a part of that which he had lost, at least that part of *joi d'vivre* linked to youth.

What it boiled down to was that he was ready to do just about anything to recover his old zest for life.

"Papa." Pato fell in beside him. The boy had been painted with the marks of this clan, thus clothed against the myriad dangers of the forest.

"I see your friends dressed you up to go traveling."

"Jus' be safe, they say. You don' mind, eh?"

"No, I don't mind. You really hit it off well with Dr. Hurley and his friends."

"Hit 'em? No, never! Not dem!"

"Good man." Wade laughed and tousled the kid's hair.

"Papa? Okay mebbe I help Tiny paddle his dugout?"

"Sure. With your brains and his brawn, you two could rule the world. Too bad neither of you speaks the other's language."

"Oh, we fix dat! I teechin 'm all my Engliss."

"Peachy."

And Pato went bounding off. Wade heard his "Iss goot!" as he neared the whale. Wade picked up the bundle he had abandoned and headed down to the dugouts.

The river was up a good ten feet and rising fast, judging from the amount of flotsam and jetsam in the current. It spread itself casually into the forest, its muddy water lapping with lazy little *fwaps* at the trunks of trees that a week ago knew only birds and monkeys. Wade had no idea where the high water mark might be, but right beside him he could see, eight feet off the ground, junk that had washed into the trees last flood season.

Elinor was helping load food supplies. Good. She was the cook most of the time and ought to know where this and that were. He watched her a couple minutes. Just watched her. One of his favorite pastimes. His brain had this nasty habit of blurring her memory everytime she was elsewhere. He must anchor her in his mind any time he could.

Marcia stood around doing nothing. But then, what was there for her to do? She was a bauble, a useless but amusing plaything when out of her normal environs. Was she as helpless in the streets and alleys of New York? Surely not.

She caught Wade's eye and winked. So. Her flirtation would not be limited to soft bumps and brushes.

Wade wandered over by Cruz. The *patrão* was explaining the

route to both Dr. Hurley and the decoys. Good old Cruz. He left nothing to chance. If the party became separated, or for any reason Hurley ended up on his own, he would know where to go and what terrors lay in the way.

Cruz drew an X on a piece of paper with squiggly lines on it. "This is the first Tenuma camp we encountered. It's very close to the water. We were afraid the dugouts wouldn't make it past them undetected, and we were right. Travers and Miss Lewis, on land about here, moved in behind them to distract them. We then picked them up along the shore along here."

"What if the dugouts had slipped past?"

"We would have kept going, leaving Travers and Miss Lewis to continue on foot. He's as good as any forest Indian at moving through the jungle, and better than the Tenumas, who have been badly corrupted by white influence."

"This point you just described will be the most dangerous on the return trip."

"Unless they've moved camps, which is likely. Tingido is scouting ahead by land."

Dr. Hurley looked up at Pahoa. The Indian nodded. "Good people. They know much, wise. They will take good care. My heart is lighter."

Wade's eyes snapped to Cruz, and Cruz glanced at him with a brief twinkle. The weight of one's heart seemed to be a universal concern.

Between coughing fits, Dr. Hurley studied the map.

Wade took a peek over the doctor's shoulder, but he already knew what the sketch looked like. "Hit the river running, and don't look back. So long as we stay on the water, we should make it."

Cruz nodded. "Better, stay in the middle. The current will be fastest there. And the river's wide enough now that they'll have to come out to us in boats if they want to hit us with grenades. The distance from shore will be too great for them to throw with any accuracy."

"And stay in among the trees after moonrise. That gives us about four hours of fast moving and another three to inch along."

"I'm more optimistic about our chances of seeing home again than I was about our chances of living to find the doctor."

"Yeah. It looks so smooth. Almost easy. That's not good."

"No. It's the easy projects that go wrong."

They launched at dusk, the flotilla of decoys followed at length by the flotilla of escapees. It was Pahoa's idea (overriding Dr. Hurley's pacifist objections) to load the decoy boats with blowgunners lying flat in the bottoms. Any Tenuma coming close enough to toss one of those infernal grenades automatically placed himself within blowgun range. An eye for an eye. Wade couldn't see too much wrong with the idea himself. Smooth.

On his first of two sorties, Tingido had found the Tenuma camps nearest the no-man's land where neither Tenuma nor Christian dared to tread. Pahoa's canoes passed without incident the distant orange glow beyond the trees marking that camp.

Wade's dugout led the second flotilla. He watched the flood-drowned shoreline for any sign that they were detected. Nothing. The three dugouts—Wade and Marcia with the doctor, Cruz and Elinor, Tiny and Pato—slipped from darkness into darkness down the middle of the rolling river. One down, X number of enemy camps to go. Lying very still in the bottom of the canoe, the doctor kept coughing to a minimum. Wade had to emulate a *jacaré* only half a dozen times or so the whole night. Smooth.

According to plan, they moved in among the trees along the southwest shore as the third-quarter moon turned the sky gray. They kept close together, working from tree to tree through the inundated understory. Slow, nerve-racking going. By dawn they were clustered in three groups among dense brush within the flood area to wait out the endless hours of daylight.

Wade lay on his back on the rough-hewn floor and watched the dense green ceiling hang there. The understory never felt the occasional winds that rustled the crown and distributed the pollen and seeds of treetop fruit. In those treetops lived whole nations of animals who not once in their lives would feel solid earth beneath their feet. And here in the understory lived other whole nations of animals and plants who would never in their lives feel the full strength of unfiltered sun or see the color of the sky.

Wade thought about these things to avoid thinking about other things, such as Marcia's young and vibrant body so close. She slept part of the day, lay like he, with her eyes fixed leafward, for another part of the day. Obeying the law of the pack as laid down by Cruz, she refrained from speaking or making any sort of noise.

But towards late afternoon, when Hurley was napping and she, like Wade, was apparently bored and getting restless, her hand ventured up to tease his hair, play a sort of footsie with his ear, tickle his nose and lips. He grabbed it, kissed it silently, and sent it home. He'd have to speak to her about her rotten timing.

They waited until darkness had dissolved into utter blackness before slipping out again onto the river. They'd have longer to paddle tonight before moonrise, and even longer tomorrow night. And by the next night they should be safely within Ocaina territory, where the Tenumas presence was not so constant.

The *jacaré* cover seemed to be working extremely well. By the end of the second night's paddling, Wade felt more than a little smug. High time he shook this lethargy loose and basked in a little personal pride again.

An hour into the third night's journey, the decoy flotilla held constant in the center of the stream until Wade had pulled alongside. Wade moved in close to the only dugout he could barely see. Starlight is the same as no light, but tonight was overcast and promising rain, which is absolutely no light at all.

Pahoa pointed shoreward and whispered, "Is that a sign?"

A flashing firefly cage hung out over the water in the drowned forest of the north shore.

"Tingido. Yes. We'll let Cruz go."

Cruz, ever on top of things, had not only seen the cage but had assumed the role of investigator. He returned to Wade with the cage in the floor of his dugout. The dim almost-light was enough to illuminate Elinor in the front of the canoe.

"No one there. This was with it." Cruz handed Wade two notched sticks and a map. The map was also made of sticks, bound into configuration with crude cordage—twigs sticking out here and withes bent there, and an occasional extraneous knot.

Wade twisted it around, right side up. "I read a tree down in the channel about a quarter mile from here, in a narrow passage beyond a broad bend. He suggests we hug the north shore to clear it. The closest Tenuma settlement is about four miles away."

Marcia hissed, "All that from a first-grader's attempt at a placemat?"

"I read the same. I'll tell Tiny." Cruz took a strong backward stroke. His dugout slipped past Wade's. Elinor caught his eye and smiled, sunshine in the darkest night, as she floated past him. That gentle smile, with no effort or devious intent on her part at all, conveyed more and teased more than all Marcia's attempt at fluttering eyelids.

They rounded the broad bend, all six canoes, and by groping carefully found the downed tree as mapped. Pahoa led to the left, cleared, moved back out into the channel. The other two decoys followed. Dr. Hurley suffered a brief coughing spell, and Wade covered. From a hundred yards away an indignant *jacaré* answered the interloper's brash challenge.

Wade gave the decoys a couple minutes to gain some space and pushed in close to shore. They slid silently among black trees over black water in blackness. He maneuvered toward the nonlight of the open river channel. Behind him, Pato's paddle splacked. No problem. It sounded like a fish jumping.

With a shriek, the blackness exploded. From above, from the silence, a heavy body dropped into the dugout, barely missing Hurley. Instinctively Wade whipped his paddle out and swung it. Marcia screamed and screamed again as Wade's paddle lifted the attacker out over the gunwales.

The canoe wallowed wildly. The half-light of distant sky reflected on shiny wetness on the gunwale. Wade slammed his paddle down on it; the two hands fell away as their owner yelled. Wade dipped deep, sent the canoe plunging straight ahead.

Wrong move. The prow thudded against a trunk, glanced off, hit another. Another swimmer had the gunwale now, beyond reach of Wade's paddle. Before he could shout to Marcia to swat the hands, the fellow had dragged the gunwale down too low. The canoe tipped, rolled nearly upright, then flipped bottom up, smooth as oil.

Wade was underwater instantly, and in this darkness he couldn't tell how far for no light marked the surface. Could Hurley and Marcia swim? He had never asked. He struggled first to pull his pistol free. Almost immediately he tangled with lianas that were probably ten feet off the ground in drier times. He was fast running out of air.

*Don't panic. One thing at a time. The vines around your legs first; now this other one. Kick free. Good. Head for the surface.* He popped up in total darkness as legs and arms thrashed all around him. Which was friend, and were any foe?

He thrust the pistol high to get it out of the water and yearned for daylight—for any light. Where were Cruz and Elinor? A pistol blasted somewhere to his right.

"Hurley? Hurley!"

No coughing.

Marcia cried, "Help me!" from somewhere. He couldn't even tell the direction.

Cruz's voice yelled, "Get out!"

"Hurley?" Wade didn't wait. The gunshot—probably blood in the water. Cruz's shout—probably piranha. He scrambled, splashing, for the nearest tree trunk and shinned up it.

The first limb was only a couple feet off the water. He bellied out along it. This was probably the very limb from which that Tenuma had dropped into his dugout. A smoky white spot in the blackness came hovering by below.

"Elinor! Straight up!" He flipped the pistol to his left hand and thrust his right down down as far as he could. He saw movement in the nothingness and grabbed. Her wet hand grasped his. He gripped her wrist, sat up, hauled in. Her legs swung up and wrapped around the limb. She was safe.

She proved again she was a better climber than he. From the impossible position of hanging by arms and feet from the underside of the branch, she managed to scramble around and clamber up onto it. He had only to keep from falling off himself as the limb swayed drunkenly up and down.

"Dr. Hurley . . . ?"

"I don't know. I didn't hear—"

Coughing!

Wade holstered his pistol, made sure the flap was snapped down tight. The thing had been soaked once already. One more dunking wouldn't do much more. He judged by ear where he'd heard Hurley; eyes were useless.

"No, don't!" she cried, and a small wet hand gripped his arm with the strength of a boa constrictor.

"I'm chosen, remember? Charmed life. Be ready to haul him up." Wade jumped in feet first because you never dive into someplace you can't see.

Pahoa's voice called out something. The reinforcements with the blowguns were here! More gunfire. Wade felt totally abstracted from the struggle all around him, even as he groped to find a dark needle in a black haystack.

The coughing—right here—he kicked, lunged out, grabbed, and latched onto lightweight fabric. It was either Hurley or Marcia, and either one would do. Wade backstroked, towing his handful. The resistance told him it was Hurley.

"Elinor!"

"Here. Do you hear me?"

"Keep talking." He sucked in a mouthful of water and gagged.

Elinor's gentle voice began a soft, constant purr, easy to home in on. Wade recognized belatedly that she was reciting the Twenty-third Psalm he had memorized as a child.

Hurley was coughing uncontrollably now. He stopped beneath the voice and gave Hurley a boost straight up. The doctor hung there; she must have him.

Wade slapped the soppy pants leg. "Keep your feet up!" He swam to the trunk in three hard strokes and shinned up it. Elinor might be able to climb like a monkey. He couldn't.

They struggled and grunted and made the limb bob like a channel marker. How many people would this branch hold? They'd soon find out. By the time they got the doctor hauled up and draped over, like a jaguar's latest kill, the war in the darkness around them seemed about over.

Who had won? How many friends had died? Who cared? Wade felt so totally spent nothing really mattered much. The constant fight, the perpetual struggle wasn't worth the victory. They were all on the brink of death now, whether the war be won or lost.

His lungs ached, his muscles cramped, every bone in his body hurt, and surely the worst was yet to come. As Wade's mind struggled as well, it suddenly occurred to him: that voice on the ledge hadn't promised a quick clean death.

# chapter
# 19

THE RAIN DRIZZLED DOWN the back of his neck and ran in rivulets around his ears. The decoy business was over, and he was wearing his own shirt again, but that didn't slow those mosquitoes up a bit. No sirree, Bob. They still treated him like a voodoo doll. How did they manage to find their prey in total darkness in the rain? Frequently. That's how.

He perched in the fork of a massive cedro with his legs bent double and pretended that humans were meant to fold this way. Whoever came up with that human-being-evolved-from-monkeys hooey never sat in a tree for four hours. He tried to keep squirming to a minimum, but there was not a comfortable square inch in the whole tree.

And he wanted to sleep. Oh, how he wanted to sleep! No matter how many hours of broad daylight you lie around in, it's not the same as one good night's sleep.

He detected movement below and behind him. Without taking all his attention from elsewhere, he followed it with his ears. Elinor. He could tell. How could he tell? He didn't know. But it was she.

"Wade? Dinner."

"Up here. The cedro. Yeah." He straddled a horse-sized limb and reached down. A bowl touched his fingers in the darkness. He grasped it, brought it up. "You coming?"

"I'll watch while you eat, if you like."

"I like." He stretched his hand down over the side, but she was already clambering up the back of the trunk as he had done. She seemed to float as easily above as she floated at ground level. She settled into the fork near his left hip and rested a delicate arm on his leg.

He talked with his mouth full and didn't care. "I sure appreciate this. I thought they were coming at us with a couple of those big, white dirt-hauler trucks, but it was just my stomach growling. What time is it? I can't see sky."

"Close to two A.M. Maybe one-thirty."

"Cruz find Tiny yet?"

"Yes. We're all accounted for. No injuries."

Wade nodded, though in the darkness she couldn't see it. He sat in silence and ate in silence and listened to the silence awash all around them. He heard, of course, the internal sound of his own chewing and swallowing. Even that was silence, for he doubted Elinor could, although she sat so close. Strange, the sounds one makes within.

Somewhere along the river and a good mile downstream, a *jacaré* boomed. Leaves flittered overhead. Finally the creatures of darkness were becoming active again, the night world returning to normal by slow degrees. Wade welcomed normalcy. With night sounds back, he could spot intruders more quickly by detecting sudden silence.

He tried to scrape his bowl soundlessly. It can't be done.

She whispered, "May I stay a while?"

He answered by laying his arm across her shoulders. Her body warmth seeped into him through her rain-soaked dress. She tilted just a little and settled her head in against his side. He rubbed her shoulder, massaged the base of her neck.

Suddenly, for a fleeting instant, he was content. Actually content. You eat, and a few hours later you hunger again. Sleep, and half a day later—or sooner—you're weary. But this—this had the feel of permanence, and it was nothing more than simply being with her. He'd never felt this contentment with a woman before.

They both heard it at the same time. She stiffened as he turned his head toward an alteration in the silence to his right. With his tongue he clicked the way a bat ticks as it flitters amid the trees. A bat responded in kind.

167

"Cruz?"

Moss whispered on the forest floor. More than one person was coming this way. Wade handed the bowl to Elinor and pulled his pistol, just in case.

"Travers."

"Up."

Cruz spoke in Portuguese. "Tiny's here to relieve you. Anything moving?"

"Normal stuff." Wade dropped to the ground. "Tiny?" He reached out, groping. A whale the size of that one wasn't hard to find even in darkness. Wade splacked his pistol into Tiny's hand and unbuckled his holster. "Here. Strap this around your arm—or wherever it'll fit."

The holster left Wade's hand as Tiny grunted. "Not going up there." The whale wandered off to pick himself a spot.

Wade didn't want that uncharacteristic feeling of contentment to fade, so he wrapped an arm around Elinor's shoulder again. It wasn't quite the same, but it was better by far than aloneness. He fell in beside Cruz, and they groped through the dripping darkness and the multitude of leaves toward the water.

Cruz slipped back into his faultless Princeton English. "Dr. Hurley's on his way down the river again. Pahoa and I agreed that a single canoe with blowgunners and the doctor has the best chance of making it. Anyone watching our position here is not likely to have seen them go, nor to suspect we've split up."

"That the *jacaré* I heard a while ago?"

"Probably. We're going to continue acting as if we have him. But we can concentrate now on surviving rather than on protecting the frail doctor. Lord willing, we'll reach Minho soon after he does."

Wade stared through the darkness and nearly stopped in his tracks. *Lord willing*? He'd never heard that from Cruz before, nor anything close to it.

They slopped into water. Cruz kept going, so Wade kept going. Weeds and water grabbed at his ankles. And now they stepped out onto land again. Tomorrow this bit of island would be inundated, probably by a good four feet of water.

Wade held Elinor firmly and rejoiced in clinging to this one piece of reality in a nightmare world. "What about Tingido?"

"Lost. I think we should operate on the assumption that he's dead." His voice was bitter, sad.

Marcia's harsh contralto broke the blackness. "What do you mean? What's happened?"

With sentinels on the outskirts, it was time to get his bearings. Wade struck a match and in the brief, flickering light saw Marcia, several dugouts pulled onto the bank, and a variety of Christian Indians standing around. The match winked out.

"Where's Pato?"

"Asleep in a dugout. He's all right."

"What about Tingido?" Marcia persisted. "We need him."

Wade left Elinor and crossed to Marcia. "The group who attacked us knew about the decoys. They let the decoys through and waited for us. It's a safe bet they got that information from Tingido and his nephew."

"Turncoats?"

"Torture victims."

"I thought Tingido was loyal."

"He would die rather than endanger us. But his nephew might not be that strong."

Her hands touched his chest, his shoulders, wrapped around him. She leaned heavily against him. He put a comforting arm around her. Belatedly, he realized she just wanted to converse very privately.

Her voice dropped to a low murmur. "Remember my offer? Now's the time."

"Now? Bottled up by Tenumas who know exactly where we are?"

"Cruz and that Indian figured it was safest for Hurley to slip away quick. Think how much safer it'll be for us to slip away in the other direction. Those bozos would never expect anyone to go sneaking off *up* the river. They'll be waiting for us to go down. Travers, I want that scoop!"

He pushed her away to arm's length. "I want to live a while yet, though I don't have the foggiest idea just why anymore. But that's not a bad idea you have there."

He left her standing in blackness and moved closer to Cruz, assuming Cruz hadn't wandered off somewhere. "Remember that half-submerged patch of second growth about a quarter mile

169

upriver on the south side? Let's hole up there for the rest of the night."

"Think we can make it there before moonrise?"

"If we gather up everybody and scoot quick. We probably have the whole Tenuma nation waiting for us on the riverbank downstream. Our disappearance should confuse them enough they'll have to spread out tomorrow, thin their ranks. Make it easier to slip through tomorrow night."

"Good. Elinor, will you call in Tiny and the other two? Let's load up here quickly. Someone waken Pato. I don't want him to stir halfway across the river and make a noise."

And here they went again. It wasn't just the physical exertion of paddling a canoe at full speed against the current that wearied him. Even more, it was the tension, the fear. Wade's muscles tightened, stayed knotted, drained his energy. Not many years ago, lust for adventure would have quelled the fear and stuffed it into some small, easily ignored pocket of his mind. His muscles then would have been loose and free to handle whatever might come along. What had happened?

They reached deep shadow just before moonlight turned the charcoal sky to gray. Like an armed camp, they stationed sentinels on the periphery. Like an army, they sent trusted scouts out to reconnoiter the enemy. Unlike an armed camp, however, they shared only seven bullets among three guns. More than seven of the enemy were out there somewhere.

Dawn brought good news. Wade could at last see their circumstance, and it looked good. Their flotilla was tucked deep in a thick, twenty-acre tangle of half-submerged bushes and leafy young trees. A small knoll toward the center gave them some bare ground to sit on. They were nearly half a mile from where any Tenuma could rightfully expect them to be. Here they could rest, plan, regroup, prepare for the wild dash down the Minho that tonight would bring. Protected by sentries they could even speak, in whispers.

Marcia didn't speak. She sulked in front of everyone but Wade. For him and for him alone, the coy and charming smiles came out. Sure, she was transparent. She was also undeniably tempting. He had to keep arguing with himself to ignore her.

With no tobacco plug to shave, Wade took to whittling sticks after breakfast. It wouldn't hurt a bit to fashion a couple spears with hardwood points for that time when the bullets gave out. Cruz materialized presently and hunkered down close beside him.

"Move out tonight?"

"Sounds good." Wade tested the point of his newly honed weapon and almost stuck himself. "I suggest sending the Indians home. Now that Hurley's on the road, we don't need them. No use exposing them to unnecessary risk."

"I agree." Cruz sat. He stared, unseeing, at the tear in the knee of Wade's pants.

"What else?"

"Tingido."

Wade glanced at the impassive Spanish face. "If he's still alive, you want him."

"Yes."

Wade had known this was coming, perhaps because he knew Cruz. "How?"

"I don't know. He could be anywhere in a thousand square miles. He's probably dead. There's no way of finding him. Even if we were to capture a Tenuma and try a little torture ourselves, we probably wouldn't get anywhere. Not only are they tough, none of us here knows the dialect."

"We're close to the Ocainas. Might be able to swap a few words that way."

"Doubtful."

Wade put his spear point aside and started another one. "Bet that's not going to stop us from trying, though, is it?"

Cruz grimaced, his version of a smile. "You know me well, friend."

"Too well. I don't want to do it, Cruz. I understand your sense of loyalty. Tingido's one of your own, and by extension, I suppose one of mine, too. We're all in this together. But I just want to get out. I'm tired. I don't want to run anymore. It's not worth it, the struggle."

"Your conscience will plague you the rest of your life if you turn your back on him now."

171

"Nice try, chum, but you're not going to work a guilt thing on me. You admitted it's hopeless to think you'd find him. You admitted he's probably dead. I'm sure he is, because they'd kill him before he'd rat on us. It's not worth risking all these lives for the one-in-a-million shot that he's within reach. Get Pato to safety. And Elinor . . . Nope. My conscience will sleep just fine tonight, on the way out."

Cruz sat silent, staring beyond the mud in front of him. Another of the *patrão's* ploys, Wade knew. What infuriated him was that it worked even when he knew what Cruz was doing.

Elinor came over and brightened the morning by sitting down cross-legged close to Wade's boot. She looked haggard, wearied by the trek and burdened with worry.

Cruz scratched his ear. "It's safe to assume Tingido was captured, dead or alive."

"I'd say that."

"And his nephew."

"Yeah. Tingido wouldn't abandon the boy."

"And the yellow dog."

Wade's hands paused. Something was coming, and he wasn't sure what.

Cruz pulled his knees up, rested his elbows on them, and began that habit of lacing his long, slim fingers in and out. "I will search for Tingido by looking for the dog. Unless they butchered him for meat, he should be somewhere near where Tingido was or is."

Wade sighed. "That big camp we first hit coming up the river was on the other shore—they probably moved it, but there'd be no reason to move it across the river. Therefore, their main bunch is likely still on that side of the river, and we're on this side, which means you can't cross until dark. But you'd need daylight if you want to look for the mutt, which means spending another idle day here. For no good reason. He's gone, Cruz."

"Perhaps. You may come with me if you like."

"I *don't* like. I already told you that."

"I'll go with you." Elinor's voice had that flat, fearless softness she always used when she was being obstinate.

"Oh, no, you won't." Wade snapped his knife shut.

172

She looked at him mildly, blankly, the way Tiny looked at anyone who spoke English.

"I'd prefer you not," Cruz purred. "Tingido isn't yours."

"But I care about him, as you do. And I can be of help. You know that."

"Yes. You're capable. Still, I prefer not."

"I'll go." Here was that same matter-of-fact tone of voice that had once told Wade *Yes, you will* when he refused to seek out Hurley.

Wade pocketed his knife and glanced at Cruz. "Excuse us a minute." He lurched to his feet and dragged Elinor to hers by one arm. He hauled her off ten feet, backed her up against a tree, and hissed, "What's the matter with you?"

"Nothing." Those disconcerting blue eyes poured all over him and made him wonder why he was bothering to disagree with her.

"Cruz is talking about a suicide mission, and you know it. I'll break your leg and carry you out on my back before I'll let you go with him."

"It's not your decision." The finality in her voice enraged him.

He had to think. He had to manage this intractable woman, and he didn't know the first thing to say. This was most unlike him, too, for usually he was very good at cajoling a woman into anything he needed—or wanted.

She smiled suddenly. "But I'm pleased that you care."

"I care. Yeah." Frustrated, he reached out to lean against the tree above her head and rubbed his neck. His muscles were tightening up again. "Look. I never felt like this about a woman before, but I care more than you know. If you go with Cruz, I won't be able to think about anything or do anything until I know you're safe again. And if you go with him, you won't be safe again. There's no way he's going to go trooping off across the river and get out alive."

"We can't just leave Tingido and his nephew."

"Then let Cruz go looking. He's the one trying to find something. He's the desperate one. Not you. Maybe he'll even find what he's looking for over there. I don't know. Neither does he. But you've already found it. Don't go. Please."

The gorgeous eyes clouded suddenly into tears that bubbled up and tumbled over the pre-Raphaelite lids. Wade was well aware of that little trick—some women dissolved instantly into tears and thereby got their own way. But he was wise to it, and he wasn't going to let those tears sway him a bit. He knew the game. Somehow, though, this didn't seem like a ploy.

She took his face into her warm, dry hands, a soft palm caressing each cheek, and smiled through the tears. "Señor Cruz? No. You're the seeker. I know what you're looking for, and I'll think of some way to help you find it." She stretched up suddenly and kissed him a warm, soft peck on the lips. "We'll go, we three, and find what you are seeking."

# chapter
## 20

CAESAR. First among equals.

Where'd he get that? High school history, probably. Julius Caesar tired to be emperor instead of first among equals, and died in a hail of daggers. Wade remembered his Shakespeare, too.

Now here he sat in the stern of a half-ton waterlogged dugout, paddling like sixty while "Caesar" paddled in the bow. First among equals, Cruz would be quick to bill himself. Cooperative leadership. Beans. Bernardo Caesar. Cruz was running this show, manipulating by word and gesture to obtain whatever he wanted.

Cruz's bullheadedness infuriated Wade. He was angry at Elinor for her bullheadedness, too. It was insane of her to come along. There she sat amidships, calm and composed as always. He was angriest of all at himself for letting Cruz do this to him and her both. He didn't want this. He didn't want more danger and struggle and useless effort. Tingido was dead.

Futility.

They had chosen the narrowest stretch of open water between shores, and they had chosen midday for their mad dash across the river. There was no way of knowing whether enemy eyes had seen them. They were on this side now, for better or worse.

The dugout floated among long-suffering shoreline trees. Orchids and bromeliads, which cling to trunks and limbs two stories off the ground, drifted silently by at eye level. Sprays of gentle little rubbery flowers adorned some of them, the muted colors barely noticeable. Vibrant splashes of purple, white, and gold marked others. The bromeliads erected bold red and green and blue spikes. No human eye until now had seen these exquisite beauties.

If God created all beauty for the benefit of people, why did he stick so much of it out of sight, where only interlopers during flood season could hope to appreciate it? A single tree might harbor twenty varieties of orchids alone. They bloomed in reckless abundance everywhere, more of them than anyone could imagine. How many zillions of flowers bloomed and died without being appreciated by any but a few nectar-slurping insects? How many washed away in the flood waters without serving any purpose whatever? Was God in the futility business, too?

Just look. Even Bernardo Caesar's insoluble philosophical riddles were rubbing off on Wade now. Disgusted, Wade shipped his paddle and let the canoe drift.

Silence. Hunters with hand grenades had rendered this part of the forest barren, also. No monkeys, no cotingas, no scolding oropendolas broke the quiet. Unnatural. Irritating. That eerie feeling Wade had on the ledge months ago started to grow again behind his breastbone.

Cruz stopped the canoe by reaching out and grabbing a tree. He listened. Wade listened. The water was too murky, the canopy too dense, to tell how deep the flood was here. Wade guessed about five feet, judging from the height of bushes. They were now perhaps a quarter mile from the river channel.

Cruz pointed off to the northeast and shoved against the tree. The dugout drifted backwards, and Wade dug his paddle in. They swung out and around a hoary, moss-covered trunk and headed in a new direction.

For an hour they prowled the varzea. They idenified one Tenuma settlement beyond the leaves, a small camp of perhaps a dozen men with a few women. No dogs. Wade broke into a cold sweat as their dugout cruised silently past it, just beyond ken amid the vegetation.

About five in the afternoon they found themselves very close to the river again and to the east of the only two settlements they had found.

Sudden surprise robbed Wade of tact. "What in the world is *that*?"

Like an anaconda in need of a shave, an undulating flotilla of vines and branches rippled and tugged on the river current. It extended very nearly from shore to shore and was anchored, apparently by more brush, on a high spot near the south bank.

A dozen Tenumas in dugouts paddled back and forth along it, inserting whole saplings, throwing thirty-foot sections of vines here and there. They chattered like monkeys when a section threatened to break loose. It started to drift downstream. With lianas and branches, they struggled to reinforce the weak spot. The thing was a monster, an engineering nightmare.

"A net!" Elinor whispered incredulously. "Look at that!"

Wade grimaced. "It's a killer. The dugouts hit that tonight, we'll be dead in the water—Stopped long enough to catch a dozen grenades, or whatever they plan to throw at us. And no way to see it in the dark."

"A good sign, actually," Cruz mused. "They know about where we are, but not exactly, or they would have put their energies into an attack, not a barricade. And they must believe Hurley's still with us."

"You think he got away?" Hope springs eternal in the female breast.

"Absolutely. They couldn't have started this before daybreak, and he was gone long before that."

"And we know where the action's going to be. And most of their fire power." A sudden crushing sense of futility whopped Wade again. "No way we're going to get back to Tiny in time to warn him. Took us too long to get here."

"That's right." Cruz dipped his paddle and stroked backward. "So we'll break the net. We have the advantage of knowing it's there. Let's get back off the river and wait 'til dark."

They buried the dugout in the midst of a cluster of some sort of bushes Wade had never identified. Clouds of shiny dark green leaves hid them and most of their canoe. They were ten yards from solid land, and if these shrubs averaged five feet in height, the water was only a foot deep here.

Wade shivered in hundred-degree heat. "They spot us now, we're cooked."

"They won't. They're not looking for us here. Who would think the lamb would hide in the lion's den?"

"Yeah. Who'd think a thing like that?" How did he get into these messes?

Dusk brought the usual plentitude of mosquitoes. Elinor grew a dozen angry red bumps on her delicate skin. She didn't seem to notice.

The Tenumas certainly expected no spies. They built a fire up bright in the center of their compound, laughed, and talked aloud. It was, in fact, a carnival atmosphere. The dancing fire rendered the three canoeists invisible in the gathering gloom, so long as they didn't venture into the circle of red light.

They did move in a little closer. Elinor huddled up against Wade, a welcome tenderness. The rising flood seemed to trap hot dank air between its surface and the understory, making the heavy night hang even more still and oppressive than equatorial nights usually do.

Wade reached around Elinor and jabbed Cruz. The *patrão* nodded. A fellow in a blue shirt was hauling a familiar-looking crate up beside the fire. Wade had robbed a crate just like that of its last half dozen grenades. This one, though, was full. With much jocularity, its contents were distributed liberally among the revelers.

Wade's stomach churned. There was enough powder there to blow half the state of Amazonas into the river. He weighed that arsenal against the three .45 shells he and Cruz shared between them, Tiny having been given the other four. They definitely lacked firepower.

Cruz whispered, "I want some of those."

Elinor nodded against Wade's arm. "So do I."

Wade stared at her. "The pacifist has wised up."

"To blow out the net before Tiny reaches it."

Maybe Cruz was Caesar, but Elinor was Napoleon.

Wade let one end of his brain do a little planning while the other quenched the terror welling up in his breast. Neither end was doing its job well. "Elinor, you wait at the boat here. If I can get hold of a couple, I'll toss them into the dugout. So long as the pin's in, they can take some raps. I leave it to you to blow the net, unless I find a good clear opportunity."

"Yes." She nodded firmly.

He looked at Cruz, and Cruz held his eye calmly. Maybe that's why he liked to work with the high and mighty emperor, even when Cruz infuriated him. The man was without equal for aligning his thoughts with yours, unspoken.

They slipped over the side and waded in opposite directions through foot-high water. Wade kept the bushes between himself and the bonfire, but he wasn't too worried about being spotted in the gloom.

He froze. Two of the revelers were coming this way; it must be changing of the guard time. Between them they had eight or nine grenades dangling from their G-strings. Perfect. He calculated more or less just how clearly those two could see him at this distance from the fires. Not very clearly, he decided, with their eyes still full of firelight and unadjusted to the dark. He stood boldly upright and moved forward, slopping just as noisily through the water as those two were, amid the bushes, straight toward them.

He knew one word that might pass as an expletive in the Ocaina tongue. Just one. He used it loudly now as he stopped, stared at his knees, and stooped over. So far, so good. Here they came toward him, relaxed and laughing.

One of them said something to him and giggled. How should he respond? No need to; they were close enough now. He rose up suddenly with both fists ready and caught them both in the bridge of the nose. One of them sucked in air, but neither screamed. They plopped backward into the water.

Wade plunged in, armpit deep, groping for grenades, snatching at them. He stuffed his pockets with them, he jammed them inside his shirt, he ran sloshing through the muck with a whole handful of them.

Elinor stood waiting as instructed, not in the boat but beside it with one hand on the gunwhale.

He dumped the armload in the dugout. "Go!" he snapped and he continued on at a slopping jog, the fastest pace he could muster in this goo. When he glanced behind a moment later, she was already shoving off into the blackness, headed for the river.

A few by the fire had heard the noise. They were looking this

179

way, peering vainly from orange light into blackness. One of them called out something that ended with a warning inflection, brandished a grenade, and hooked his finger in the ring.

Wade knew *wait* in Ocaina. He tried it. The threatener hesitated.

The water was maybe eighteen inches deep here. If only Wade knew where Cruz was, he could toss a grenade into that crate and duck to safety underwater. But he didn't. And what if Tingido were miraculously alive somewhere here in camp? As silently as possible, Wade worked backwards until he could get behind a tree.

Still no grenade came at him. He slipped into deeper water to where he could frog paddle and pray there were no *jacarés* in the immediate vicinity, waiting to get him for playing vocal tricks on them.

Pray. Elinor frequently went into some sort of gentle trance with her eyes closed, sometimes even with them open. She was a woman of prayer, conversant with God, Cruz called it. Woman of light. Wade had been raised on admonition to pray, though the God to whom one prays was never clearly defined. He ought to pray now. Now of all times, with death and mayhem so close at hand . . .

The bottom sank out from under his reach. He saw the lighter sky of the river just ahead, a fern-clad knoll near the shore, still above water. He hauled out like a tired walrus on an ice flow to catch his breath and try to detect Cruz somewhere.

The revelers weren't reveling now. Quite agitated, they yelled at each other a lot and dispersed here and there into the forest. They were wading out now to here he used to be—at least he thought they were; it was hard to tell with all the vegetation and the darkness.

He was tired, so tired.

The river exploded in a burst of yellow fire. In the light of burning sticks he saw the net, that ominous net, waving and tugging in the current, stretched like a black anaconda across the dark river.

The current ripples picked up bits and pieces of the tiny dancing flames.

Another grenade exploded in the net. More fireworks spattered the night. Parts caught fire, sagged, snuffed their meager light into the black river as the anaconda parted company with itself. Ponderously, lazily, the tangle swayed and rolled over. The middle of it picked up the speed of the current and arched downstream like a bow being drawn. It ripped loose near the far shore and continued its silent drift in two great pieces before it dissolved into the nothing of total darkness downstream.

"Elinor, you beautiful doll."

Behind him, a dandy imitation of hell howled up through the trees. The Tenumas were pouring this way screaming. Some took to dugouts beached near the rain shelters. Others splashed into the flood a-running. No dogs barked, yellow or otherwise.

From somewhere in the distance a gun fired, and almost simultaneously the whole compound filled with brilliant flame. Cruz's only bullet had blown whatever was left in that crate.

Time to leave! Elinor most surely had pushed off by now and was safely away in the darkness, but Wade didn't want to leave that to guesswork. If the canoe was gone—and he dearly hoped it was, with Elinor gone into the night as well—he would take to the river, risking jaws of fish and reptile, and swim to safety. If she was still close, he would help her paddle, get her out of here.

The blaze behind him thundered as one rain shelter caught fire, then its neighbor. A grenade exploded in the forest downstream of him. Another. Grenades were popping now like corks. He must be nearly at the end of this little knoll by now. The ferns opened up enough to let him run. There was the river bank, and safety, right there.

Rifles went off somewhere between him and that conflagration. Who was the target, he or Cruz? Or Elinor? Agonizing fear inside him burned brighter than the inferno behind, but this was fear not for himself but for Elinor. She must be saved at all costs. Another gun fired from out on the river. He paused, hesitating—not even the river was safe now.

The left half of the universe blazed white and lifted him through the air. It paralyzed him as it tossed him carelessly into the mud. Sluggishly, casually, his body slid downhill through the slime, pushing his face into the tepid water.

And he gave up.

For the only time ever in his whole life, Wade Travers, intrepid adventurer who never failed a task, quit fighting.

He relaxed. His weary muscles melted. He couldn't move, but that didn't matter, because he didn't really try to. He didn't care any more. *Beware, Wade Travers. You'll die.* You're about to expire in an unmapped tributary, drown in an insignificant backwater of the world's greatest river. And there's not a thing you can do about it even if you wanted to.

The battle was no longer his. Someone else would have to shape his destiny.

Warmth trickled down the side of his head that was still out of the water. The cold river, water and mud, swamped the other side and crept up into his nose. He could hear shouts and screams and the roaring fire. And more explosions.

He heard sobbing and was pretty well certain it wasn't him because his mouth was full of mud.

Strong hands gripped him and lifted. Someone vindictive was about to throw him to the *jacarés*. Fitting. Out of the river you were made, and to the river you will return. Or was that dust? No dust in flood season. He bobbed wildly, suspended in darkness.

His wits, scattered like a covey of trumpeters, came tiptoeing back, one by one. He was unable to move or see or speak, but then again, he didn't have to. Someone else was doing for him what he himself could not. This being ministered to—this being totally dependent on unknown others—was something new to him, and in an incomprehensible way deeply satisfying. Very well. He would let them take care of things. They could do all the worrying. He was tired, so tired.

What had Elinor said? The Holy Spirit was working in his life. That was it. Speaking to him. Crazy notion. Where was she? Was she safe?

Pain in a thousand places was starting to replace the blessed numbness. He could see; he thought he could. Those might be stars in a moonless gray sky up there. As vision returned, sound abated; or perhaps the world was simply getting quieter.

A dark shadow blotted out the stars right above his head. Someone struck a match. In its fluttering yellow light, the shadow became Cruz. The *patrão's* face, normally impassive, bespoke the loving concern of a father. His long slim hands gently tipped Wade's head aside. He said something to someone nearby. Then the match went out, and his face returned to shadow.

Funny, how safe he felt in Cruz's shadow. No fire, no death could get him now. It probably wouldn't last, but for these few relaxed moments, Wade Travers was at peace.

## *chapter*
# 21

THE HUMAN BODY CONTAINS 206 BONES. Every single solitary one of them ached. Wade even ached in places where there weren't any bones. He started to draw a deep breath and choked on grit in his throat. Grit lined the creases between his teeth and made his eyes watery.

He lay in the bottom of a moving dugout, its roughhewn sides wrapping up and around like half a coffin. From the feel of its balance and motion, he could almost tell who was paddling—Tiny's power strokes in the stern and Pato up front. Heavy gray mist was beginning to blank out the stars of morning—Regulus, Spica, Arcturus. The trees were too tall for him to see the Cross. Probably somewhere around three A.M. The moon was not above the trees yet.

The canoe surged forward. Yes, definitely Tiny. Tiny would know. In Portuguese Wade asked, "Where's Elinor?"

"Open your eyes."

He hadn't lifted his eyes quite high enough. There she was, smiling down at him, her lap cradling his head and shoulders. The modest white dress was all blood-stained in front. Her blood or his?

"You all right?"

She nodded. "Fine."

His.

"Cruz make it through okay?"

"Yes."

"He find any sign of Tingido?"

"I don't know. We just barely escaped; no time to ask yet."

"Wass beeg ess-itemen'! We t'row you inna boat here, off we go, eh? Krenates all over, wham. Lahss eh-splosions, then Tiny he sees you got all dose krenates in your shirt. Tiny iss t'row krenates right back at 'em. Tiny t'row so far Tenumas dey hafta wait 'way back not get close, off we go clear like wheesle. He t'rowss like sisty!"

Oh, for the enthusiasm of youth! Wade smiled. "You all right, too, sport?"

"*Sí.*" The voice hesitated, sobered. "When I see you boat Iquitos, 'member? Say dere's goot papa, take care me. No more work in fields, meeshin, eh? You look important, rubber boss mebbe. Goot life now." Pato hesitated, groped for words. "Didn't know get so much life so queek, eh?"

"Guess you should have found out how I make a living before you latched onto me."

"Naw, iss okay. I like ess-itemen' lahss. 'Sep one t'ing." Again his thoughts seemed to be getting ahead of his English. "One t'ing. When Señor Cruz iss hurt, an' Tiny in ribs, eh? And Tingido's sobrino dead. All dat, still I don' never t'ink iss gonna be you or gonna be me. Ever'one else mebbe, not you, me. Know what I say?"

"Yes. I know." Take normal precautions, and you'll live forever. Death, even ennui, was for others; not him. Youth.

"So when I see you go so down hard, I get ess-tra eh-scairt. Issn' eh-'spose, can't happen to you."

"Or you."

"*Sí!* Dass what I say."

Gruffly, Tiny suggested that the loquacious boy engage himself less in conversation and apply himself more to propelling the craft. Wade translated to Spanish for him. Apparently Tiny's English lessons had not progressed yet to the point of permitting a free exchange of information.

Wade drifted, dozing fitfully in the world's nicest lap. The dugout bumped, scraped through bushes, jerked to a standstill in leaves too thick all around to see anything. He sat up on his own, but he needed lots of help to get out. He left behind stains and puddles of blood. Marcia would be appalled.

185

He slept through dawn. He awoke briefly to notice Cruz sound asleep in the hammock beside him. He slept through breakfast. When he finally roused himself, outrageously thirsty, the sun appeared to be high overhead. The canopy here was too thick to let more than suggestions of sunlight through.

How did Elinor know how much he wanted a drink? Here she came with a gourd of something cool and rather sweet-tasting. The sunshine smile warmed him. "Do you want to eat now or wait?"

"Wait."

"I'll return momentarily." And she was off, tending him and mother-henning the rest of the crew as well, no doubt.

He detected movement to his left, but it took him a long, hard moment to get his head turned that way. Cruz sat down heavily on his hammock facing Wade, dropped forward with his elbows on his knees, and laced those fluid fingers together.

"See anything of Tingido?"

"No." The man's face was drawn, tight. "The boy is dead."

"The nephew?"

"I found his head in the forest. They'd thrown it away, but it lodged in a bush."

"I'm sorry."

"I couldn't find any other remains. I brought it, of course, for the relatives to dispose of properly." The dark eyes, infinitely deep and sad, rose to meet Wade's. "I should have listened to you; heard what you were saying. I should never have let you and Elinor come with me. We very nearly lost you both because of my foolishness."

"Nearly . . . ? Was she—?"

"No. But when she saw you fall, she came back, knelt there in the thick of it keeping your head out of the water. She wouldn't leave you. And had any of that shrapnel hit the grenades you were carrying . . ." He sighed and wagged his head. "Tiny was making his run then, opened fire from out on the river and scooped us up."

"You're not apologizing for all this, are you?"

"Of course. I should never have—"

"Caesar mustn't grovel."

"What?"

"Forget it. Sounds like it all went the way it ought to. We all

186

would have died in that net if we'd come down on it not knowing. You learned about the nephew and about Tingido by inference, since he'd probably be where his nephew was. That's what you went over for. We're all together again, and we might not have got past them at all if we didn't have those grenades. At least, that's what I hear from Pato's wild and hairy description. It worked out almost as well as if it'd been planned that way."

"Elinor says it was. God's plan."

"She said I was chosen, too—same authority—but I sure had my doubts there for a while."

"A woman of God."

"She is that." Wade stared at the countless leaves above until his eyes grew weary of holding themselves open.

Cruz stood slowly, stiffly. "Can I get you anything?"

"Thanks, no. Yes. How about another long drink, and some extra water to swish around? I'm going to be three days getting the mud out of my teeth."

Woman of God. God's plan. Wade tried to analyze Cruz's tone of voice. Either Cruz was very, very tired, or he was resigned to believing, without artifice or intellectual baggage, that Elinor's God was exactly as she saw him—a divine Master in charge of every phase of this Hurley operation.

Wade would love to believe that, too. It would be so easy, so comforting, to turn the project over to a divine director and follow orders. Elinor did that. He remembered her sitting calmly in the dugout when they crossed the river, totally confident that things would roll along as planned by God. He remembered her complete lack of fear whenever danger reared its ugly head. But how can you feel certain about something you can't pick apart, dig up proof for, see hard courtroom evidence of . . . ?

She was so sensible, so rational, in every way but that. Without a shred of proof she stood foursquare for her Jesus.

She also stood right beside his hammock. "Cruz would have brought this, but I was coming over anyway." She gave him another gourdful of the sweet liquid. She looked so exhausted Wade felt ashamed to have asked anything of her.

He flexed his knees and drew his legs aside. "Sit. You look ready to fall over." His left hip screamed at him for making it move. He rested the gourd on his breastbone at sipping distance.

She sagged into the far end of the hammock, let it sling her at any angle it chose. She studied him smiling. "The color's finally coming back to your face. That's good. I was afraid for a time that there might be some internal problem. And the rip in your arm is probably going to leave quite a scar."

"Something to boast about to my grandkids."

"Grandchildren. Yes. And your son. Last night in the dugout, when he was talking to you . . . Whose son is he, really?"

"I have no idea. Doubt he knows, either. And I never met his mother."

The most wondrous glow of admiration lit her face. "What a beautiful thing!"

Wade felt his cheeks get warm. "Well, uh, nothing big. He's bright. Lot of fun, with that goofy English of his. Pulls his full weight. I don't mind his hanging around. Quit looking at me like I'm ready for sainthood, will you?"

"I didn't mean to embarrass you. I'm sorry. It's just that every new thing I learn about you makes me li—" She bit her lip as her ears turned pink. The charming way she blushed tickled him.

"You didn't. It's okay. It's just that I don't do beautiful things. I'm not very beautiful inside at all. In fact, if you could see inside, you probably wouldn't speak to me again."

"Oh, that's not true! I mean, everyone is ugly from God's point of view—God sees the inside, you know—until the sin problem is taken care of. I mean, when he's . . . But then you . . ." She pressed her hand across her mouth and looked almost ready for tears. "I just don't understand. I have never had difficulty talking about my Lord with anyone, ever. But with you . . . I just can't . . . I mean . . . And yet, I see your aching heart, and I know what I should be saying. But the words get all mushed up and . . ." She ripped herself away from the cozy sling and stood up. "I must start dinner." She hurried off.

He watched her until she disappeared beyond the leaves, then watched the memory of her there. Every time they talked, they ended up talking about God or the Holy Spirit or some such thing.

Was that all she saw in him? A potential convert to her religious fanaticism? He was ready to love her on her own terms. Yes, love. For the first time in his life, Wade had found someone he could say that about. He didn't feel any pressing need to change her, to swing her to some new way of thinking. Why did she have to be that way with him?

He had forgotten to thank her for staying by him in the war zone last night. Rats. He should've done that, and he hadn't. One more example of the ugliness inside.

His son, the fisherman, came bounding out of the forest with a couple small, black catfish and a turtle. Grinning, he proffered them to Elinor almost like a peace offering. Or love offering. She took them graciously—there weren't many women who could accept a couple slimy dead fish that elegantly, let alone an algae-covered sideneck.

Tiny came slogging into the camp. He gave Elinor his catch, too, a single fish half the size of Pato's. Pato and Tiny. They looked ludicrous together, the utmost extremes of big and small, quick and sluggish, bright and slow. And yet they got on so well, complementing each other, that you didn't notice the disparity. Now, if they could just learn a common language . . .

He slept some more, off and on. He awoke in a deep gloom that told him day was nearly over. Cruz would want to shove off in a couple hours. He let Elinor force a little catfish down him and went back to sleep.


Morning. Morning? Here they were, still in the same place. Cruz's hammock was empty, so it wasn't even early morning. Why hadn't Caesar sounded the clarion call to move on? The whole camp stood vacant. Where was everybody?

Wade felt far stiffer today than yesterday, and yesterday he would not have thought that possible. He could barely move anything, neck and shoulders especially. He'd better, though, or he'd never move again. Besides, there was no one around to help him. He lurched to sitting, plunked his legs over the side, and spent a few minutes assaying his aching body.

Elinor had mentioned a rip in his arm, and it was a beauty. Its ragged edges were pinned together with the jaws and heads of a dozen soldier ants. Whoever had done the pinning—holding the huge squirming ant just so, pinching together the ripped skin until the ant chomped down on it with its massive pincers, then clipping away all but the head—was as highly skilled as any forest Indian medicine man. Elinor, probably, or Cruz.

A jagged gash in his left hip was similarly stitched. In fact, he noticed that someone had stitched the corresponding tear in his pants with ants as well. Clever. Poor old Pato must have been out hunting soldier ants for hours. Scuffs, scrapes, a cut over his left eye, a couple welts and bruises—no wonder Wade felt like he was flogged by a windmill.

He was almost afraid to stand up. What if he got dizzy, or his tortured hip gave way? He'd fall over, that's what, tumble onto soggy ground covered with soft moss. So what? He stood. He made it the three steps out of camp to take care of business. He made it back, past his hammock, to the dying embers of the morning's fire. With extreme caution he eased to sitting beside the firepit and picked through the breakfast leavings. Here were some plantains, a couple pieces of fruit he thought were probably wild plums, two leftover broiled fish filets.

He heard someone coming out of the forest and recognized the footfalls. He didn't have to twist around to look.

"Good morning, boss."

"How'd you know it was me?" Marcia plunked down beside him and picked up a plum. She was sopping wet, revealing every detail of her form.

"Lucky guess. Laundry time again?"

"Fell in. Cruz is doing some work on the dugouts. Guess we're gonna be in 'em a while. I can hardly wait." She slurped plum juice.

"No solid land at all between here and Minho?"

"Apparently not. All flooded. What's it called?"

"Varzea."

"Yeah. Hey, you know, I found out what 'minho' means. It means 'mine,' as in belongs-to-me. That's a pretty cocky thing to call a plantation that big. Just plain pompous."

"He's not a farmer, he's an emperor, and he built it himself out of

190

virgin forest. If anyone has a right to name a place 'mine,' he does. But that's not why he calls it that."

"It's not?"

"In Europe, the Minho River forms part of the boundary between Spain and Portugal. He grew up in the Minho valley on the Spanish side. Farm boy of humble circumstance."

"Horatio Alger stuff."

"Exactly. Spoke Portuguese as fluently as Spanish, even considered studying in Lisbon, but he was sent to Salamanca instead. Grew up on the border between two cultures, you see. Now here's his Minho in the Brazilian jungle, the border between two cultures. Part old world and part new. Part Portuguese and part Spanish. Part European and part Indian. And it's all his, as you say. *Minho.* Perfect name."

"Mmm. Still, I should think he'd want to name his place something more imposing. Jefferson's Monticello, for example, or Wheatland—Buchanan's estate. Something a little classier than a possessive pronoun."

For no particular reason, he had the strongest urge to kiss her. In fact, if the others weren't apt to pop in any moment . . . Others. *Elinor.* The height of shame would be Elinor catching him with a woman. Any woman. Not the reverse, though. Were Marcia to catch him with Elinor, he'd just tell Marcia to beat it. Strange, the difference.

"You're a million miles off. What're you thinking about?"

"Don't ask. Cruz leaving tonight, then?"

"Maybe tomorrow night. Says we're all awfully tired. That's bul— . . . not true. He's tired. I feel fine. Wanna get going."

His gashed hip begged piteously to return to the comfortable sling of the hammock. He was going to tear it open if he weren't careful, and Pato would be back to ant-hunting. Now, how to stand up without doing damage? He shifted weight and reached for the last fish filet, a snack to take along to bed.

Marcia gasped. Her shocked eyes stared past Wade's shoulder. He yanked his belt knife free as he wrenched around to meet the danger. With stunning, searing pain, every ant-jaw stitch in his hip ripped loose.

Tingido's yellow dog stood on the brink of the green wall. Its ribs showed plainly through its soiled, ragged coat. Black flakes of dry blood matted its side and rear end. It stood a long moment watching Wade, trying to call into memory its friends of yore. The sorry tail stiffened and rose, but the poor pooch was past tail-wagging.

"*Eh, perro. Ven. Pescado, eh? Ven.*" Wade extended the fish, waved it to send the smell off quicker.

The dog tottered forward.

"Get Cruz. Hurry!"

Marcia jumped to her feet and ran off. The dog crouched warily, then returned its attention to the fish. Here it came. It plopped on its belly near Wade's foot. He broke off a bit of fish and halfway forced it between the dog's teeth. The next piece went in easier. It bolted the rest of the filet in proper dog fashion and had wolfed down a plantain by the time Cruz arrived.

It cringed as Cruz settled to one knee beside it, but it didn't attempt to run off. Cruz laid a slim hand on the dog's head, scratched it behind the ears, patted its back. Gently he pulled the back end around a bit, craning for a closer look. "Grenade, I'd say. Ragged tear."

"Why here?"

"The high ground to the northwest narrows down to something of a point here. It was probably headed home . . ."

"Its Ocaina settlement."

'Yes, which is under water now. The high ground, with a few swamped spots, would funnel it down to here instead."

"Tingido, too, if he's alive and moving overland?"

"I've never been too sanguine about miracles." Cruz's dark eyes drifted up to Wade's. "Until now."

# chapter
## 22

WADE LAY ON HIS RIGHT SIDE in the hammock and listened to the dog whimper. He knew the feeling. Elinor held the dog's head securely as Cruz and Tiny worked on its backside. With tweezers of two *caña brava* splinters, Pato passed a soldier ant to Tiny. Tiny touched the ant to just the right spot as Cruz held the edges of the wound together. The dog would whine, Cruz would pinch off the ant's body with a thumbnail, and Pato would pass Tiny another.

The only difference between Wade and the dog was that Elinor wasn't holding his head. When Cruz was working on him, she was off washing and mending his trousers.

Cruz sat back and nodded. Pato rubbed the dog's chin and purred in sympathetic Spanish. Elinor made an even bigger fuss and hand-fed it some juicy tidbit from the stew pot. Wade envied the dog.

So did Tiny. He made pointed comment on the high quality of the dog's treat, so Elinor mollified him by hand-feeding him a few tidbits also. Tactful lady, Elinor. Tiny wandered over to his little corner of the world and lowered his bulk into his hammock. He kicked something egg-shaped. It rolled.

Wade propped himself on an elbow. "What's that?!" He pointed.

Tiny peered over the side. "Souvenir. Had one grenade left. Thought I'd keep it."

"Oh, no, you won't. Get that thing outta here. Now!"

"Besides, maybe come in handy. You don' know."

"Get rid of it!" His voice was far too strident. Everyone was staring at him. "Out in the woods, in the river. Just do it. And do it silently."

Tiny studied him a minute, shrugged, and dumped himself out of his hammock. " 'Fyou say so." With casual slackness he scooped up the mini-bomb and walked off into the forest.

Cruz came wandering over to his hammock. He poured himself into it, stretched out.

"Souvenir. One've *them*." Wade rearranged his sore backside. "When are you going out to look for Tingido?"

"As soon as the dog is fully active. After lunch, perhaps."

"I dunno. Tingido didn't have the dog very long—not much time to build a strong bond. Think it'll take you to him?"

"Who knows? Who knows if he's still alive? The dog is probably alone, trying to go back to his old people. But I want to be sure." The voice drifted off to other days and distant places. "Tingido was a superb woodsman. The best. And a good friend."

"Think Hurley's at Minho yet?"

"No sign of him along the river. Pahoa seems competent. No reason to believe otherwise."

"Those weren't the only Tenumas."

"True. In fact, they may look here next, if they know enough about the country to realize everything terrestrial collects on this little peninsula. We should have left yesterday. But we're all tired, and you're incapacitated. It's not safe to stay, nor is it safe to leave, as weak as we are. . . . And now that dog."

"You, too, huh? And here I thought I was the only one responsibility was mashing into the ground with its big fat thumb."

Cruz snorted. "Just one of the many imps bedeviling me."

"Hurley's library didn't help? Or his conversations?"

"He posed solutions I cannot accept—at least, not yet." Cruz sighed heavily and rubbed his face with both hands.

Wade could not imagine the man getting old. Cruz was ageless. There was a day, and not long ago, when Cruz could run circles around him. Back when Wade worked for him, Cruz would still be rumbling along, freight-train strong, while Wade faded and lagged. And yet now the *patráo* looked so drained, acted so weary. Part of it was his injury surely, not yet healed. But it was more than that. Cruz was no longer invincible. Death, even ennui, threatened the indefatigable Bernardo Martin Cruz as inexorably as it was closing in on Wade.

A movement by the firepit caught Wade's eye. "The dog."

Cruz raised his head.

The dog was walking, a bit unsteadily, off in the direction whence it had come. Cruz swung his legs to the ground and watched the dog disappear beyond the leaves. Firmly he took off following.

Did Wade believe in miracles? Maybe so. He was tempted to call someone to go help Cruz, but everyone was off doing other things, like preparing to survive a while longer. Wade got his legs over the side without tearing his hip open again and climbed shakily to his feet.

Cruz was too quiet to follow by ear, the growth too thick for eyes to be useful. Wade walked a hundred feet and stopped frustrated. Then a passing flock of indignant aracaris told him where the action was. He fought his way through the growth with about as much finesse as Marcia. His left arm wouldn't lift, his left leg wouldn't step over things.

Aracaris. The gaudy little toucans were the first good birds or wildlife Wade had seen in eons. He welcomed the harsh babble of their voices and privately cursed the grenade-happy Tenumas.

He struggled along for maybe a quarter mile, but his body complained like it was walking halfway to Ecuador. No more. He had to give up. He had given up once before, and it had felt so good. He melted against a tree trunk and thought back to that. Had it just been his imagination warped out of shape by the awful moment, or had he truly found a measure of peace then?

The dog barked in the distance, canceling any notions about giving up. Wade lurched erect and tried to quicken his step, but it wouldn't quicken. He doddered. He heard laughter of a sort—tense chuckling—and he knew what it meant: forest Indians respond to pain with laughter. And he realized how often he had used the word *miracle* loosely, and how miracles actually happen now and then. Like now.

Cruz rose from kneeling by a kapok buttress and watched Wade approach. "You sound like Marcia."

"And I feel like a hundred and ten."

"I'm glad you came. I was afraid that if I left him to fetch help, he might wander off. He's not fully coherent. Wait with him." And Cruz pushed off through the forest, making not much less noise than Wade. Or Marcia.

Devoid of either paint or fabric, Tingido lay curled up on his side in the smooth arc of the tree buttress. Whatever man can think to do to inflict pain on another, men had thought to do to him. Marks Wade didn't want to consider analyzing covered the warm brown body. Even Tingido's fingernails oozed pus where slivers had been jabbed in.

The dog went to the ground by the Indian's head, panting. Tingido stirred and patted yellow fur. He said a word resembling the Portuguese for *fix* or *mend*.

Very, very carefully Wade settled beside the Indian, to wait. Cruz wasn't going to be back soon, not as slowly as he was moving. What an outfit! Wade, Cruz, Tiny to an extent, and now Tingido—the invalids would soon outnumber the well. Theirs wasn't a flotilla, it was a floating infirmary.

So Elinor attributed all this to God's plan. God planned to subject Tingido to excruciating suffering? God wiped out his two nephews, both fine young men, because he wanted to? God decided who should bleed and who should die and who should mop up the remains, and then, like a demented chess player, moved his pieces at random around his board? How did God do his planning, Elinor?

If God decided to monkey around with Wade's body, apparently he had the prerogative. But why did he have to tear up Wade's hip? This was worse than that broken leg. Wade would scarcely be able to handle a canoe, sit down without working out a lot of logistics, or walk very far. God's plan for the Hurley project required a fit and hale Travers, didn't it? Or *was* there a plan? Or maybe the Hurley project was successfully completed, and Wade Travers was now expendable, a trifle to be toyed with and teased.

He flopped back against the buttress, disgusted. Elinor was responsible for this. He was already mixed up, despondent even, before she got him speculating about God stuff. He didn't need this new dimension of confusion. He had enough problems without adding in a bunch of spiritual question marks.

Holy Spirit indeed.

His eyes drifted shut. Going the way of his eyes, his mind drifted, too. He'd be asleep in a minute if he didn't drag himself to standing or something.

He had been speculating on God, had he? Even making fun? God was now getting back at him for that. God sent angels to sing to Wade. They were distant angels, of course; after all, the canopy stretched 250 feet off the deck, and the very tall emergent trees extended up still farther. Angels, being creatures of flight, wouldn't want to come down too close and risk damaging those great silver wings. Wade even recognised the hymn from his childhood, something about bringing in sheaves.

Tingido grunted. "Cant'."

Wade's eyes popped open.

Either the angels were teasing a helpless, tormented Indian as well, or . . . or what? He got his good right leg under him and hauled himself to his feet with the help of the buttress. Vegetation so deflected and filtered the faint sound, he couldn't guess which direction it came from. But they weren't angels, because it wasn't from above.

It was a good bet they weren't his crew, either. He couldn't imagine Marcia singing a hymn, though such songs would flow naturally and sweetly from Elinor. And Tiny didn't know the English word for *sheaves*.

American hymns in the forest? Wade might be bringing the wrath of the Tenumas down on himself. This might be a magnificently conceived and executed trap. He would risk it. He waited, his heart pounding, for the song to cease. This was insane! The silence arrived, filtered through the trees. As loudly as he could muster, he sang out the first line of the chorus, the only line he could drag from the cobwebbed closets of his memory.

The ersatz angels began another hymn. The tune was vaguely familiar, but the words had him stumped.

He pulled his shirt off and hung it from a high bush a yard from Tingido's head. *"Perro. Ven, conmigo. Perro."* He wiggled a hand at the dog. The dog started to rise, then flattened out on its belly, its chin in the damp moss, and followed him with eyes only. "So don't go. Just be sure to tell Cruz where you are when he comes."

Wade started walking. Where? He didn't know. He glanced back occasionally and stopped when he lost sight of the shirt. He tried his only line of bringing in sheaves again. Silence. He backed up against a tree and listened.

A solo voice echoed through the forest from a distant but identifiable direction. Over there. Wade recognized the tune that always appeared as "doxology" on the church program, following offering. It had ever been the same, week in and week out, and he remembered its words, now that he heard it. "Praise God from Whom All Blessings Flow." Indeed, he was among those who sang it the loudest, his mother having sent him to church weekly for years. It was proper that a child get religion, everyone knew, although she herself was too tired by Sunday to go along.

He didn't mind church when he was a kid. He liked the singing, felt important dropping his pennies in the plate, and found the sermon a convenient rest to prepare for the mischievous afternoon ahead. He had praised God weekly and voluminously as a child and never remembered it until this moment. He didn't even know God then. He certainly didn't now.

The towheaded boy just before the turn of the century who garbled words in church could not have dreamed that today, in 1922, he would find a use for those words in the steaming rain forest of Brazil, matching choruses with, he hoped, a Christianized Indian. Wade belted out the first line and paused, suddenly uncertain about the lyrics of the second.

Like a rival bellbird, the singer answered, closer.

Wade couldn't hope to blend into the shrubbery the way Tingido could. For one thing, his shirtless torso wasn't the right color. He tried anyway. He stood motionless against the tree, waiting.

Waiting.

His hip burned, his muscles ached.

The mystery singer possessed an extensive repertoire. Now he started something about "Savior, do not pass me by."

There he was, on the far periphery of visibility. The Indian stopped and disappeared instantly. He moved again. Wade could just barely make out the paint marks.

"Over here!" Wade waved an arm.

The Indian jumped. He literally popped straight up. He started this way much too quickly for good sense, paying scant lookout for things with fangs that might be lying in wait. Hurley seemed to think Christian influence had not altered their woodsworthiness. Wade was not so sure.

The Indian was one of Hurley's, all right. He stared at Wade a long, long minute, then lifted his arms and praised God over and over.

"Hurley?" Wade asked.

"With us. There." He pointed behind him. "All you?"

"There." Wade pointed. "What happened?"

The Indian raised both hands to make up for a lack of words. "First, we slipped past that place. We stayed unseen."

"Where we parted. Were they building a net anywhere along there? A fence across the river?"

The Indian frowned. "Net. Fence. No. Nothing. We traveled through the night. All is well. The varzea makes many good places to hide in day. We found a good place on this side. Darkness, we went again. Where is river?"

"The main channel. The open part. Current."

"Yes. We struggled through many trees and thick places. We found the river. In the dark we, uh . . ." His gesticulating hands groped for words to pluck from the air. "We struck bushes. Our enemy was the forest. The paddles were wrong; the canoe went over. *Jacaré* came, caused great grief. We lost a man. We lost the bundles. The papers. But the doctor is safe."

"My condolences for your man. Join us. Bring Hurley. Bring you. All of us can go together."

"Yes!" Radiant, the Indian smiled out from under this thick, squared bowl haircut. "Yes, brother Travers. God is good! God is good!"

He is, is he? God is surely ironic. Wade would give him that. He watched Hurley's Indian hurry off through the growth until the man was out of sight, then returned to Tingido. He was buttoning his shirt when Tiny and Pato arrived, with Cruz well in the rear.

"Pato, got a job for you. Hurley and his Indians are off that way somewhere. I want you to go lead them in. Can you handle it?"

"*Sí*, Papa!"

"Don't bother too much about staying silent. They've been making enough noise to delight the hearts of choirmasters in Manaos. Get 'em in quick and keep an eye out behind."

"Gotchit!" The boy bolted off through the brush.

Wade hollered, "And watch out for snakes!" to the butternut-colored back. Pato. Death was for others, not him.

Cruz stood near Tingido, staring at Wade, the word *Hurley?* formed unspoken on his face.

Wade crossed to him slowly. His hip hurt. "You were speaking about miracles."

"This definitely qualifies." Cruz watched as Tiny knelt and pushed the loose hair off Tingido's sweat-sticky face. "I'm convinced Hurley's and Elinor's concepts of God are essentially accurate. That he does exist and he does intervene."

Wade raised his eyebrows, as much in doubt as in surprise. "Make this a minor miracle, though. You said the lay of the land channels everything terrestrial to this point."

"Hurley wasn't terrestrial when we parted."

"True." The pain in his hip was going to slay Wade right here if he didn't lie down soon. In Portuguese he spoke to Tiny. "I sent the other litter carrier off into the woods. Sorry. Wasn't thinking."

"Don' need 'm." Tiny worked his massive arms under Tingido and lifted. "Quicker, easier this way." He stood up, carrying the stricken Indian as a housewife might tote a laundry basket out to the line. "Take him to Elinor." With a resigned sigh, the dog lurched to its feet and followed stiffly.

Elinor, the physician. What would they do without Elinor?

Wade walked for maybe ten feet before his ragged body cried *enough*. Cautiously, he lowered himself with his good leg and flopped out on a soft bed of moss. "I'll be all right by the time Pato comes by. I'll come in with them."

Cruz studied him with eyes that miss nothing. "Don't leave this spot. I'll bring help." He stared into the distance. "I'm not sure yet, but I think I may have been betrayed."

"By whom?" Wade raised his shoulders enough to pull his shirt off again. He tossed it up onto a bush to mark his position just in case he should fall asleep while Cruz was gone.

"Good question. You see, any concept of God I or anyone else comes up with still leaves numerous questions unanswered. For example, why is Tingido suffering? Why are you there—a strong, able man—laid low? Why Tingido's nephews? Or Hurley?"

"I don't think you're the first one to ask 'Why is there suffering?' "

"Nor am I the first one to come up with this response, probably. Either there is no God and I will never find a concept that fits God because there is no such thing—"

"Elinor would fight you on that one."

"—or God takes a certain perverse pleasure in making himself inconceivable. I will never know him because he won't let me. If I should assemble a given set of facts into a concept of God, he alters the facts or inserts others. Opposites."

"So you're betrayed—either by your own desire to know a god that isn't, or by the God playing tricks on you. It's an interesting theory. Pretty discouraging theory, it looks like to me." Wade chuckled.

"I look forward to approaching Hurley with this one." Cruz spread Wade's shirt a little higher in the bush.

"We won't need matches. You'll make enough friction to start fires for three days. I hope you're wrong. I hope Hurley argues the socks right off you."

"So do I. Rest easy. I'll return shortly." He turned away toward camp, muttering, "So do I."

Wade closed his burning eyes. He adjusted his body, stretching it out, trying to find a comfortable position. A comfortable position? There was no such thing outside a hammock.

He felt befuddled, but Cruz sounded far more befuddled. Cruz was the philosopher, the thinker. Wade was the simple jungle guide. Cruz was right, though. This finding Tingido and Hurley both within the same, oh, say, five square miles of high ground rated as a miracle.

Not only that, there was a still bigger miracle. It appeared Wade wasn't expendable, after all. Apparently they were all still part of—if there was such a thing—God's plan for the Hurley project.

# chapter
# 23

SHOULD A LEVEE BURST along the Mississippi, the flood might spread out over several square miles. The Ohio River every now and then made news with its spring overflows. And then there was shocking, tragic Johnstown. Still, nothing in America, or anywhere else in the world, for that matter, could begin to prepare the observer who first encounters "flood" in the Amazon.

The river itself spreads out for forty miles beyond either bank. Its waters gush forth through the furos to deluge forests twenty or thirty feet deep. Eighty miles wide by two thousand miles long, give or take an area the size of Texas, submerged in twenty feet of tepid water—now that's Flood.

For two months, any plant or creature on the ground will be under water. The plants and animals have adjusted to that. Nearly all are arboreal. Some go dormant until the inconvenience passes. Many don't even notice the flood below, much less appreciate its stupendous size, for they never touch foot on solid ground at all. Their be-all and end-all exists in the treetops.

The myriad aquatic creatures appreciate the flood in ways no human can imagine. Crowded together two deep along ragged shores during low water, the *jacarés* can at last cruise wide open spaces. Swimmers large and small go forth among the trees joyously, freed for a time from their cramped existence in a river a mere two or three miles wide. Schooling fishes and great snakes and curiously flexible pink dolphins swim for miles among bushes and trees that will be three stories up in the air six months from now. Flood.

Many of the Amazon's tributaries are innundated as well, losing their identities for a time in the great general deluge. One such was Cruz's river.

Were they following Cruz's river? Cruz said so, and he must know. He said that, in three days, they should be safe and comfortable, resting in the imported chairs and beds of Minho. But the varzea looked all alike to Wade. The dugouts slipped silently among identical trees over motionless water, occasionally brushing the tips of submerged bushes. There was no respite from the crowded canoes, either, for Minho herself was now the first and only high ground they would draw anywhere near.

Paddling a dugout, when you come right down to it, is a boring way to travel. Infinitely more boring, though, is riding idle in one. Wade welcomed the rest and inactivity at first. By the end of the second day, he loathed it. He wanted to take over the bow paddle from Elinor in this canoe with Cruz and Tingido. He wanted to take Cruz's stern position; let the *patrão* sit inert a while and ruminate. Instead, Wade squirmed, trying to find a comfortable position in a crude, cruelly shaped hollow log that bore no resemblance in shape or form to human anatomy.

Pahoa and the singer paddled the canoe with Marcia and Dr. Hurley. Marcia became pretty annoying as she tried constantly to engage the doctor in long conversations. The man was fading rapidly, taxed by the difficult trip. He didn't need the extra ordeal of lecturing nonstop on people and places in the slave trade.

In the third canoe, one of Hurley's Indians handled the bow while Pato and Tiny took turns in the stern. Tiny's relinquishing his position fifty percent of the time to a mere kid told Wade how weakened the whale had become in the last few days.

Lunchtime. They roped together the lianas and floated in the sunspeckled bower of a tree Wade didn't know. Its points, waxy leaves and drooping branches cascaded around them, embraced them in living green splendor.

Wade accepted a couple plums and a slab of fish left over from breakfast. "You know, I'm almost to the point where I miss manioc.

Haven't had it in so long." The dog had awakened. It uncurled from near Tingido's legs, stood, and stretched its front half. It started nosing around Wade's fish.

Marcia stared. "You mean that gritty paste stuff?" She shook her head and went back to her plantains.

Tingido sat up for the first time that day, looked around a moment, and smiled. With a long, stretching reach, Elinor handed him a small pot. Wade didn't remember anything edible coming in a pot that size. Tingido peeked in the pot and smiled again—two in a row, for one who counted Tingido's infrequent smiles. He dipped a finger in and with slow, leisurely strokes, dressed himself in the green and white markings of his clan.

Elinor turned her sunshine smile to Hurley's Indians. "Thank you," she said to the source of the paint.

Cruz addressed the canoe beside him. "Dr. Hurley, do you feel inclined to talk a few minutes, or would you rather rest?"

"Talk about what?"

"God."

"Much inclined, my friend." Hurley coughed his lungs out a minute, then wedged himself crosswise in his boat, the better that he might regard face to face his challenger. "Do you disagree with my arguments that God does not play pranks with them who would know him?"

"You made your case." Cruz halved himself another piece of fruit.

"Ah, then what can I explain for you?"

"In a few succinct and lucid sentences—the meaning of life." Hurley chuckled. "I can do it in two words. Jesus Christ."

Wade's back was partly turned to Hurley, but he sat right by Elinor and could see her without twisting at all. She was draped across the gunwale in that delicate way of hers, rapt. Her eyes flitted from man to man. Her interest, even say delight, glowed in her lovely face. What a splendid lady!

Tingido finished his turtle drumstick, gave the bone to the dog, and lay down again. Philosophical discussions in a language he did not know could understandably put him to sleep.

Cruz finished his plum and reached out over the gunwale to rinse off his hand. "Might you elaborate?"

The doctor chuckled. "If you wish. Let's say there's a sloth up in this tree."

"There is, in fact, a sloth in that one." Cruz pointed beyond the bower.

"Excellent. If you would, please, go explain to him how an airplane works. Not just what it is. How it works."

Cruz studied the man, and for a brief and shining moment the fatigue lines in his face softened. He was off in hot pursuit of his favorite pastime. "First, tell me why the sloth should know."

"He wants to know. I'm shipping him to a zoo in one."

"One can ride in an airplane without knowing how it works, but that would miss the point, am I correct? Your point is, there is no way to show him something as complex as airplane mechanics because of the intellectual gap between sloth and man."

Dr. Hurley smiled as wide as Texas. "And its corollary?"

"There is no way God can explain to us something as complex as himself because of the intellectual gap between him and man. Very well. Then, if God created people, why did he put in our hearts a yearning to know something that is beyond our capability to understand?"

The doctor built his hands into a teepee, fingertips together, and studied his thumbs a moment. "God is all things to all people, Mr. Cruz, because people are so different. Each human being is unique, with a unique frame of reference toward life. Elinor and I have discussed you more than once—and you, Mr. Travers. Elinor feels inadequate to answer your questions because—well, let's see— because her concept of God is based on her frame of reference, not yours, and therefore would fail to meet your needs. You would see it as too simplistic; although in reality, I assure you it's not."

Wade found himself sucked up in this discussion almost against his will. "If God's God, we should all see the same God."

"No. That's my point. God is so much greater, no one can see him entirely. That sloth's concept of me would differ radically from a jaguar's. And a monkey might see me as a possible ancestor but certainly not as its equal. I failed tree-climbing even as a boy. Even you do not understand all my complexities, and I'm but a man like yourself."

"I destroyed a jaguar several months ago, a child killer. That cat knew me as an adversary. The sloth would see me only as another creature passing on the floor below. The same man."

Suddenly the old Cruz was back. The resilient, competent, vibrant Cruz filled up the hollow, Cruz-shaped shell Wade had worked with these last weeks. A light had dawned within him, and Wade knew without knowing how he knew, that this was the light he himself sought so desperately.

"Let me anticipate you." Cruz stared past Wade's ear at Hurley. "God cannot hope to reveal all of himself to us. So he places in us the desire to know him, a yearning. But it's not important that we know everything about him; only that we know that part of him that affects us personally. Directly. The yearning is to know the part of him he wants us to know."

"Yes! Yes!" Hurley started to speak and ended in a spasm of coughing again.

"So he begins by showing us that part of himself that's important and leaves it to us to seek out other facets if we choose. Elinor told me once that we see the Father by seeing Jesus. That's our starting point for knowing God."

"Go on! Go on!"

But Cruz bogged down. His face worked as he tried to push ahead. In desperation he looked at Wade.

Wade waved a hand helplessly. "Maybe, uh, if God is as efficient as Cruz here, Jesus isn't just the starting point. He has a purpose of his own besides simply tipping us off to the nature of God. God intended him for more than one reason."

"Beautiful! Beautiful!" Dr. Hurley coughed more when he grew excited. "Go on!" he gasped.

"Jesus' most common title is 'Savior,' not 'Beginning.' I assume that's the dual purpose."

Hurley took a couple minutes to reassemble his shattered insides before speaking. "Yes. Mr. Cruz, you could take it from here without my further urging, except that I know something you don't. A person's spirit becomes soiled by wrongdoing."

"Sin."

"Sin. And not just criminals and liars, but all people. The soiled spirit cannot see God well, even under the best enlightenment. It must be polished, if you will. Cleansed. For reasons of his own, God decreed that such cleaning must be done with blood. He permits the blood of Jesus to serve that function. This is what theologians call salvation."

Cruz was starting to tense up. "Then a person can't see God outside of salvation?"

"He may, perhaps, but not well. Not enough to satisfy the yearning. And not with any help from God. You see, good, by nature, can't co-exist with evil. God's good Spirit can't join with a person's dirty one until it's cleansed. But once you are made clean, God's Spirit helps you know him better. It adds a whole new dimension to your life, a spiritual dimension you had no way of dreaming existed. God is not at cross purposes with you, Mr. Cruz. He wants to help, if you will only let him in."

Wade was staring at Elinor. "You mentioned a couple times about spiritual insight, stuff you didn't think I'd understand. That what you were talking about?"

She nodded. "Another way you may have heard it phrased is rebirth. The old spirit dies, in a sense, and God's Spirit takes over. You die to self and live to Christ."

Cruz began untangling the stern from the liana thrown across it. "This brings us back to where we ended our previous conversation, although by a different route."

"And our next conversation will end here also, because Jesus Christ is the center and linchpin."

Cruz threw the vine over the side. "You're dangling a carrot in front of a goat, doctor. You promise me new insight if I will become religious according to your definition. You tempt me— bribe me—with something desirable to me."

"If bribery would only work, I'd be out on the street corner passing out twenty dollar bills. I'm telling you about a benefit. Now, I'll tell you something you don't want to hear, the thing with which I began this discussion. God is for all people, including Tingido here. Yet Tingido is not equipped intellectually as you are. His gifts are in other areas. You cannot reach God intellectually. I'm sorry. That's not how he set it up. You must approach God as

Tingido would, or as this child, Pato. As Elinor did. With no proof at all, no intellectual insight."

The old, vibrant Cruz quietly faded. The bitter Cruz of late reached for his paddle.

Dr. Hurley pressed on. "Put aside the intellect you depend upon and place your dependence on God directly. When you trust your ability to sort facts, you are putting trust in yourself, not him. Trust him. Accept him. Accept his gift, cleansing with Jesus's blood. He'll return your intellect to you, I promise. Multiplied. But first you must yield it. And I must nap."

The doctor scritched himself around, started to lie back and sat erect again. "Oh, and Mr. Cruz, would you waken me please as we approach Minho? I've heard so much about it, I look forward to seeing it loom suddenly into view."

"I don't understand."

"Of course you do. Tingido betrayed you by painting himself. He knows we're close. Excellent ploy. Promise Minho in three days and then *poit*! There she pops unexpectedly into view, beckoning with clean sheets and a well-laid table. And should we be delayed, no one is disappointed. Morale is a very important consideration. I tip my hat to you. Now good night."

Cruz glanced at Wade like a puppy caught with the dinner pork chops. He dipped a paddle. The dugout lurched sluggishly forward.

Wade quit leaning on one gunwale; he was pulling the boat out of trim. His head was all amuddle, and he couldn't tell which direction it was taking. He knew one thing. Bernardo Martin Cruz didn't polish his intellect for a lifetime simply to put it aside now. And yet, where had Cruz's intellect gotten him so far? He wasn't any better off than Wade. Worse maybe, even. With his deeper thinking, he was digging himself deeper holes.

Wade searched in vain for some landmark. Treemark. Whatever. Something to tell him how close to Minho they might be. Tingido had recognized this faceless waste instantly. Of course, Tingido had been born and raised here.

He might be yearning for God, but he was also yearning for a plug of tobacco. Nothing would please him better than to be able to pack his pipe and set fire to it now. The rote procedure helped his thinking, kept his hands busy. He could sit idle no longer. He scooted carefully in behind Elinor, arranged his bad leg just so, and tapped her on the shoulder.

"Gimme that."

"What?"

"Whatever you're holding at the moment." He took the paddle from her small white hands, settled a bit more at an angle, and stroked deep. Felt good, so good, to do something again.

"Please. You shouldn't."

"'S okay."

She hesitated the briefest moment. There was no hostility in her eyes, and no anger. But that didn't soften them any. "You'll not risk tearing stitches. No." She snatched the paddle away with unexpected strength and resumed paddling.

He learned something he should have guessed much, much earlier: this fox-fire, this will-o'-the-wisp possessed a core of iron.

He sighed. "Cruz? You were saying about intractable women?"

"Strictly your problem, friend."

She twisted instantly and abandoned paddling. "Intractable!"

"Yeah, you. Soft as summer smoke, so long as everything's going exactly the way you think it oughta. Someone disagrees with you and whammy! Your nostrils flare and you get tough. No room for somebody to want something a little different. Besides, it's harmless."

Her nostrils flared. "I'm paddling, and you're sitting there because I have some idea how painful your injuries are. I care very much about . . . I mean . . . Besides, it's *not* harmless. You're starting to heal, and it's foolish to take any chance of reopening either . . . I mean, you're doing very well. Don't take risks. I mean, I'm not trying to be obstinate—'intractable' as you put it. I just . . . just . . ." She snapped around front and sliced the paddle into the flaccid water. "Don't do that again."

Mildly, Cruz purred, "I could have handled it that well."

Wade risked the pain of motion to rotate enough to glare at Cruz.

But Cruz had abandoned banter. He was studying with concern the flood ahead and around him. He stopped the dugout and motioned, *Wait,* to the boats behind.

Wade put his senses on alert. They told him nothing.

Cruz leaned forward and tapped Tingido's sleeping head. He hissed something unintelligible.

Tingido aroused himself quickly, crawled to sitting, and looked around. He asked something, and Cruz replied. Tingido shook his head.

"What's cooking?" Wade muttered.

"Three or four of my people should be in the cove fishing. It's the season and the time of day."

Stroke by stroke, he pushed the dugout forward. Elinor shipped her paddle, watching and listening. Wade glanced back. Everyone but the napping Hurley was on alert. Good. Let him sleep. Less coughing.

Tingido said a single syllable. He raised his hands above his head and clapped. Silence.

Cruz stopped again and motioned the others in beside. "Something's wrong. We should have flushed a dozen screamers out of those thickets, if not with the dugouts, then with Tingido's noise." He pointed behind. "The rest of you wait back there, under the coloca tree. We'll go ahead and call you if it's safe. Elinor, will you hop into Pato's canoe there?"

"No. I'll go." The woman was maddening.

Bernardo Caesar knew when he'd met his Rubicon. Or Waterloo. Or however that went. He studied Elinor impassively. "You'll stay with the dugout at all times."

He turned their boat aside and wound it through close saplings. Wrist-thick tree trunks scraped along both gunwales. They glided past rubber trees, and Wade was beginning to recogize where he was. The ground rose to where he could see it beneath the clear water. They were in Cruz's backyard.

He turned carefully to look behind at Cruz and Tingido. The Indian held the dog's muzzle firmly. Its ragged yellow tail beat back and forth a mile a minute.

Cruz whispered. "No laundry on the line."

Wade strained his eyes. Barely through the trees he could make out the stately white expanse of Minho. The place looked deserted. They moved in until the prow nudged into soggy mud.

Cruz stepped into the water and beached the dugout as Elinor climbed out. He helped Wade over the side. Tingido stood erect on the soil of his birth, and his eyes were misty. With a snap of his fingers, he brought the dog to heel.

Cruz whispered to Elinor, "You're our safety net. Have the boat ready to go." He turned away and started up the gentle incline toward the house.

Her smoky eyes rested on Wade. "I wish you wouldn't go. You aren't fast enough right now."

"Cruz needs more help than just Tingido, and I know the place well. Been around before. It's okay."

She grabbed his hand suddenly and kissed it.

She deserved far more than that obeisant little gesture. He pulled her in against himself and kissed her long and properly. He wished he could forget about Cruz for a while. It would be easy, wrapped around a woman as splendid as this.

He gave her wet eyelids a little peck, smiled, and followed Cruz up the bank.

Cruz stood behind a strawberry guava watching . . . what? Guards!

A man with a rifle stood near the little row of houses that were the servants' quarters. Another waited at the kitchen door. It didn't take a sprawling intellect to figure out there more than these two around.

Wade slipped in beside him.

Cruz's eyes never left the house. "Considering courting?"

"You don't miss a trick, do you?"

"I've been thinking about it myself."

Tingido materialized beside Cruz and whispered.

Cruz nodded. "No fieldworkers out. All the servants and hands are penned up inside. Tingido sees a guard out front. That's three, with probably several more inside. Any idea who?"

"Yeah. The uniforms are Colombian border guards."

Tweed.

# chapter
# 24

WADE FREQUENTLY REFERRED to Cruz's planning sessions as war councils. This really was one. Floating in two canoes, they gathered, with heads together, muttering strategy in hushed tones.

Here came the third canoe with Tingido and two of Hurley's Indians. It nuzzled in against its brethren. Tingido murmured to Cruz.

Cruz translated. "Our clue about the screamers was valid. A launch with several guards is patrolling the river channel on its approach to Minho. They expect us to appear from that direction."

"The only way they could have gotten that is from the Tenumas." Wade rubbed his cheek. "The Tenumas must have a direct link with Colombian officials—Tweed himself, most likely—in order to pass the information on so fast. You know, I'm getting pretty sick and tired of grenades."

"How many enemy in all?" Pahoa whispered.

"At least seven. But if they came in that launch, that's about the maximum."

Tingido muttered again.

Cruz corrected the record. "One or two came in an airplane. He reports a craft in addition to mine sitting out on the strip."

"Tweed's gone modern. No, wait. Can't be Tweed. He didn't have an airstrip, remember? Wanted me to build him one."

"We also surmised that he planned your death before you could start the project. Perhaps he does."

"Seven. Guns." Pahoa wagged his head. "And Morris is very ill. We must hurry with him to his people."

"I know." Marcia leaned forward. "If it's Tweed, he doesn't have any fight with me. I'll take a couple of Hurley's Indians here and come paddling in. Say I'm alone and find out who's in there and what's going on—"

"You couldn't get back out to report." Wade shook his head.

"Maybe, maybe not. I could also feed him any tidbits of false information that might help you out. I'm not afraid of that buzzard. Guys like him are a dime a dozen in New York."

Cruz's dark eyes riveted on her. "He'll have immoral designs on you, possibly on your life as well. He no doubt considers himself above the law. Particularly since, under normal circumstances, I am the law at Minho."

"Immoral designs." She smirked. "Cruz, you're too d— . . . too polite, in your language. I tell you, I've dealt with the top of the line when it comes to sleazy creeps. I can take care of myself."

Wade made an appropriate noise. "I've heard that before. Just prior to yanking you out from under Tiny. You know, though, she could be a pretty good distraction."

"Distraction? I'm the best." And Marcia smiled a smile that could only be described as lascivious.

"Just keep him busy long enough to let us get in the house."

"No." Elinor didn't have to whisper. Her voice was soft as a spring breeze anyway. "Too many guns. Let's ride the flood around Minho and go out to the river. We can find a freighter or mail boat or something out there. Avoid the confrontation."

A rock-hard core surfaced in Cruz's voice, a menacing edge Wade hadn't heard for a long time. "No one usurps Minho as these men have done. No one. I will sleep in my own bed tonight."

Wade need think only a moment about this man who carved an empire and built a dream. He understood. "So how do we work it?"

"You know where the woodbox is up against the back of the house. There's a small door, about a yard wide by a yard high, in the house wall, linking the woodbox with the kitchen. Its purpose is to give the cook access to stovewood without leaving the house. We'll enter that way, if you think your injuries will permit."

214

"They'll permit."

"Then this is the plan."

Julius Caesar's forte was trouncing barbarians. Bernardo Caesar upheld the tradition well, and he'd do the trouncing without benefit of the legions and slings and huge catapults—the only thing Wade remembered from high school Latin. All Cruz had were a couple gimpy sidekicks and Elinor's prayers. She told him so. It would be enough.

Tingido waded ashore and positioned himself. Wade and Cruz slipped in behind bushes a hundred feet apart. Now here came two Indians in a canoe, with Marcia, up to the muddy slope beyond the back door.

Marcia should be an actress in moving pictures. She bounded out of the dugout as soon as it touched bottom. "I can't believe it! Civilization! A *gen-you-wine* house! And people with clothes on! Oh, brother, am I glad to get here!" Then again, maybe it wasn't all acting.

She jogged, slipping in the wet dirt, straight up to the astounded backyard guard and hugged him. He stared agape at her. He glanced about, gripped her elbow, and ushered her inside.

Cruz reached the woodbox first. Fluid as floodwater, he poured into it and disappeared. By the time Wade got there and lifted the lid Cruz was gone. The little framed door, hinged at the top, swayed slightly back and forth. Wade managed to stuff his body inside and get the lid about down by the time the guard stepped out again onto the back stoop.

He waited for a count of ten. He must make no sound; especially, he mustn't scrape the sides. This woodbox, like a drum, would magnify the slightest noise. Finally, he could take the dark stuffiness no more. He pushed on the little door. He pushed further. No one in the kitchen. It took him a while to draw his crippled hip through.

He was halfway to the dining room door when Magdalena walked in. Cruz's cook knew Wade as he knew her. The wide half-Indian clapped her hand over her mouth. Silently she ran to him and wrapped around him in a hug any bear could take lessons from. Wade returned her embrace, chose two butcher knives from her

215

collection by the stove, and flattened against the wall near the dining room door.

Magdalena met his eye; she knew what he needed. She squared her ample shoulders, took a deep breath, and marched back out. Wade listened.

In Spanish, Magdalena asked how many she should expect to serve at dinner.

Tweed's voice replied she had already asked that.

She was upset; she did not remember. Very sorry.

Tweed's voice commented bitterly on incompetence. Only the three. No, add one more. A young lady had just arrived. And serve it elegantly.

Elegantly. Of course, sir.

Magdalena came popping back in the door. She whispered, "One in the salon and two others in the study. And that lady."

"Remember Marcia Lewis? No lady. But *you* are, Maggie."

He slipped out into the silent, vacant acre of dining room, past the ornately carved chairs and the serpentine sideboard from Seville. It was good to be home, to work in familiar, civilized surroundings once more. He revelled in solid walls and the elaborate vaulted ceiling. Cruz knew how to build, and Wade appreciated all over again the man's desire to reclaim Minho from its usurpers.

He peeked through the great double doors into the salon. Marcia perched on the edge of the red horsehair sofa, waving her arms and describing the Great War. And in the overstuffed chair across from her, like a king enthroned, sat Tweed with his back to Wade.

"You wouldn't believe it! These bomb things going off all over! They yelled at us to come get them, but those two Indians and I weren't about to come close to that mess. We took off. It wasn't our fight anyway. And then we got lost. And we about starved. I don't know this country at all and neither do they, you know. And so much water. It was just horrible."

"Yes, yes, I can see it was dreadful."

"Oh, Mr. Tweed, you can't imagine how glad I am to be here in your home and out of that horrid jungle! And it's a lovely home, too, I must say. So elegant. So Old World. So—so welcome in the midst of all these *bushes*. Your other home in Colombia is lovely, too, of course, but this one . . . You have fine taste."

"Thank you, my dear. Of all my estates, I think I like this one best. I believe you'll appreciate the bath amenities here. Porcelain fixtures, indoors. You'll want to freshen up before dinner, I'm sure, but I've a few questions first, if you're not too weary."

"Sure. Anything I can do to help those people." She settled deeper into the sofa. "Anything short of going back there, that is."

"No. That won't be necessary, rest assured."

Wade didn't listen as Tweed started pumping Marcia, except to notice that she could play dumb with the best of them. He listened more for action in the study.

There it was. Someone beyond the far door dropped something heavy. Wade slipped inside the double doors, moved silently across the plush carpet toward Tweed.

Marcia never once glanced at him, bless her. "Oh, and Mr. Tweed, you should have seen some of the things we had to eat! You wouldn't believe it! Why, back in New York we call that stuff 'vermin' and put a bounty on it." She giggled, leaning forward to tap him on the knee. If that didn't distract, nothing would.

He was behind the chair now. A distraught voice in the study cried out. Tweed sat erect. Wade reached around and grabbed the septum of Tweed's nose between finger and thumb. He hauled the boastful head back, and poised a butcher knife just so at the flabby throat.

Quick as a fox, Marcia bolted forward and jerked Tweed's pistol from the official-looking holster at his side. She ran to the study and threw the door open. With a broad, hearty grin, she flashed an okay sign to Wade before she disappeared inside.

Moments later Cruz steeped out into his salon. Cruz always carried himself with grace, but when he was in his home, master of his hearth, there was a special mien about him. You looked at him and knew without question to whom this opulence belonged. With measured stride he crossed the salon and handed Wade one of two pistols.

Only then did Wade release Tweed and step back. He tucked the knife in his belt.

Tweed twisted in the chair. "You!"

"Why not me?"

217

"Of course. She hired you. I should have expected you."

Marcia leaned in the far doorway watching. Tingido pushed past her and brought Cruz a drapery cord.

Cruz slipped his pistol into his belt at the small of his back. The long, graceful fingers began coiling and uncoiling the cord with excruciating slowness. "Explain your presence in my home, Mr. Tweed."

"Ah, yes. Bernardo Cruz, am I right? I've heard of you, sir." Tweed started to rise with hand extended. Wade jammed him back into the chair. The handshake died aborning. "Your hostility is misplaced, sir. I'm here on official business. I've heard of your legendary hospitality and presumed to make myself comfortable awaiting your return. This man," he pointed to Wade, "is an escaped suspect. I might add he's without papers. I certainly have no argument to pose with you, sir, official or otherwise, but you do ill to harbor him."

Cruz tossed the cord to Wade. "Mr. Tweed, I'm not finished with you. In a sense, I haven't started with you. But we'll deal later. Right now you will do exactly as I say, in the way I say it. Keep in mind that, though your people may by chance kill some of us, you will be first to die."

"You're not under suspicion—yet—Señor Cruz. I strongly recommend your cooperation in this police action."

"Hey, chum." Wade flicked the back of the thick neck. "You're in Brazil now, remember?"

"And the men with whom you dealt so harshly, Sr. Cruz, are Brazilian officials."

The black eyes snapped to Wade.

Wade poked Tweed again. "Why?"

"To find Dr. Morris Hurley and fly him to safety." Tweed twisted his bulk around. "The very job I so graciously offered you, Travers. You should not have fled. Glory could have been yours. Now it will be others'. In fact, I no longer have work for you building an airstrip. You may recall that you said you had built a road near Manaos capable of taking heavy trucks in the dry season."

"Yeah."

"Using that germ of an idea, I built a four-lane road, a magnificent piece of engineering. Perfect landing strip."

"Good. Then I can have my passport back."

"Alas, we still have to discuss charges of unlawful flight and crossing international lines without papers. However, the speed with which these problems are dispatched may well depend in large part upon your cooperation now."

"Yep," Marcia chimed in. "Sounds just like your average New York City councilman."

Cruz dipped his head toward Tweed. "Stay with him. I'll see who the others are. We can plan from there. Where's Tingido?"

Wade pointed. The battered warrior stood by the door ready for his next assignment. The man's resilience amazed Wade. That Cruz permitted the dog inside the house also amazed him. Cruz, Marcia, and Tingido disappeared into the study. The dog wandered off toward the kitchen.

Tweed fulminated about his sidearm and other things, but Wade didn't listen. He didn't understand this mess, and no way he sorted it came out right. Just like religion.

An official in a perky beige uniform came out of the study presently with Tingido at his side. He marched outside without so much as a nod in Tweed's direction. Wade noticed his sidearm was back in its holster.

Cruz and Marcia emerged with the other, a man in his late twenties, it appeared. Wade returned his sidearm to its rightful owner. Cruz handed Tweed his and offered Marcia the chair. With uncharacteristic tact she refused and sat down on the sofa.

Cruz flopped, exhausted. "Be seated, gentlemen."

Wade lowered himself into one corner of the sofa.

Cruz waved toward the young man perched on the sofa beside Wade. "Hernando Vargueza, Wade Travers. Sergeant Vargueza is with the Brazilian consulate out of Manaos."

"Your servant." Wade used English because Cruz did and extended a hand. The man's grip was firm and confident.

"The sergeant's companion is instructing Tweed's guards regarding our arrival. We may now move about freely. Tingido is ringing in the rest of our party. Also, I asked him to send Hector up here. You remember Hector."

"Of course." Cruz's foreman, his second-in-command. Only by

chance of birth were their roles not reversed. Hector was nearly as brilliant as his master.

The sergeant smiled. "Señor Cruz, you are a legend of sorts, and I can see why. To best the both of us so quickly."

"I am not Macunaima."

"In some quarters you are."

"Who's Macunaima?" Marcia looked from face to face.

"Paul Bunyan. Super hero." Wade threw in another Northern European name for Cruz to file. "Peer Gynt."

"The military advantage lies with the side fighting on its own familiar ground, and with him who can employ the element of surprise. I had both," Cruz said.

Turning to Tweed, he continued, "The sergeant tells me that when Dr. Hurley is found, he is to be flown out immediately in your airplane using your pilot. Written orders to that effect. I assume that's your craft waiting on my strip."

"Correct." Tweed smiled at Marcia. "I will instruct my pilot to return and bring you out also, so that you might join Dr. Hurley. I assume you've been talking to him, but almost certainly you'll want a more formal and private interview."

Marcia glanced at Wade. She smiled at Tweed. "Why, thank you. Very perceptive. I appreciate it."

"Then you may ready your plane and aviator. Dr. Hurley is here." Cruz rose stiffly. "Excuse me momentarily. My foreman." He got up and crossed to a nimble and athletic Indian no younger than he. They muttered head to head several minutes, shooting glances at the others as they talked. With a brisk nod, Cruz ended the conversation, and Hector left the room.

Cruz ambled back. "By restricting my staff to their quarters, Mr. Tweed, you put normal daily operations considerably behind. I have gotten the wheels rolling again."

How should he say this tactfully? Wade threw tact to the winds. "Wait, Cruz. Let's use your plane and pilot. You fly Hurley out, and then we'll know he's going straight to Manaos."

The sergeant pulled a large foolscap envelope from his inside tunic pocket. "Written instructions specify Mr. Tweed's craft, sir. We are not authorized to use any other plane."

Cruz's dark eyes riveted Wade's. "I live under Brazilian authority and submit to it cheerfully." Was he saying something else? Wade couldn't tell.

Ragged and worn, battered and torn, and coughing uncontrollably, Dr. Morris Hurley appeared in the doorway.

"Miss Lewis," Cruz purred evenly. "You owe me three thousand dollars."

*chapter*
# 25

AVIATORS DURING THE GREAT WAR flew resplendent in helmet, goggles, jacket, and scarf. When temperature and humidity shoulder each other around the hundred-degree mark, jackets and scarves are extraneous. But aviators are aviators, and, perhaps as an extension of his penchant for putting servants in brocade livery, Tweed would have his aviator correctly attired, or bust. Wade couldn't understand why the poor man didn't bust.

Nattily encased in jacket and so on, the pilot climbed into the front cockpit of Tweed's delicate little bi-plane and began fiddling with controls. Various parts moved back and forth, up and down. Cruz himself helped Dr. Hurley into the rear of the two cockpits and strapped him in. They exchanged words, nodding. Cruz stepped back.

With a mighty heave, one of Tweed's men gave the propeller a spin. The engine coughed like Hurley and took on the third try. Blue smoke billowed. Dr. Hurley's head disappeared briefly as he endured a coughing fit, then popped back up. The helmet and goggles waved a signal to Tweed. Bucking and lurching across the uneven ground, the airplane trundled forward.

Wade had watched airplanes before, but not many. His only intimate contact with one had been that crash he had ferreted out in the rain forest. Once those birds go down, they lose any glamor they might have had in the sky.

But this one . . . Like an ungainly condor it waddled to the far end of the strip. As stiffly as Wade with his hip, it turned. Another cloud of blue smoke boiled up. The engine howled. And here it came, at a walk, at a trot, at a run—bumpety bumpety.

Then, smooth as glass, it skimmed the ground, lifted above the trees, disappeared beyond the green wall.

Wade wagged his head. "Cruz, I think you just made a fatal error."

The Sergeant scowled at Tweed. "It's flying off to the west. Manaos is east."

"Just swinging out and around so as to follow the river. We won't be able to see it from here, of course, but rest assured it will fly east above the river."

Marcia gave Wade a shove, her eyes blazing. "Don't you see? This jerk's not going to let Hurley live to see Manaos! And he thinks he's going to fly me to oblivion next! Cruz, how could you—?" She stopped and craned her neck skyward.

A whining howl drifted in from beyond the trees. Here it came soaring east, three hundred feet off the ground and still climbing. Something brown came tumbling out, and Wade's heart leaped into his mouth. It was only an empty jacket. Moments later, a yellow scarf floated down through the air.

"What—?" Tweed gaped.

Cruz turned and started for the house with the smugness of a victor, so Wade fell in beside him. Marcia latched onto Wade's other arm, gripping tightly.

Cruz briefly laid a hand on Wade's shoulder. "You worry too much, my friend."

Wade listened to the distant eastbound hum. "I've known you ten years, and I still keep underestimating you."

Tweed burst between them, shoved them apart by the sheer force of his bulk. Marcia staggered aside, wrenching Wade's arm. His hip stabbed so painfully that sweat popped out on his face.

"That's not my pilot!" the man screamed.

"Your pilot was indisposed, so I substituted mine, Mr. Tweed. Hector is competent at the controls. I assure you, your plane will arrive safely in Manaos. That is the destination we all want, is it not? As specified in the written orders."

Tweed glared with a fury Wade could not have imagined. He began to see how Tweed might send the troops out to skewer the simple foreigner whom he thought was crossing him.

Sergeant Vargueza frowned. "I fail to see a reason for your ire, sir. Except for the minor matter of which aviator—"

Tweed yanked his pistol before Wade could move and waggled it under Cruz's nose. "You're under arrest for obstructing the duty of an officer and—"

"Now just one minute!" The young sergeant had starch, all right. "You've no arresting authority in this district, Mr. Tweed, nor will I let you intimidate a citizen of—"

Words to the wind. The enraged Tweed was in control, and he knew it. It was his guards with the firepower. The sergeant had only one other officer with him, a youth even more callow than himself. And Cruz's motley crew? Forget it.

Tweed flapped arms and barked orders with the hysteria of a man possessed. He sent troops out to find his pilot. He sent troops to ready his launch. He sent troops to guard these "impudent scum."

Unintimidated, Cruz stood quietly watching the frenzy. He glanced at Wade. "I suggest our Mr. Tweed is driven by some extremity greater than circumstances in the corridor."

Wade nodded. "As frantic as he is, I'd guess Hurley's mess might extend clear up to Bogotá."

Marcia pressed in against Wade. "You mean, he's afraid the people above him'll give it to him in the neck if he doesn't get rid of Hurley?"

"Maybe."

"And me?"

"Also maybe."

"What are we gonna do?"

Cruz studied the distance. "Tweed had the initiative. Let him act, then respond."

Wade lowered his voice. "Where's Elinor?"

"On the edge of the field a few minutes ago." Marcia looked around. "I don't know. Pato or Tiny, either."

"Good. Hope they stay out of sight. Pato especially. One of Tweed's men is walletless because of him. The guy could be here."

Tweed's men found his pilot much too soon. They escorted the fellow, still groggy and staggering, to Cruz's bi-plane and boosted him into the seat. A tall, tough-looking lieutenant hopped into the seat behind. Someone passed him a large-bore rifle.

Flaps wagged, the engine coughed clouds of smoke. In a pattern now familiar, the little craft lumbered to the end of the strip and turned around.

"Which one's faster?" Wade asked, not certain that an accurate answer was possible.

"This one. Newer, larger engine, more power."

"In other words, as soon as your bird gets airborne, Dr. Hurley's gone."

"I don't know how to warn Hector. This airplane will reach him long before we can."

Wade sized up the enemy and saw nothing reassuring. None of them stood close enough to make an easy grab for a gun, and Tweed was already headed for the temporary docks. Wade would have to run and dive to snatch a gun, and hope that Cruz wasn't thinking of doing the same thing in the same direction. His hip would never forgive him for this.

A movement at the far end of the field caught his eye. As the plane began its taxi, Tiny steeped out into the clearing. He hauled back, his arm extended behind his head.

Cruz's voice, tight and controlled, muttered, "I believe Tiny's about to dispose of his souvenir, as you requested."

The plane came licking down the bumpy field at full gallop, engine screaming. Its stout little wheels lifted free of the grasping, greedy, binding earth.

Wade knew what was coming and steeled himself, but the blast threw his gun-shy nerves into a panic anyway. With a flash of orange Tiny's grenade exploded under the skybound creature's belly. Silk and dope ignited instantly in a whooshing cloud of plane and dense black smoke.

The two men tumbled out, hit the ground running, scurried for cover as the fuel tank blew. Cruz's bird melted, quickly and gloriously like a moth in a candle flame, in a stupendous fire that roared to heaven.

Wade didn't wait to watch the pyrotechnic display. He lunged for the nearest rifle, let his momentum carry the fellow to the ground. His left arm, though, was much too weak and this fellow much too strong for his right alone to handle. The guard wrenched away and swung his rifle toward Wade's belly.

With a banshee shriek, Marcia pounced on the guy, her arms and legs flailing like those airplane propellers. It spoiled his aim; the rifle fired harmlessly at distant treetops. And it gave Wade time to line up one solid punch that flattened his opponent.

"Good girl, boss!" Wade scooped up the rifle and struggled upright with his one good leg. "Where's Cruz?"

"He shouted something about the wireless. I don't know."

"The docks. Stop Tweed."

The whole Brazilian navy was embarking on the temporary docks Cruz used during flood, when his permanent dry-season docks and the village itself lay underwater. The guards were pouring into the launch they probably had arrived in. Tweed and a couple of his minions were scurrying aboard another, a pretty little boat with Brazilian registry.

From somewhere to his left, Wade heard Sergeant Vargueza's distraught tenor: "He's absconding with my vessel!"

It took Wade a while, hopping and waddling, to get down to the docks, even with a helpful assist from Marcia. Tiny and Pato were already there. Cruz came running out of the house with a shotgun in each hand. Where was Elinor? It didn't matter. Better that she stay behind, in safety.

Cruz waved toward the only other power vessel in sight, his tired old launch that passed as a tugboat. He used it to maneuver freighters in the narrow confines of his docking area. Wade couldn't imagine it grinding all the way to Manaos.

Apparently Cruz could. He jumped aboard with Pato and Tiny right behind him. Impatient with Wade's delay, Vargueza grabbed his arm and manhandled him to the boat.

The Brazilian vessel pulled away. Her engine whine rose a notch. She churned her way three hundred yards down the channel, and the guards' launch had not yet cast off.

Wade grabbed the edge of the cabin roof and swung himself the three steps down into the cabin. His left arm reminded him he shouldn't have done that.

Cruz was fiddling vainly with controls. "Pop the hatch, and prime the fuel pump."

Wade grabbed the brass ring and yanked the cover at his feet. "Might have water in your line, too. When's the last time you lit this thing off?"

"Six months ago."

There is no way to upend oneself, head below floor level, and avoid pain in a torn hip. He did his best to ignore it. The job now was to get this junk moving.

Why was Tweed so obsessed that he'd go to such lengths to pursue the ailing Dr. Hurley? There had to be more to the doctor than simply a few notes on possible slave trade. And how much further was Tweed prepared to go?

The motor wheezed and sputtered and made a noisy protest, but it ran. And it stayed running.

Cruz yelled, "Cast off!" at almost the same moment Pato yelled "No, Elinor! Don'!"

Wade abandoned the hatch. He lurched frantically to his feet and discovered himself capable of running, after all.

Pato stood at the railing near the bow, screaming at the river. The guards' launch had left dock, finally. It was a hundred feet out now, and rapidly picking up speed. And out of the drowned forest, directly in front of it, came Elinor in a dugout.

Either the launch pilot failed to see Elinor, or he failed to realize that a dugout that size weighs a good fifteen hundred pounds or more. He bore down on her full throttle, and she on him full paddle.

Now Wade was out on the bow railing with Pato, yelling just as loudly. There was nothing he could do. He watched helplessly, hopelessly, as that insane woman threw her life away for nothing, and his world turned an ugly gray.

Futility.

The dugout slipped from view beyond the launch's hulk. The launch jolted. No harsh crash—just a crushing, rushing sound with muted edges. Men cried out as the launch listed gently to port. Her stern began a slow, graceful swing to starboard until the boat lay wallowing nearly broadside to Cruz's tug. Guards were jumping off the slanted deck, like fleas abandoning a sinking dog.

The dugout had stove her almost squarely at the cutwater, and her shattered bow had swallowed the front five feet of it. She took the canoe along, like a grotesque cigar in her mouth, as she continued her idle circles through the flat, listless water.

Elinor—

A white head bobbed to the surface.

Cruz had the engine wound up tight enough to send pistons through the hull. Pato dropped to his belly and stretched his arms down over the side. Tiny hung onto a rail and leaned far out. The sergeant tried unsuccessfully to hook his leg around a hawser bitt, the better to reach farther. Even Marcia was in there ready to grab.

Wade sat on the bow deck, braced his good leg against a stanchion, and gripped Pato's ankles. Emboldened, the boy put his life in Wade's hands and squirmed out over the water until only his thighs touched wood.

Pato lunged and jerked against Wade's grip. "Gotchit! I gotchit!" His soprano pealed joyously.

Wade's left arm felt the fire of a thousand branding irons. But this was one handful of light and life that he would not let go.

Then many willing hands were there, dragging Pato back onto the deck, reaching for the white head, crowding around so closely they jostled one another.

Pato looked at his ankles, then at Wade. "S'okay, now."

"Right." Wade turned him loose. He tried to hop to his feet, but his body rebelled flatly. Through the confusion of legs, Wade glimpsed the launch. She listed nearly ninety degrees now, less than two hundred feet from the dock with her slimy green keel peeked casually out of the water.

Cruz was pouring it on, picking up speed. They slowed out onto the river proper now; another hundred feet off shore and Cruz would have good solid current under him. Wade looked for Tweed's launch and was shocked to see it so far ahead.

Elinor sat leaning against the cabin wall, all dripping wet, with her legs stretched out across the deck. The deck here was shorter than her legs; her bare feet dangled over the side. She was trying alternately to breathe and to clear her waterlogged lungs. She didn't seem to be accomplishing either very well.

Wade plopped down heavily beside her.

The endless blue eyes rolled over to him, and she smiled almost apologetically. Speaking did not come easily; she nearly gagged trying to inhale. "When Tiny stopped . . . stopped the airplane, I knew Tweed would use a motorboat next. So I ran down . . . down to . . ." She coughed. "I was going to stave in the other. Tweed's boat. But I couldn't get in front of it in time, before it pulled away."

"*Why*?!"

"Cruz had those two guns. You carried a rifle. Tweed's men were all armed. I was afraid of a . . . a gun battle. A war. Too many people have died already."

"And you risked . . . Just to . . ." Wade sighed and rubbed his face. He couldn't look at her lest he strangle her. Of all the insane, foolish, magnificent . . ."Pato, go put the cover back on the hatch, will you? Before someone breaks a leg."

She had shed some of the water in her lungs. Her voice was stronger now. "I'm sorry you're angry with me. I did what I could. What I had to."

"I know. I'm not angry with you. I'm mad at me for being upset with you. I just—I don't know how to say it." He forced his eyes to meet hers. "Don't pull something like that again."

She smiled. "I doubt I'll ever have the opportunity."

Suddenly he wanted to kiss her more than he had ever yearned to kiss Marcia—or any other woman, for that matter. But with four other people standing around watching, he dare not. It wouldn't bother him. He was ready to tell the world. But Elinor, modest, sweet Elinor, might burn with embarrassment. He'd hate himself if he did that.

He had to do something, though, so he stood up. And he knew what else he wanted to do, now that the excitement was past and his blood had cooled. He worked his way aft and limped the three steps down into the cabin.

Cruz perched on a stool at the wheel, his left hand draped over the wheel and his right diddling dials, trying to fine-tune an engine with basically two speeds—running and not running.

229

Wade settled into a corner and braced himself to take the weight off his left leg. "She did it to avoid a firefight."

"She's all right?"

"Think so. Alert. Her voice sounded steady enough. No visible marks or problems."

Cruz squinted silently at the river ahead.

"Where we going?"

"Hector will set down at Tefe to refuel, eat, perhaps rest overnight. We'll go there first."

"Couldn't raise Tefe on the wireless?"

"Tweed destroyed it."

"We have enough fuel?"

"Yes. Tweed might not. His craft burns more, and he's pushing harder."

"You're not exactly lollygagging. Think you might blow something?"

"She runs better cranked up." Cruz sighed. "It appears I'll not sleep in my own bed tonight, after all."

Silence.

How should Wade put this? Directly. That's how.

"Hear you're considering courting."

Cruz glanced at him for the first time. "What are your intentions?"

"Honorable. Serious."

"This isn't another of your annual infatuations?"

"No. Marcia mighta been. But this one's real. You know, you coulda phrased that a little nicer."

"That *was* the polite phrasing." He studied the glistening water, the dancing ripples as they caught the golden evening sun. "You never met my wife."

"She was ill and not receiving guests when I first met you. No, I never knew her."

"Ill. I thought it only fitting to go back to the region of my ancestry for a bride. She was of a well-bred family whose lands were only two miles distant from the house where I was born."

"Romantic."

"But not practical. European women, by and large, do not adapt

230

well to the rain forest. She didn't. She spent the most miserable eighteen years of her life at Minho, from when it began as little more than a grass hut, until I built the house you know. Rest assured, she informed me of her misery quite regularly."

"And now you think you've found a noble lady who thrives in the rain forest. The perfect mate. No complaining."

"Noble. Yes. Brave and noble. What she did just now was noble. Her whole being is noble. Without artifice. Such women are rare beyond imagination."

"Love her?"

Silence. "Yes."

"Then we got a problem. 'Cause so do I."

"Enough to fight for her?"

Wade didn't have to stop and think, but he did pause a brief moment to consider the possible consequences. "Yeah."

"So do I."

It was the slightest noise, almost not distinct enough to be called a noise. Wade's head snapped toward the cabin doorway. Cruz twisted on his stool.

She stood there, backlighted radiantly in evening light, with her hands pressed to her cheeks, and she was staring at them with her unbelievable eyes brimming. Shock. That was the only way Wade could interpret her expression. She was shocked, as if it had never occurred to her that a man might care about her.

Cruz woke up first. "Come in."

She shook her head. The brimming eyes spilled over. "I never want to hear anything like that again. Not from either of you." She wheeled and ran back up the three steps, though on a boat this size there was nowhere to run.

"Y'know, Cruz, unless one of us gets a whole lot better at managing intractable women, we might both lose her."

*chapter*
# 26

IF YOU THOUGHT ABOUT IT, there are far worse places in the world to work. Here was the broad, silver expanse of the river, swimming in starlight. The night had cleared crystal bright, and in the sky overhead, this was the most dazzling time of year. And in just a short while, dawn would alter the whole scene into a brand-new tapestry of vivid colors. Sure, you had a lot of fangs and jaws out there waiting to get you, but there was magnificent beauty, too, and grandeur.

Grandeur. The endless reaches of velvet green rain forest; the great river herself, vast beyond imagining, a symphony of superlatives. Wade was lucky to be here, let alone be able to forge an exciting career here. He could be bolting handles onto cooking pots in Cleveland, or something.

The only thing he lacked now was a pipeful of tobacco.

This little old jalopy of a motorboat was performing a lot more admirably than Wade would have expected. It churned on and on, plowing ahead, but hating to as its engine roared in contralto and occasionally hiccupped. How far were they from Tweed? How close to Tefe? Wade couldn't judge their speed well, but Tiny claimed he knew Tefe when he saw it.

Wade sat on the forward deck with his tired legs stretched out, leaning back against the edge of the windshield. Tiny at the wheel could see around him well enough. He would have supposed Cruz to be asleep, sprawled on deck somewhere like the others—it was past four in the morning—but here came the *patrão* wandering forward, looking lost.

Cruz paused and squatted beside him. "Mind?"

"Welcome."

The weary Spaniard settled himself against the side cabin window, pulled his knees up, and draped his arms over them. In the humid silence he stared at infinity off their starboard beam.

Wade yearned for some tobacco. "Saw you talking to Elinor earlier. Didn't hear words, but I watched her face. She's upset."

"Very."

"Funny, the difference between those two women. Marcia'd love to hear two men fight over her. She'd goad 'em on and watch the spectacle. Shoulda been born a classical Roman. Perfect Colosseum patron."

"She'd cheer for the lions."

"Yeah. And Elinor'd be out in the arena with them."

Cruz nodded. "And that, my friend, is the difference between them."

They floated alone together in silver splendor. This little tub was moving right along, yet the river sprawled so huge that the distant shores passed languidly.

A meteor drew a yard-long chalk mark across the vault overhead. It reminded Wade that there are such things. Casually, he began watching for others. "When we got to Hurley's stronghold, and you were still pretty stove up, you and he did a lot of conversing in his library. Anything helpful?"

"Let's see. To start with we discussed favorite authors. He seemed dismayed that mine is Joaquim Marcia Machado de Assis."

"Never heard of him."

"Hurley did, which surprised me because Hurley's American. Few Yankees can discuss Brazilian authors intelligently. Machado died about fifteen years ago. For example, in his *Memórias Pótumas de Brás Cubas* . . ."

"'Posthumous Memoirs of a Small Winner'? Or 'Epitaph of a Small Winner'?"

"Elements of both, actually. Brilliant work. After his death he is balancing the pluses against the minuses of his life. He says, 'I found that I had a small surplus, which provides the final negative of this chapter of negatives; I had no progeny. I transmitted to no one the legacy of our misery.'"

Wade snorted. "Yeah, I can see where Hurley'd be dismayed."

"From that he told me that my favorite book of Scripture is Ecclesiastes. He's correct."

"What's his?"

"The Psalms; and in the New Testament, Philippians."

Wade twisted his top half to stare at Cruz. "You remember every syllable of that conversation?" He straightened around again to the front. "Don't know why that keeps surprising me. You always do."

"This one especially vividly. He's so profound intellectually, and yet so simplistic in some theories. Too much so. I found it impossible to accept his approach to religion. I couldn't find the answers I want the way he says they should be found."

"Depends, I suppose, on how desperate you are." Wade watched the river and sky and knew without turning that Cruz was studying him.

"You forget nothing either."

Wade smiled. "Don't I wish. I do remember Hurley saying you have to surrender your intellect. Don't try to think Christ out logically, just buy what he has to offer. I'm about ready to try it, but then I don't have as much to surrender as you do. Never was big on philosophy and that stuff to start with. I sure need to do something, though."

There went another chalk mark, fainter this time because the sky's gray was turning to pearl. The eastern horizon beyond the river glowed purple-pink.

"Do you ever pray?"

Wade watched the sparkling sky fade dot by dot into uniform brightness. "I've been known to mouth a heartfelt 'Lord, get me out of this!' When the Jivaros are trying to make your head into a paperweight, it cures atheism real fast. But no. Not the way you mean."

"I grew up reciting beads and saying novenas. It was part of the natural order of things. I never, as a child, wondered to whom I was reciting. It didn't matter then."

234

"Maybe that's what Hurley was talking about when he said, 'Like this child, Pato.'"

Silence, but for the drumming engine.

Surrender. Giving up. Diverse memories, from *McGuffey's Readers* to the last month's horrors, arrayed themselves in front of Wade's thoughts. "Cruz? Tell me what's wrong with giving up."

"It prevents you from reaching your goal, whatever the goal may be."

"I know, I know. You never would have built Minho if you'd given up. You're not the one to ask. Every reader we went through in grade school pounded into us never to give up, too."

"Perseverence is a virtue."

"And surrender's a vice. But it feels good, Cruz. No burden. The struggle fades away. You're at peace."

"When did you ever give up? I've never known you to quit."

"Yes, you have. You were there. When I went down under that grenade. I was just thinking about that."

"Down. I doubt you realize how down you were. Absolutely limp; no muscle tone at all. I thought for a while your neck was broken. We were out on the river and well on our way before your eyes opened. I wouldn't call it surrender when you can't move and you're unconscious, or nearly so."

"That's the whole thing, dontcha see? I couldn't do anything. Nothing. I *had* to let someone else handle everything because I couldn't handle it myself. Now extend that. Hurley says to see God we have to be cleaned with blood. But that's not something we can do by ourselves, so we have to surrender and let God take care of it. Like I did. Give up because you can't do it and let him handle it. Same thing, Cruz. Exactly the same thing."

"How did you just describe it? Peace? The struggle fades?"

"Yeah, only stronger than the words sound like. Deep. Real deep. Intense."

The rosy splash across the east turned yellow. The sun was here again.

Tiny thumped on the windshield from inside. He jabbed a finger off toward the south shore.

"Tefe coming up." Wade squinted and marveled at Tiny's sharp vision.

Cruz rolled to his feet and offered Wade a hand.

He accepted. "Wake up the troops?"

"When we're closer. Ask the sergeant to look for his vessel there, send a message ahead to Hector if Hector's continued on already."

"Will the wireless be open yet?"

"Probably not. We'll pound on doors."

What Wade wanted even more than pipe tobacco was breakfast. Or lunch or dinner or something off a guava bush. Anything. And if he were famished, poor old Tiny must be downright hollow inside. Thoughts of religious philosophy and God's role in the scheme of things slipped away, displaced by more immediate demands.

They cruised the waterfront first, looking for the boat Tweed had commandeered. The flood this year was as high as Wade had ever seen it. The houses upslope from the floating waterfront were nearly up to their bellies in water, despite their being perched high on stilts that usually kept them above it. Most of the waterfront activity didn't change with flood. The houseboats and fishermen and floating stores and businesses bobbed year round at whatever water level the river deemed their lot.

A couple decent vessels were moored along the Tefe River side of town. None resembled the sergeant's launch.

Apparently Tiny knew the town better than Wade did. He refused to relinquish the wheel until he had nudged the boat in against a slim little planked craft with rotting bumpers. He threw a line across and hopped over onto the flat gray deck. The whale then jumped up and down until a sleepy head appeared from a reed-roofed cabin amidships. He gave his breakfast order clearly and insistently and sat on the weathered deck to wait.

Wade smirked. "Tiny has his priorities, and business is hardly ever at the top of the list."

"I like the way he thinks. I could almost eat worms." Marcia dug all ten fingers into her scalp to scratch. "*Almost*, I said. I suppose worms are available somewhere in this . . . this place, but I don't expect to see any, all right?"

"You're learning. Still got your boodle?"

"Yeah."

"How much Brazilian currency's left?"

"I don't know. Let me step below and look." She paused in the cabin doorway. "How much you need?"

"Breakfast and some wholesale bribery, probably." She disappeared beyond the doorway.

With the sergeant tagging along, Cruz bounded gracefully from this deck to Tiny's and onto the floating dock. They walked rapidly beyond sight among the hodgepodge of boats and rafts.

Breakfast arrived on deck in a big bowl with little bowls. Scoop your own. The sleepy Indian woman set out a basket of papayas and guavas, too, so they were dining at one of the more elegant restaurants in town. Wade thanked her in florid Portuguese, and she radiated into the nicest smile.

Marcia plopped a big glob of the goo into a bowl and studied it in consternation. "What is it? Manioc, right?"

Wade sniffed. "Right. Farinha cooked in goat's milk."

"That's disgusting. But I'm too hungry to care." She popped a spoonful into her mouth and swallowed it without taking a breath. "If only Harry could see me now."

"Gonna be glad to get back to music and motor cars?"

Her voice softened. "Isn't it weird? Yeah, I guess so. But this adventure—that's what you'd call it, an adventure—is the greatest thing that's ever happened to me. It's just so completely different from anything I ever experienced . . . And I get to *do* things! Like when you tried to take that guard down, and I jumped on him."

"Pitching grenades."

"Yeah! And shooting a rifle and helping haul you up over the side of a dugout. Jiminy, you're heavy! And at Cruz's place. Hey, I had a major part in that Tweed thing. Big part! You see? Not just talking and talking and talking and then writing down notes and beating out a story on the oldest Royal standard in the office because the bigger cheeses all get the newer typewriters." She inhaled deeply and downed another gob.

"Keep at it. Maybe someday you'll be a bigger cheese."

"A woman? Forget it. We fetch the coffee and do the fluff stories. Even if I score real big with this Hurley story, it won't last. I'm not fooling myself. We don't become editors. Except maybe of the Society section, and after all this? Dealing with society snobs? No thanks. That's what I mean. Right now I'm just as much a part of the operation as you or Cruz. That's what I mean about doing." She waved her spoon at Elinor across the deck. "You, too. You know what I'm talking about. We're not women here. We're people."

Elinor smiled, a touching, haunted look. "Yes, I know."

Marcia kept babbling, but Wade didn't listen. He sifted back through those last few sentences, trying to figure out what would bring such a poignant note of sadness to Elinor so unexpectedly— for she seemed to be more or less getting over her upset of the night before.

Wade saw a black head navigating among the reed roofs and scooped two more bowls of breakfast glop. He handed one to Cruz as the sergeant and *patrão* climbed aboard.

Cruz waved a finger at Tiny. "Can you obtain from her enough food to last us a day or two? And quickly."

Wade purred in Portuguese, "Our boat isn't big enough."

"*Sim.*" Tiny stuck his head inside the reed-roofed cabin and commenced a heated argument with the lady inside.

Wade shifted to English for Marcia and Pato's sakes. "What's on?"

Cruz settled down cross-legged with his bowl. "Tweed ran out of gas and had his people paddling for four hours. They lost much of their time their faster boat gained on us. He's less than an hour ahead and running low-grade fuel."

"Think his engine'll foul up before he reaches Manaos?"

"Devoutly to be hoped, but I doubt it. However, it should slow him down some, unless he has a good mechanic aboard."

"What about Hector?"

"No one on the wireless yet this morning in Manaos. The operator here will deliver a message as soon as he can. The night was clear and Hurley so very ill that Hector decided to refuel and continue on immediately, while flying was good."

"Direct?"

"No. Coari and in."

Up on the floating dock a boy Pato's age arrived with a push cart. He unloaded three drums, waved to Cruz, and jogged off.

Tiny suggested that Wade take charge of the provisioning. The dock wagged gently as the massive longshoreman climbed onto it and brought the drums aboard one by one.

Wade looked at Cruz. "You said low-grade fuel. How does this little beauty react to low-grade?"

"Well enough. During the war she ran on brandy."

Wade subcontracted provisioning responsibilities to Pato. The boy had more of a vested interest in food than he. Wade would work on the delicate task of getting his body back onto the correct vessel without falling in the drink. Cruz's tug had drifted a couple feet out from the restaurant barge.

A slim white arm reached out full length; its fingertips just touched the molding. Gently, that touch brought the boat sliding, bobbing lazily, up against the bumpers. She held it firmly as Wade convinced his left leg to make the long step. Marcia might crow about being part of the operation, but here was a lady who *looked* for ways to help, ways no one else noticed.

She didn't need it, but Wade gave her a hand into the boat anyway. And when her feet touched the deck, he didn't let go. He led her by the hand to the stern and sat on a coil of decaying hawser. She perched on the very edge even though he gave her lots of room.

"We didn't mean to offend or upset you last night, either one of us. I want to apologize for us both."

"No apology is necessary, although Cruz said much the same thing last evening." She folded her hands in her lap, didn't seem to like the arrangement and refolded them. That one apparently didn't appeal either. "After I thought about it a while—I lay awake for a time last night—I realized that it was actually quite flattering. Not something to be offended by. You and Cruz are accustomed to fighting, to violence. It's the way you think." The pearlescent blue eyes met his for the first time. "You two wouldn't really come to blows, would you? You're such good friends. You admire each other so much."

"I don't know. I really don't know. I do know that he's a cunning fox, much too cunning to match wits with. I'd never win the contest, if it came down to plotting and conniving. But I'm his equal in some areas, or almost so."

"But not a physical fight."

"I can't imagine that happening. But if it did, I can't tell you who'd win. He's the best."

She was starting to cloud up again. "How can I prevent you two from . . . from . . . from being children about this?"

"You can't. We're big boys, both of us. If we decide to get stupid, that's our problem, not yours. You have to learn that you can't save the whole world."

She studied him a moment. "I can try." Her hand slipped out of his, and she jogged down the three steps into the cabin.

Now what? Obviously he couldn't afford to let Cruz take the initiative. Cruz was a formidable adversary in any arena, including this one, even thought he wasn't what some would call a ladies' man. And somehow Wade wasn't a real big hit with the lady right now. He'd think of something. He had to. He'd be diddled if he'd let the *patrão* whisk this bright will-'o-the-wisp out from under his nose. Wade saw her first. More important, she was the one woman in the world—the first one ever—Wade cared about enough to fight for.

Hurley was a lamb in the wilderness out here. Wade had a moral responsibility to protect the doctor from Tweed's evil. If he and Cruz and the rest of this goofy gang didn't reach Hurley, the man would soon be dead, and with him any good he might have done. But once that responsibility was discharged. Once Hurley was on his way somewhere—anywhere—Wade would apply his full attention to wooing and winning the gentle fox-fire that charmed him so.

There was a day, and not long ago, when he thought Pato and the women and Cruz and such were a heavy responsibility. How he hated this responsibility now!

As soon as the basket of fruit and the manioc came aboard, they were out on the water again in this headlong race for Manaos and Hurley.

They had cleared the Tefe River channel and were three miles down the big river before Wade realized his error. He had been mooning so much about the bewitching Elinor that he had forgotten to run ashore and pick up some tobacco.

# chapter
## 27

THE RIVER, like the rain forest she drains, displays a moody and petulant personality all her own. And why not? She is so unimaginably huge—too immense to be called simply a river—that she can do anything she wishes without fear of reproof. At the pace of a person strolling, she moves more water than all the rest of the world's rivers combined. She challenges the sea itself by shoving all that fresh muddy water hundreds of miles out into the blue salt, and the sea retaliates by nudging her with its endless tides for hundreds of miles up her course.

She wedges her emerald banks so far apart that they recede into the mist. She makes her own weather, annually drowns her intimate companion, the forest, harbors hosts of curious creatures found nowhere else on earth. Does she wish to pout or smile or randomly alter the affairs of human folk? Who is to prevent her?

Wade Travers, mere human being, perched on the stool at the wheel, in charge of the helm for the moment, and pondered the ramifications of immensity. And there was no better place on earth to do it than here on this so blatantly immense phenomenon, the river. The sprawling river, the endless forest, the arching vault of star-struck heavens crushed him down and made him feel much smaller and less significant than he hoped he was.

He wanted to be finished with this Hurley project and lacked the power to end it. He wanted to sway a certain woman to him, and it looked as if he weren't even sharp enough to pull that off. What sharpness he had was dulling rapidly. He still burned with disappointment whenever he thought about Tingido standing right beside him undetected. You're losing it, chum. What you had wasn't much, but even that's slipping away. Then what?

*Beware, Wade Travers. You'll die.* That's what.

"You look like you just found out you're an orphan. Want me to spell you at the wheel a while?"

She made him jump; he hadn't heard her. And when he failed to hear leadfoot Marcia, he really *was* slipping.

He turned a little on the stool, to talk without twisting. "Know Manaos when you see it?"

"You wait 'til the water turns black and hang a left." She frowned. "It is a left, isn't it?"

"Yeah. North shore and up the Rio Negro a ways. You been there before."

"That's amazing, you know? How black the Rio Negro really is, and how it dumps into the Amazon but doesn't mix with the main river for the longest time. Different colors. We came through that in the daytime—you know, when I was coming up the river for the first time?—and I just hung over the side of the boat gawking. Couldn't believe it. Now I'll believe just about anything. I doubt that much about this river would surprise me anymore."

"Wait'll you smell your first hoatzin."

"Those big ungainly birds with the fright wigs? They smell?"

"See? Told ya." Wade listened to the grinding hum below. The little tug didn't like low-grade nearly as much as Cruz thought.

"Want me to steer or not?"

"I'm fine. Tell me something. Ever consider living down here? Just staying?"

She shrugged. "If I could keep doing the kind of thing we're doing right now, it'd be fun. But no. Not really. 'Cause I think what we're doing is a one-and-done situation. There'll never be another time like this. We spirit Hurley to safety, and I write his story, and when I hit the thirty, it's all over. Hey, I don't like the climate *that* well. I don't like it at all." She frowned and studied him closely. "Why?"

"Don't stare at me like that was an overture to a marriage

proposal. It wasn't. Curiosity, is all. City-bred girl. I just wondered."

She still looked suspicious. "Quit scaring me like that."

Was Elinor hostile toward marriage also? Wade couldn't quite imagine a relationship with that woman based on anything less than a wedding ring. Strange that Elinor should strike him that way when the saucy lady standing beside him . . . well . . . didn't."

"When we gonna get there?"

"Midmorning sometime."

"When's Tweed gonna get there?"

"Probably docked already. Do you remember whether Sergeant Vargueza's companion made it aboard that boat with Tweed?"

"He didn't. I saw him standing on the dock looking mad."

"Good." Wade nodded. "I don't think Tweed knows Portuguese. He's going to have trouble finding what he wants in Manaos."

"Don't most people there speak Spanish, too?"

"Most of the bilinguals have moved on to greener pastures, and the locals who are left aren't impressed by Frank Buck suits. It's practically a ghost town. But you should have been there in its heyday."

"Bustling, huh?"

"Opulent. Babylon in its prime. There were rubber barons who sent their laundry to Europe. Every paving stone in the city is imported—there's no local rock—and most of the city's paved."

"The opera house. Saw pictures of the opera house. And that tiled plaza out in front of it."

"Once we get this Hurley thing settled, take some time and just wander around the city. She's still glorious."

"You take me around. You obviously know the place." She moved in closer. Maybe she still had in mind to penetrate the interior with a simple jungle guide.

"Think I'll have another project going." *Courting a lovely lady. Sorry, Marcia.* Achieving a goal through perseverence before a certain Spanish plantation *patrão* reaches it first. How do you tell a perfectly willing woman she's not good enough any more?

The engine sputtered ominously. Wade kept half an eye on the river and listened with the rest of his attention. "Go get Cruz, will you? He knows better'n I do how to cajole this crate." Was Cruz as good at cajoling ladies? No doubt.

She groped her way out to the door. He throttled down a bit. The engine dropped back a lot, and began spitting smoke.

From the darkness came Cruz's voice. "Cut it."

Wade did so. Sudden, startling, penetrating silence rang in the darkness. They bobbed dead in the water a good two miles offshore.

He had the hatch cover off and was looking for the electric torch when Cruz came barefoot down the three steps. Elinor's pale form hovered by the door.

"Now what?" Wade peered down at the engine and saw nothing but blackness—not even engine. "Can't find the torch."

Cruz flopped down on his belly and let the hatch swallow him from the shoulders up.

Tiny paused in the doorway and completely blocked the faint starlight. "What's happening?"

"Engine's down."

"Crescent wrench and a bucket of water." The maw muffled the mechanic's voice.

As Wade groped for a wrench, like magic Elinor appeared with a pan of water.

Cruz extricated himself from the jaws of darkness and sat up. "Thank you." He plunged his hand and wrist into the pan. "Burned myself; it shouldn't be that hot. Must have blown a seal. Oil all over down there. I can close down one side. We might make it in on half an engine."

"Then again, we might not." Wade had more or less been caught up in the thrill of the chase. Until now. Now his enthusiasm was chilled again, back to its usual sorry state.

"We gonna hafta paddle?" Tiny asked wearily.

"No." Elinor's voice took on that same flat confidence she used whenever she explained to Wade or the rest of the world that something absolutely was going to be. "Don't you understand? We're on God's business. He'll take care of the things we can't. Why won't you trust him?"

Surrender to him. Give up and let him do . . . do what? The smell of hot metal and overheated oil rose thick on the stuffy air.

Suddenly overcome by the sheer futility of it all, Wade flopped onto the stool and stared out across the starlit water.

This was the same overwhelming sense of hopelessness that had been nipping at his heels for months. It had him treed now, good and proper, and baying up at him in the darkness. He leaned an elbow on the cowling by the wheel and rubbed his face. His eyes burned. His heart sagged.

He didn't want to be here, but there was nowhere else he'd rather be. He didn't want to be doing this—any of this—but nothing else appealed more. He turned to watch Cruz upended in the hole. A kindred spirit.

Cruz came up for air. "Keep us in the current. This time of year we're still going three miles an hour out here."

Wade nodded listlessly.

From somewhere Marcia had dug up a candle. She lit it and leaned down, holding the light as Cruz plunged once more into the breach.

Elinor disappeared, off somewhere.

The cabin felt constantly hot and stuffy under the best of circumstances, but the heat and stink from the engine hatch was making it unbearable. Wade had hired Tiny; let him take the heat and smell a while. He wiggled a finger toward the whale and turned the wheel over to him.

Outside the cabin, the uncontained dense, dank night air felt better. Not much better, but better. He stepped over Pato, all curled up on the stern decking, and made his way forward past the slumbering sergeant. He sat down carefully with his feet pointing toward Manaos and leaned back against the edge of the windshield. Thinking position. He pulled his pipe out of his pocket and stared at it the longest time. How could he have been so dumb? He jammed the pipe back in and buttoned the flap.

On all sides stretched blackness and flat water. No running lights, no possible tows or lifts to Manaos. The overhead vault was turning almost as dark. The stars were fading, blotted out by the handful, behind a thickening cloud cover. Not even the rising silver moon shown sharply.

A soft breath of light settled in beside him. Elinor sat cross-leggedly and watched him as she so often did, with great and glowing gray-blue eyes. "I'm sorry," she murmured.

"Why are *you* sorry? Now that engine down there—that's the sorriest thing I've seen in a long time. But you have nothing to be sorry about."

"I'm not apologizing for anything. What I mean is, I feel sorry. Sad that you're so tormented."

"Tormented. I don't think I would have used that word. Kinda strong. Direct, powerful. I feel just the opposite."

"It fits."

"Yeah. It fits." He leaned his head back against the windshield post, bone weary, and watched the last of the stars wink out overhead. The moon near the horizon disappeared completely. Total darkness enveloped them like a vast, vacant bubble.

"It doesn't have to be."

"Maybe so, but it is, all the same."

He expected preaching. Instead, he got a quiet sniffle. She was crying again, or near it. That hurt him worse than if she'd yell and scream at him.

"Before nurses' training I went to a Bible school two years. In Chicago. One of the things they teach you is how to show your Savior to people who don't know him. How to evangelize is the word. It all seems to work so well in the classroom. But this. You and Señor Cruz. I know all the methods, but none of them fits."

"I resent that." He abandoned his study of atmospheric conditions to look her right in the eye. "Five years ago I barely avoided death up near the Marañon. Headhunters. It's one thing to almost die, another to know that if they get you, they're gonna cut your head off. There's just something about it. Something . . . I don't know. More final than final."

"Repulsive."

"Yeah. That, too. Well, I'm getting that same feeling now. It feels like you're a headhunter—one of those church people who loves to brag about how many people he's saved—and you're after my head. And Cruz's. And soon as we say the right words, you get to run another shrunken head up on a pole. Another notch in your gun for Jesus."

Her voice was icy. "And is Dr. Hurley a headhunter, too?"

"Not sure."

"I ran the dugout into that boat to protect you. Protect us all. It was the best I could do. I could, I suppose, simply cower in the trees until the fight was over and then count myself lucky to be alive. I didn't hide because I care about you."

"And we apprec—"

"If you were walking down a trail, and I knew there was a spiked pit in the trail—and certain death—I would do my best to get to you before you reached it. Save you from sure destruction, and for the same reason."

"Yes, but—"

"And I want so intensely for you to yield to God and accept his Jesus for exactly the same reason. You're walking right toward that pit—eternity in hell—and I want so desperately to stop you. But every time I talk to you, the words somehow come out wrong." The cloudy eyes poured up and over.

"You really think I'm doomed to—"

"I know you are. From your despair and your lack of understanding about Jesus. I'm sorry you feel like it's headhunting. What it is is fear. I'm so afraid for you, because I know what your end will be and I—" She sucked in air and murmured, "And I love you."

"And Cruz?"

"Yes, I love him. But it's different. The same word, but two very different feelings." She wiped off her glistening cheeks.

He had heard the "Love thy neighbor" admonitions throughout childhood and sensed she was talking about that, but for whom? What sort of love did she feel for him and what sort for Cruz? Was he behind or ahead? He was too afraid of hearing the wrong answer to ask.

The engine belched. Pungent black smoke drifted forward on the sullen air. As the motor picked up a rapid, clumsy two-beat, the boat began moving forward. Her engine hammering, the little tub increased her pace, but her running lights were only half bright, and the big spot mounted on top of the cabin didn't shine at all. It glowed a quiet, morbid yellow, leaving the river ahead of them in darkness. Wonderful. Now how would they see where they were going in this ink?

247

The question became academic, as the philosophers say, for with a wheeze and a bang the engine quit. The lights went out. For all intents and purposes, God's Hurley project had just ground to an ignominious halt.

The only light sat beside him. Light as in hope, the light at the end of the tunnel. Light as in revealing; you can't see dirt in the darkness, and next to her Wade looked filthy. Light as in guidance; she told him the way, but he couldn't bring himself to follow her. Light as in purity and holiness; above all else, she was that.

Jesus is the Light. Wade had heard that somewhere, long ago. She had claimed once, and not boastfully, back before the horror of that first raid, that she was Jesus' representative in the Colombia corridor. No, not *representative*. What word did she use? *Presence*. That was it. And she was just as much his presence here now. Everywhere she was, he shone in her. It made Wade uneasy.

He hauled to his feet and groped, stumbling back toward the cabin door. He just about splacked into Cruz in the doorway. Only the smell of hot oil warned him in time. "Nice try."

"Thank you." Cruz's voice was tight, weary, that of a man who had just lost after expecting to win a hundred percent of the time. "My same to you."

"What?" In the darkness Wade barely saw him glance at Elinor by his elbow, then back to him. "I wasn't making time, Cruz. We were talking religion."

"Of course. And when a chance presents itself, however unfair or inopportune, so shall I."

The hair on Wade's neck prickled. He didn't mind if someone like Tweed questioned his honesty, but when Cruz doubted him . . . "Hey, chum, you just do that. Because, according to this lady, we're both going to hell, and I don't think I'm gonna like sitting around a fire with you for eternity while you feel sorry for yourself. 'Cause you're a real mess when everything mucks up; you don't even believe your friends. And I hear there isn't anything can get worse than rotting in hell. Don't kick Pato. He's right behind you."

Wade limped the three steps down into the cabin and groped his way to the wheel. He poked Tiny's shoulder and took over the helm. No reason to. They sure as blazes weren't going anywhere in this nothing.

The whale mumbled, "*Boa noite*," and staggered off to resume sleeping. Why not? Sleep or worry, it all pays the same.

Huge hard drops pelted the windshield. Peachy. Just peachy. Now the whole mob would come crowding into this stinking cabin to get out of the rain. Wade locked the wheel in place and headed for the door. He struggled out against the tide of sleepy incoming fugitives, like a salmon swimming upstream to the spawning ground.

He reached fresh muggy air in the doorway and slogged up the steps. Suddenly, impudently, sheets of driving rain pounded him. It beat against his skin and pierced his shirt, soaking him instantly. It drummed wildly against the deck and cabin roof; little rivulets formed here and there from the pour-off and hurried across the deck toward the river.

He could hear the numberless, clumsy raindrops splashing into the river, into waters so limitless they wouldn't even notice this tiny addition to their ranks. From the pain and the warmth he could tell that his seeping hip had opened up again. The thing was never going to heal. Never.

Too weary to stand, he settled onto the soggy, rotten pile of thick mooring rope and listened to the thundering blackness all around him.

Futility.

His eyes burned hot and wet. He was tired, so damned tired. Damned tired? No. Just damned. According to Elinor, according to Hurley, according to everything he had ever heard in church as a child or from occasional preachers he'd stumbled onto here and there in life, he was damned.

What if hell is reality?

In anger at Cruz, he had treated hell flippantly. There is nothing, absolutely nothing, flippant about an eternity in hell.

He was as nowhere as this little boat engulfed in wet blackness. Nowhere to go, nowhere to reach out, nowhere to turn. He was done fighting. Quietly, so quietly he almost didn't notice, the last shreds of his resistance dissolved in the beating rain.

He would do it Elinor's way—Hurley's way—because he must. Whatever came next, he couldn't do it himself. He must assume there is a God and let that God take over. Let God do it God's way, for Wade, mere human being, was even weaker and punier than the immense river and the endless forest and the vaulted sky insisted he was.

After all those years of fighting man and God, Wade Travers gave up.

And the thrusting, slathering rain washed away his tears as peace, at long last, poured over him.

# chapter
# 28

SHOUTS. SOMEONE WAS YELLING. The world wagged side to side. Wade lifted his head and ordered his eyelids open. His brain and his senses lurched falteringly into gear, but his left arm remained asleep. Its fingers tingled. He was still on the hawser coil, curled into a sorry little ball as soggy as the rotten hemp. His hip burned.

The boat wagged again as Tiny leaned out over the starboard rail. The Iquitos mailboat filled sky and water beyond the bow. You didn't realize how small Cruz's little tug was until you put it up beside a real boat. Tiny waved a flipper high.

The boat lurched, almost throwing Wade off the coil. And here they went, moving again, on their way to Manaos under tow. Stiff all over, he hauled himself to his feet, hung onto the rail a moment until all his parts were awake, and limped forward to join Tiny near the bow.

What time was it? The thick sky made time-telling difficult. Wade guessed dawn, or thereabouts.

He bellied up to the rail by Tiny and asked in Portuguese, "How'd you get the tow? The mailboat never does this."

Tiny shrugged. "I hailed 'em, and they hailed me. Said since they're 'way ahead of schedule they might's well."

Pato pushed in between the two of them. "Tink dey got food mebbe?"

"Only if someone's willing to share. You've been on that boat before. No dining salon. Just goats all over."

"I can hold rope. Go 'cross mebbe, eh?"

"Absolutely not."

"Betch' I can. Hand, hand like dis, eh?"

"You can't do it with a broken arm, chum, and if you try a stunt that stupid I'll break it for you. *Comprendes?*"

He muttered a resigned "*Sí*, Papa" and watched breakfast churn the water a hundred feet ahead.

On the line where sky meets water, the sun found a crack in the cloud cover and stuck its fingers through. It wedged the crack wider and streamed rosy light into Wade's eyes. He rubbed Pato's head, warned "You stay aboard now, hear?" and wandered aft. He was just as hungry as the bottomless boy.

But he felt good. For the first time in what seemed like eons, he felt great. Should he mention something to Elinor? No. Not yet. For one thing, he didn't know what was going on. He couldn't discuss spiritual things intelligently because he still didn't understand it at all. He knew it had happened, but he couldn't say how. For another, it might sound silly, trying to explain feelings. Feelings are volatile, unreliable. Better that he wait and tell her when he'd make less of a fool of himself.

Jesus Christ, huh? Whoever would have thought Wade Travers would throw all his trust onto a person he could neither see nor hear nor touch? Not an ounce of proof. That in itself was crazy.

Cruz was stretched out on the cabin floor with his head and shoulders down the hatch again. His shirt was off, and the muscles of his bare back tensed and twitched. The rips in his body inflicted during that shootout at the Ocaina settlement had not yet healed much better than Wade's hip.

Wade stepped around and over oily engine parts and settled carefully beside the hatch. "Morning."

The back wriggled, twisted. With a few clunks belowdecks, Cruz hauled himself out and sat up. He reached for a well-used rag to wipe his hands and arms. "Morning."

"Any hope?"

"I think she's dead forever. I'll see whether I can get her rebuilt in Manaos, and how much, but I have my doubts. Too old, too tired."

"I know *that* feeling."

252

Cruz was studying him with those dark eyes that miss nothing. "Not today you don't."

"No. Not today. And if this spiritual rebirth thing is the way Elinor and Hurley describe it, not tomorrow, either."

Cruz leaned back against the locker behind him and stared a while at nothing. "I think I'd be a lot happier for you if I didn't know it will improve your relationship with Elinor."

"That's not why I did it. I didn't have anywhere else to go. I was tired of struggling."

"I've been accused of not believing my friends, so I suppose I should take that at face value. Very well, I do." He jerked erect. The long slim fingers cast the rag aside. Then he dived into the hatch again, back to whatever it was he was trying to salvage down there.

Strange, this. Wade felt suddenly, inexplicably alienated from the man who so recently had been a kindred soul. Cruz was still the haunted, desperate seeker of yesterday. Wade was not. A gulf had ripped open between them, and it was not the iron wedge of rivalry. It was something else.

Wade wanted Cruz to bask in this same sensation of peace he was enjoying. This was what Cruz sought so desperately, and Wade wanted equally desperately to share it. He hurt for Cruz; he knew Cruz's pain firsthand. And he couldn't think of any way to spread this feeling of release onto the *patrão's* weary shoulders.

The mailboat, according to the schedule, was supposed to arrive in Manaos at 12:05. Why did schedules always promise exact minutes, when the boats in question were lucky to arrive within half a day of the appointed time? Why couldn't the table simply say "noon"? That was surely close enough to the mark.

This day, the mail arrived in Manaos precisely at 10:43. So much for exact schedules. Tiny sculled Cruz's launch in the last fifteen feet, Wade threw a line over the pier post behind the mailboat, and Cruz cast off the tow. The *patrão* crossed from boat to dock to mailboat, no doubt to thank the skipper and offer a bit of sweetener for his coffee. It's the way things are done in Brazil.

Instantly the sergeant trotted off to report and obtain an arrest order, just in case his radio message had failed to get through. Wade sent Pato, with instructions not to get lost, with Tiny to scour the

253

north end of the waterfront. Cruz and Elinor disappeared uptown. That left Wade and Marcia to cover the south.

Marcia held up well until she passed a little street vendor with a pushcart of hot empanadas. She screeched to a halt. "What're those?"

"*Papas sabrosas.*"

"Right. So what are they?"

"Sweet potato turnovers."

"I want three. No four. What're those?"

"Chicken, looks like. Chicken empanadas. Also turnovers."

Wade dug into his pocket for the cruzeiros she had given him in Tefe. "How about a couple of those? I think you'll like them."

"I'll eat the cartful. You can't believe how hungry I am."

"Oh, yes, I can." Wade bought a dozen of the little goodies, various flavors, and pointed to a crate. "Lunch break."

She plopped down and stretched her long legs out. She was through one empanada and into the next before she spoke. "This your favorite town?"

"In Brazil? Yeah."

"Anywhere."

"Rochester, I guess. Probably go back someday."

"Funny, y'know? Rochester's a nothing town, right?—when you compare it with this." She waved a hand. "Exotic. Half the town here floats during flood. Dirty, crowded, bobbing on a black river that's flooded how many feet deeper'n usual?"

"Close to sixty."

"Right. And charming. Exciting. You said so yourself. You can't dream of anything like this in New York. Not even the city. And yet the people here wouldn't like living in New York, and we don't want to get stuck here forever. Wherever you grew up, that's the best place, in the end."

"Usually."

She popped the last of an empanada in her mouth. Her eyes grew wide. With bits of empanada crust flying, she cried out "Mp! Phht Mmph!" and stabbed a wildly pointing finger at the water.

Beyond the tangle of dugouts and scows, a white launch cruised by at low speed.

"Good girl! That's— . . . no, it's not. The numbers on the boat Tweed swiped ended in a nine. This one's a three. That's either harbor patrol or some of Sergeant Vargueza's people, maybe looking for Tweed. Come on. Let's walk while we eat."

She tucked a couple empanadas in her pockets, and he slipped his last three inside his shirt. They hurried double time along the dirt-crusted dock. It creaked and swayed in places. In other places a plank might bend or a knothole gape, hand-wide. The thing was actually in pretty good condition, considering.

Nothing. Perhaps they'd missed it. A big green lunker of a boat chugged past, and the natives in their various scows and dugouts were out in force. No police craft. The way back didn't turn up the launch either. Tweed must have docked at the other end of town. Wade was probably missing out on all the fun right now, simply because of the luck of the draw.

They spent five extra minutes at the main wharf, stocking up for dinner. Scores of long, narrow boats full of local produce, some of them roofed in reeds and some open, shouldered each other impatiently, trying to be closest to a pier big enough to hold at most a dozen. "Casa Uniao," the locals called it.

Wade called it heaven. He'd been hungry too frequently and too long lately to pass up all this food. With Marcia tagging along wide-eyed, he hopped from deck to deck, from scow to scow, picking and choosing, haggling in slurred rural Portuguese. All this hopping was wrecking his poor old hip, but he didn't care. Food. They left Casa Uniao with fresh fruit, crisp vegetables, and a couple fat chickens.

"Live chickens!" observed the New Yorker incredulously.

"How else do you keep poultry meat fresh in this climate?" rejoined the simple native guide, and they returned to Cruz's boat with light hearts and laughter, and the chickens making purring, crowing sounds from deep inside their doomed throats. They stowed their trove in the cabin, poultry and all.

Tiny and Pato arrived back seconds before Cruz and Elinor returned. She'd been crying again. Her eyes were puffy.

Pato perched on a mooring post. His mouth and hands were all greasy. "Nada. Nobody. Iss they didn' come mebbe."

Cruz sighed. "We stopped by the sergeant's office and then out to the airstrip. His boat hasn't been reported back, and Hector isn't here. No sign of the plane, no sign of Tweed."

Elinor nodded. "We asked at the infirmary, too, just in case."

Wade watched her tight face a moment. He yearned to tell her that what she had wanted so much had happened, but this was not the time or place. "Eaten yet?" He didn't wait for her to answer. He pulled the remaining empanadas out of his shirt, gave her two and offered the other to Cruz. "Fruit on board. We went shopping."

The *patrão* accepted and thanked him with a bare nod.

"So now what?" Marcia looked from face to face for answers, even though she surely realized there were none.

Cruz finished a mouthful. "Our objective is Hurley, not Tweed. At Tefe, Vargueza radioed a complaint of theft of official property—his boat. There was already a warrant out for Tweed's arrest when we got here."

"Won't hold water." Wade looked for a comfortable resting place for his hip and saw none. "Tweed'll cite some gibberish about commandeering the vessel for purposes of official pursuit or some such nonsense and squirm out from under it."

Cruz brushed his hands off, nodding. "But it should delay him long enough for us to see Hurley to safety. Vargueza's pride has been injured. He's fit to draw and quarter Tweed; he'll make plenty of red tape just for spite. Then, with time to work, we'll get Tweed turned around and sent home, empty-handed. At the infirmary I asked them to send an ambulance up to the airstrip. I suggest we wait there, be there when the plane comes in."

He didn't say *if* the plane came. Wade was glad of that.

Tiny made the short hop from boat to dock, bristling with arms and fruit. He handed a shotgun each to Wade and Cruz and gave Pato two papayas.

They stopped only once on the way out to the little landing field Wade remembered from the past as a potato patch. It was at another of those innumerable pushcarts for some grilled lamb skewers too aromatic to pass up. Pato ate two more than Wade did.

Fairly new houses crowded in on either side of the long, narrow landing strip. Apparently modern Brazilians considered it prestigious to live next to an airfield. He couldn't remember that they had been so eager to build around the potato patch. Half the town, including some ornate and elaborate old mansions, lay vacant and decaying while new buildings both grand and shoddy cropped up all around its edges. Curious people, city folk.

At one end of the strip by the wind sock stood the radio shack. No fancy building here. A thatched roof on poles covered a bare dirt floor. The walls were a four-foot-high fence to keep the hogs and chickens out. Unless the radio operator left his station long enough to do a little clear-cutting, the jungle would soon crawl in and take over. Already, heart-shaped liana leaves flittered in under the roof.

Cruz stuck his head over the wall and asked in Portuguese, "Have you raised Coari yet?"

The operator shook his head. "Still trying."

Wade moved closer to look at the place. On a rickety table sat the radio set, a huge box adorned with dials and levers. Red rubber-coated wires connected it to two battery jars on a shelf behind. The jars contained water tinted the loveliest blue. Stand-by jars lined another shelf.

A broken, hissing voice erupted from the round, fabric-covered speaker. The operator leaned close to a microphone the size of a breadfruit and shouted in Portuguese, "Manaos, Coari. Go ahead."

Snapping, crackling sputters surrounded the voice-like noises. Wade couldn't make out a single word of it. No wonder no one knew what was going on. Wireless wasn't half what it was cracked up to be.

"Roger, Coari," the operator snapped. "Over and out." He turned in his chair to Cruz. "Your man left there at first light. He should be here soon."

"He should be here already." Cruz walked off.

Wade scowled. "You got all that out of that noise? You're sure that's what he said?"

"Yes." The operator looked at him blankly, as if all those frizzled voice sounds were the stentorian tones of a stage actor. "You heard him."

"Right." Wade walked out onto the strip and into sunlight. The cloud cover was breaking up rapidly. Patches of blue in the gray were fast becoming a few gray patches in the blue.

He tucked his shotgun in the crook of his arm and jammed his hands in his pockets. He had ample time now to reflect ruefully that in all this hustling about, he still had not purchased any pipe tobacco. It didn't have to be a plug; loose tobacco, moldy tobacco, last year's cut—he didn't care anymore.

"Here comes!" Pato craned his neck skyward. "Iss here!"

Wade heard nothing. Wait. Yes, he did, too. A distant whining hum became a drone. Long minutes later, Tweed's airplane roared in above the trees and arched around in a lazy circle. Cruz glanced at the wind sock and came walking toward this end.

Burping and sputtering, the craft hummed low across the forest and dropped down rapidly at the far end of the strip. Its wheels hit the grass, bounced, settled in, from smooth grace to ungainly waddle. It lumbered to a standstill very near the trees at this end. Hector popped up out of the front cockpit and straddled the fuselage facing the rear seat.

Cruz and Wade reached Hurley as Hector unbuckled him. Hector spoke rapidly, but Wade wasn't listening. The doctor's wild ride had brought him not just to Manaos but absolutely to death's door. His waxy, translucent skin looked like an onion skin stretched tight. Blood spattered the front of his shirt and stained one corner of his mouth.

Gently Wade supported as Hector lifted. Then Tiny was there beside him. The whale picked the man up and brought him over the side without so much as touching the plane. It almost appeared that Dr. Hurley had lost weight since leaving Minho.

"Put him down a minute, please, until the hospital's hack arrives." Elinor knelt beside the stricken man and tenderly arranged his head in Tiny's lap.

With a wan smile Dr. Hurley acknowledged everyone present, including Pato. He sighed. "Friends. Delightful." The watery eyes drifted closed.

Wade stood near Cruz watching the vacant road. "We're gonna lose him. You know that. You can help him die happy by telling him you've put your whopping big intellect in the closet and committed yourself to God, his way."

"Lie to him?"

"Naw. Do it first. Then tell him." Wade held Cruz's eye steadily and tried to keep it from being a hard stare. It was Cruz who broke the gaze and turned away.

By Wade's elbow Marcia sniffed. "Did I say 'exotic'?"

Here at last came the ambulance. Wade had expected one of those boxed-in trucks, perhaps a surplus vehicle left over from the war, painted white with a cross on it. This conveyance was a simple open buckboard behind a ragged old roan horse. Were it not for a mattress thrown down in back, you'd think it was a farmer selling manioc.

Effortlessly Tiny scooped up the doctor and arranged him on the mattress on his side, with his legs drawn up. He thrust a thick, threatening finger toward the driver's nose. "Gently now, you hear?"

The driver nodded, saucer-eyed.

As the ambulance turned slowly, carefully, and started down the road, Wade nodded toward the airplane. "Should we tie that thing down or something?"

Hector wagged his head. "Let Tweed. It's his plane."

They fell in behind the wagon. "So you think Tweed's here? Or will be?"

Hector nodded. "I had engine trouble at Coari. Delayed. Finally I got on my way. But I had to set down again shortly at a little landing field fifty miles east. They had a wireless at that little field, and I heard Sergeant Vargueza's message to arrest Tweed at Tefe or Coari or Manaos. Then I knew he was pursuing me, but I didn't know if it were by boat or by plane."

"Wait'll you see what Tiny did to your plane; he pulled the pin. Good thing, too. They would've blown you right out of the sky if they'd gotten airborne."

A dazzling blue morpho butterfly flittered by with great lazy flaps. It coasted into the darkness of the forest beside them.

"We in that sluggish craft, and they in our airplane? Indeed! Tweed's is terrible. Just terrible. Very badly maintained. Slow. Pity, too. She could be such a light, responsive little aircraft if he would only take care of her. Why, the engine was . . ."

259

"Later. Tell me why you were so late coming. We broke down in the tug and still beat you here by two hours."

"The tug!" Hector exploded in laughter. The merriment died. "Constant engine problems. Fortunate I know all the little strips along the river. I believe I didn't miss any. And the poor doctor. All those take-offs and landings nearly killed him. On one occasion he fell into a restful sleep, and so I waited until he awakened naturally."

Pato crowded in at Wade's elbow. "Sir? Señor Hector? I can ride fly one time sometime mebbe?" His eyes sparkled. Youth.

How do you recast that into intelligible Portuguese? Wade tried. "I understand our airplane had been damaged."

Simple, easy translation.

"Iss gone good, *sí*. Señor Cruz he needs one, new, eh? Get one mebbe here Manaos, fly home. Howzzat, eh?"

Wade translated dutifully. He expected to see some sign of dismay from the company aviator. After all, the company plane was now but a pile of smoking rubble.

Instead, Hector brightened. "Gone, eh? Please explain to the boy that I think it would be a wonderful idea, but my *patrão* controls the purse. Ask the boy to convince the *patrão* of his need for a new aircraft. He might specify the new Lepere, or perhaps a Verville Packard. A hundred and seventy-eight miles an hour, the Packard. Minho to Manaos in four hours."

"Man wasn't meant to go that fast."

Hector smiled softly. "Yes, I was."

They wound now along narrow little streets between ill-kept, flaking buildings. Playing children paused to stare at the strange procession and the foreign woman in the culotte. Dogs barked. The roan tossed its head and rolled its eyes. Tiny moved in beside its neck. It wouldn't step out of line now. Probably the whale outweighed the old horse; the man was certainly stronger.

"Wait." Cruz stopped and looked around. He addressed the driver. "Why are we down in this end of town? We're going out of our way."

"The infirmary, yes?" The driver fidgeted with the lines.

"The infirmary is north of us. Turn aside on that street."

"Excuse me, señor, but that way."

A moment ago Cruz slung his shotgun carelessly under his arm. He held it balanced in his hand now. He nodded to the north. "Go up that street anyway. Let's see where it takes us."

"I fear . . ." The man's face twisted as if working on a problem too complex for him. "I fear for the health of your friend. Pray go this way a bit farther. Then we'll turn up on a broad street, easy way to the infirmary."

The eyes that miss nothing moved in closer to study the wretched fellow.

Wade picked up the drift, too. He nodded and used English. "Let's take Hurley—let's see—how about Sergeant Vargueza's office?"

Cruz bobbed his head slightly. Affirmative.

Marcia frowned. "Why?"

"Tweed's been to the infirmary. He got to this fellow somehow. Bribe, threat, whatever. It's no longer safe to take Hurley there."

She looked from Cruz to Wade, scowling. "You know it really is creepy the way you two talk to each other without saying anything out loud. You even think the same thoughts."

*And love the same woman.* But Wade didn't say it. He glanced at Cruz. The corner of the *patrão's* mouth tilted up. He was thinking exactly the same thing.

"He needs professional care." Elinor stared at Dr. Hurley, her mind elsewhere. She nodded. "I suppose you're right, though, until we find out where Mr. Tweed is."

"Mr. Tweed is right here."

Wade spun around; his hip howled in protest. He started to swing his shotgun up without thinking and stopped himself barely in time. He let the muzzle drift back down to the ground.

Tweed and his two remaining minions stepped out into the street, out onto the imported cobbles from a wealthier era. One of them moved quickly to the horse's head as the other swung wide around to take gather up the shotguns.

For there would be no arguing with the man just now; he held Pato in a vice-lock grip, and his official-looking pistol, fresh from its official-looking holster, was pointed at the boy's head.

# chapter
## 29

FROM THE SMALLEST little neon tetra in a side eddy of the world's greatest river to the largest jaguar in her endless forests, the instinct for self-preservation runs like a lifeline, knitting all the river's wonderful creatures together into a common web. Most of them shared also an instinct to preserve their young. Men certainly did— men of the forest and men of the city, including Rochester. And it wasn't even his young. But Pato might as well be; he was Wade's now.

Wade watched Pato's face a moment and felt proud of the kid all over again. The boy was scared, sure. But he was alert, too, and wound tight as a spring. Should the call come to move, he'd act quickly and correctly, Wade knew. Did Tweed underestimate the boy? Almost certainly. Good.

From behind, one of Tweed's own tugged at the shotgun in Wade's hand. He forced himself to loosen up his tensed muscles and let it go without a fight.

He thought Hurley was asleep on his bumpy pallet, but the man opened his eyes and looked right at Wade. " 'Cursed be the man that trusteth in man and maketh flesh his arm, and whose heart departeth from the Lord. And blessed is the man who trusteth in the Lord.' That's Jeremiah; Chapter 17, I think."

"I've learned not to make flesh my arm, but that shotgun was comforting." Wade spread his hands wide. "You've got us, Tweed. Turn the boy loose."

"I think not. Continue, driver."

In halting, bumbling Portuguese, one of his guards translated. Wade wondered how they managed to get through to the driver, if this were typical of Tweed's communications. The fellow clucked to his roan. The buckboard lurched into motion, headed toward the riverfront.

Tweed literally tucked Pato's head in the crook of his left elbow and more or less dragged him along. The kid was managing to keep up so far with no real distress. So far.

So. Wade's new commitment required him to trust God. Elinor did so consistently. So did Hurley. There must be something to it. But whether there was anything to it or not, it was now to be Wade's course of action also. And it came hard, much harder than he would have thought, to turn everything over to an unseen power and simply wait for a cue to leap into action. On the other hand, it eliminated a lot of worry and fear. Wade felt curiously at peace, even in the midst of this royal mess. He was beginning to understand Elinor's strength.

He moved in close enough to Tweed for comfortable conversation. "Your bosses up in Bogotá are going to be really pleased with you. You've shown brilliant preseverence . . ." He glanced at Cruz. "And perseverence is a virtue, as we all know. You've gotten yourself in hot water with Brazilian officials. Oh sure, the sergeant's a fairly minor official. But he's got clout. And you've made an absolute fool of yourself. All for them. All to help ease their silly little fears."

Tweed turned to look at him, and the expression on the pudgy face told Wade clearly that the man had absolutely no idea what he was talking about. Whatever Tweed's interest in Hurley, it had nothing to do with cover-ups or higher-ups in Bogotá.

This required some rapid and major re-thinking. Wade looked to Cruz. Thinking was more the *patrão's* forté than Wade's.

Cruz tucked his hands in his pockets and wandered along the tail of the buckboard. "Señor Tweed, Travers is circling when perhaps directness would serve better. We are extremely curious as to the reason for your intense interest in Dr. Hurley. It far exceeds the limits of mere official interest."

"The same interest you have, Señor Cruz."

"I seriously doubt it, since our motives were simply to bring the doctor out to safety and medical attention. Were your motives ours, you would be content to see him tucked comfortably into the infirmary here. You would not have traveled here from Minho, much less from the Colombia corridor. Why is his death so important to you?"

"Not his death, señor. His life, since I've not talked to him yet."

"Then why try to send your lieutenant up in my airplane to shoot him down?"

"No. Turn them around and force them back. Or perhaps follow them to their next landing and bring the doctor back. Señor Cruz, would I, a Colombian official, do such a thing as shoot him down? It's your man, not mine, who destroyed your aircraft."

Cruz fell silent and contemplated the rolling wheel in front of him.

Alive. If that be true, Hurley then must know something Tweed wants to know. Surely not. What could Hurley possibly know that Tweed would work so desperately to learn? It couldn't be anything religious, and that was about all Hurley really knew. Something concerning the Ocainas? Tweed already knew more than Hurley did about them. The Christian Indians? Why should Tweed care? They didn't live that far into Colombia, if at all.

The buckboard rattled out onto the dock, rang hollow on the rotting planks. The early afternoon sun burned down as only the tropical sun can. They'd better get Hurley into the shade soon.

"This way." Tweed motioned.

Wade recognized the big green boat tied here—the lunker he and Marcia had seen go by this morning. They must have watched Tweed cruise past and never knew it.

Tweed waved them aboard. "All of you. You all had ample opportunity to talk to him. You especially, Miss Lewis. Come."

Wade reached out and slapped the cabin roof as he boarded. "Nice vessel. Trade up from the sergeant's launch?"

"The launch used too much fuel. The second time we ran dry, I conscripted this vessel. Official use."

"Right. Except you aren't on official business. Whatever this

264

thing is, it's as far from your official duties as you can get it. That's why you wanted to hire me. Keep it unofficial."

"Of course." And Tweed's haughty tone of voice suggested that Wade had just mouthed a truism that could go without saying.

Gently Tiny gathered up mattress and all.

"Wait." Cruz laid a hand on the mattress. "Señor Tweed, it's time to deal."

"I have no deals to make·with you. Bring the man aboard."

Cruz's hand stayed the mattress. "Yes, you do. Concerning the gold. Hurley can speak to you only in generalities. I can give you specifics. But I shall do so only if the doctor here is sent instantly to the infirmary."

"No." Tweed gave Pato a shake and gestured with his pistol. "I read his letter myself. Bring him aboard."

Tiny's eyes never left Pato. He brushed past the long slim hand and carried the mattress, doctor and all onto the green boat.

"Gold?" Wade muttered as Cruz came aboard.

"A shot in the dark. What would best pique Tweed's greed?"

"Looks like you hit the mark."

When Tweed had commandeered this vessel, he must have put the rightful owners ashore. Only Tweed, his two minions, and these kidnappees seemed to be aboard.

"Sit. There, that corner. All of you." Tweed wiggled the gun impatiently. Elinor blatantly ignored him. Instead, she helped Tiny arrange the doctor as comfortably as possible along the cabin wall.

Wade wished Tweed would let go of Pato before he wrenched the poor kid's head off.

One of the guards stepped into the wheelhouse, and the other disappeared belowdecks. It must take a minimum of two people to torch this clunker off. With a cloud of black smoke worse than the tug's, the engine belowdecks decided to live again. Its bass rumble vibrated the whole vessel.

"Wait! Hey, wait." Marcia pointed an arm downriver. "We just stocked up. Fruit and stuff and even a couple chickens. It's aboard our boat down that way. Send one of your people down and get the food first, huh?"

The Portuguese-speaking guard came up out of the hold to cast off. Tweed snapped orders at him and turned to Tiny. "You will go."

Tiny looked at Wade. Wade nodded. The guard wiggled a finger and, with a last glance at Pato, Tiny followed the fellow out the door.

Wade was getting impatient. If God was supposed to be in charge, why hadn't he done anything yet? His doctor was going to be dead soon. That would end his Hurley project, all right.

"Mr. Tweed?" Dr. Hurley looked asleep, he lay so lax.

"Yes."

"Your business is with me, is that correct? Therefore, you may release these others."

"I can't be certain how much you told them, or how little. They come also."

"I'll not talk to you until they're free."

"But then you would not talk at all."

"You read my letter, you said. What letter?" And the doctor doubled up with another spell of coughing.

"Your letter to John was intercepted. I'm rather surprised at your naiveté, doctor. You should never have committed something like that to the written page."

"John. John. Dr. John Marchand at the college?" Dr. Hurley's eyes opened. "Of course!" A stunned look paralyzed his face. "So much tragedy! Lives lost, difficulties, suffering. All for a simple misunderstanding. All over a simple misunderstanding!" Were the tears in his eyes from this sudden realization—whatever it was—or from this latest coughing seizure?

"Misunderstanding?" Elinor laid a gentle hand on his face.

Hurley's voice was fading. "I can't remember exactly what I said. Just tragic. And sad that John never received it. It would warm his heart so. He's very much burdened with spreading the gospel. Let's see. I recall, yes. The letter, Mr. Tweed, said, 'John, they believe. They don't just believe. They know. Corinthian gold, the solid foundation, that will smelt out pure when tried by fire.' Was that it?"

"An excellent memory, Doctor."

"Pahoa's people," Elinor whispered, and the bottomless eyes filled with limitless sorrow. "So much hurt. Pahoa's people."

Wade yearned intensely to gather her up in his arms and comfort her. "I don't get it."

The pearlescent eyes rose to meet his. "First Corinthians, third chapter. The apostle Paul charges us to build only on the foundation which is Jesus Christ himself. Everything we build—of gold, silver, wood, hay or stubble—will be tried by fire. Tested. The dross—worldly interests, selfish works—will burn up when the fire tests it. Only the pure faith will remain, but it will be all the purer for being tried by fire. That's the gold. That's what he meant, Mr. Tweed. No precious metal. Precious faith."

"Beautifully spoken," purred the doctor.

Cruz sat down cross-leggedly on the deck and rubbed his face. "A whole tribe converted. That was your gold."

"Yes. You see, it's far more difficult for them to commit themselves to Jesus than it is for us." Hurley paused for a coughing fit. "Much of their healing and medicine invokes various spirits. To put away all the spirits and cling to one God places their health, and their children's health, on the line. Someone is injured, becomes ill, and the temptation is instantly to call up the appropriate spirit. Just this once, mind you; so human when someone's life is at stake. So easy. And yet, they've steadfastly resisted. They build with gold, not hay and stubble. John Marchand will understand the depth of the reference."

"Tragedy of the first order." Cruz studied the pegged wooden planking. "You went to all this for nothing, Tweed. There is no gold. Not the kind you're seeking."

Tweed smirked. "You're very clever, both of you. I presume this was rehearsed. It's too well orchestrated to be spontaneous. I'll not be drawn off the track so easily."

"There is no gold." Cruz's voice rose a notch. "You've no doubt heard rumors of a quartz reef south of the Uaupes, and from it a whole shining riverbed of gold, untouched since the beginning of time. You're hoping that the doctor's discovery might be that very lode."

Tweed said nothing. He didn't have to; his face told all.

"I heard them, too, and sought it for a full year. I found the quartz seam. It's not quartz. It's very brittle shale. Flint. The

267

streambed shines just as the legends promise, but it's all iron pyrites. All."

"Fool's gold." Wade was staring at him.

"I sent Hector up the next year, for he's much better at communicating with wild tribes than am I. Just to make sure, you see; it sounded so good. Nothing. Futility."

"I can tell by Tweed's face that he doesn't believe you, but I do." Wade shifted his weight a little. "You just saved me years of squirreling around the Uaupes trying to dig up a retirement fund."

"Your personal business?" Cruz looked interested.

"Yeah."

"This exchange, and your tale, Mr. Cruz—these attempts to discourage me tells me that you're all in it together. You all share the doctor's secret. Before disposing of the unneeded members of your party, I must first make certain that the ones I keep know all the necessary details. It could be any of you. But I certainly don't need all of you."

Tiny and the guard came back aboard stomping, each with a squawking chicken in hand. Tiny dropped his load, pointed a menacing finger at Tweed, and rumbled almost under his breath.

Wade leaned back against the cabin window to get some weight off his hip. "Tiny says you turn the boy loose now, or he'll break your arm off."

"Tell him to sit down."

Wade translated loosely. "Not yet. Relax and wait. You'll get your chance."

Belowdecks, the engine noises rose in tone and volume. With much sighing and lurching, the green lunker began to back out of the crowded docking area, through the jumble of houseboats, scows, and jangadas.

Backed up against the window like this, Wade could see the world go by, mindless of tragedy and heroism. The helmsman had to slow still more as they neared the *fluteuantes*, the floating city within Manaos. Shops, businesses, homes, hovels—nothing built and used by humans touched solid ground here. All the many parts of a thriving city in itself played against each other on the crest of the changing black river.

A couple small boys in dugouts paddled out to meet the boat. They waved high their wares—matamata turtles—and shouted, "*Um cruzeiro!*" The green boat pushed past them; they bobbed in its wake and waited for the next customer.

Was Wade getting a call from God, or was he simply too antsy to wait any longer? He wished he were more sensitive to that sort of thing. Once they got out into the river past all this floating stuff, they'd have a straight shot at Colombia, and there'd be nothing Wade or anyone else could do. Wade was absolutely certain they couldn't let Tweed take them out of Manaos.

He wheeled on Marcia right behind him and wagged a finger in her face. "Now cut that out!"

"I didn't do anything!"

Wade jacked his voice a notch. "Don't give me that innocent stuff. Just cut it out, you hear?"

"What'd I *do*?" Instantly, Marcia being Marcia, she shouted just as stridently as he.

"You know what I'm talking about. No more."

Her finger waved in front of his nose. "Don't you dare yell at me like that, you half-baked potato, or I'll—"

"And don't you scream at me, you little twit. Just cut it out."

Tweed and the guard were both hollering at them. Yes indeed, Marcia really ought to become a stage actress.

"I'll do anything I want with you. I bought and paid for you, you jerk, and don't you forget it!"

"Oh yeah? Did you pay for this?" Wade hauled an open hand back as if to swat her and hoped she would catch on and get the timing right. Scenes like this probably went a lot better with rehearsal.

She did. She rammed a fist into his belly. She pulled her punch. She could have hit him a lot harder, but it took most of his wind out anyway. He oofed and doubled up and threw himself back against the cursing guard behind him.

His hip did not at all like the way he whipped around to floor the guy. But by the time he had the fellow down, Marcia was on top of them both and flailing. The woman did enjoy scrapping.

Somewhere up there, a gun went off. Tiny's voice thundered

indignantly. Suddenly the boat careened to port, tilting the deck enough to fling Wade and guard and all into a corner. The boat lurched again; everything not tied down slid to starboard. She lunged and waddled and jerked to a grinding, clunking stop amid crashes and crunches and screams and angry yells. Wade knew without looking that they had just rammed the floating city.

# chapter
# 30

PANDEMONIUM MULTIPLIES. Feed it just a little, and it grows a lot. Noise and gunshots and thrashing arms and legs are some of its favorite food. That sort of pandemonium is all external, and Wade was in the middle of it, trapped under a pile of churning people. True pandemonium erupted inside him when he heard Hurley's tortured voice cry out, "No, Elinor! Please!"

That insane woman was doing something magnificent and crazy again, and Wade was buried by this mess, unable to stop her. Maybe Cruz could. Wade didn't care if it were his rival, just so long as it was somebody.

He kicked free, squirmed, twisted—and surfaced. Here was one of Cruz's shotguns free. Wade grabbed it.

The deck tilted at a wicked slant. Hurley had been thrown into the corner, mattress and all. He sat up, clutching his chest, and waved a helpless arm toward the door. "She went with him. With Tweed."

"He kidnapped her!"

"No," Hurley rasped. "He was going to shoot . . . shoot some of you. He was enraged. She said she was privy to my secrets, but she would prefer seeking gold with a healthy man, not a dying one. She went voluntarily. To save you all."

Wade was beginning to appreciate the rage Tweed expressed now and then. It boiled up in him now, scarlet and delicious. She was God's person. *God, why do you let her pull fool stunts like this?*

271

He left pandemonium behind without trying to sort any of it out and scrambled up the tilting deck to the door. He literally dragged himself out and crawled up over the gunwale.

Here was pandemonium just as wild and tangled as that inside. Millions of sticks of ragged, shattered lumber poked out in all directions. A dozen people yelled and shook their fists, some at him and some at each other. He recognized most of the words they were using, too. Marcia would have felt right at home.

The boat's ugly green bow had torn into someone's parlor. Chintz curtains tangled in her plow anchor. A fully occupied clothesline draped across her bow railing. There, in the black water beside her trailboards, floated a chair.

The police were just arriving. Their paddy wagon came chugging to a stop up on the dock thirty feet away. They had a newer vehicle than Wade remembered from his last time in Manaos; this one was an open truck with a metal cage chained to the bed. Good. Let them deal with this mess. Where was Tweed? And Elinor?

"Dere go zem!" Pato was hanging onto the gunwale by Wade's elbow. "Up street!"

Tweed's latest commandeered conveyance was a little open jitney, one of those boxes on wheels with a motor in front and packing-case seats in back. The snowy white head gleamed in the sun beside him, and rage flooded Wade all over again.

"The paddy wagon's still running!" Wade struggled forward over splinters and broken dreams through the tangle. Pato, nimble as a possum, reached the distant dock before he did.

One of the officers approached him and motioned toward the shotgun in his hand.

Wade pointed toward the green boat. "Talk to Hector, and get Hurley to the infirmary! Hurry!" Without hesitating he rushed past them and hopped into the truck seat. He popped the brake handle. His hip screamed and shuddered whenever he moved his foot to work the pedals, but he didn't really notice. He left the officers' tortured cries behind and roared up the hill.

Pato flopped into the seat beside him and gripped with white knuckles. He laughed joyously. "So great! Dis iss so great!"

"I don't want you around if shooting starts."

"I stay okay, Papa. Almost as goot ride airplane iss, eh? Where they go? I know! Airstrip, *sí*?"

"Airstrip, *sí*."

This truck was by far the better vehicle than the old jitney. Wade was gaining rapidly on this run up the steep bluffs. And now the two were nearly neck and neck as they clattered over the cobbles scattering chickens, goats, and angry fishwives. They were less than two blocks from the open airfield now.

The jitney rattled around a corner. Wade followed, and the heavy iron cage on back tipped them over to two wheels. Pato whooped gleefully.

Wade slammed both feet on the brake and yanked the hand brake. The jitney had smashed into the back end of a horse cart, completely blocking the narrow street. Even so the paddy wagon almost missed them. Wade turned it aside, clipped their back end, and slammed to a stop against a brick wall. Loose bricks and dirt rained over the engine cowling. The street was littered with bowls and jars and ollas, some broken and some just rolling around. The scrawny bay carthorse waltzed in place, anchored by its cart shafts, its eyes rolling wildly.

"Elinor! Where . . . are you?" Wade scrambled out and nearly fell when his bad leg hit the round cobble stones. As Elinor's voice shrieked, "Don't!" he swung the shotgun toward Tweed, who had leveled his own pistol on Wade.

Elinor pushed in beside Tweed. "I promised to go with him, and I will. Turn around. Go back." Her face and nose were wet. She sobbed, choked, and begged, "Please, Wade!"

To save Elinor, Wade should just blast this clown and take his bullet. His own death was better than her going away with Tweed. But what if stray buckshot hit her? God forced himself into the periphery of Wade's thoughts, but Wade couldn't bring himself to think that God could be in control of a mess this nasty and confusing.

From the alleyway a policeman came running. "What's going on here?"

Elinor translated from Portuguese to Spanish for Tweed's sake. *Hah! Maybe God had a few cards up his sleeve, after all!* Wade

273

mused. "There's an arrest warrant out on this man, officer. Signed by Hernando Vargueza of the embassy."

Tweed's gun never faltered. "I am an officer of the Colombian border guards sent to arrest this man. He is an American in Brazil without papers. A fugitive."

It probably would never have occurred to Elinor to lie in her translation. She did a good job of it, although her voice wavered. Wade wished he had half her discipline for simply following such divine edicts as "Thou shalt not fib."

That passport. Wouldn't you know it would crop up now. For the briefest moment Wade sifted through various possible bluffs, the simplest of which would be to attempt unaccented Portuguese and claim citizenship in Tefe or something. His conscience nagged that God was supposed to be running this show, and God didn't like liars. Elinor hadn't lied; he shouldn't either. Still . . .

Pato laid a hand on Wade's arm. "Ess-cuse me, Papa. I take him your passport, eh? You don' put gun down." He stepped behind Wade, brushed his hip pocket, and appeared on the other side. He crossed smartly to the officer and handed him—Wade's passport!

Wade stared, dumbfounded, and hoped it didn't show on his face.

"Thank you." The officer studied the battered little book, page by page, nodding. "All in order, sir."

The most wondrous look of utter perplexity flooded Tweed's pudgy face. He patted all his pockets. He dug, he searched, shifting that pistol from hand to hand. A fat trembling finger shook at Pato. "You picked my pocket!"

Pato cringed against Wade. "Papa—?"

"Stop frightening my son!" Wade abandoned English for Portuguese. "Officers, this man doesn't even speak Portuguese, and he accuses me of being the alien."

Then the police officer unwittingly broke the stand-off. He stepped between Tweed and Wade. Instantly Tweed's elbow whipped around the poor fellow's throat. The man was sure one for putting his gun to people's heads. Tweed waggled his gun muzzle. Wade laid the shotgun on the truck seat and stepped back.

Elinor's voice purred by Tweed's ear. "You'll remember our mutual promise. Hurt anyone, and you'll never see my gold."

"You promised to stay with me."

"And I shall. Let's go."

"Papa . . . ?"

"Wait. Just wait easy."

Dragging the callow officer along, Tweed hustled, stumbling toward the corner.

Elinor stayed close beside him. Suddenly she stopped, turned back this way. The woman was coming to her senses at last! But no. "I see the change, Wade. I'm glad you found *your* gold."

"How'd you—?"

But she wheeled to scamper off after that animal. They were gone around the corner. The sunlight fled.

Wade snatched up the shotgun and ran. His hip objected strenuously to running. It slowed him down against his will. He turned the corner and tripped over that officer, sprawling out across the rough cobbles. They both clambered to their feet, but the officer was apparently too groggy to run.

The cobbles gave way to soft dirt as they topped the rise. Easier running. He had only a few hundred yards more. . . . As he reached the open grass, he heard a galloping horse come drumming up the road behind him. He didn't bother to look—no time.

Tweed's airplane sat right where Hector had left it. Elinor scrambled into a cockpit as Tweed spun the prop. It lit off instantly. So where's engine trouble when you need it? And now Tweed was hopping into the other cockpit. In moments they would be airborne, and Elinor would be dead. As soon as Tweed learned the only kind of gold she had to offer, he'd kill her. He was a greedy man and not the least forgiving.

Wade ran out into midfield and hesitated. He must be very careful. That flimsy craft of wood and silk was not protection for Elinor should he misfire. He had two shells. He must take out the propeller and possibly the engine without hitting anywhere near the cockpits. He raised the shotgun to his shoulder.

And now, at this moment, this absolutely worst moment when he least thought it would happen, Wade's hip quit. His whole left side from the waist down buckled under him like a paper housepost and sent him tumbling. He heard the engine howl and rev. The airplane was starting its taxi this way.

He'd fire from prone position. He rolled to his elbows and brought the gun back up as the horseman rode barreling out onto the field—Cruz, on that bay cart horse!

Tweed came faster. He'd blow his engine right out of the cowling, he had it cranked so tight. Cruz never hesitated. He rode in hard beside the plane, horse and aircraft in a wild and ragged race. With a mighty lunge Cruz reached wide to snare Elinor and drag her bodily out of the cockpit. Pato's vibrant soprano cheered lustily.

Wade saw no more of horse or rider or woman. All he could see was a whole lot of airplane coming at him. He barely had time to roll aside to avoid the whirring propeller.

Some spare part—probably the wheel strut—caught the side of his head and bowled him over. He struggled desperately to pull himself upright again, at the very least to get oriented. He couldn't even see well enough to know which way the plane went.

By the time he wrenched around and propped himself up to kneeling on his one good leg, the plane was airborne. He emptied both barrels at it, mostly out of frustration. The plane disappeared whining beyond the trees, leaving behind its constant blue cloud of oil smoke.

"*Wade!*" Pale thin arms, remarkably strong, wrapped around him as he flopped down to sitting on his good side. "Wade?"

Gentle fingers touched the side of his head. Very nice, but he didn't want that now. He kissed the soft skin of her hand and sent it back. He let the useless shotgun fall away.

"It's all right." Her milky blue eyes were laughing. "God doesn't really need your help to take revenge, you know. He can handle it."

"Yeah, I know. Still, I'd love to help him out with that one." Wade happened to glance up. Cruz was off the horse. He stood there twenty feet away, and the eyes that miss nothing were staring at them, staring at Wade and Elinor. Wade could meet this better standing up.

He struggled to get his good leg under him, but it was Cruz's strong hand that brought him to his feet. Wade held both hand and eye. "What do you see?"

"The writing on the wall." The dark eyes misted. "The way she

276

squirmed free of me to reach you. Her face and tone of voice. She's not once addressed me as anything other than Señor Cruz."

"Stop!" Elinor pushed between them. "Don't either of you dare start an argument or . . . or anything."

"No argument. No." Wade dropped Cruz's hand. "She'd be dead soon, Cruz, if it weren't for you. Tweed's not interested in her kind of gold. Dead, and worse. You saved her, and besides, you need her. You need what she has. I withdraw my nomination."

"Do you mean . . . ?" For the first time ever, Wade saw fear on that delicate face.

He'd better elaborate a little. "Tweed's got it in a way, Cruz. He's willing to risk everything—money, position, even his dignity—for a chance at ultimate wealth. Risk beyond measure for gold beyond measure. I admire that in the man.

"But there's a time to quit, too. For years I've been trying to grasp what I want. Seize the dream at any cost. Same as Tweed. Didn't work for him, and I'm beginning to see it never worked for me, either. The most important things, like Elinor or God, I can't get by by force."

"You said peace, I remember. The struggle fades." Cruz took a deep breath. "I don't know how to quit."

"May I suggest . . . ?" Elinor looked from face to face, apparently not quite certain where the conversation had been before. She tipped her head in that charming way and spoke to Cruz. "Talk to God. Try not to listen to what the inside of your head is saying. It's difficult, yes, but wait for him. Listen for him."

So where are the police when you need them? Here came that officer in the paddy wagon, its hood still all gray with brick dust. Marcia and Tiny hung from the running boards.

Tiny's feet hit the ground before the truck stopped. With the lumbering gait of an anxious whale he ran to Pato, and Pato to him. Massive arms wrapped around the butternut-colored boy; the rumbling bass enquired as to the child's health in a language the lad did not yet know, while Pato, gesturing like a windmill gone berserk, babbled on and on about the excitement of the hour. Death and ennui were for others, not him.

And not for Wade. Not any more.

Marcia came bounding up like a knight victorious. "Hector's seeing to Hurley. That Hector's quite a guy. Y'know, Travers, I've revised my opinions of the whole human race. Except Tweed. His ilk I've seen before. He got away, huh?"

"From us, yeah. He'll pay up, one way or another."

"Those two officers down at the dock, y'know? They came aboard, and Hector explained what was going on and Hurley backed him up, and they congratulated me! They congratulated *me* for helping collar those buzzards. What a story!" And she slipped with one of her favorite words. "Harry'll never believe this!"

But Wade was watching Pato. He would have walked over to those two, but he dare not trust his left side. "Pato? Hey." Let the boy come to him.

Pato came trotting over, and his eyes were dancing. "*Si?*"

"You look terribly pleased with yourself, sport, and with good reason. When did you do it?"

"When he holds me this." Pato demonstrated with his elbow crooked. "My arm do this . . ." He swung and slapped at nothing. "An dere iss all those things in his pockets they say, 'Here I am, Pato. Take me wit' you.' "

"Thought I told you not to."

"You say 'don' steal.' The passport, thass no steal. Thass yours. Tweed, he steals it. Steal-back isn' steal, *si*? Oh, here." He dug into his loin wrap in back. He handed Wade a tooled leather wallet. "Tweed he hass lahss money dat purse, but we send it back, *si*? Send it to him?"

"Would you have kept it?"

"Mebbe not." The big dark eyes drifted up to Wade's. The kid had great eyes. "Okay, No I don'. No more."

"That's right. Cruz, Elinor, me, Tiny—all of us are honest, and most important, God says he wants you to be honest. Got it?"

"*Si*. Okay. But you lose somebody your passport again, you jus' tell me, eh?"

Tiny laid a fat hand across Pato's shoulders as he spoke to Wade. "I was real afraid when he left with you. You attract too many things that explode.

"Don't I though. You and he make a good pair. And he'd be safer with you. Wanna keep him?"

278

The tiny black eyes widened, brightened, almost emerged from the pudgy face. "Sure! What's he say?"

Wade shifted to English. "How about Tiny being your papa instead of me? It's okay with us if it's okay with you."

The huge liquid eyes flitted from face to face. "Dass great, *sí*! You sure iss fine you, him?"

An expletive burst in Wade's ear. "You can't be serious! You couldn't give your own son away!" Marcia stared at Wade. "You *are* serious! You'd really do that."

"Bet Harry'll never believe it."

Pato glanced beyond Wade. Involuntarily Wade looked back. Cruz and Elinor stood in earnest nose-to-nose conversation. And now they were walking this way.

Pato grabbed Marcia's wrist. "You come fin' out how I get my papa. Harry don' believe dat one neither. You get lahss goot stories here. Put me in one mebbe, eh?" And he dragged her off more or less against her will.

Wade should walk over to meet them, but his hip warned him not to. He waited until Cruz approached to within easy speaking distance. "Does it work, listening to God?"

Was there a sense of wonder in his voice? It almost seemed so. "It works, though I suspect he'll speak to me better through books and Scripture, and Elinor agrees."

Elinor's marvelous eyes studied the green grass at their feet. Why wouldn't she look at him?

"So wha'd he say?"

Yes, it was a sense of wonder. "It didn't come from my mind. I would never have dreamed or guessed, never have thought of it on my own. God loves me."

Cruz's voice tightened. "This, though, I already guessed. Elinor loves you. Even if I claimed her, she'd not be mine. She's yours." He stepped back. "I'll see you later at the infirmary." And he walked away quickly.

"That is," Elinor murmured, "if you still want me."

"If I . . ." Actions speak louder than words, they say. He wrapped around her and pulled her in tight. It felt good, it felt so good. "I really do love you."

"Some Scripture scholars say one should never marry a person outside the faith. That's one reason I was so happy to see the Holy Spirit working on you. I was hoping and praying you were for me, and . . . uh . . ." She sighed. "My words just went wrong again."

"Marry. Yeah. About time I gave up my rambling ways."

She pulled her head back to look at him. "Oh dear, I hope not. Do you remember soon after we left Minho and encountered those forest Indians? And Pato and I went to talk to them?"

"Yeah. Why'd they come to you like that, anyway?"

"They'd heard of me. A woman of God, they called me. You told Señor Cruz you can talk to the Indians south of the Uaupes."

"Pretty well. I was gonna go gold-seeking there."

"We still can, you know, among those Indians. The kind of gold Dr. Hurley sought and found. The two of us. Will you?" She blushed again, that pink glow that delighted him so. "I mean, of course, if we first . . . uh . . ."

"Yeah. I'm ready to 'uh' if you are. Let's."

The more he thought about it the more enthusiastic waxed his spirit. *Beware, Wade Travers. You'll die.* He did. Dead and now Alive, and the zest was back. Zest and purpose and no more futility. He gathered Elinor close against him, and he kissed her under the sun in the middle of a green airstrip he did not build.

# ABOUT THE AUTHOR

SANDY DENGLER, a consummate storyteller and popular Serenade author, has written five books for the historical inspirational romance series. *Jungle Gold* is her first SuperSaga.

An Ohio native, Dengler earned a master's degree in zoology/ecology at Arizona State University and then married a National Park Service ranger. She and her husband have lived in national parks from coast to coast, raising two daughters along the way. They now live on the flank of Mount Rainier in Washington.

Dengler describes herself as "a writer, who moonlights as a housewife." Her hobbies include gardening, classic needlework, miniatures (ship models and doll houses), and painting. "And I've been known to dabble in active pursuits involving horses, canoes, skis—although not simultaneously."

# *A Letter to Our Readers*

Dear Reader:

Welcome to Serenade Books—a series designed to bring you beautiful love stories in the world of inspirational romance. They will uplift you, encourage you, and provide hours of wholesome entertainment, so thousands of readers have testified. That we might better contribute to your reading enjoyment, we would appreciate your taking a few minutes to respond to the following questions and return to:

> Lois Taylor
> Serenade Books
> The Zondervan Publishing House
> 1415 Lake Drive, S.E.
> Grand Rapids, Michigan   49506

1. Did you enjoy reading *Jungle Gold*?

   ☐ Very much. I would like to see more books by this author!
   ☐ Moderately
   ☐ I would have enjoyed it more if _____

2. Where did you purchase this book? _____

3. What influenced your decision to purchase this book?

   ☐ Cover          ☐ Back cover copy
   ☐ Title          ☐ Friends
   ☐ Publicity      ☐ Other _____

4. Please rate the following elements from 1 (poor) to 10 (superior).
   ☐ Heroine      ☐ Plot
   ☐ Hero      ☐ Inspirational theme
   ☐ Setting      ☐ Secondary characters

5. What are some inspirational themes you would like to see treated in future books?
   _____
   _____

6. Please indicate your age range:
   ☐ Under 18    ☐ 25–34    ☐ 46–55
   ☐ 18–24    ☐ 35–45    ☐ Over 55

*Serenade / SuperSaga* books are inspirational romances in historical settings, designed to bring you a joyful, heart-lifting reading experience. *SuperSagas* are longer, more developed stories than the regular historical Serenade novels, or Sagas.

*Serenade / SuperSaga* books are available in your local bookstore:

#1 *Dearest Anna*, Deborah Rau
#2 *Tachechana*, Jack Metzler

The following *Serenade / Saga* books are also available:

#1 *Summer Snow*, Sandy Dengler
#2 *Call Her Blessed*, Jeanette Gilge
#3 *Ina*, Karen Baker Kletzing
#4 *Juliana of Clover Hill*, Brenda Knight Graham
#5 *Song of the Nereids*, Sandy Dengler
#6 *Anna's Rocking Chair*, Elaine Watson
#7 *In Love's Own Time*, Susan C. Feldhake
#8 *Yankee Bride*, Jane Peart
#9 *Light of My Heart*, Kathleen Karr
#10 *Love Beyond Surrender*, Susan C. Feldhake
#11 *All the Days After Sunday*, Jeanette Gilge
#12 *Winterspring*, Sandy Dengler
#13 *Hand Me Down the Dawn*, Mary Harwell Sayler
#14 *Rebel Bride*, Jane Peart
#15 *Speak Softly, Love*, Kathleen Yapp
#16 *From This Day Forward*, Kathleen Karr
#17 *The River Between*, Jacquelyn Cook
#18 *Valiant Bride*, Jane Peart
#19 *Wait for the Sun*, Maryn Langer
#20 *Kincaid of Cripple Creek*, Peggy Darty
#21 *Love's Gentle Journey*, Kay Cornelius
#22 *Applegate Landing*, Jean Conrad
#23 *Beyond the Smoky Curtain*, Mary Harwell Sayler
#24 *To Dwell in the Land*, Elaine Watson
#25 *Moon for a Candle*, Maryn Langer

#26 *The Conviction of Charlotte Grey,* Jeanne Cheyney
#27 *Opal Fire,* Sandy Dengler
#28 *Divide the Joy,* Maryn Langer
#29 *Cimarron Sunset,* Peggy Darty
#30 *This Rolling Land,* Sandy Dengler
#31 *The Wind Along the River,* Jacquelyn Cook
#32 *Sycamore Settlement,* Suzanne Pierson Ellison
#33 *Where Morning Dawns,* Irene Brand
#34 *Elizabeth of Saginaw Bay,* Donna Winters
#35 *Westward My Love,* Elaine L. Schulte
#36 *Ransomed Bride,* Jane Peart
#37 *Dreams of Gold,* Elaine L. Schulte

*Serenade/Saga* books are now being published in a new, longer length:

#T1 *Chessie's King,* Kathleen Karr
#T2 *The Rogue's Daughter,* Molly Noble Bull
#T3 *Image in the Looking Glass,* Jacquelyn Cook
#T4 *Rising Thunder,* Carolyn Ann Wharton
#T5 *Fortune's Bride,* Jane Peart
#T6 *Cries the Wilderness Wind,* Susan Kirby
#T7 *Come Gentle Spring,* Irene Brand
#T8 *Seasons of the Heart,* Susan Feldhake
#T9 *Ride with Wings,* Maryn Langer
#T10 *Golden Gates,* Jean Conrad

*Serenade / Serenata* books are inspirational romances in contemporary settings. The following Serenata books available in your local bookstore:

#1 *On Wings of Love,* Elaine L. Schulte
#2 *Love's Sweet Promise,* Susan C. Feldhake
#3 *For Love Alone,* Susan C. Feldhake
#4 *Love's Late Spring,* Lydia Heermann
#5 *In Comes Love,* Mab Graff Hoover
#6 *Fountain of Love,* Velma S. Daniels and Peggy E. King
#7 *Morning Song,* Linda Herring
#8 *A Mountain to Stand Strong,* Peggy Darty
#9 *Love's Perfect Image,* Judy Baer
#10 *Smoky Mountain Sunrise,* Yvonne Lehman
#11 *Greengold Autumn,* Donna Fletcher Crow
#12 *Irresistible Love,* Elaine Anne McAvoy
#13 *Eternal Flame,* Lurlene McDaniel
#14 *Windsong,* Linda Herring
#15 *Forever Eden,* Barbara Bennett
#16 *Call of the Dove,* Madge Harrah
#17 *The Desires of Your Heart,* Donna Fletcher Crow
#18 *Tender Adversary,* Judy Baer
#19 *Halfway to Heaven,* Nancy Johanson
#20 *Hold Fast the Dream,* Lurlene McDaniel
#21 *The Disguise of Love,* Mary LaPietra
#22 *Through a Glass Darkly,* Sara Mitchell
#23 *More Than a Summer's Love,* Yvonne Lehman
#24 *Language of the Heart,* Jeanne Anders
#25 *One More River,* Suzanne Pierson Ellison
#26 *Journey Toward Tomorrow,* Karyn Carr
#27 *Flower of the Sea,* Amanda Clark
#28 *Shadows Along the Ice,* Judy Baer
#29 *Born to Be One,* Cathie LeNoir
#30 *Heart Aflame,* Susan Kirby
#31 *By Love Restored,* Nancy Johanson
#32 *Karaleen,* Mary Carpenter Reid
#33 *Love's Full Circle,* Lurlene McDaniel

#34 *A New Love,* Mab Graff Hoover
#35 *The Lessons of Love,* Susan Phillips
#36 *For Always,* Molly Noble Bull
#37 *A Song in the Night,* Sara Mitchell
#38 *Love Unmerited,* Donna Fletcher Crow
#39 *Thetis Island,* Brenda Willoughby
#40 *Love More Precious,* Marilyn Austin

*Serenade/Serenata* books are now being published in a new, longer length:

#T1  *Echoes of Love,* Elaine L. Schulte
#T2  *With All Your Heart,* Sara Mitchell
#T3  *Moonglow,* Judy Baer
#T4  *Gift of Love,* Lurlene McDaniel
#T5  *The Wings of Adrian,* Jan Seabaugh
#T6  *Song of Joy,* Elaine L. Schulte
#T7  *Island Dawn,* Annetta Hutton
#T8  *Heartstorm,* Carol Blake Gerrond
#T9  *After the Storm,* Margaret Johnson
#T10  *Through the Valley of Love,* Shirley Cook

Watch for other books in both the *Serenade/Saga* (historical) and *Serenade/Serenata* (contemporary) series, coming soon.

# Date Due

| | | | |
|---|---|---|---|
| SEP 2 0 | 1987 | | |
| JAN 3 | 1987 | | |
| JAN 1 7 1988 | | | |
| JUN 2 4 1990 | | | |
| JAN 2 7 1991 | | | |
| MAR. 7 1993 | | | |
| NOV. 7 1993 | | | |
| | | | |
| | | | |
| | | | |
| | | | |
| | | | |
| | | | |
| | | | |
| | | | |
| | | | |

BRODART, INC.          Cat. No. 23 233          Printed in U.S.A.